PELHAM ON PAROLE

PELHAM ON PAROLE

Carl Plummer

Pelham on Parole
Copyright © 2020 Carl Plummer

Content Editor: Kevin J Topolovec
Copy Editor: Meagan Daquan
Cover Art: Krystina Hamilton
Editor-in-Chief: Kristi King-Morgan
Formatting: Kristi King-Morgan
Assistant Editor: Maddy Drake

ISBN- 978-1-947381-35-3

www.dreamingbigpublications.com

Failure is unthinkable. Failure is unforgivable.

Failure is not an option. Failure is highly likely.

CONTENTS

1.	Greta	6
2.	After that Strange Release in The Spring Of 1939	11
3.	From a Body in The Barn…	17
4.	…to a Baby in The Bathwater	21
5.	Some Autobiography and The Letter	29
6.	Home, and The Soiled Persian	38
7.	A New Sidekick and the Obligatory Broad	47
8.	Concatenations and Conflagrations	55
9.	Interrogation, Kedgeree, and The Off	60
10.	The Four Oarsmen	70
11.	Dolly Orbs	75
12.	Stranglers on A Train	85
13.	A Suit and A Suite	97
14.	The Suit in The Suite	109
15.	An Interlude	118
16.	Manifestations	126
17.	Crises, and Trouble Down Below	138
18.	Don't Shoot Him; He's Only the Piano Player	151
19.	On Considering the Three	165
20.	You Can Swim but You Can't Hide	171
21.	Home Truths	179
22.	That Sinking Feeling and The Normandy Landings	189
23.	French Leave	199
24.	The Hammer Blow	209
25.	Equals	218
26.	Dundee Cake	222

CHAPTER 1
GRETA

"This stuff is dynamite."

"That good, is it?"

"No, Hardy, it's dynamite."

Dan unrolled the newspaper wrapping; I think it was the *Daily Mirror*, a parcel not unlike one keeping warm a hearty serving of haddock and chips with extra malt vinegar, and bits.

I croaked, "Dynamite?"

He selected an explosive tube, complete with fuse, as his eyebrows squeezed in to touch. I waited for him to growl. He growled. "It ain't sticks of bleedin' Blackpool rock, is it?"

"Dan," I continued in what I hoped was a mollifying tone, "all you'll be able to do is blow the cell door off. The window is not an option…" I wavered a moment before continuing. My cow-pie-eater of a cell mate commanded a certain amount of verbal tiptoeing. "We're four floors up. Only blowing the doors off isn't going to do it. After this door, there are many others."

He tickled his chin with the fuse. "Got more of 'em, loads of 'em, well, six sticks. An old mate worked in a quarry."

I formed a small-talk type of question as I envisaged my limbs and organs plastering the grey and cream painted bricks of our little cell. "Worked or laboured?" I inquired. "What I mean is, whistle and flute, a Peckham Rye and a pencil behind the ear, or the arrowed pyjamas and pickaxe in hand?"

Dan leant against the steel door, covering the spy hole with a broad shoulder, and a very broad shoulder it was indeed. My cell mate had the physique and aura that, if down by a Rocky Mountain stream, would persuade a grizzly bear to hand over the prize salmon and slink off into the woods, happy to fish and feed another day. "He was my mate. Done ten years, done his time. Now he's 'elping me be a free man, an' I am gonna be a free man. Don't you wanna be free?"

"Not so many months stretching ahead of me, old chap," I said. "I've got less than a year left to do…keeping my nose clean…being a first timer and all that…I'm nearly done."

He pointed with the stick of dynamite. "I gotta see 'er."

I turned to view, for the thousandth time since my incarceration in the summer of 1938, the curly-cornered photograph above Dan's bunk. There, in black and white, with sultry eyes shadowed by glossy blonde hair was the woman from *The Kiss*. I faced him once more, feeling my heart sink. I'm sure you'll agree, there's nothing worse than trying to reason with the lovelorn; it is an endless highway of listening and nodding until you wish the poor blighter would gallop off to Beachy Head and finish it all: once and for all.

That said, I am prone to lend a keen ear to a man in need. I tried once more. "Dan," I implored, "you arrived with that photograph nearly ten years ago. You've only another five to do. Don't go and spoil it. Tot up your years of good behaviour and…you know she wants to be alone."

"I must see her, now, and if I can't see 'er…"

"Come on, Dan," I said, still venturing with my mollification of his ire and hunger for freedom. "All this for a woman who doesn't know you, won't want to see you, doesn't want to see anybody?"

"That's as maybe, Hardy," he said with another wave of the dangerous sticks. "I've waited long enough. I'll get to see her if it's the last thing I do, that's after I've seen…"

"Your dear, grey-haired old mother?"

Dan stiffened. His eyes narrowed as his fist tightened its grip on the dynamite. "No, not my grey-haired…she hasn't got grey hair. Not the last time I saw her, anyway."

"Oh," I said. An 'Oh' in these situations is not much to say, I'll admit. Dear reader, and welcome to you, let me explain. As you get to know your hero – Pelham Hardimann – you will understand my keenness to keep emotions at bay. Best to avoid such things, be they filial, maternal, or worse, the going gloopy and weak at the knees over a set of high cheekbones, dainty ankles and a slim waist. You won't find such fault with me. Back to the matter in hand…in Dan's hand. "I know," I said. "You were diddled, stitched-up by your gang members. They ran off with all the loot?"

"No, it wasn't them what stitched me up. It was Quill?"

I am rarely one to take a step back, but I took a step back. "Quill? Detective Inspector Quill?"

"Yeah, Quill. He got me banged up for something I didn't do."

"Really?" I was tempted to lift an eyebrow of irony or incredulity or some such thing. "Dan, you robbed a Royal Mail train. His Majesty, God bless him, does not take kindly to his subjects messing about with the postal service. From post box to letter box, all mail is property of The Crown."

"He had me up before the beak for robbing a bank. I never robbed a bank. I robbed a train. He had me down for something I didn't do."

"That sounds like Quill," I said.

"So, you know him?"

"You could say that," I said.

"He got you for bank robbing?"

"No, nothing as adventurous. Breaking and entering, with a bit of theft post breaking in."

"Lucky for you he didn't pin bank robbing on you," said Dan. "I mean, you send people to prison for something they've done, something they is guilty of, not something they ain't done. That's how the law works."

"That's how it's supposed to work, Dan, yes. I'll see you right on that one."

"Bet he tried something…good for his clean-up rate and getting promotion."

"Well, I think he made sure another couple of months was added, for my smacking him in the mouth."

"You should've strangled the bastard."

"A bit much, don't you think?"

"Not for me, Hardy." He poked the sticks of dynamite at me. "Strangling his scrawny neck is the first thing I'm gonna do. Then I'm on a boat to America." Another poke with the dynamite. "First things first, eh? We blow down this wall and escape."

"You'll blow us to smithereens," I said, wondering if his torso would offer me enough shelter from the blast.

"I'll be free. Is you in or is you ain't?"

"Well, I'm in and I can't get out, so I suppose I'm…"

"In." He pressed a paw against my chest. "My bunk."

"Your bunk?" I asked, considering the idea that sharing a prison cell and slop bucket for such a short time was no basis for a relationship.

"Get under it." He dug into his overalls and pulled out a box of England's Glory, jammed a finger into the box and selected a match. "Cover yer lug 'oles."

Resigned to the fact that all remonstration was over, I turned to nod goodbye to Greta, went down on my hands and knees then wormed and wriggled my way under Dan's bunk, my nostrils catching the burn of cheap floor cleaner and the mossy waft of damp bed linen. I flattened palms against ears, closed my eyes and said a silent farewell to a friend who had impossible yearnings for a better place.

After the shuddering, the smack of compressed air and the boom making light work of my improvised ear muffs, I opened my eyes and turned my head to see blustering dust and the snowing of paint flakes laying a gentle cover over the supine and serene mass of my once desperate friend.

It was perhaps a minute or so before the polished boots and sharply creased shins of a warder arrived. One boot kicked against a flank to test for death, unconsciousness, or heavy sleep.

"Still breathing." Some silence followed. "5271, you in here?"

I edged sideways, stuck my head out from beneath the bunk, jamming an elbow against a boot. "Just about, Mr. Kay," I chirruped, catching the light from the gaping doorway as it glinted against the warder's necklace of keys.

"Get out of there."

"If you could just…"

"Come on, 5271, up you get," came the reply as the boots inched back to leave me the minimum of space in which to slither out and render the back of my head a nasty smack from the rusted frame of Dan's bunk.

It was about thirty seconds before I could stand up straight and peer into the eyes of Mr. Kay, a man who had that pinched face of a fellow suffering a shard of peanut cutting into a gum.

"I couldn't stop him, Mr. Kay. He was determined."

The warder looked down to the slumbering figure at his feet. "You should have stopped him, should have called for assistance, 5271. Bloody fool."

I thought the accusation a little stern. "I spent some time talking him out of it…"

"Bloody talking is all you're bloody good for, 5271."

"But…"

"Wouldn't surprise me if you put him up to it. Just the sort of thing a chinless, smooth-talking upper-class twit and twister like you would…this poor old dimwit…"

"Steady on," I exclaimed. I felt judgement on my cell mate a little premature and unfair; he was in no position to defend himself, or me for that matter. As for the upper-class twit thing, well, it has always been somewhat of a contradiction in terms as far as I'm concerned. After all, were the ruling classes to be such twits, power would swiftly slip through their well-manicured fingers. It hasn't yet. I was keen to put this dialectic across to Mr. Kay, but I thought better of it.

He gave Dan another groan-prompting kick before taking a step towards me, to squint, a hand twirling his keys, somewhat akin to a miffed gunfighter with the sun in his eyes. "I am on the horns of a dilemma, 5271."

"A dilemma?" I asked.

"I would be happy…no, I would be delirious with joy to see you suffering another five years for your part in this…"

"My part?"

"Shut it."

"But…"

"Quiet, 5271. I am in no position to question my superiors and *you* do not question *me*. You are out of here."

"Out?"

"Shower."

"Of here?"

"Get cleaned up. Use plenty of soap. Your clothes will be brought here. Say farewell to Dan. Then pick up your belongings…and I do not wish to see you…"

"What about the delirious with joy…?"

"5271. Shut up before I call my superiors and explain your need to be held in the infirmary for a week."

"I'm on parole?"

"Something like that, not that I'd ever trust a word of yours."

"I'm free?"

Mr. Kay was in no hurry to answer. After another cursory check of Dan, he clanked his way across the flattened door of my cell and planted himself on the landing of my wing before doing a smart about turn to offer me a finale of a scowl. "I don't know what this country is coming to, 5271, I really don't."

I was ready to concur, to give one of my hell-in-a-handcart lines. "Well…" I was not allowed to continue.

He sucked in dust-free air. "Just consider this on the outside, 5271. You've let your country down, you've let this prison down, you've let your cell mate down, and perhaps most important of all…you're a blithering idiot!" He marched away with a *"Gawd 'elp us all."*

CHAPTER 2
AFTER THAT STRANGE RELEASE IN THE SPRING OF 1939

I wandered a little way from the small huddle of newly released inmates, giving myself time to adjust to the coal smoke and diesel of the open air. I disdained the jubilation and downright raucousness of the others; they were bolstered by the warmth of outstretched arms, hugs, and kisses, and all that other gooey stuff ladies and their offspring insist on sharing with their prodigal males. After all, is not every murderous villain just a loveable rogue who is good to his mother?

I blinked in the early morning light. I had plumped to be alone, left not stranded but calm in the knowledge that I was a free man in all senses of the word. At least, that was my hope and intention, despite a nagging feeling, the sort that limbers up in your stomach before sprinting to your nape, causing hairs to stand to attention.

I strode up and down and all about, from left to right, and then in ever decreasing circles until sure of my solitude. Once the brouhaha died down, I halted to enjoy the resounding clunk of the closing Judas gate.

I untied the brown paper parcel, hoping my cigarette case still contained a couple of gaspers. It was a small parcel and I wondered why they had bothered with it. It was the end of August when I went to court with nothing but a lightweight grey suit; matching suede shoes and grey fedora, and pockets weighted down with the usual paraphernalia: cigarettes, lighter, a wallet with some crisp ten-bob notes, some loose change, a handkerchief, and a comb hewn from an elephant's tusk. From court, I was hustled off to clink without a by-your-leave. The law of the land can be a cruel and vindictive mistress.

I could have just lolled there for a few moments, refilling my pockets instead of allowing the screw to practice his round turn and two half hitches, counting as he did so. But, I mused, that's the way they like to do things in chokey: everything by numbers. Eat, clean your teeth, and get the compulsory seven bells kicked out of you by numbers. It all makes you a better person, is what they tell you. I had added to my already consummate skills of breaking and entering and safe-cracking; some excellent teachers were available at a nominal fee. *"You write me a letter to my missus and I'll give you the low-down on a Chubb Special,"* was the usual way lessons were arranged.

11

I'd learned not to spend too much time looking for the soap, and mastered tucking hospital corners around the sparsely stuffed palliasse of my bunk. It's like being back in the sodding army. We've made a man of you, shown you the world and taught you how to kill people. This time, we'll make a man of you, show you four walls and hope you don't strangle the filthy slob sleeping above you. No doubt you have met the type of slob to which I am referring; he fidgets like an ape gleaning for fleas to nibble, spits like a camel and spends half the night tossing and turning with the free hand gently nursing a stiffy.

I gave a moment's thought for Dan.

Eight months later, here I am, with my belongings returned.

I shivered. The warm glow of freedom and a felt hat were not enough. A coat would have been nice; perhaps I should have asked. I don't know if the early spring of 1939 was going down in meteorological annals as the coldest since such annals began, but it was making a dashed good effort. I stamped my feet, sending shock waves juddering through my bones.

Having emptied the parcel and fed my pockets, I tucked the paper wrapping under an arm, needing both petrified thumbs to work my Ronson. I sniffed frozen air and the smoke of stale tobacco as I looked up at the façade of His Majesty's Prison. My guess is they'd done their best to build it to look like the Tower of London, only with cheaper and redder bricks because the inmates were to be less illustrious. There is also an uncanny resemblance to the main tower of my old home, Eton: a reminiscence that does not sit well with me.

A gentle cough caused me to turn around. It was the cough coves of breeding use when they want to give their three-pennyworth.

He was at least six-two tall and dressed in a morning suit without the topper. The ramrod erectness of the man prompted me to guess he had left the hanger in his suit and the horn still squeezed into the heel of his shoes. His long thin face was the whitest I'd ever seen, which was strange considering I was the one meant to be sporting the prison pallor. He looked like death that hadn't bothered to warm up. Making a stab at his age was not simple, but I settled at no less than a good three score. I consider myself a generous man and I had no wish to lumber him with another decade, although others with darker souls may have done so.

I gave my cigarette a suave Bogart flick out into the road: another skill mastered in the prison yard.

"I get a chauffeur?" I asked. I wasn't sure if things were looking up or not. I had been let our early, before completing half my sentence, which is all well and good, and now someone was putting a cherry on the already iced cake. That line of surprise is always worrying in my trade. Villains, especially the big ones with broad shoulders and fat cigars, do not dish out favours for nothing. I tossed the balled-up parcel paper back at the prison, with my thanks, before looking back at my new friend. "Smashing Rolls Royce you've got there," I added. I wasn't lying; it was as devoutly polished as his shoes and giving the sun's meagre rays a sturdy return passing shot.

Words slipped from his mouth like Lyon's Golden from a hot spoon. "I am a valet, sir."

I chanced a guffaw. "His Lordship fall out on the way here, did he?" I watched the corner of one eye twitch, firm in the belief he was aching to snarl at me. No; that was all he was prepared to give.

He checked a piece of paper as he looked me up and down, like a coffin-maker on a busman's holiday.

I thought I'd better help him out. "Pelham Hardimann," I chimed. "Born in Chelsea, 1900, so a skilled mathematician, most probably like your good self, would ascertain I am but a gnat's whisker on the desirable side of forty. Six-foot in stockinged feet, blue eyes, short, light brown hair: the type girls call mousey as they run their fingers through it. The medical profession would say I have well developed muscles. Athletic is the word I use. I was a wet bob, you know." I waited for a response, but he was still checking. Maybe he needed more. "The small scar running from my right earlobe to the hinge of my anvil jaw was etched by a beer glass. The said beer glass was at the time in the hands of a tart who forgot she owned a heart. She called it getting fresh, I called it being friendly."

"That seems to correspond with what I have here, sir," he replied at last. After a pause nearing on the pregnant, he added an ominous, "So far."

I bent a little to lift a left trouser leg. I stuck the leg forward in a dainty fashion, somewhat akin to a night watchman making a defensive stroke off a medium pace flagging at the end of his final over. "Shrapnel," I said with a modicum of pride. Like any good Englishman, I am always happy to display pride in the inventions of his fellow countrymen. "Some of it still in there: Vimy Ridge. I was busy helping our Canadian cousins. By whom the offending missile was delivered, the better half of Herr Krupp or Field Marshall Haig himself, who knows? There was a great deal of confusion at the time, and I am never one to go laying blame."

The syrup flowed once more. "Very good, sir." He folded the piece of paper with fastidious neatness then slipped it into his side pocket. "If sir would like to embark?" He duck-shuffled to the rear door of the Rolls Royce. "I took the liberty of leaving the engine running, sir, in order for the heating apparatus to maintain a comfortable ambiance."

"You mean it's toasty?"

"I would venture to say it is cosy, sir."

The chance of defrosting my extremities won me over. I flung my hat in, slid in after it and bum-skated on the pristine red leather to the other side. I smiled affection at the decanter and selection of smokers' requisites and assumed I was entitled, no, expected to help myself. There being no yardarm to pour scorn on my choice of early morning refreshment, I wasted no time in doing just that. I was generosity itself, adding a squirt of soda for decency's sake.

The valet planted himself in the driver's seat, reached back to close the glass partition, made great art of donning his leather gauntlets and revved the engine. The Rolls Royce pulled away with the clatter you get when a feather collides with a lawn.

Now, as a gentleman in a land fit for heroes, I have always believed that one should never cut the working man off from one's association. I leaned forward and opened the partition a smidgen, enough to shovel a question into his shell-like *auris* and sufficient to scoop up his rejoinder. I signalled the opening of the conversation with a gentle tap on the glass with my whisky tumbler. I didn't want to start spouting off and send the man, my good self and his magnificent black and yellow beast into a spin.

His head didn't move, and for a moment I wondered if his neck needed a drop of 3-in-1. This man kept both hands firmly on the wheel and both beady eyes on the road. "Sir?" he eventually asked with a tone that could have slid under a door.

"Any chance of a hint as to where we are heading?"

"I am not at liberty to divulge the destination, sir. However, I can assure you of our arrival within thirty minutes."

Sufficiently satisfied with his return I slid back the glass, slipped back to press my bones against hide and nestled my whisky in warming and grateful hands. It occurred to me at this point that my friendly, though rather lax hosts had not bothered to pass an iron over my strides. I like a good crease.

Deeming it better to concentrate on the brighter side of things I watched the world go by as sunlight did its dappling between branches, hedges grew higher, and through their gaps I glimpsed the rolling hills dotted with beasts at the cud. I finished my whisky, regarding it as something of an ad hoc nightcap.

The man was true to his word. After thirty minutes of dozing in the back of the Rolls Royce I opened a lizard-like eyelid to find us sweeping between crumbling brick gateposts. There was no gate, but the vandal had been kind enough to leave the rusted hinges.

It seemed my new friend, this valet-cum-chauffeur, was a devotee of the wireless and my awakening was accompanied by Jack Hylton and his orchestra wishing for a talking picture of some young filly. I, who had not enjoyed the touch of the fairer sex for more than half a year, felt the warbler protested a little too much. I promised myself I would open my little black book as soon as I pressed a leather sole down in my London mews once more, hoping it would not be too long, and praying I would still be complete in limbs and digits. I'd always had my reserve chorus line for the rare occasions when I found my crooked arm lacking a charming companion.

That final worry concerning my limbs and digits was brought about by the new surroundings. Now I'm all for the good healthy sod, the honest sweat and toil in England's garden, stout yeomen and all that, but this farm had an immediate air of disrepair and neglect, with hints of foot and mouth, swine fever, and all those other diseases from which we dwellers of the city are protected. The villains with the broad shoulders and fat cigars also came back to mind.

The Rolls charged, with some petulant splashing, across slurry-covered concrete and came to rest beside a black Austin Ten saloon. I know a flatfoot's runabout when I see one and this one was propping up its own sample of the aforementioned biped.

The leaning constable looked a little out of sorts, but I put that down to his having to stand in a puddle that had ambitions to be a lake. He didn't reach out to open my door, so I took it upon myself, not wanting to interrupt my companion's musical reverie.

I shared the growing lake with the rozzer, but before closing my door had second thoughts. I peeked back in and caught the attention of my driver with chirpiness. "You're not joining us?"

"I am required to wait here for you, sir," he said, using the rear-view mirror to allow me a glimpse of his eyes. A positive crossed my mind; he may have the face of Dracula but at least he has a reflection. He spoiled it. "I will be here when they have finished with you."

I straightened; words can have such impact. As an ally and helpmeet, my new friend and driver had collapsed at the first hurdle and I needed another. I closed the door and turned to eye the bluebottle, searching for some humanity in his chubby face, a face I first met during a spot of violence at the moment of my arrest some months before: Studely.

"Follow me." He further displayed his wishes for me to move with a stiff clockwork arm, at the end of which was a wooden truncheon adorned with more pits than a fly fisherman's cork rod-handle. He paddled away in his rubber galoshes and I followed with a creeping tiptoe, a thin cat stalking a swarthy mouse across oily mud and manure. Well, at least I wasn't yet up to my neck in it, but the foreboding was there. I ran a pinkie around my collar and gulped good thick country odours.

I shadowed the man for fifty yards, at the end of which we found ourselves in the gaping doorway of a barn. It was a dark structure, with its wooden slats clinging for dear life to the cobwebs and creepers around it. The roof was peppered with holes, the sort a more romantic soul would find delightful at night, watching the stars and catching the hay dust in the streaks of silvery moonlight.

You can imagine the sort of rot I mean, and I'm all for such slushiness when it is called for, but this was not the time.

And there he was: Inspector Quill of The Yard.

CHAPTER 3
From a Body in The Barn...

"I ask you again, Hardimann. Can you identify this man?"

My heart sank to my sodden socks, not so much from being *mano a mano* with Quill once more, but from the tableau at his feet. The subject on display was a body half-covered in dank and slimy straw, with a thick rope snaking from the noosed neck.

I lifted my gaze to the cross beam of the barn and studied the dangling tether. "Did you cut the rope and let him down?" I asked.

Quill spoke again, flat and nasal, as though he went through life suffering a permanent cold. "We shall get to that later." His weedy moustache rippled along the smooth beach of his upper lip as he produced a torch from his coat pocket and flashed a white spot on the bruised visage. "Take a proper look at the face."

Despite my sentence at Eton and education in Wormwood Scrubs, I must confess that I have rarely found myself supine next to another man's face. I went down on all fours and peered into the wide, open eyes of a dead man frozen in the shock of gasping his last.

The tightness of my throat rendered my *"poor Clackett"* almost inaudible. On rising, I turned from Quill and feigned dust in the eye. Never let these bastards know your true feelings; they always use them against you.

"Do...you know this man, Mr. Hardimann?" His "*do*" was long and deep enough to have had an *m* attached to its ominous ending.

I turned to look the detective in his steely eyes but found my sights focused on the dental gap: the one I'd given him some months before. "My batman," I said after some time. "Yes. Clackett."

Quill did that heel-to-toe rocking so beloved of officers of the law. "Clackett, you say."

I nodded. "Yes, that is what I say."

"Your batman?"

I was in two minds about speaking again, feeling it better to save Quill the labour of repeating my utterances any further. But, someone had to move the plot along or we'd be standing there for a lifetime and Quill had never been down in my book as someone in the running to share the rest of my pitiful existence. "I met him the day my fist clasped the King's shilling in 1917," I said. "Good fellow, he was."

"I'm sure he was." A cloud must have passed over the barn; there were no longer sunbeams spiking through the holes. "And when did you last see him?"

I was tempted to say *"when I was on my hands and knees,"* but the coldness in his stare warned me off. Rather like all those chaps who tell you *"I like a good joke as much as the next man,"* Quill was not a man to jest. I watched him light up a Player's Navy Cut as I scrabbled around in the old grey matter for an honest answer. "I can't give you an exact date," was all I could say.

"Roughly, Hardimann. We could start with a year then work our way to a month, if you like."

"Twenty years ago, if I can recall with accuracy. It was some three months after the Royal Families of Europe finished their hissy fit and sat around the table to smoke the pipe of peace before running out of subjects to subjugate."

Quill was a snarler. "When!"

His abruptness urged me on. "Early spring, March 1919. We shook hands on landing at Dover then sped off on our merry ways."

"And you never kept in touch? You have heard nothing from him since?"

"Never been one for all that keeping in touch thing," I said, holding a gentle wave of remorse within me. "He had his road to follow, to Newcastle if I remember, and I had my way…"

"So why would he be looking for you now?" Quill sprang to his right as a fresh beam of sunlight sped through a hole in the roof to slap him a golden one in the face.

I used the intermezzo to look back down to the head, down the length of the torso then up to the dangling rope. "One hell of a drop," I said.

"Hanging is a very scientific form of execution. If the drop is too short the victim can take an hour to die, and if the drop is too long the head and body can be separated."

"One thing does seem odd."

"And what would that be?"

"No chair," I piped up. "There's always a kicked-over chair."

Quill blew solid smog. "We're in a barn, we are not in a gentleman's parlour." He nodded to a ladder propped against the wall of the barn. "And I doubt he had the good manners to return that to its proper place."

"Not suicide is what you are telling me," I said.

I was answered by another. "Even a bloke with *two* arms ain't going to tidy up the place after topping himself, is he? And he's only got *one*." With a foot on the first rung of the ladder was a rotund constable, the

18

one who had whacked me across the head on the evening of my arrest: Constable Studely. "And only one ear."

"The Great War," I said as though the disfigurement should be of no surprise. After all, it was nigh on impossible to walk down a city street or through a quaint English village without passing some poor soul blinded or crippled, physically and mentally destroyed in some way or another: the hell did not cease with the ending of the tolling bell.

The constable batted on. "So, you haven't seen him for twenty years? How can you be sure it is him?"

"Exactly," said Quill with a glare warning Studely to keep his nose out of the inquiry.

I looked back to Quill then with near-closed eyes nodded down to death. "I would know that face and body anywhere."

"You would? Even bashed up like that?"

"Of course. The man saved my life on several occasions and he was always ready with soap and badger, even when standing up to his snake belt buckle in mud, blood, and guts. A German sniper removed the right ear. The round went straight through his helmet."

The moustache hinted at some incredulity. "And it didn't kill him?"

"He always drank his tea from his helmet. He was holding the vessel up high to keep it from the mud and rats. After a good about turn he was ready to plonk himself down on an ammunition box when the bullet zinged its way through the helmet, did a smart ricochet, and slapped him in the ear. Poor Clackett didn't even get his first sweet sip of the day. You should have heard the blighter curse. Never mess up a working man's cuppa, that's one thing you should always remember, Quill…"

"Inspector."

I ignored the correction. If there's one thing I cannot abide, it is the puffing out of one's chest with rank. I never do it.

I looked back down to my dead friend then back to Quill. "Next thing, he's up the ladder waving a white-knuckled fist and letting off cusses. The arm was removed by the second shot. Those Hun snipers were pretty determined to get their man, you know."

"I reckon…I deduce…he was given a beating then knocked unconscious before being carried up that ladder to the noose. Maybe they tried to make it look like suicide but…" Quill fell silent as though contradicting his thoughts.

I prompted. "Why am I here? I didn't murder him. Like I said…haven't seen him for years…dead or alive."

"Ah, yes, but you knew the man. You admit that much."

"I most certainly did but that was twenty years ago, Inspector. And…" I stressed this point with a twirling finger, "you'll also remember, if you ponder for a mo., I have been safely locked up at His Majesty's pleasure…"

"He was on his way to see you, Hardimann."

"Mr. Hardimann," I added for him. "So you said."

Quill offered one of those wasp-chewing Bulldog *"don't push it"* scowls. "He needed your help, didn't he?"

I shrugged. "But in what way could I help him?"

"Makes me shudder to think. A man of his calibre sacrificing so much for the pale and shoddy over-indulged likes of your class." He pulled himself to full height and prepared a Fabian fusillade. "For four years…" He relaxed a little and shoved his hands in his pockets. "There was a letter."

Now, I'm sure that you, like me would have expected Quill to do a bit of the old *légère de main* and supply me with some missal. No such luck. I gawped with disappointment. "Where is it?"

"I no longer have it about my person, Mr. Hardimann."

Isn't it odd the way policemen seem to lack a 'self' or a 'me', and view themselves as inhabiting a "person"?

"Well?" I taunted.

Quill, for some strange reason, felt this news best reported by another. "Studely?"

Studely waddled over. "It has been delivered, sir. By motorcycle, sir."

"If you mean dispatch rider, say dispatch rider."

"Dispatch rider, sir," sulked Studely.

Quill grinned. Now, I don't mind a chap blowing his own trumpet from time to time, and would encourage him to do so should the appropriate victory demand it, but Quill was armed with the complete brass ensemble, no matter how flat the notes. "We have found our missing man, we have found the letter, and now we have you. A tidy little result, even if I say so myself. Now, you have a duty to perform, Mr Hardimann." He unpocketed a hand and waved at the barn doors. "Your transport is waiting for you."

"Home?" I chanced.

"Someone else is reading the letter. You are invited to share in its details before exchanging your arrowed pyjamas for the cloak and dagger. Get back in the car."

Ice dribbled into my veins and my horizon was swallowed in cloud.

I left the scene and headed for the Rolls Royce and the driver who had delivered me to that strange meeting. He was holding open the passenger door. "Not far to go now, sir, you will soon be at your destination," he drawled.

CHAPTER 4
...to a Baby in The Bathwater

After thirty minutes of my driver's gentle murmuring along with the wireless, and his occasional attempts at shared harmony – he seemed to be an aficionado of the trombone – I alighted on the driveway of a large estate.

It was a strange red-bricked affair, as if the architect had begun in earnest to create a stout Victorian school before changing tack and heading for a castle. The garden was not yet in full bloom, but snowdrops were edging their way up to the tendrils of weeping willows. Kent's patchwork of greens wallowed for miles, as far as the eye could see, and in the distance small white clouds did their gambolling thing.

My stomach grumbled, calling for late breakfast or early lunch, as I watched my driver creep away towards the tradesman's entrance.

I followed suit in the hope we'd enter through the kitchen. "Eggs and bacon would not be pushed aside," I chirruped as I caught up with the man.

"You are invited to luncheon, sir," he replied as he opened a paint-chipped door and signalled for me to enter a boot and gun room. He closed the door behind him and wafted past. "If you would be kind enough to follow me, sir?"

I followed, took in the smells of gunpowder and gun oil, brushed fingertips along oak panelling and patted two inquisitive but rather docile black Labradors, before breaking into the cavern of a hallway where we came to a halt at the foot of a stairway.

"The first door on the right, sir." He flapped his gauntlets at the stairway. "Just knock and enter."

My empty stomach plummeted as I began my ascent. I crept on soft red carpet before coming to a landing of buffed oak boards. They creaked a little.

The door was ajar and along with the grunts emerging from the room was a mixture of visible gases. I can't provide you with a scientifically accurate ratio, but I guessed it was fifty percent steam and fifty percent smoke from the barrel of a thigh-rolled Montecristo.

As commanded, I knocked and pushed at the door, allowing more cloud to drift out and add sheen to my face. The steam and smoke billowed, most of it sweeping out onto the landing, and there, sitting in a bath with most of the bulk shrouded in a mountain of bubbles was...a baby. When

I say a baby, imagine one nearing twenty stone. Elbows were perched on the side of the tub and in one hand was the cigar, in the other was brandy in a balloon large enough to lift Montgolfier and his extended family.

Chins and shoulders wobbled, the baby's voice rumbled. "Enough, Milly."

The sparking bits of the old grey matter went into overdrive and I pushed the door open a little further. There in the corner, perched on a stool was a woman with tortoiseshell spectacles, a journalist's pad and a pencil. She was dressed primly in tweed, no doubt doubling the weight of her tiny frame with all the moisture it must have sponged from the perfumed air.

A strange expression of disappointment came across her face, somewhat akin to the look Lazarus would have conveyed if rising from the grave to find that nobody recognized him or even batted an eyelid in faint surprise at such a miracle. She arose from her stool and brushed past me without a consonant or vowel being formed.

The bather continued. "So, you are Hardimann, eh?"

"I am," I confirmed.

"Good, pass me a towel." He waved the cigar like a swagger stick. "The white one beneath the mirror."

When reaching for the towel rail at the ankle end of the tub I caught a reflected glance of the huge figure lifting from the water, all pink and bubbly and overcooked. There was a moment of awkwardness and visual avoidance as we swapped objects. I grappled with the cigar and balloon as he squinted like a child with soap in his eyes and grabbed for the towel.

He dabbed at his face as he gave more voice, so I cannot give you a perfect record, but it sounded like, "was there a suitcase? There was a suitcase. Did he get the suitcase to you...?"

Finding life more comfortable looking in the mirror, I studied my reflection. I had the drawn features of a cod misjudging the gauge of a trawler's net and coming to the conclusion that there was no return.

The bather grunted and struggled over the side of the bath before wrapping himself in a dragon festooned gown. He shoved his feet into black velvet slippers.

I felt it safe enough to turn. "A suitcase?" I asked, giving a flappy waft to clear my face of talcum powder.

He tugged at the belt of his gown then reclaimed his cigar and brandy. "Clackett was carrying a suitcase," he answered, waving me to remove myself from his bathroom. I inched back out onto the landing and was about to give him the negative riposte when he boomed. "Milly."

From the top of the stairs I looked down to the tiny figure of the secretary who was still armed with pad and pencil.

"Sir?"

"My bloody glasses, woman."

"You left them in your studio, sir," she answered, with a shock-inducing bellow up the stairs, before she scuttled away in her sensible clogs.

The old man plugged the Montecristo into his mouth, picked up his walking stick and started his slow swaying progress down the stairs. I followed, trying not to sneeze or bump into him.

A few minutes later – I told you it was a slow journey – I found myself in an artist's studio. The walls were covered in pastoral scenes and the furniture was smudged with a rainbow of colours as if he'd used the whole room as his palette.

He slumped into a high-backed chair, put on his glasses, and squinted at me. "Clackett was looking for you, Hardimann. We have found him, or at least his body, but there was no suitcase."

I pinched at my strides and perched a quarter of my rear on a stout and sturdy table. "I have no idea why, sir," I offered in all frankness. "It's been a score of Christmases since we parted."

He grumbled, turned the cigar, removed it, lifted the brandy balloon, returned the cigar. His face was still pink, and his cheeks glowed as though having been pinched by an aunt: one of those busty aunts who squeeze you ferociously and tell you how much you've grown – every bloody weekend.

I can be quick once the starting gun has cracked, but I had no idea why Clackett would be looking for me, let alone be murdered, or why he should have been armed with a suitcase. I chanced a question. "The suitcase is important? More than a spare pair of socks, a clean shirt, a regimental tie, and a starched collar?"

My stomach rumbled and a rectangle of sunlight broke into the room. A budgerigar twittered in a corner and the two Labradors slunk in. One of the dogs traversed the full length of the room to sit at the feet of its master while the other seemed to regard the journey as too demanding a task and felt satisfied with struggling a yard or so before planting itself on my grey suede shoes, clamping me to the carpet. My feet felt slow warming: a little too much warming.

The old man did some patting then looked back to me. "He was carrying a piece of scientific equipment. A state secret."

"Did he steal it?"

"No, he damn well didn't, Hardimann. He was working for me."

"Well, well," I said. "Old Clackett playing spies eh?"

Now, I'm not one to judge a man, but I could have sworn that baby face was scowling at me as he spoke. When I say spoke, let me explain. It was a low rumbling voice, sure in its delivery but rather too slow for my liking. I'm a great lover of zippy badinage, the cut and thrust of argument even though I am commonly viewed by members of my club as somewhat taciturn and laconic. That's most probably because I'm a great listener who always holds sway for another fellow who wishes to spin a yarn. But of course, there's nothing worse than a cove pricking over the hills and dales of verbosity just as you are inwardly pleading with him to get to the point before the Port and Stilton arrives.

As I say, he spoke. "Clackett may have put down his rifle as you did at the end of the Great War, Hardimann, but he went on to greater things, always ready and willing to serve his country. You, on the other hand…" The cigar morphed from swagger stick to headmaster's cane. "You have spent the last twenty years in the smoking rooms and billiard halls of Knightsbridge. That is, when you have not been incarcerated at His Majesty's pleasure for petty larceny."

My jaw took a tumble towards the floor. Damn it. Stealing diamonds, pearls, and priceless art is not exactly petty. It takes a craftsman; an artisan, a man with perfect timing, the most acute of all five senses, and a light touch. But I held my tongue.

"We will soon be at war with Germany, Mr. Hardimann."

"Really?" I enquired. "How so?"

I don't know what I'd said to get the chap all a fluster, but he arose like a bear that had just realized Goldilocks had been messing about in his house. His grumble took on the tone of an awakening volcano as he staggered towards me, all red and shiny and coated in gold dragons. A man of less fortitude and thinner wit would have chuckled with a failure of the nerves at such a scene, but I kept my guard as he erupted. "While you were slopping out and mopping the tiles, Mr. Hardimann, our beloved Prime Minister handed the Sudetenland to Hitler, on a plate. And the nasty little corporal will want more very soon."

It took me a moment to free myself from the swirling fug of the brandy and cigar smoke. "And that's down to Clackett and a suitcase?"

We were almost *nez à nez*. "No, it bloody well isn't. What it means is that very soon we'll be going through hell once more." I must have appeared a little nonplussed to him, prompting him to add, "We will be at war, Hardimann. Time for you to play your part, do your bit."

I gave the shoulders a ripple. "I did my bit twenty years ago. I gave my blood, sweat, toil and tears."

He withdrew from me, taking cigar and brandy, and went over to his table. He brushed aside some paint pots and spent a moment searching. A look of delight came across his face. I half expected him to giggle and present one of those rattling chuckles toddlers produce when coming to terms with an oversized gobstopper. He picked up a pencil and scribbled something down on a scrap of paper.

Having dropped the writing implement and rearranged his face to its original grimace he looked back at me. "And you'll be doing it again. No doubt you've managed to gloss over more than *The Sporting Life* in your quieter moments, and you may have seen what the war machine of the German National Socialists did to Guernica. That's what they will do here, Hardimann, and they will be swarming all over us after the bombing."

He had a point, so I gave my approval. "Not so much sitting in the trenches, but fighting on the beaches, in the fields and in the streets this time." Well, dash it all if he didn't start scribbling again. "England expects…" I added. He didn't write that one down. He'd probably heard it before off that Jenkins fellow, you know the one I mean: the one who lost an ear at Trafalgar.

He wiped his hands down his gown, ruffled the dragons, tightened himself up and waddled back to me. I counted it as a blessing that he'd left smoking and drinking at his table. It's always nice to have a clear view of a fellow when he's trying to stake his claim. I allowed him to continue.

"We need the Americans, Hardimann, and we'll need them on our side a damn sight quicker than the last time, I can tell you." I was in no position to tell him he couldn't tell me, so again I let him continue. "Chamberlain is an ass, and Halifax is a…"

I have never been one for cabinet, frontbenchers, backbenchers or even those in the shadows. "Another ass?" I offered, always ready to help a chap halted by a papercut as he flicks his way through his mental dictionary.

"If there is a war, Chamberlain will resign, and Halifax will take the helm. He'll want to do a deal with Hitler." His face expanded with a beetroot hue. "Never, I say. We shall never do a deal with Hitler. We cannot do a deal with Hitler. We shall have to fight until the very end."

I shoved my hands in my pockets and felt the friendship of my cigarette case. I was gasping for one but thought it better not to ask. I slipped the case from my pocket and watched his reactions. He nodded. All well and good. I lit one up and puffed a pungent blue towards him. "We will never surrender. Is that what you're saying? Good show."

"I've been making plans, Mr. Hardimann."

I beamed and donated another "Good show." I respect a chap with plans. "Saves a great deal of mishap and bother."

My interjection must have blown him off course a little. He put fingers to his bottom lip as if preparing a blubber or gurgle. "I've been making plans, secret talks with some Americans. They know they must get involved eventually but they will hold off as long as possible. The important thing is that they provide us with arms and munitions, and above all cease trading with the Nazis. We are in a sorry state of affairs, a sorry state of affairs. We should have been rearming ten years ago, and would have been but for that miserable red weakling, MacDonald, and Baldwin with his belated sense of urgency..."

I'd heard that argument before and could see his point. "But will they play ball?"

He nodded with solemnity engraved on his brow. "They will, at great cost to us, but dare I say it, a cost much lighter than that of bending to the Nazi will. We are no position to pay with ready cash or even with ready gold, and I cannot go to parliament with cap in hand, I cannot even go to parliament. I am using another coinage. Science, science and engineering. That is something I can trade in secret without the likes of Chamberlain and Halifax getting wind." He took a moment to oil the vocal cords with brandy. "We are a few years ahead of the Americans in some of our engineering. Our man Clackett was to make the first delivery of a vital piece of defensive equipment as a down payment."

"In a suitcase?"

"Yes, Hardimann. In a suitcase. He was coming to see you, to enlist you as a companion on his voyage."

"But I was..."

"Yes, you were locked up. We didn't realize that until today, but it seems Clackett did."

"Done his homework, eh?"

"You were to travel with him, without you knowing about the suitcase, of course, to New York. It was to be under the pretext of some business adventure, and you were to lend moral support."

"I can readily dish out the moral stuff," I said, perhaps with a little too much enthusiasm.

His face hardened. "Good. You are to take his place."

I coughed smoke. "Take his place?"

He came over all fatherly, and I must confess that first name terms with chaps do not readily put me at my ease. "Time to do your duty again, Pelham." He winked and added a sly sentence: the sort that kicks you when you're down. "England expected before and England expects again."

"Like a bally woman," I said. "You make sacrifice after sacrifice, give her your all, the shirt from your back and the blood from your veins, and just as you recover she comes back for more." I take this truth in good faith, for I have never allowed myself to succumb to such weaknesses with affairs of the heart.

"Precisely," he said with a fulsome grin that allowed the glint of wiring on his bottom plate. He wobbled for a moment as if his shoulders were balancing a yoke. "Of course, should you wish not to assist your King and country, your King has in all kindness allowed your prison bunk to remain reserved…for you to lie upon… as long as he deems fit."

Of all the nerve, I thought. It may be true what our good man William said about mercy dropping from the heavens like the gentle rain, but I, Pelham Hardimann, was roasting beneath the furnace of a cloudless sky. And the yoke was mine.

"Patriotism is swelling in my breast as we speak," I said in the hope my larynx had not done the constricting it had suffered earlier in the presence of Quill.

He smiled before shouting. "Hammer." He softened. "Oh, Hammer, there you are."

A voice came from behind me, a voice near enough for its breath to warm the back of my neck. "Yes, Mr. Churchill, sir. I had just arrived to inform you that Mr. Halifax is on the telephone."

I began his sentence with feet on terra firma, spent most of it in the air, and landed on what would have been his full stop. I turned.

The driver-cum-valet smiled. "I apologize, sir. It was not my intention to startle you."

"Hell's teeth, Hammer," I said, practising his name for the first time. "You could bottle smooth-and-silent-gliding and sell it to swans."

"It is something in which I take great pride and something for which I have been well trained, sir."

Hammer and I were just about to shake warm hands, pat each other on the back and do the manly "glad to be friends and we must have a beer sometime" thing when Mr. Churchill came between us.

"This is Hammer. He will accompany you, Pelham."

"I see. You want me to take another piece…"

"You must find the suitcase. Retrieve it, guard it with your life then deliver it into safe hands."

Hammer (as I shall now refer to him, for he offered me no other name) used some hocus pocus to supply me with an ash tray. I stubbed out and he hid it. I needed both hands free for what I was about to say.

"But Clackett was murdered for that suitcase. It's dashed clear to me that some villainous sort does not wish for the said vessel to arrive at port on the other side of the pond."

Mr. Churchill placed a firm hand on my shoulder, but I did not give way. "Exactly, Pelham. I shall enlighten you. There are a few members of Parliament with some inkling as to what I am doing. There are many Americans who do not wish to be once more embroiled in European squabbles, and Nazis who know what we are about. None of them, I assure you, wish to see that suitcase arrive in New York in your hands. However, they all want it for their own purpose, gratis."

As I often do in my more stressful moments, I came over all peckish. "I wouldn't mind something to eat before setting off," I said with hope in the pump.

Hammer sniffed. "Milly is preparing sandwiches for us now, sir. You can take advantage of that time to read Mr. Clackett's correspondence."

Followed by his favourite Labrador, Mr. Churchill wandered from the room after giving a nod to Hammer. The second dog, the one using my favourite suede shoes as its resting place, gave leisurely chase after stopping a moment to look up at me with what can only be described as a wide-eyed expression of guilt.

I looked down at my darkened shoes then back up to Hammer.

"A most discriminating hound, sir," was all Hammer had to say on the matter.

If a forlorn look washed across my face, I am sure you can understand why. England may expect, has a right to expect and is expected to expect. But not from a badly shod man fuelled with only sandwiches. And a man on a mission could have expected better reading material.

CHAPTER 5
SOME AUTOBIOGRAPHY AND THE LETTER

I must beg your forgiveness. In the previous chapters you hugged me tightly to your breast and trusted me as I recounted how I arrived in this situation, in the gripping company of one of our former Honourable cabinet members and his dedicated major-domo.

My failure to notice your trembling, your need to understand how I became the man I am can only be excused by my desire to get things rolling along. There's no fun in getting oneself bogged down in all the tiny details, the whys and wherefores, the whens and whences and other things, unless one has done the tickling. I trust I have tickled you enough. Let me set things out, put the cards on the table and confess before the bodies start piling up.

I was born with the old *argentum* spoon highly polished and wedged into the maw and as soon as the brain had some worthwhile reason for connecting with the vocal cords, the fruit of the genus *prunus* was shoved in. I took to the tails and topper with ease; learned how to pass the port, be vicious at croquet, bully my fag and avoid paying my tailor. By seventeen I was the *honnête homme* and ready to be squeezed into uniform. I will gloss over the two years as a sword-waving subaltern, only noting that I was one of the few of that rank to see the chalk cliffs again.

In 1919, pleased to be back in civvies, I parted company with my batman, Clackett, wished him and his Newcastle all the best and headed back to Oxfordshire to see how the old flint ruin was doing.

"All seems rather rosy so far," I hear you grumble. Do not be sour. Keep your chagrin and class envy at bay for a while. Life is not always as easy as it appears when viewed from outside the circle of perceived comfort. Have you ever played croquet? And let us keep in mind what that chap Tolstoy said about families: *every unhappy family is unhappy in its own way.*

Home, for want of a better word, was an impressive estate more than large enough for Mrs. Bennett and her daughters to rattle around in, but their snobbish friend Mr. Darcy would have deemed it a little cramped. Oaks and cedars, lawns and lakes, and a ha-ha. Along with a full corps of staff, ornate furniture and silverware, we had a good mix of oils and watercolours, the pastoral stuff, the obligatory family portraits and some of those awful ones of horses with heavy, shiny bodies and spindly legs.

The first collection to be noticeable by its diminution was the company of servants; the rot set in at the beginning of the war. The buggers gave notice at the rate of at least one a month. By the beginning of 1920 we were guarded by one butler, a driver with only one Rolls to polish, and a cook. The cook, the portly Mrs. Allingham, was no worry. She was in the fourth quarter of her century and we rested assured the Good Lord would soon be handing in her notice on her behalf.

The paintings were reduced in number at a speedier rate, first the oils, mainly the horses, and then the watercolours. The portraits were not so easy to dispose of. Who, let us be truthful with each other, would want a cracked daub the size of a screen at Lord's Cricket Ground of someone else's great uncle?

The reason for these losses was a simple one. Father was hooked on the hoof and the hooch. The more he imbibed, the more he bet, and the more he lost, the more he imbibed. Not so much swings and roundabouts, but a helter-skelter, at the end of which was a bottomless pit. He wagered and he invested when it came to nags, and soon-for-the-glue-factory nags they invariably were. He diluted his pain with the best clarets, champagne, and malt whiskies.

Father was never one to skimp, unless it concerned the tax man. Wars and the debts they incur must be paid for and our government could not expect the common man to dip into his pocket; had not the brush of state been too heavily dipped into that blood already? The tax man was regular in his correspondence: soon to become a regular visitor. And let us not forget the pile. Upkeep is the word. These ancestral homes have their draughts, most of them sweeping up notes of the realm as they go.

It was a crisp March morning in 1920, a Saturday if I recall, when father sat down to break his fast, still dressing-gowned and slippered. He'd scraped some Cooper's Oxford onto cold toast, stuck the knife in the edge to clean it, poured his coffee, and settled down with the post. I wouldn't say he was agitated, but he was not as still as usual. He spent some moments shifting about on his chair, rocking from cheek to cheek the way a maiden aunt does when she's trying to let loose a silent trouser cough.

My father was no trilling lark in the morning, had not been so since the day of my birth, but once settled he managed to mumble something. "Banking, boy; we could make good use of someone in banking."

I lifted my gaze from *The London Charivari*, in which some wag had suggested that all the great men were dead, and I returned my father's rare morning vocal lob. "Well," I volleyed, "it's always fun to play with other people's money."

That seemed to be the end of the conversation, so I went back to my reading and father attacked an envelope with his recently wiped knife.

I could state, in order to step up the drama a notch that his face whitened with shock. However, it was difficult to tell. His face had been hangdog and sallow for forty years. He grunted, mumbled something about the Purdeys then informed me of his desire to be left alone in the library.

I, busy tucking into the Cumberland sausages, eggs and bacon, thought it best to grant him his wish. Besides, my mind was on other things: some sour comments in that week's edition about Winston Churchill, and my hope to trade in the Singer 'Ten' for something a little sportier. It is also worth recounting that father, by this time, went to the library after calling to Mrs. Allingham to deliver the Purdeys on a weekly basis.

My concentration was interrupted by a shot, a yell, and another shot. You would not be wrong in assuming the second shot was the coup de grace. It was a very long Purdey. It is not easy to shoot oneself with a shotgun at the best of times. My guess was that practice had been called for.

The first cartridge had emptied itself behind my father, punching a dartboard size hole into a frowning Mortimer Hardimann. It was not one of my favourite portraits, but old Mortimer had been a jovial sort of fellow, full of tales of how only armed with the Maxim he had quelled uprisings in the Congo, the Sudan and Zanzibar, and many other pink places where warmongering natives brandished the assegai.

"What of the second shot?" I hear you ask. I am no artist, no connoisseur, I am more the dilettante, but I think you'll agree with me when I say that the rear half of my father's splattered cranium did not repair the hole in Uncle Mortimer's bulky frame with any aesthetic charm… but it did fill it.

It did not take long to view the tiny massacre. I went back to the dining room to read the letter – to find it the catalyst of all the damage, and to hear a shriek of horror and a wail of grief, followed by the thump of a collapsing body as God handed Mrs. Allingham her cards.

Having read the letter pertaining to our financial predicament, I felt I had little chance of receiving references from the great and the good as far as a career in banking was concerned. I did, however, like the idea of playing with other people's money.

I sense you are judging me, even pointing the finger, perhaps donning the black cloth and praying God may have mercy on my soul. Let me explain. I am not without feeling by choice. I was meat for the gallows before gasping for my first lungful of nursery air.

"Your mother died giving you life," my father would remind me as he sent me off to schooling and noticed my return from schooling with a grunt and an *"oh, you're back, then."* I was never permitted to put the matter to the back of my mind. In his eyes, I was a murderer. The need for penance and self-flagellation was always on the front burner in the Hardimann household, from the day I was born.

I'm sure you know how we use incidents as reference points in our reminiscences. *"Do you remember…a year before your mother died…just after the death of…not long after…?"* Even my brother, Grenville, three years my senior was trained to keep the subject raised at all opportune moments. He was taught to hate and bully, excelling on both fronts as only children can. Grenville cashed in his chips on the first day of The Somme, along with 58,000 other British and Commonwealth fodder. I may have been suddenly blessed with the loss of a berater, but Father did not stint in the pursuit of his *raison d'etre*. Father, with his ache of loss multiplied, continued the *'giving life'* routine and though adhering to fatherly duties in terms of education and ever-diminishing finances, his heart was kept at more than an arm's length.

That thing about giving life has always hung heavy with me. Life is not given to us like some jolly ribbon-and-bowed *cadeau*. We are shovelled into the world like coals into the furnace of a steam engine, without warning, without being questioned, and asked to be forever glowing with gratitude. Our parents, if you are lucky enough to be pestered by two, fatten us and fill us with their unfulfilled dreams and scorn us with their nightmares, slaver over us with baby talk, wave us at the world and boast of our gifts and natural talents, never ceasing to remind us that it is they who did it all for us. But if we fail to live up to their standards and dreams, we let them down. We drop the ball in a game we never asked to join. Do not misunderstand me; I do have my softer, tender places, but if I am a little *en retard* in slapping the old *cardio* below the leather patches of the Harris Tweed, I have good reason.

Enough of that. We can tarry a little later if you devoutly wish it. I have an inkling you are itching to garner knowledge of my criminal lifestyle. You must wait. We must go back to Kent, to Chartwell, and on with the plot.

The letter – perhaps the second most important letter in my life – was handed to me by Hammer as I followed him through a low door into the kitchen where I fell back into a solid chair, rested my unshod and still damp feet on the rail of the range. A willow-pattern plate of sandwiches perched on the near corner of the great oak table. A kettle, recovering from a long and energetic bout of whistling, let off little puffs of steam.

I grumbled something about duty being foisted upon the good self by external forces.

Hammer checked I was comfortable, edged the sandwiches and teapot nearer and said "Kant." I believe it was Kant. He then made to leave me, humming and brum-brumming *Saint Louis Blues* as he backed from the kitchen with the stoop and pensive look of an aged man struggling over the threshold with a nubile bride counting the days she had to suffer before getting a decko at the will.

Talking of will, his was most certainly ill. Let me explain. There are some fellows one can read like a book. Hammer was the book opened at the correct page with the appropriate paragraph neatly circled in red ink, and a note saying: *"Read this!"* The paragraph? I would guess it to be something savage, full of spite, contempt and bile concerning his new position as my guardian, valet, keeper, bodyguard, servant, lackey, and a string of other meaningless forms of employment.

He had more to say. "I am endeavouring, on your behalf, to take possession of more suitable attire, sir."

I eyed him in the hope he was not about to create a twin for himself. I have never come across as dashing, handsome or debonair in black. It's my colouring, you know. "Something sporty," I said. "Shoes would be good." I wiggled a wet foot. "Size…"

"I am well aware of your stature, sir." He recovered from the strange stoop and pulled at his cuffs. "As I said: suitable."

I'm never happy with that phrase *"As I said"*. It has a tone, a ring about it. Not as under-the-belt as *"with all due respect"* but certainly jabbing towards *"do I have to repeat everything, you blithering idiot?"*

He prepared a sneer as he finished his way through the door then trump-trumped to catch up with where he'd left William Christopher Handy to his own admirable devices. He closed the door firmly behind him.

I am adept at my own dirty looks, so I presented him with one to enjoy *in absentia.* I watched the brass knob rattle to rest before changing focus to nod a hello to Milly – the girl in tweed in the bathroom if you recall – who was practising the raising of individual eyebrows, the sort of thing that demands a great deal of concentration and should only be done in private and in front of a mirror. I remember having sacrificed such time and energy to the old flicking-the-cigarette-to-the-lips routine. A waste of time you may feel, but let me assure you, such a skill has introduced me to a pretty face and shapely ankle a lot speedier than wittering on about the latest MG or a recently purchased mashie.

I gave my dog-pee-soaked toes a wriggle over the bar of the range and caught Milly's eye. "A little damp?"

"I'm quite at ease, thank you," she said.

I landed a finger onto the folded letter and pulled it across the table towards me.

Milly ceased the eyebrow regime and began another one, taking it in turns to adjust her glasses and the lay of her skirt as she sat perched on a tall ironing stool in the far corner of the kitchen, squashed between the range and a shelf of copper pots and pans. "It was stitched into his collar," she said.

"Was it, by George?" I quipped, unfolding the letter. To be honest, I was unsure how to answer. "He was always a cautious man," I lied. Clackett was never a cautious man; he was stuffed from head to toe with the bravura most of us can only dream of, but I always feel ill at ease when someone darkens the memory of another. He had been my batman and had served me well, and that is good enough for me.

"It is common practice in the service," Milly continued. "There were two messages. One for us, and one for you."

I pinned her with an ocular stab. "I can see the other?"

"No."

"Well, I suggest you leave me in peace to read." It occurred to me as odd that she should make the error of mentioning another letter, especially if it was so obviously not for my perusal. I left the irritation as something to be scratched at a later date.

I feel I must comment on Milly at this point. You know when you shake a beautifully wrapped Birthday present – you know the sort, large with lots of paper, ribbons and bows – and it teases you, plays with your imagination? Well, there are other presents, neatly wrapped but solid and you know it's going to be a bloody book, or it's all squidgy and you're sure you are in for an ill-fitting and gruesome hand-knitted pullover. That's how Milly struck me the second time of espying her. She needed a shake, just in case she was what I'd always wanted. But part of me was sure she would be the dour and wholesome book, something like a volume from Gibbon's *Decline and Fall*...

I tempted a smile in the hope it would at least loosen a bow. It wasn't my birthday. She said nothing, slid from her stool, gave me a glance filled with the malice one would have seen on the face of a disciple coming across Judas counting his silver, and for the second time in twenty minutes she marched off to relieve herself of my presence.

I bit into soft brown bread, thick cheese and a spicy pickle as I began the missal. It was not an easy read. I recall Clackett's writing having something of the arachnid about it, and the scrawling beast seemed to have lost a couple of legs over the passing years. I don't feel it wise to transcribe the complete opus; I think the gist will suffice.

It began: *I am writing this slowly. You will understand why am writing this slowly. I never was able to write fast. I don't know if you remember. I was left-*

handed. I still is left-handed. But at the same time, I have to be right-handed. It rambled on for a few lines about a docker squashing the bed springs with his good lady wife while he was fighting for King and country – that sort of thing happened a lot. Then some cryptic stuff – cryptic through lack of grammar if nothing else – about working for some special people, but not getting the really special jobs because he hadn't been to Cambridge and you can only trust people who have been to Cambridge.

It appeared that Clackett had taken delivery of the case from two clever chaps in Birmingham. Scientists, the sort with extended foreheads and unruly hair, I imagined. Nothing verging on the adventurous there, I mused. But on further reading I learned that poor Clackett was the rabbit, on the run and hopping from burrow to burrow, with his pursuers hot on his unlucky heels.

As for the farmers with their guns? One, Clackett explained in his scrawl, was *a square-jawed and monocle-wearing German fellow, identifiable by a missing small toe on his left foot.* Nothing as easy as a missing finger or an arm, I clucked. And how did Clackett get to know about this missing toe?

I spent a few moments contemplating how I could put myself in such a position as to check for the deformity. As Mrs. Beeton would have advised: *first, catch your German.* "No, no, Mrs. Beeton," I mouthed in silent rebuttal. "First, let your German catch you." I shivered at the thought. I have spent many a long day avoiding traps and there I was setting mine own. It is an extremely thin line stretching between heroism and foolishness. And I could feel a 'twang' and a 'snap' coming.

On I read. *I am being followed by an old woman. She uses a bicycle and knitting needles.* Little chance of harm there, I thought. Perhaps Clackett was losing it, a touch of trench foot in the brain or the old shell shock coming back to haunt him. And on I read. *Americans, in long raincoats: chain smokers, and hat wearers, and gum chewers.* Nothing to worry about there, I thought. Chicago hoodlums were not at this point making waves in the calm tributaries of England.

Clackett went on to explain that he'd visited my sometime colleague, Sam the Spot, who had advised him of my short holiday at the King's expense.

I folded the paper and attacked another sandwich. There was no mention of the suitcase and that puzzled me. Isn't that what all this is about? I was a little disappointed. Clackett, with his letter, a chore worthy of Sisyphus on his part, had scrawled a great deal but informed me of little. The letter put me in mind of those witnesses of events interviewers drag before us. "*Well,*" the witness begins, full of bluster and pride, "*I was in the back yard putting out the washing. Gerald was in the kitchen scraping the dinner plates like he usually does on a Sunday; he's very good like that. We had a leg of lamb and I always use the leftovers for a Shepherd's Pie on the Monday or Tuesday; you can't leave lamb too long. When all of a sudden I heard…a bang. I said to Gerald…"* You know the sort of thing? Full of Macbeth's whatsits and signifying nothing.

Deciding one mouthful of the next sandwich was enough, I dropped my feet from the bar of the range and stood to stretch the legs. I swaggered about the kitchen, made a few circuits of the table, opened lids, sniffed at pots then lit a cigarette.

Half a Pall Mall's amount of boredom passed. I was turning events and recently acquired knowledge over in the old lemon, concentrating mainly on the missing toe and the knitting needles, when I heard a regular clipping sound: the metronomic snapping of heels adorned with metal resounding on floorboards then floor tiles.

The doorknob rattled and I turned to see Hammer doing his erect thing. He had the air of a man who'd enjoyed the luxury of a wash and brush up, his hair neatly oiled and pressed, his eyes cleaned of the dust and clutter of the morning's exertions.

It was at this point when something struck me. His ears. There was something about the angle and size of them that must surely cause him concern in strong winds. That may seem of slight importance to you but stick with me; I am a keen observer of the species *homo sapiens*. Picture the clean-cut arch of bare skin between ear and trimmed hair. Not the sort of thing one would normally notice, but the angle of his head had caught the light. The man had dyed his hair and omitted to clean the excess of solution between ear and hair, the way a chap can, in times of confusion and interruption such as the doorbell clanging or phone jangling, fail to wipe away that little strip of shaving soap that has escaped the slice of the blade.

A thin black rivulet made its way from the outside of the pinna – if I remember my anatomy correctly – down the side of his neck and within reach of his starched collar. The flow was staunched with surprising speed as Hammer whipped a handkerchief from his top pocket, flicked, dabbed and wiped. His pained smile was enough for me to ascertain we were in one of those *I know you know, and I know you know that I know, and you know I know…* situations.

Someone had to chuck a brick through the hiatus, if that's what you do with hiatuses. I volunteered with reinforced cheeriness and an artistic flourish of cigarette to show that all was tickety-boo and we were well towards the end of the beginning, if not the beginning of the end.

"We must head to Knightsbridge, Hammer." I gave my hands a clap of resolution, get-up-and-go. "I need my little black book." Forgive me if I glossed over my little black book some paragraphs ago. The time did not call for your need to be appraised of more than my list of charming girls, but within the hardboard covers of that little book also lay my other connections; let's call them business connections. "Sam the Spot is the man I need to see, Hammer. We will soon have the suitcase in our hands. I can then take dinner at my club while you settle in the spare room of my commodious mews house, the suitcase sitting pretty on your knees, while you consider our next move, perchance a drive to Southampton where we may embark on a steamer to the Americas."

Hammer clicked into the kitchen and came to attention. "There is a liner leaving within the next few days, sir. I shall pull strings."

"Very well," I said with glee. It had been some time since I'd worn my deck shoes and blazer. I'd never been one for the cap and scrambled egg; that would be taking things too far, but the whiff of a salty breeze and the skid of quoits on a swabbed deck as the sun dips with an imagined hiss into the horizon brings a joyous flutter to the heart. An iceberg entered upon the scene as I remembered we were out of season. No matter, I thought, ever the optimist, there is always *chemin de fer* and the cocktail lounge. I exited my reverie and noticed Hammer still standing to attention. "Very good, Hammer. Just need to spruce up a bit and change the togs."

"A bath has been run for you, sir, and clothes arranged. You may continue through to the guest bedroom once you have finished your *toilette*." He did a smart about turn and signalled to the door. "If you will allow me to guide you, sir."

Hammer followed me from the room. Once upstairs, he introduced me to what I felt to be a rather dark and heavy worsted, and a highly polished pair of brogues. He presented me with a sturdy walking cane, brass handled and adorned with two triggers. One, he informed me, was for the blade and the other for a few .22 rounds.

"This is necessary?" I fumbled a little before squeezing the first trigger, sending a Toledo into the knee of a dainty cabriole-legged dressing table.

Hammer steadied the table as I retrieved my blade. He gave me the old fisheye look as he uprighted a selection of colognes. "If I venture to take the liberty, sir, despite the recent death of your former friend Clackett, I feel you are not fully cognisant of the dangers. Enemies are without."

"Any within?"

"I trust not, sir."

CHAPTER 6
HOME AND THE SOILED PERSIAN

An hour later after my chat with the good man Mr. Churchill – I have always enjoyed a good soak – I swept a Mason Pearson across the crown then cut a dash downstairs, neatly dressed and shod. I had something of the Robert Donat about me, if you discount the lightness of my hair and lack of moustache…and the lack of Canadian accent.

I marched out onto the driveway to find Hammer loading the Rolls, stretching straps and fixing buckles. His trunks were impressive. There was, however, something of the tired automaton about him.

"What ho, Jeeves," I called out as I watched him tug at his gauntlets. "No Milly?"

"No, sir," he answered with a tone prompting me to wonder whether I should pinch him to jerk him out of his soporific state. "She is destined to join us later."

"Are you with it, Hammer?" I quizzed. "Down in the dumps?"

"I am rarely lionized for my exuberance, sir. We have a perilous journey ahead and I must consider all the consequences, all the concatenations that could befall us." He straightened and adjusted his lapels. "And as for your most recent little witticism and mocking sobriquet, if I may stretch the meaning of mirth, I am also trying to recount how many times I have murmured *if I had a shilling for every time someone…*"

"I see, I see, Hammer." Wishing to alleviate him of his travails, I opened the passenger door and slid in, finding myself once more in the presence of good liquor and temptation. I abstained. I sat slightly forward with my forehead touching the glass partition, my chin on a fist, elbow resting almost Rodin style on my recently acquired explosive walking friend.

I'm sure, like me, you have spent many an uncomfortable hour at your local Regal, Rex, or Savoy, taking in all the Pathé news stuff then trying your best to settle down and watch the hero catch the villain, free the sweet heroine from the tracks before the Flying Scotsman arrives, and have that final fidget during the clinch and closing credits. Let me gripe for a while. Put yourself in the usually safe hands of Hitchcock or

Korda. Imagine our hero, Mr. Templar with that comma of black hair over one eye, leaving the scene, a murder, his hideaway, whatever you wish. Out he comes, closing the door behind him, onto the pavement then along the street. He heads for his red and cream Hirondel without a second glance, a double-take or even cursive look up and down that shadowy, ill-lit, foggy boulevard. As his taillights are swallowed in the mist, we hear another engine being gunned. Out from between parked cars or from the thicket on the corner pulls our villain, lamps blazing, tyres squealing. Will our hero notice? Not a chance: not a snowball's. Well, dear reader, you will not find such fault with me. Your hero is professional, constant in his vigilance…on the ball.

As we swept from the drive, in fading light, and onto the lane I checked from left to right, and behind. We were alone and I was able to settle down in safety and peace, apart from Hammer's droning. He began the long medley, one which was to last from beginning to end of the journey, with Benny Goodman until he relieved Bunny Berigan and Gene Krupa of their tasks. I kept the partition closed firmly enough for my little mobile salon to be almost airtight, but it was not enough. I prayed, with some premature thanks, he was not a devotee of the psalm or Gregorian chant and lifted my spirits with the thought that once upon the ocean-going steamer we could relieve each other of our company by choosing ends. I had already done a baggsy for the bow, away from the stack and belching smoke. There is invariably a brass band and a semi-circle of deckchairs on the stern of these vessels, so Hammer would not be alone.

I took travelling time to consider my life so far, and the people in it. You have been wondering about what happened to me after father ruined the fabulous Mortimer Hardimann portrait and triggered – excuse the pun, I use them sparingly – the demise of Mrs. Allingham.

Nothing exotic, I am afraid.

I sold the stately ruin for a reasonable sum to an American businessman in lingerie. I could have married his daughter or one of the plethora of American heiresses looking for an English *pied-à-terre*, double-barrelled name, and a coat-of-arms to go with them, but I could not sit comfortably with that eternal heartfelt gratitude I would be expected to offer. You may have been told that it is greater to give than receive: of course it is. The giver can revel in the unceasing adulation and apple-polishing, while the adulator and polisher lives with the constant reminder of his need.

So, I sold to the man in lingerie. Let us not veer towards that old chestnut of a crack. I heard, through the grapevine, he later jumped from the highest turret of the pile, having lost his all in The Crash. In what I viewed as an elegant touch he lowered the flag to half-mast for the occasion. Despite his Colonial roots he was not a man lacking in manners or style.

You would expect, after the death of my father, for all the family to rally round, hug and support, console, and comfort. Not a hope. He was as much despised by them as he was by me, and I was guilty by association. They did the hedgehog, curled up into a tight ball and remained spiky until I was gone from their lives forever. Never fall for that old *'blood is thicker than water'* routine. It isn't thicker; it just leaves a more stubborn stain.

The sale of the estate gave me funds to purchase reasonable accommodation, an elegant two up, two down in a Knightsbridge mews. There were no birds of prey to be evicted and their ancient lodging was used to garage the new motorcar.

Housed and happy, you may presume. But what of an income? You'll recall banking was a no, no, and doors to family businesses were slammed shut. I had a light bulb moment. I had recently flogged and fled the stately pile and all there was within it, some paintings, the odd Persian carpet, and a selection of silver. Father had not completely scraped the barrel. The American, the one in lingerie, had mentioned during our dealings that he would be attending the international lingerie fair in Paris. He was pleasant enough to offer me an invitation, which I declined with due gratitude and respect. It was to last for a week.

Housebreaking was new to me, I was the *voleur manqué*, but I had inside knowledge on my side. I knew the contents, the secret passageways, even where the ladders were kept. All I needed was a mentor, a teacher. I scoured the seedy saloon bars of the East End of London and soon found myself inveigled into the criminal fraternity where I came upon Sam the Spot.

I am appreciative of the fact you'd like to understand the reasons for his name, but come on, it isn't that demanding a quiz, is it? Fair enough. It was on his nose and it sported hairs. Rest assured, it had something of the *diptera* about it. I can recount no introduction where a newcomer of his acquaintance was not tempted to roll up an edition of *The Daily Record* and give the beast a good thwack!

He was a little wiry weasel of a man, but I was persuaded he was the best in the business. I proposed, and he accepted. I gained a partner in crime, and a fence.

The first job was simple enough and with practice I improved. We did well for nearly twenty years. My downfall, albeit it a little one, the one which led to my incarceration was brought about by snagging a buttonhole on a window catch – often a problem with sash windows. I heard the shrill whistle of a flatfoot, turned smartly with tool bag in hand, stuck a foot out, nudged my head against the upper half of the window, and as I backed out, down it slid, clamping my hopsack jacket with the grip of a vice.

Sam the Spot, with swag over his shoulder, had slid down the ladder and legged it before the clomping size tens of the local constabulary came around the corner. One flatfoot, Studely, was decent enough to ascend and free me before I could make my way to the pavement and prepare myself for a good hiding. Be that as it may, I did land Inspector Quill a tooth-loosening sucker punch. So, there you have it; that is me, your hero, Pelham Hardimann.

Now, you may picture me sitting with some apprehension in the Rolls as we sped towards London. Would Sam the Spot be waiting for me, happy to hand over my share of the loot, even more considering I had taken the fall? No need for concern. I have never been one to trumpet on about honour amongst thieves and all that rot, but I relaxed safe in the certainty that Sam the Spot was a fellow on whom a man could rely. After all, he had the skills, but I had the contacts, the details; I was in the social circle, knowing when the mark was off to the opera or away for the season.

Anyway, enough of this. On we must go with what I think is now referred to as our *journey*.

I had dozed off for a while and came to just as Hammer was making the tight right-hander into my mews. There had been some light drizzle during the evening and the cobbles shone handsomely, reflecting the dull yellow of the lamp a few yards from my front door.

I clambered out, slapped the thighs to get the blood flowing and fumbled for my key. "Sort out the trunks later, Hammer," I said as I stuck the key in the door. "A stiff scotch is called for."

"Are you sure, sir?" Hammer asked. "I feel I must park the car somewhere less inconvenient to your neighbours, and then I would imagine the dampness of an empty house over the winter months would call for a good fire to be charged."

I was surprised. Hammer didn't strike me as the type to refuse a stiff one when it was offered. I turned to find him standing uncomfortably close. Like any proper English gentleman, I guard my personal space with adamant jealousy. "A couple of fingers each is called for, Hammer." I beamed. "Grab my coat and stick, will you?"

I put the *gambade* then near goosestep as he ventured back to the Rolls down to his sudden flush of happiness brought about by my generosity of spirit with the spirit. Let it never be said that I ignore the comforts and well-being of the working man. If there's one thing my service in the trenches taught me, it is that history proves the bonds and shackles of servitude and class should be unlocked and unhinged, to some extent.

Hammer was back with me in a moment. I opened the door, giving it a bit of a shove to remove the dune of post that had gathered behind it. I switched on the light and said hello to my home, my hall table, my stairway, my Picasso, and a rather fetching Gauguin. I was also pleased to greet the rare Ming Vase on the sideboard, one of the few things I'd never had the heart to sell.

Hammer did the limpet thing as I tapped on the first door on the left. "You may use this room, Hammer. It is quaint and feminine, being the room of my housekeeper, Mrs. Glendower. She is, thanks to my generosity, on a long holiday somewhere west with her nephew. He's in coal, I am led to believe."

He handed me my coat and cane. "I am sure it will be satisfactory, sir. Talking of coal…"

I unfurled a digit and pointed. "Upstairs. In the scuttle, next to the fire."

"In the lounge, sir?"

"Naturally." I bound, two steps at a time, to the landing. "Come on, Hammer. Those legs of yours need a stretch after all that driving."

I flung open the door and stepped into the lounge. I reached for the light switch and…click…nothing. I remained cloaked in darkness.

Hammer halted behind me. "It appears the bulb is not working, sir. The fuse wire, perhaps?"

"Perhaps," I chipped in. "Make your way across and open the curtains, Hammer, the streetlamps will throw some light on the issue. There are some candles in the kitchen."

He had made but two paces when he fell, ungracefully from what the noise told me, flat on his face. I listened to grunting and grumbling as he pulled himself up and continued his way to the window. He opened the curtains and a soft yellow crept in.

The light worked in the kitchen and I was soon in and out and armed with two lit candles. There was little need. Hammer had found the two table lamps I have, one either side of my Chesterfield. He was standing stock still and staring down. I blew out the candles, giving myself time to view the scene upon which he had settled his eyes.

There in the centre of my lounge, lying peacefully on my most cherished Persian, was Sam the Spot with two rods sticking through his neck in the shape of the cross of St Andrew. A dark pool encircled his head, but I assumed it to be dry; there was not the shine one gets from warm wet blood. Twinkling like stars amidst the dry pool were fragments of the shattered light bulb.

I was no Simon Templar and could not look upon a fresh corpse squared-jawed with the comma of hair over one eye and a jovial tip backwards while offering up a hearty laugh. I need time to gather the wits, and the self.

The pause was long.

Hammer was the first to break the silence. "Shall I relieve you of the candles, sir?"

"No, no." I shot back through the swing door of the kitchen, chucked the candles to the sink and returned to find Hammer crouched, doing the mirror to the nose, the listening for the heart and the feeling for a pulse routine. "Is he dead?"

Hammer rose with gravity. "After a brief inspection, sir, I have ascertained that Mr. Spot is lacking in all the vital physical signs pertinent to sustaining life."

"Well, dash it all," I said. "The man was in possession of my ill-gotten gains. He had them in safekeeping for me until my return."

Hammer released a gentle cough. "I respect the importance of the arrangement between the two of you concerning your joint profession, sir, but I feel I must remind you that he was also in possession of the suitcase."

"The suitcase, Hammer?"

"Yes, sir. The suitcase. The suitcase you are charged to retrieve before taking it to the United States of America."

"Ah, yes. The suitcase." I plonked myself down in the wing chair near the kitchen door. It was my favourite chair, the one where I sit with a scotch and peruse *Variety*. "Dash it all, again, Hammer," I said with feeling. "We have taken a step back." The geography of my room, and where I was sitting, reminded me of something. "*Nunc est bibendum*, Hammer. A good three fingers each is called for, two will not suffice."

I watched him turn and open the cabinet, take out two cut glasses and pull the cork from the neck. "Very good, sir." He poured, and he was generous with my whisky.

One thing about Hammer, I thought: he is quick to get the layout of a room once it is lit. I received the offered drink.

"We have taken a step back, Hammer," I repeated. "A step back. And what are those things sticking through his neck?"

Out of some bizarre respect for the dead, and keeping hold of his drink, Hammer leaned across to whip my *Variety* from the cabinet. He rolled it tightly, leaned down and gave a great sweeping thwack to Sam's nose. He stood back up, a man defeated. He tossed the out-of-date copy of *Variety* aside and hunkered back down to scrutinize the cadaver, the still spotted nose and the metal cross embellishing the neck. After some time, he arose with the confidence of a man with an answer.

"They are knitting needles, sir. Double pointed, a size seven and a size nine." He sipped. "Does your Mrs. Glendower knit, sir? It is a common pastime for aunts with nephews and nieces to clothe."

"I suppose she does," I offered.

"If I recall, sir, the front door took some effort on your part to open owing to a barrage of post behind it. I could not help but notice two postcards from Oxfordshire. I did not take the liberty of reading the other side, I take secrecy and privacy very personally so I could not discover the date on which they were posted but I would imagine a postcard from Oxfordshire – second class – would take the minimum of two days."

I was sharp. "Your point, Hammer?"

He sipped once more. "Judging by the coldness of the cadaver and the dryness of the bloody halo around his head, I think we can safely surmise that Mr. Spot has for a good few days been not of this earth."

I hoisted myself from my chair and held out my glass for him to replenish. I was sorely tempted to boil but I kept on simmer. "Mrs. Glendower is a septuagenarian, plump, heavily-tweeded, a baker of cakes and a rider of sturdy basketed bicycles, Hammer. She is not a murderer."

"No, sir."

"Or a murderess. Another thing, Hammer. Dear Mrs. Glendower is a woman of correctness and exactitude. If she were, I repeat were, to murder someone with knitting needles, she would go to great pains to use a pair and not end up with a pair of two odd needles in her knitting basket, size seven or size nine."

"An odd pair cannot be a pair, sir." He handed me my replenished glass, taking care not to step on the body. "I apologise, sir. I have an aversion to oxymora. I am only looking for answers."

"Well, we should be looking for clues, Hammer. Sam the Spot was a careful man, I'm sure he has left some sign for me."

He drained his glass. "Something has struck me, sir."

"Speak, man, speak, Offer up. We are in the dark, and in the longest of tunnels. Give us some light."

He took the liberty of helping himself to some more of my scotch, but I let it pass. I put it down to pressure and nerves. We must allow men their weaknesses.

"The front door has not been opened for some months, sir."

"Yes, yes," I said, feeling I had some understanding as to where he was heading. "The pile of post."

"So how did…how did your friend Mr. Spot…?"

"There is a through door to the garage, Hammer, from the hallway, opposite Mrs. Glendower's room. To the stable of my SS."

I don't know if you recall the twitch in the corner of Hammer's eye when our paths first crossed; think back. Well, blow me if it wasn't there again: just the slightest of twitches that a man with lesser observational skills would miss, but for me, noticeable enough.

He went to the window. "There is a car down in the street, sir. It has just pulled up."

"So?"

"I recognise it as that of a Mr. Quill, sir."

"Quill," I gasped. "Quill of the Yard?"

Hammer turned away from the window and finished his second shot of whisky. "The very same, sir. He began following us as soon as we left Mr. Churchill's residence. I managed to lose him on the straighter roads owing to the superior power of the Rolls Royce."

"But I didn't see…"

"No, sir, you didn't."

"We are in a corner, Hammer."

"He will not enter the premises, sir."

"Don't you believe it. Warrant, or no warrant, Quill will make his way in." I gulped my whisky and croaked with excitement and hope. "The SS, Hammer."

That twitch again. "Sir?"

"My car, Hammer, my Swallow Sidecar One Hundred. We can get to the garage and make our escape."

"I feel we would need to employ a decoy, sir, some form of diversion."

"I think I can hold him up a while with some banter, some verbal obfuscation, while you fire up the beast." I was about to come up with a plan or at least voice the beginnings of it, when a heavy rat-tat sounded on the solid oak of my front door. There's no need to rattle my way through the whole plan but it ended with "…and then you pick me up around the corner."

"But the engine block will be frozen, sir. The battery will be flat. The starter will be seized."

"No, no, Hammer. Sam the Spot used my car quite often. We had an arrangement. It will start on the button."

Hammer nodded in agreement. The rat-tat upon the door sounded once more.

"Off you go, Hammer," I commanded.

He left, and I listened to him make his way down the stairs and through the side door to the garage. Having allowed Hammer enough time to get himself ready, I went downstairs with lightness in my step. I opened the front door.

"Quill, Quill, old chum," I gurgled as the man stood like a tallyman on my doorstep. I lowered my tone and looked past Quill's sloping shoulder to get a view of my favourite puddle-dweller leaning against his runabout. "Evening, Studely." He saluted, fine fellow.

Quill took a step forward, pressing me back into my hallway. "May I enter?"

"It appears you have," I replied. "Care to step further?"

He did not refuse. At that moment, I heard the growl as two-point-six litres of hearty British engineering came to life. I reached up to the top of the sideboard, grabbed my favourite Ming vase and launched a swooshing arc towards Quill's head, and it was a good enough swing to worry an

Olympic Hammer thrower. Down he went, with a slow slump, a bit of a drag on the hallway wall, then a gentle nestling to the carpet to sleep the sleep of the innocent. I was pleased to see the vase in one piece. The Chinese used to make some quality artefacts in those days. I put the vase back on the top of the sideboard and turned to see Studely springing to some directionless action and reaching for his whistle.

Just as I made my way through the door, I caught sight of the garage doors crashing open, and my SS100 lurching for freedom. The black and silver beast skidded out onto the cobbles, missed the Rolls by an inch then charged down the street.

Studely, obviously a little stunned, danced a jig of quandary for a while, unsure whether to help his boss, collar me, or make chase for the disappearing roadster.

I, as planned, legged it to the other end of the mews where I was able to scale the wall and drop down onto the street on the other side, to freedom once more. I stooped to catch my breath.

So, all went well. In the drizzle and yellow light of a Knightsbridge midnight I turned my collar up and shivered. I waited for a good few minutes, sure I could hear the roar of my roadster above the shriek of Studely's whistle. My heart rested as I saw headlamps come around the corner and race for me.

Now here's the rub. Those great bulbous headlamps headed for me then swished past at high speed before turning onto the Brompton Road and…who knows? And, I had forgotten my cane.

I called out. "Hammer!" There was no way he could have missed me. I was there, standing alone, against the wall, on the corner as planned.

The roar of my SS100 died away. A church bell struck midnight. The drizzle changed gear and became a downpour.

Quill's drunken call echoed and bounced around the wet London gloom. "Studely, stop that bloody whistling!"

CHAPTER 7
A NEW SIDEKICK AND THE OBLIGATORY BROAD

Why they are designed so, I shall never know. Opening the doors to England's most beloved and traditional red telephone box requires the strength of ten men. On closing they are sly, creeping a little before snapping through the last few inches to break ankles, catch turn-ups and rip the laces from your best dress shoes.

I heaved then launched myself in, lucky not to catch any bodily parts or item of clothing as the devilish jaw clamped shut behind me. My head dived for the telephone apparatus to receive a good clean slap of cold metal. The receiver sprang from its cradle with the ferocity of a disgruntled viper and wrapped its wire around my neck. I flattened my hands against the sides of the kiosk and strove for dignity. The mouthpiece toppled and supplied me with a knock to the skull: the aforementioned mazzard resounded with such a clonk as to make your good man wonder if he really was an empty vessel above the neck. I had gone from pouring rain to noose in one fell swoop.

Untangling took a while. It was as rising from my discomfort, putting the receiver and mouthpiece back in place – I am no hooligan – when I saw another set of headlamps come swinging into the street.

I was momentarily illuminated in my box, stung with the foreboding and dyspepsia of a big-game hunter who's nonchalantly wandered into the Serengeti only to find he has omitted to bring his blunderbuss, just as he hears a nearby roar of hunger.

The beams flashed past, giving me an instant to see Quill's usually poker face, no longer pokerish but wide-eyed with the mouth stretched in rage. The car swept past and I was returned to near gloom with just the weak yellow streetlamps to spread the rain-glister around me.

It is not a simple matter trying to find comfort with nothing but a concrete floor, iron framed windows and the pungent whiff of puddles caused by those gentlemen of the late-night drink and the easily relieved bladder. I wedged myself down onto the haunches. That was my position, concertina-like, for a few minutes before the cramp set in.

Should you be the younger reader, and welcome to you, you may well wonder why I should be suffering such pains after so little exertion. All I had done in those moments leading up to my incarceration was a hundred-yard dash, scaled a wall, and prised open the door to my cage. Trust me here. There is a switch, a natural trigger perhaps, for the knees and the back, turned or flicked just before you reach the part where you are *in fair round belly, with capon lined, with eyes severe, and beard of formal cut, full of wise saws and instances.* It is furtive in its onslaught. There you are with a spring in your step, all ready to rush for the bus, take a scissor leap into your jalopy – the ladies love that – forego the opening of the gate, or skip lightly onto the dance floor to whisk her through the French windows and out onto the balcony for a whimsical moon at the stars when, wham! It gets you in the knees, cracks you one in the lower back, or that shoulder stiffens and the pain hikes up your neck, leaving you perched at a jaunty angle like the yardarm hit by the first cannonball of battle.

Something took my mind off the pain. It was Constable Studely's Horse Chestnut truncheon rapping on the iron framework of my prison. Judging by the animation of his face, the squat little man was shouting. I was well and truly sealed in, so spared the volume of the tirade. He pulled and I pushed.

"Studely," I gasped through the widening gap. "Nice of you to stay." I squeezed out onto the pavement to be blessed by even harder rain.

Studely heaved like a grampus, holding a hand to his stomach in the style of a man overly sated at a policeman's ball buffet. He banged out the syllables of his orders with his truncheon, missing my nose by an inch. "You are to remain with me, sir."

Your hero did not flinch. I felt the situation needed some qualification. "Am I under arrest?"

The baton stopped mid-swing. Studely waited for the message to be telegraphed from over-taxed cerebrum to mouth. "I was not told, sir."

I looked to my left to study the wall over which I'd recently leapt. Judging it to be too much of an effort to be tackled alone as before, I signalled to Studely that we should together take the shortest route to the cover of my mews house. "Any chance of a leg up, old man?"

Studely took some time to consider the request. He was, I concluded, in a cleft stick. I was his quarry, his prisoner, but somewhere deep inside him was, I believe, some comradeship borne out of his hatred towards his boss: Quill. There was something of the *'mine enemy's enemy'* about the situation.

He needed help. Let it never be said that I turn my back on a man in need. Had I been blessed with a middle name it would be Samaritan. "You can stand guard over me in the warmth and shelter of my abode," I said, cleaning my face with the coal-filtered pouring of late night and early morning London. "I make a good cuppa."

"You give your word?"

"My word is my bond, Studely."

He grunted, tucked his trusty truncheon beneath an arm and bent low with his hands enjoined, fingers intertwined, ready for the leather sole of the sinister half of a good pair of Church's. Grunts continued as I rose to stamp the right foot against brick and reached both hands up to the top of the wall. I pulled with all my might, gaining extra power by planting the loosed left firmly on his helmet. I felt it give a little – the helmet, that is. Once perched on the top of the wall I managed a brief survey of my surroundings. Below me was Studely, staggering a little and straining all muscles to dislodge the helmet from his head.

Taking advantage of the brief respite while balanced on my vantage point, I turned to get a lengthy view of my mews.

It could have been the shadows playing tricks, or perhaps some hallucination caused by sudden exertion, but I did see the elegant figure of a woman walking away from my front door. I say a woman, and I was sure.

Picture if you will, the silhouette behind the frosted glass door of your down-at-heel Los Angeles gumshoe. There he is, a little bourbon-soaked, leaning across to smudge the dog-end of his last gasper into a dusty cactus on the corner of his desk when he hears heels, followed by gentle taps of delicate knuckles on his painted name. He knows his once broken and now steely protected heart is about to melt, for twenty dollars a day plus expenses.

She was all in black. There was a flirtatious swing of the hips, a waspish waist, and one of those hugely brimmed hats ladies wear to avoid the irksome chore of having to arm themselves with an umbrella. Had the light been better, I'm sure I would have spotted a pair of ruler-straight seams running up extraordinarily long legs. But, as you are no doubt aware, there are times when the imagination does the filling-in of details on our behalf. She turned the distant corner, leaving a gentle rain-punctured billow of cigarette smoke wafting into the halo of the streetlamp.

My reverie was interrupted by Studely. "If you could be givin' me an 'and, sir," was his plaintiff cry.

Heels of dilemmas were legion. Here was the chance to make my escape. I had two minutes grace in which time I could surely gather up a few items of clothing, stash them into a sturdy overnight bag, snatch the wedge of crisp notes I keep hidden for emergencies into my pockets, and hot foot it into the remains of the night. But no; Studely had done me a service.

I reached down and felt his clammy clasp. The hoisting was more strenuous than expected. Sure, he was round and lumpen, but he carried with him the weighty stodge of a public-school pudding, sweet or savoury, take your pick. He was no climber and I felt most of the effort was made on my part.

With the struggle over we sat like Jack Spratt and his wife atop the wall. Studely still needed time to free his head from his helmet. It came off, not with a 'pop' as you'd imagine, but with the succulent slurp one hears when a serving spoon emerges from a stubborn blancmange. The one who would eat no lean fidgeted, banging his boots against the wall as he tried to knock his helmet back into its more regular shape should any passing woman with child need instantaneous but discreet relief. He spoke. "You said somethin' about a cuppa."

I gave him a gentle nudge and down he went. He was no cat.

I dropped with more grace, taking care not to use his bulk to soften my landing. One can never be too accurate about these things. Blaming my ill-judged landing on the darkness and rain I strode away, giving him the dignity of freeing himself from the gutter without sniggering onlookers, of whom, I suspect, there were none.

I was a little perturbed to find my front door wide open, so I quietly reprimanded the absent Quill for his lack of care concerning my private property. One never knows who is about. I stood in my hallway, sniffing, taking in the sweetness of a perfume I did not recognize, which was disconcerting because I'm usually good at that sort of thing and have often used it as a line. I've never met a woman who doesn't lift a tingling leg at the mention of her fragrance. You know the leg-lift I mean: the one she does during the final embrace before the credits roll and the fire curtain descends.

Studely arrived, stamped his boots on my welcome mat, folded his arms and joined me in perusal. I was still sniffing and checking my art collection. He focussed on one of my favourites while enjoying his own bout of sniffing.

Never let it be said that I am one to dismiss another fellow's opinion. I gave an investigative sniff and enquired. "A rather pleasant fragrance, don't you agree, Studely?"

He turned and pressed his back against the wall, the back of his head against a portrait. "Not the sort of thing you should be discussing with an officer of the law, perfume and stuff, if you don't mind my saying so, sir."

"Not mine. I just thought…never mind."

He reversed his earlier turn. "What 'appened to her?" he asked. "Face like a roofer's nail bag." He puffed out his chest as if to confront the painting and demand some explanation from it. "In an accident, was she?"

"No Jimmy James, are you, constable?" I managed to stop him prodding it with his truncheon. "It's a Picasso. Spanish artist," I said.

"Bloody ugly women them fascists hang around with."

There are times when one cannot argue, cannot educate, and it is best to leave the issue well alone. Not all are blessed with a passion for the beauty or strangeness of art. And this masterpiece had cost me only as much as a grazed shin. "Maybe," I said, "but it will be worth thousands one day, I'm sure."

Studely pulled away, unfolded arms, and nodded to the stairway. "You hope. Cuppa?"

I closed my front door. "Lead on," I prompted. "I'll follow." I began the fortification of my castle with a dull and heavy sense of the horse having bolted.

I cannot recall if it was an effort to feel more at home in my house, to loosen up for some coming exertion or to prepare himself for a bar room punch-up, but Studely unbuttoned his tunic before setting off. He hesitated on the bottom step. "Expecting intruders, are we, sir?"

"We've already had them, Studely." I gave the third bolt a goodly shove as I watched him wobble his way up my stairs.

It was not exactly one of those situations where one watches someone go up the stairs only to forget his reason for doing so, but I realized at this point that something had slipped my mind. Studely's reminder came in a whisper of reverence. "There's a body lying on the floor of your front room, sir."

I'm no Mick the Miller, but my sprint up to the landing would have left the hare a poor loser and praying for retirement. My thoughts were just as agile. "Sam the Spot," I announced as I pushed Studely into the room. "Hammer and I found him here. As much stuffed with surprise as you, dear man."

"I know who 'e is. Quite a regular down the station, but we never got him on nothing." Studely sniffed, gave his trousers a tug and his braces a stretch, before venturing towards the stiff. "Is this why you done a runner?"

His calm, let's call it his aloofness, puzzled me. Where was the shock? Was the appearance of a corpse an everyday occurrence for Studely? I did not push home the point. My mind was on his tacit accusation. "It was not I who did the runner. It was Hammer. I'm beginning to wonder if your man Quill has something on him."

"He's got plenty on you."

I set my eyes to a steely stare, unsure if they would flash in the milk-and-water glow of my living room. "But not murder, constable."

"That be true, sir. Not your style. Not the gentlemanly sort of thing to do," said Studely. I was tempted to thank him, but we cannot become too appreciative of our public servants; it gives them ideas above their station. I let the matter rest. He did not. "Mind you, there's such a thing as the falling out of thieves, and you…" He made his way into my lounge, crouched with an arm resting against my Gilbert mahogany gramophone, and came over all Sherlock Holmes. I was suspecting him to whip out a plate-sized magnifying glass as he shoved his free hand into a trouser pocket, but it was a torch. "Interesting, sir," he mumbled.

Concern enveloped me as I pictured Studely taking a hefty swipe at poor Sam's already over-trammelled nose. Calm returned as I realized the man was only doubling his efforts at detection with the help of the beam. Besides, if Sam the Spot had been a regular through the doors behind the local blue lamp, a man like Studely would own all the facts concerning the nasal deformity.

"Certainly not routine, finding a corpse on the Persian," I quipped. With a crack of the knees, Studely brought himself upright and I waited for the excess corpuscles to drain from his face. "Anything?" I asked.

"Marks around the neck, sir. Quite apparent, even in this light."

"Knitting needles, size seven and size nine," I offered. "Bound to leave some trace."

He shook his head. "Not through. Around. Other marks, a chain, a necklace, like it was snapped from his person."

That person thing that our police force has, I mused. I raised an eyebrow of respect. "Good detective work. I know he wore something, a talisman, a pendant of some description."

Studely squinted at me, lifted himself up on his toes and flooded my face with the golden wash of his torch. I saw spots. He switched it off. "A Saint Christopher, that nature of adornment, would you say, sir?"

"It was a saint, yes." I needed a few more moments to finish blinking. I mulled, thumb to chin. "Not a Saint Christopher. A woman."

The constable beamed. "Ah, the blessed virgin herself. I know Sam the Spot was a godly man despite his waywardness. A generous man, as well. He once gave the good wife and me a silver cow creamer for our wedding anniversary. Lovely thing it was, but we 'ad no use for it. We flogged it and splashed out on a weekend in Morecombe."

"I wondered what had happened to that, a fine specimen and nothing to sneer at," I grumbled.

Studely rubbed at his forehead with the torch. "Mind you, it was only our tenth. Yes, our nipper must have been eleven."

I'm not sure if he blushed at the mathematical frankness, but I let his latter comment pass. It is all well and good showing a modicum of human warmth and kindness to the lower ranks, but one can coddle them too far. Before you know it, you are grazing your knees on the bark of every branch of their family tree until you know the smallest twig and freshest sprig as though it were from an acorn of your own.

Familiarity can breed contempt, and it can also be the thief of time. "It was a Mary, but not that one," I said, getting us back to the trunk of our discussion.

"Sorry?"

"Not the Mater Dolorosa," I pressed, regaining full vision and landing an eye on my drinks cabinet. "Are you sure you wouldn't prefer something stronger than a Rosie Lea, Studely?"

"Just a cuppa, if you'll beg my pardon, sir, thanks all the same. I'm on duty. Mind you, the rain...perhaps a brandy would..."

I thanked God, did a seven-leaguer over the corpse, and played the goodly host. As pouring, I spied Studely twist a thumb down and run fingers along my gramophone. I crossed over the cadaver, and we chin-chinned. "Maybe this will help bring some Marys to the fore," I said.

The man drank with the enthusiasm of a too-small-for-the-pan haddock being tossed back into the frothing ocean. He scrolled down his list of Marys. "Let's see. There's Mary Magdalene...Mary of Bethany...Marie Antoinette...Marie Celeste..."

I feared the poor soul was to drift down the Nile of his own meanderings. "Saints, Studely. Saints."

"Doing my best." He shoved the depleted brandy balloon at me. "Much obliged, sir. I trust..."

I raised a halting hand. "Quill will know nothing of it, old man." Something clicked. I snapped my fingers. "Saint Mary of Mead."

Studely gave me the look one would give a man telling tales of how he'd spent the last evening with Martians and learned of their culture and all things green. "You sure you don't mean Saint Mary Mead, sir?"

"Not an of?" I enquired.

"A village, sir, about forty miles from here. A pretty place."

I must have looked askance. Never let it be said I question another man's geographical scholarship, but why a flatfoot born of a Plaistow salmon-smoker would be cognisant of the rose-scented environs of middle England did cause some astonishment. "Go on," I pleaded.

"I had a great aunt who lived there, sir. Was in service to some toff out Oxfordshire way before he went and topped 'isself. From what I heard, the cook passed on only moments after the tragedy. Shock, I wouldn't wonder."

I did not stagger. "A tragedy," I offered in condolence. It's always good to mirror, to repeat the words of a fellow converser when in conference. It shows empathy. Did I mention before that I am a great student of the species *homo erectus*?

Studely smiled. "Well, I suppose not really, sir. She did manage to stash some oddments away for a rainy day, borrowing the odd bit of porcelain and that from the old buzzard. And from what I heard, as a young man delving into the ways of the world, he'd remunerated her quite generously for her ministrations. She 'ad a sister, but I don't know what become of her. The cook, that is, not my aunt. Word has it and far be it from me to gossip, but she had to go and disappear for a while. In confinement, if you get what I'm getting at."

I did not baulk. There is no such thing as coincidence; there is only the ignorance of connections between actions and their consequences. Besides, if considering the possibilities running through my mind, a detective such as my nemesis Quill would only regard them as long shots, and extremely far-reaching ones at that.

It wasn't so much a matter of changing the subject, but I felt things needed moving on. "Constable," I began, "a quick wash-and-brush-up is called for, on my part."

"Not gonna go sneaking out the bathroom window, are we, sir?" asked Studely, with perhaps a hint of humour; it was difficult to tell.

I offered a chuckle and gave a wave as wide as my generosity. "Help yourself to food and drink. The kitchen is all yours."

Not having my housekeeper, Mrs. Glendower, to run a bath for me, I made do with one of my most recent acquisitions, a shower. An American fad, I was led to believe, and one of the few of their ideas worth latching onto.

Thirty minutes later, I stepped back into my lounge, in a grey suit, a rather fetching yellow paisley cravat, grey suede shoes, a black woollen overcoat and fedora, all neatly brought together with the white silk scarf that usually rests on the shoulders and lapels of my dinner jacket. I was ready to face the world.

Studely was force-feeding himself mutton, leek and potato broth with the vim and vigour of a humpback whale scooping up a shoal of herring. For a moment, his gaze was transfixed on a carriage clock and the tiny ballerina giving a twirl as it chimed two. He took a break from scooping and pointed the spoon. "I think we should have the body removed, sir."

"Of course," I said.

"I'll call it in, via your telephone, if I may." He went back to his shoal.

"Are we to wait here?" I enquired.

Studely wiped a sleeve across his mouth and gave a sigh of satisfaction. "Very good soup, sir. Found it in the larder. You cook it?" I disabused him of the assumption, informed him about my housekeeper and Sam's freedom to come and go as he pleased. He let the spoon rattle into the bowl, turned his upper half, and rested the ensemble on my gramophone. "Whassat, then?" he quizzed, prodding at the corner of the equipment. "Putty?"

I followed the line of his finger, recollecting he'd been fiddling about in that area before. "Well," I exclaimed. "Of all the bally..."

"Sir?"

"Some blighter has discarded his chewing gum and thumbed it into the corner of my…"

"Disgusting habit, if I may say so," said Studely. He looked down at Sam the Spot and spat disappointment. "Disgusting habit."

"Sam did not chew, gum, or tobacco," I replied. "And Mrs. Glendower would certainly never entertain such a thing."

"Mrs. Glendower?" Studely's face ran through a gamut of momentary expressions, ranging from inspiration to utter contempt. "These bloody American inventions, sir. Poisoning the world."

I felt the accusation a little strong, but a bell clanged. "Clackett, in his letter, said something about Americans…" I clamped the mouth. It was not that the dear constable could not be trusted with the facts, but I was not yet sure how *au courant* he was with recent occurrences. Had Quill brought him up to speed, and what did Quill know anyway? And, come to think of it, what was Quill doing pounding upon my door. Why had he followed me from Mr. Churchill's residence? I put the matter to the back of my mind for later contemplation. I went back to the matter in hand. "Something about Americans. In his letter…Clackett's letter."

"Clackett," said Studely. "That's the body what we found in the barn, your old army chum…"

"Whom I did not murder."

He nodded, once again, to the knitting-needle-adorned cadaver on my Persian. "And it is him what passed the suitcase, the suitcase what you is searching for, to Sam the Spot, here."

"Whom I did not murder."

"And now, your man Hammer is on the trail."

I protested. "Not my man. Churchill's." I did thumb to chin. "He has gone into the night, left me stranded, so to speak."

Studely stood then paced, hands clasped behind his back. Using Sam the Spot as a small roundabout, he travelled some distance before asking his question. "He got a good look at the body, did he?"

"Oh yes, most certainly," I assured him. "Down to the very size of the needles."

"But he didn't mention there being anything around the neck?"

The penny dropped. "You mean he knows about St Mary of the Mead?"

Studely gave a cough. "Saint Mary Mead, sir." He came to a halt. "With Hammer at the wheel of your SS100, there is not much chance of Inspector Quill catching up with him."

"So, Constable," I pressed. "What do you suggest?"

"I suggest, sir, we speed our way to Saint Mary Mead. Mr. Hammer's Rolls Royce is outside."

I picked up my lethal weapon: my cane, stuck it under an arm and donned my string-backed driving gloves.

CHAPTER 8
CONCATENATIONS AND CONFLAGRATIONS

The journey would have been more relaxed without Studely's rabbiting. There is much I can tell you about his wife; her cooking, her church duties, her swollen ankles, and the gyp she gets in the small of her back, but we can leave all that for another time. While he talked, I turned the cogs, searching for answers.

Imagine my dilemma. My original helpmeet, Hammer, had deserted me; Inspector Quill was looking forward to pinning two murders on me or grabbing the suitcase for his own devious ends, my housekeeper was perhaps a murderer, and two unknown Americans had snooped about my humble abode. Most disconcerting of all was the realization that my new sidekick was none other than Constable Studely. There was also the mysterious woman who'd exited my house.

The beam of the Rolls Royce illuminated the church clock as we delved into the bosom of Saint Mary Mead. It was three o'clock, the rain had ceased, and the world was dormant. It was, at scant perusal, a quaint little village with a pond and Post Office, a pub, a trough with pump, flint walls, neatly combed thatch, and a telephone kiosk. I suspected, if one were to fling a shillelagh down the main cobbled thoroughfare just before opening time, one could reliably catch a brace of retired colonels and majors on their selective bonces.

I parked abreast the telephone kiosk. Forgetting myself for a moment, I kicked some loose stones into the pond to annoy sleeping ducks and fired an explosion of quacking. I surveyed the moonless scene. Studely, at my side, and after giving me a finger-to-the-lips hush, was the first to spot something interesting. I was impressed: here was a man who ate his carrots. I had seen the motor car parked on the other side of the telephone box, but I had taken little notice of it.

After a moment's tugging, Studely removed his torch from his back pocket. He whispered. "A Cadillac, sir." He swept yellow across the windscreen of the car, bashed the base of his torch with a palm and cussed. "Bloody batteries. This is a diplomatic vehicle, sir. American Embassy."

56

I took a few steps and tapped my cane against the front bumper. "So Mr. Joseph Kennedy has friends in the village," I remarked. "Very interesting. I wonder if he chews gum."

Studely's torch illuminated my face. "What, sir?"

"The man from RKO, Studely, the American ambassador to our fair isles but no friend of England. He's the man who will stop at nothing to block American support for poor old Blighty should hostilities commence," I said, letting my new pal know I had some acquaintance with affairs of state. He was not to know its limitation. "Now flick that light around and see if we can't spot anything else."

The weak circle of torch light danced. "That looks a lot like your motor car, sir." Studely pointed then nudged. "Inspector Quill's car is down there on the corner, parked up against the hedge."

"Very good," I said, stepping forward to peer down a lane. "Doesn't tell us much though, does it? We need the house." Hope swelled in the breast as I made out the faint sheen of light behind a heavy curtain. "This way, down the lane, Studely, and watch your step."

He put his best foot forward into a puddle and cursed the world and his wife.

We made our tentative way down a hundred yards of raindrop-heavy, privet-lined lane until we arrived at the glow. A small wooden gate barred our way, on the other side of which was a path of crazy paving.

I opened the gate with caution, fearing any clicking or squeaking would awaken the village and reinvigorate already irritated waterfowl. My movements were lost in the inundation of another sound: the whirring of a starter motor and the firing of six cylinders as someone somewhere started their motorcar.

Studely shadowed me as we made our way to the drawn curtains. Only a few stones crunched. There was a thin strip of gap in the wall of cloth flowers.

Hunkering, with gloved fingertips touching the wooden window frame for balance, I peered into the cottage. "Well, stone the flipping crows!"

"What?" Studely wormed his way in to catch a glimpse. He breathed potato and leek across my face before pressing his nose against the rain-spotted glass. "Gawd almighty! My aunt... Is that your Mrs. Glendower, your housekeeper?"

"It most certainly is," I proclaimed.

"Then why is she all binded up and gagged, sir?"

Feeling a concoction of numbness and pain oozing into my thighs and calves, I dropped a little lower and leaned my back against the wall. "Well, Studely, as for her being gagged, I can well and truly understand and would not reprimand a fellow for taking such action, but as far as her being bound, I have no idea."

Studely was still studying. "There's a big picture on her wall an' all. Ugly looking bugger with a moustache. Her husband, her late husband, you think?"

I overcame aches and twisted around and up to purloin another furtive decko. "Uncle Joe."

"Ruddy big picture for only an uncle," said Studely. "You'd 'ave thought a small silver-framed photo on the sideboard would be more than enough."

I enlightened him. "Uncle Joe Stalin."

I was about to go into mini-lecture mode, as is my wont on occasions when I feel a man deserves my wisdom and learning, when Studely ducked away from the window, just saving himself from a backward roll onto the flowerbeds. "Cripes! There's a bloke just walked in."

I was made of stronger stuff, but surprise still hit me. "Hell's teeth. That's Hammer. And he's holding a pistol."

Studely was up snuggling again. "That ain't no ordinary pistol, sir. That there is a Luger."

I wasn't about to question Studely's knowledge of side arms, but I deemed it necessary to quiz him on the whys and wherefores a man such as Hammer would be brandishing a Luger. What is more, why aim it at my harmless, plump, grey haired housekeeper?

I opened my mouth then closed it. This speedy closing of the mouth owed nothing to any nervousness, lack of assuredness, or problem of vocabulary: far from it. My collected thoughts and prepared sentences were engulfed in a crashing explosion of light and noise. A hundred yards away, in three separate locations at the far end of the lane, great balls of flame ballooned, rocketed skyward, and dissipated to be followed by a downpour of motor vehicle parts.

In the wondrous glow I watched a bonnet drift in the air like a breeze-blown leaf before twirling to the ground. Two headlamps arced and spun like rugby balls before plopping with gusto into the pond. Ducks flapped, quacked, and flew with more ardent rage than that caused by a few kicked stones.

Studely and I were back down the path, through the gate, and onto the lane before other parts landed, the largest of which was the boot lid from Quill's runabout. The most horrific sight was the fuel tank of my beloved SS100 suffering the indignity of being tossed in the series of explosions before being granted some grace and allowed to lodge firmly in the sturdy arms of a beech tree.

We stood stock still in the lane. We looked down the length of it to the centre of the village, the burning Rolls Royce, the brightly lit telephone kiosk, and the duck pond being pockmarked with fragments of metal, rubber, and leather. A white-walled tyre rolled and bounced towards us then twirled and twirled with ever increasing speed like a tossed and uncaught coin before flattening to rest inches from our toes.

"Someone's blown up all our cars," said Studely.

I was tempted to pour ironic scorn on Studely's observations, but let it pass. "The Cadillac is not there," I said.

"No, but summit's there," he answered.

At the far end of the lane, glorified in the backdrop of flames, were two figures, silhouettes. One was tall and grand, the other solid and squat, but both statuesque in raincoats and Homburgs.

"I bet they chew gum," I said.

The figures disappeared as speedily as the flash in which they had appeared.

A noise came from behind. We turned. Like a gunfighter, Studely whipped the torch from his pocket. It failed him. Drifting away into the darkness, with a long shadow spreading from her feet brought about by the flames at the other end of the lane, was the tall slim figure of the woman I'd seen leaving my mews house. She melted into the cloak of the trees.

CHAPTER 9
INTERROGATION, KEDGEREE, AND THE OFF

You may be aware of the stumped writers' trick of having a man entering the room with a gun; it works on occasions but is becoming rather old hat. Be that as it may, and there is nothing I can do to change things, the man was already in the room and holding a gun: a Luger.

That is what Studely and I saw before things took a turn for the worse. Events had shunted us from our crouching voyeurism to the centre of the lane some yards from the house.

The conflagrations resulting from the three automobile explosions at the other end of the lane were dying down, leaving a pleasant glow beating hearty warmth into the cold early spring morning of Saint Mary Mead. The jingle-jangle of a fire engine filtered its way through the woods towards us and, I was sure, the coarser tones of the local constabulary were adding discordant harmonies.

The two figures, Americans, I assumed, had disappeared into the night, no doubt comfortable in their Cadillac. The prim and elegant silhouette of the mystery woman had slipped away into the trees at the end of the lane.

Studely, with most of his bulk flopped down onto the lane, and there was some good deal of bulk, one could have mistaken him for a collapsed vaulting horse, had his helmet in his hands.

"No time for that," I quipped, ever armed with the stiff upper lip. I tapped at his knees with my cane. "The door is opening."

"Sorry, just recovering. Came as a bit of a shock, them explosions."

"Understandable," I said, offering comfort. We must be shoulders for our troops at times of stress, I have always thought, but there must also be the firmness of a man in control. "Come on. We have a woman to save."

Up and down he went, somewhat akin to a procrastinating cow unsure of the weather forecast. His lack of grace, brought about partly by his volume, was also the result of trying to keep one hand in a trouser pocket. He cussed a while.

"Hurt, Studely? Holes to be patched?"

He was upright at last. "Squashed my Tunnock's, sir. And…" He removed the hand from the pocket and flat-palmed to show me something glinting reflections of the strange surrounding firelight. "…found this monocle thing in the glove compartment of Mr. Hammer's Rolls Royce, sir. Thought it might be yours, I forgot to give it to you earlier. Busted, 'fraid." He donned his helmet.

"A monocle? Not mine," I assured him, hoping to put him at his ease. "Too ostentatious and Teutonic for my style."

He flipped the hand to let the brass ring and broken shards tinkle to the puddled grit of the lane then retrieved the squashed Tunnock's from his pocket. He launched them afar to be scoffed by hedge fauna.

"Shall we go and investigate, sir?" he said with punchy enthusiasm, the get-up-and-go of a man refusing to succumb to past defeats. He nodded towards the cottage door. "That were your Mrs. Glendower in there and your Mr. Hammer pointing a gun at her."

I stiffened with resolve. "I have not forgotten, Studely. I have been thinking things through. There must be an explanation."

The constable ratcheted up the suspense. "Hammer didn't come out of the house. Strange, considering the rumpus what has 'appened."

"Exactly, Studely. Let us go and pound upon the door to see how the cat jumps."

We went through the gate through which we'd passed some five minutes beforehand and marched with mustered bravado to smack the hefty metal knocker against the oak door.

Studely skipped aside a little to get another peek through the gap in the curtains. "Just the old lady in there now, sir."

"Alive?" I considered it a worthwhile enquiry. I banged upon the door with added firmness and it opened a fraction. A gentle push with my cane opened it fully and allowed me to peer into the gloom of Mrs. Glendower's hallway. I called out. "Mrs. Glendower?"

Studely, swift to close the distance between us, whispered in my ear. "She's gagged, sir."

"Not about the ears, Studely."

"Yes, but even if she can hear…"

"Good point."

We crept, in step, along the hallway to the open door on the left through which a blanket of firelight was flickering. There she was, sitting rigid and wide-eyed. It's not easy to tell if someone is smiling with relief when they have a handkerchief stretched across their mouth, but I suspected a modicum of palliation as I stepped across her threshold.

Studely, a trifle speedier, kept low as if expecting a missile to zoom through the window. He launched himself towards the stricken housekeeper and caroused her with a volley of "there theres" and "oh, my words," as he untied her hands and feet. Her voluble mumbling led me to believe she would have been happier to have her mouth freed in the first instance, but I let Studely continue. Never halt a man in the midst of his heroic deed, is my creed.

Once un-gagged, Mrs. Glendower opened wide, gasped, and aahed! with the vigour of a man blessed with his first ice-cold Carlsberg after a month of Saharan dunes. I've never understood why chaps do that in the saloon bar of any local inn, but it seems to be an unwritten rule: Take a swig, wipe a sleeve across the old north and south then let out a gasp of appreciation. A chap never does it solo; it is not the action of the lone wildebeest. It is a ritual of the group at a watering hole, as compulsory as the sudden need to slap shoulders, hug, laugh at the most inane of comments before falling *en masse* into the pastime of tottering down the pavement homeward-bound, professing undying manly love to the chap who shares the same lathe or workbench with you but irritates you throughout the working day to the point where you could clang him a good one on the nugget with a bastard file.

Studely, with surprising decisiveness – surprising to me anyway – poured from a water jug near the mantelpiece and offered her a refreshing glass. "Get that down the hatch, my dear," he said with the assuredness of a man who had spied land and grabbed the tiller. "Then you can have a brandy before telling *uzall* about it."

She drained the glass and watched Studely unleash some of Napoleon's finest.

I sensed a little peevishness in her eye as Studely finished pouring. "A decent shot is called for, Studely," I commanded, taking the interlude to find the light switch near the door, to kick the prancing shadows from the room. "The dear woman is in shock."

The light from the single shaded bulb was weak but it bathed Mrs. Glendower in a circle of warmth and comfort.

I brought myself to the centre of the room, rested on my cane, purveyed the scene then suggested Studely should draw the curtains to keep out the show emanating from remnants of the dying fires down the lane, along with the kerfuffle of fireman wielding their hoses. We needed to be *in camera*.

Always mindful of good manners, I removed my grey fedora and plonked it gently onto a shiny bust of Vladimir Illich Ulyanov, for a moment wondering why the chap wasn't wearing a sturdy but weather-beaten worker's cap above the sharp cheekbones and finely trimmed beard. Headwear is important. It has often caused me some consternation that our famous bard is always portrayed *sans chapeau*. Nothing worse than a bald pate skirted by overly grown locks: it gives the genius the appearance of a straw-sucking bumpkin.

My sartorial and literary meanderings were dammed by my housekeeper. "Kindly remove that piece of apparel and place it on the hat stand provided in the hallway, Mr. Hardimann." She scowled as she lifted with the weightiness of a castle drawbridge.

Studely danced a little, perchance wary of offering her patronizing assistance or wondering if he should go fetch a parbuckle.

I removed the fedora, jinked neatly through the door, and tossed it in a perfect arc, after which it landed neatly on the top of the hat stand near the front door.

I flitted back into the room. "We saw Hammer," I said, feeling we must get to the nub.

"Your new valet, or so he informed me," said Mrs. Glendower with a flutter of her weak chin and extended bottom lip. It gave her not so much of an impediment but a unique and instantly recognizable trait. "Way ahead of you, Pelham," she added with that condescension one can only permit a great aunt.

I stuck hands into coat pockets and did the bat thing. "Well, Mrs. Glendower, he is as hot as mustard. A touch overzealous, would you say?"

The stout woman relieved Studely of the Napoleon and replenished her medicine cup. "I would say, a forceful and forthright man who was under some misapprehension."

"Misapprehension?"

She staggered a little, lifted her well-stockinged knees to remove cramp and give her rotund chassis a thoroughly energetic twirl. She jumped slightly as though warming up for a *gopak*. Having come to a rest, she downed her brandy and shoved the glass at Studely, allowing her the opportunity to settle with her hands firmly imbedded into her padded hips. "His misapprehension, Pelham," she began with a devilish glint in her eye, "is that he thinks I was in possession of that wretched suitcase."

I tottered a little. "Were you?"

"Only momentarily, I can assure you." She loosened her hands and clucked with discontent. "Such antics will be the death of me. I do not enjoy being interrogated by some heel-clicking jackbooted, monocle wearing, spawn of Satan."

"Monocle-wearing?"

Studely lent support to my inquisition. "We found a monocle in the Rolls Royce, remember, the one what I broke by accident."

I stepped towards my housekeeper. "Are you telling me...informing me...that Hammer was wearing a monocle?"

Mrs. Glendower slapped at her thighs and jabbed herself back onto the chair from which Studely had recently freed her. "I draw the line at entertaining the sadistic whims of a Nazi spy."

I felt the lower mandible take a dive. "He is hardly a Nazi spy, dear woman."

She scowled. "Well he made a consummate impression of one, dear boy."

Some noises off drew my attention. "Studely, have a scout about the garden and check that all is well, will you?"

What concerned me was the local constabulary snooping, seeking witnesses and such like. I sidestepped to take a gander through the curtains through which we had peeked from the other side. There was still the faint glow of dying flames cavorting above the hedgerows and sticks of torch light fenced in the night sky.

I listened to Studely make his way out of the front door. I watched him amble about, torch in one hand, truncheon in the other. In those few moments, I gathered my thoughts and prepared my questions. Mrs. Glendower was in for another grilling.

I was tempted to glean from her an explanation as to why her sweet and gentle cottage should be adorned with artefacts from my own abode, and secondly, to ascertain some reasoning behind her love of revolutionaries, both Russian and Georgian. I have heard of reds under the beds but never had the misfortune of meeting one slouching across the counterpane of the four-poster with crimson flags draped for all to see. Aren't these people supposed to be surreptitious? And was Mrs. Glendower not a might too invested in decades for all that changing-the-world malarkey to succumb to the myth of the noble cause?

I am not a bitter or petty man but bear with me. It was galling to find many of my favourite trinkets filched by someone to whom I pay a generous monthly stipend. Perhaps the dear woman was convinced the daily waft of a feather duster around the curtains, a rub of beeswax on mahogany, and the occasional steaming of fruit and stirring of suet deserved more than what she was receiving, but I would have listened. I am always ready to embrace a compromise.

As I said, I was tempted, but there was the security of the nation with which I had to concern myself. Let it never be said that I am a man to wander from my duties. I am the Agincourt arrow once launched: with purpose and deadly. I let go the curtain, sure in the knowledge that Studely was scouting well.

I turned to my housekeeper, unbuttoned my coat, stuck hands into trouser pockets, and parked the rump against the windowsill. I left my cane against the wall, a foot or so from my right. "This interview with Hammer," I began.

She was an adroit glowerer. "It was an interrogation."

I was a syllable away from remarking that she was unadorned with the rosy smudge of slaps, fisticuffs, the red-hot poker, and her neck, well graced with pearls was far from showing the lines of taut piano wire. I let the point pass. I was to cast the limelight upon her and let her speak freely. I started again. "Of course, Mrs. Glendower. The interrogation. *Da capo.*"

"Three days ago," she began as she lifted a little to arrange the line of her tweed skirt then settled for her Homeric chronicle. "A man arrived three days ago, carrying a suitcase and looking for you. A man with one arm."

"A one-armed man," I suggested.

"He wanted your assistance but was unaware of your travels."

"And were you not to be on yours?" I enquired.

She shifted. "Do you wish for details or are you attempting to repeat Mr. Hammer's antics."

Something leapt into my mind, the way things do when one is turning the cogs on another matter. I reached out and gripped the handle of my cane.

"And what are you planning to do with that?" she demanded. "Prod me to death?"

I checked my tone, following the gentle, caressing, nurturing route. "I am mystified, Mrs. Glendower. On many points."

She followed my survey of her living room. "You are referring to my allegiance to socialism, world socialism?"

I felt a chill from the window and heard the crunching footsteps of Studely outside. "I can understand the working man...or woman...but have you not been well rewarded all these years?"

I felt a point having been scored as she wriggled. "I have no complaints as far as that is concerned," she said.

"Nearly twenty years." I felt it needed to be said. "And you came to me for employment. You could say I took you in."

"The working man, and all women have always been taken in."

I was nonplussed, to say the least. Had this fervour been beating beneath that weighty and voluminous bosom for many years, or was it a sudden thing, one sharp intake of breath drawing in all spirits manic and belligerent?

I nodded towards one of her rather large portraits. "And you believe Uncle Joe is the man to follow? Isn't it a shame that those who rebel – perhaps quite rightly – against those who damage them tend to follow the flag of mass murderers?"

"World Socialism, Pelham, will free the working man from his chains, and now it is all that can beat the evils of Nazism."

"But didn't your hero Ramsay..."

"A good man hijacked by the Tories."

"... while overseeing a rise in unemployment to three million, a refusal to re-arm, and wasn't it he who five years ago suggested that old Schicklgruber was a decent sort of chap, a socialist like himself, a man with whom one could knock jugs and share a sip at the bar? And did not Lloyd George describe Mr Hitler as the George Washington of Germany? And did not Moscow's friend in Germany, the KDP, ally with the Nazis in the Reichstag vote?"

Have I mentioned she was a skilled scowler? "You have acquired a ream of historical knowledge recently, young Pelham Hardimann."

"I learn enough to lend encouragement to my argument." I'm sure I beamed. Had I sported a moustache I would have pinched it between soft kid-covered fingers and twiddled it, if that's what one does with moustaches. "Recently had a chat with a certain Mr. Churchill, dear woman," I replied with aplomb, and I must admit, a modicum of pride.

"That old warmonger," she hissed, a bubble swelling and popping on that lower lip. "Got you in his clutches, has he? He can't even pronounce Nazi."

She had a point there, but if we were to judge our fellow man by his mispronunciations, would we not be the scourge of the plum-in-gob ruling classes before setting about the workers? "Is he not the stout fellow who gave your working man his tea-break?"

"Pah! A concession," was her swift response.

"And is not a warmonger what a country needs when heading towards another spell of unpleasantness with our Saxon cousins?"

Quietude rested upon her. Her bottom lip quivered and her wattle shivered. Her mouth opened and closed. I put this snapping of the trap down to noises at the door. Studely was returning to report. It was at this point, the arrival of Studely, when something else crept into mind. I shall come to it.

"All peaceful on the fronts?" I enquired.

The welcome mat took a pounding from his size tens as he called out. "Bit of a crowd by the pond now, sir, warming themselves by the dying fires. The local wooden-tops are doing door-to-doors. I told them there is no need to call here 'cause everything is in control and the area is clear."

I could have taken this opportunity, this lull, to rest upon my oars. I did not. "I must interrogate you, Studely."

The constable filled the doorway and the last gasp of dying firelight flashed on his face, a face flushed from exertion. "Sir?"

"Your man Quill..." I said.

Although I cannot recall any upper inflection, Studely took it as a question. "My man, sir? Ain't I his man?"

"You need not be," I said, hoping recent experience was pulling him towards me, further from his master. After all, the peasants never want revolution; they only want to become Kulaks.

I gave a swish of my cane for effect. "I commend your feudal pedantry, Studely, but you have opportunities here. Let us get to the core and shake the pips. With regards to Quill, what in the name of all that is…what in all that is holy is he up to?"

"Haven't seen him, sir."

"But his car was here?" I mulled. "Has he acquired Hammer's ability to emulate Hamlet's ghost."

"Sir?"

"To take cover in thin air."

"Sir?"

"To disappear, Studely."

"He's following Hammer, I'll bet."

"Why?" I huffed. "One spook haunting another?" I looked across to Mrs. Glendower for some support, some suggestion. She was not playing, leaving me to continue with Studely. "Why did he not enter upon the premises and apprehend the man forthwith? He must have been here a good half-hour before us. His car was parked near, the remains of which are only footsteps away." An idea slipped in. "We did not check. Was he asleep on the back seat, waiting until light for a dawn raid? He may now be in smithereens."

A clock in the hallway chimed something from Delibes. In the jumping shadows of that early morning in Mrs. Glendower's front room I saw the soft downy whiskers of her upper lip ripple as her tired limbs stretched from their dormancy. She yawned.

"Was there another man here, Mrs. Glendower?" I asked.

She gave me a pirate's parrot eye, her head cocked to one side as if a shoulder had given up the ghost. She did that thing elderly ladies do: stuck scissored fingers up a sleeve then withdrew a few square inches of embroidered and initialled gossamer.

The clock finished its fourth chime; Mrs. Glendower heaved a foghorn blast into the patch of cloth, and Studely emptied the doorway before plonking himself down near the hearth to pick up the poker and…poke.

Safe in the knowledge that everyone was sitting comfortably, and I perhaps had their full attention, I lobbed the question once more. "Was there another man here, Mrs. Glendower?"

Using the rhythm of the two short jabs with which she re-sleeved the handkerchief, she eyed me once more and spoke. "There was."

"And he was…?"

"He was outside, sneaking about, got a good look through the window at us."

"You and Hammer, you mean?"

"Yes."

"You saw his face?"

"I did."

It is no simple task pulling teeth from the long in the tooth. "Can you describe him?"

"Tall, skinny, long face and a thin moustache. Hat too small for his head."

Studely caused an earthquake in the hearth and sparks leapt. "That's him. That sounds like Quill."

"Certainly does," I said. "But the light could not have been good, Mrs. Glendower. And your curtains – were they not drawn?" You see how quick off the mark I am? I could picture it all, but the picture was not true. "I fail to see how you snatched a decent gawk at him. It's been dark for hours." I turned to pull the curtain aside a smidgen just to peer into blackness and get nothing but a reflection of my own fizzog and Studely's head hovering over an expiring fire. I let go the curtain and turned back to finish my interrogation. "His nose must have been flattened against the pane."

"We heard movement outside. Hammer made me go and close the curtains. A man was crouching, and stood up just as I was…"

Studely sniggered. "So, you got a good full-frontal eyeful?"

My housekeeper levered herself out of the chair and adjusted her tweeds. "I had a very good view of him. I would recognise him again, anywhere. He is hot on the heels of Hammer who is most certainly hot on the heels of…"

I interjected, my enthusiasm and gratitude unbound. We were moving along. "On the heels of whom?"

She was standing to attention now, with that chin and bottom lip jutting proud. "Him. That wretched…suitcase."

I smiled the sweet smile of success. She was going in the right direction.

I'll cut the story short, as I feel we must at times, although I hope I have not been snipping too much. We need the textures and senses of a story; without them, we have no story. One has to get a feel for the places and the characters. One cannot just rush like a train through a tunnel. Texture gives crescendo and crescendo leads to climax: the tunnel must be used to the full, otherwise we have nothing but some smoke and steam then darkness.

We had time to kill and filled it well with some kedgeree, homemade gooseberry preserve on wholesome whole wheat toast, and good thick grainy coffee.

Studely helped himself to some clothes left behind by the deceased 'whatever' of Mrs. Glendower. I suspected the deceased, whose name was never proffered, was a long-lost lover She insisted he was her poor younger brother who had recently died of something caught in coal mines of Wales, something that attacks and fills the lungs, but wasn't catching so there was no need to worry. The clothes fitted well and Studely morphed from constable to noble and robust working-class backbone of the British Empire, with wider braces and a wider belt. He was pleased to keep his boots.

Mrs. Glendower changed to darker tweed, stouter walking shoes, carpetbag with obligatory knitting needles peeking out, and a walking stick with a rubbery end.

You know how I was.

So, to cut the story short: During the hiatus and supping we made plans for the journey to Southampton where we would board a steamer to the Americas. Mrs. Glendower was not up to more questioning, so I refrained from the desk lamp in the eyes and thumbscrews for the time being. I was in possession of the core of what I needed to know, and I was to be happy with that.

We had our missions. I was setting out to meet up with Hammer and the suitcase while Mrs. Glendower was putting her best foot forward to slap a Nazi. Studely, I felt, was tagging along because he thought he ought to find out what had happened to his boss, although, on the suggestion of Mrs. Glendower he could have made a telephone call to his station. Studely was not up for that, thinking it more discreet just to tag along, see where things went, get a breather from his good wife's lumbago and swollen ankles. There was also the promise of a gander at the lovely green lady adorning the gateway to the United States of America, sure in the knowledge she would lay down her torch, quote Emma Lazarus at him and be open-armed to an officer of his abilities.

CHAPTER 10
THE FOUR OARSMEN

Feeling it unsafe to cut into the heart of Saint Mary Mead, with its pond, telephone box and gathering of emergency services, my housekeeper suggested we take the narrow alleyway down the side then to the rear of her cottage, to cut through a spinney and make our way along the river to the railway station

We were in single file, hidden by high hedges and thin trees. The river, she said it was The Mead, was a wide and fast running affair with banks that would have looked sublime, inviting picnics and lazy Sunday afternoons, but we were in darkness and cold.

Is the world darker in the countryside of England? Is there some indolence to delay the opening of the door to the chariot?

We tramped, methodical and rhythmic, taking care not to slide on mud and flattened grass, things we spotted with intermittent flashes from a torch up front. Mrs. Glendower led. Studely brought up the rear. I was the slice in the middle.

You, the reader and ally of the hero may wonder why the woman had taken command, and why I had let her do so. Let us not stumble and twist ankles here on the pebbles of our prejudices. We were, for the time being in her hands; she was the person in the know and it is to the person in the know where we should bend our ears until they have fulfilled our needs. I view it as a horses-for-courses type thing; but how often do we, the freemen of the world, choose the best horse?

Mrs. Glendower spoke with one of those whispers that cut through the night like the screech of an owl. "They have taken the boats."

So, they had skulked and sculled, but how many of them? Hammer, Quill, the woman, the Americans?

"Boats?" I enquired. "Is it that far?"

"It is quicker than walking, and easier," she schooled. "We can make our way over the hills for a short cut." With that she lifted her walking stick, slapped some low branches then stabbed into the darkness as though I should have espied some proud mound rising before me. Perhaps it was the mound that was hiding the sun.

Studely grumbled. "Could have waited for a bus."

"And be seen," I said.

Mrs. Glendower halted, causing a bumping of fronts and backs. "Larrison's milk cart."

I prodded. "Larrison?"

She put her best foot forward and our patrol continued. "He drives his horses and cart through the villages, collecting the milk. I've used him before. He unloads the churns at Nevercombe Lowdly Station." In the darkness, she checked her invisible watch: force of habit, I supposed. "He'll pass us as we make the final mile."

I had hoped for 'the final furlong' but made no further comment on the matter. We negotiated a stile and began our ascent as daylight bothered to make some furtive appearance. It was not so much the sun fervently chasing away the clouds of a cold spring night, but more of a sun wandering into a space vacated by clouds that had given up the ghost and slunk away.

The three of us stood upon the summit, Studely and I bending to drag oxygen into our burnt lungs, and Mrs. Glendower straight-backed and triumphant with the ease of a sprinter who'd hopped on a bus after one or two untroubled strides.

To our right we could see the train of dominoes wending their way from milking shed down the lane to field, and to our left was the muddy silver back of the River Mead slipping between the patchwork bumps and gentle slopes of southern England.

I wasn't sure which was the best foot, but I was putting one forward when Studely slammed an exclamation into the scene. "Boats!" He pointed, downhill – the obvious direction, you'd rightly surmise.

It was then that I realised the stillness and pacific mood of an early spring morning amidst the wilderness of England. There were sounds for sure, but good sounds, wholesome sounds of worms hiding from the early bird, and then came to me the rhythmic dipping of oars into tranquil waters. I even perceived a crab.

There in the slim cleavage of the valley was a chase. Not the tyre-screeching, grit-chucking rush you have come to expect in your local flea-pit, but a gentle competition of stretching arms and tightening buttocks as three small rowing boats cut their way over tresses of weed, leaving gentle wakes. In the lead, perhaps by a hundred yards or so was a single rower. In the middle was a single rower and bringing up a very poor rear was a pair. The final two were in no way Blues.

Each party was hidden from the other thanks to the tight bends of the river. But they were not hidden from us, apart from the obfuscation caused by low sunlight and long shadows of willows and birches strewn along the banks.

"We'll make it the station before them if we meet up with Larrison," said Mrs. Glendower in a whisper as though fearing her breath would sweep down the slopes and warn our prey.

Studely pointed. "That's Detective Inspector Quill."

I lifted my cane and jabbed. "Followed by Hammer who's holding the inside line." I edged my cane a little to the east. "The two Americans."

Studely scrabbled fingers through thinning hair. "So who took the Cadillac?"

"Your mystery woman," said Mrs. Glendower before turning her back on the scene and commencing the long descent. "Come. We have a mile or so yet."

The descent was speedy with that awkward knee-jarring stumbling with which one must cope when travelling down a steep incline, but we made it safely to the five-bar gate at the corner of the field with just enough time to catch the clip-clop of heavy hooves, the rumble of steel-banded wheels and the cheery giddy-up of a little man in control of his beasts.

He pulled up with an ease born of habit. He spat the last eighth of an inch of roll-up from his dry lips, laid the whip across his lap and doffed his cap. "Morning, Mrs. Glendower."

"Morning, Mr. Larrison."

"Not your usual library day."

"Not a usual day at all." Mrs. Glendower made her way down the length of the cart, heaved her carpetbag up onto it then waited for a hand up. Studely obliged, with strong arms around her rump. She parked herself on an orange box and leaned against a churn. "I'm sure these gentlemen will be happy to dip into their pockets, Mr. Larrison," she called. She sat stiff-backed with carpetbag on her knees, her chin jutting and her nose lifted to draw in the morning's freshness.

Larrison's head turned like that of an owl, and I noticed the heads of the two great Suffolk Punches turning in unison as though seeking some explanation for her companions. "No problem, Mrs. Glendower."

I followed Studely up onto the back of the cart and we squeezed ourselves in between churns, crouching down onto straw and ungleaned grain. The cart pulled away with a jerk and I received a gentle tap on the head from a churn.

I must first remind you that this was early morning and I had been without sleep for many hours, and then I must remind you that I had been without female company for a good six months. Let me be soft of touch here. Perhaps it was the rhythmic trundling of the cart that did it, sending me to the land of nod for fifteen minutes or so. The gentleman reader will understand the double whammy; I think whammy is the modern terminology. I was blessed with the combination of morning glory and the unwished for rise oft brought on by the gentle jostling one receives in the rear seat of a charabanc. While a chap near his double score would be proud of such a thing, I freely admit I was a little uncomfortable – put out, is perhaps the phrase.

I awoke from my fleeting slumber just as the cart wheeled round and conquered a sharp slope to pull alongside the loading or unloading bay of Nevercombe Lowdly Station.

I did my best to loosen up, free things, and generally arrange myself, hiding my awakening with my coat tails as Studely lowered Mrs. Glendower from the cart.

Nevercombe Lowdly station was a long red-bricked affair, long as I suppose all stations are by necessity, with a stubby clock tower somewhat akin to a poor man's *pigonnier*. Gas lamps converted to electricity leaned over the thin pathway along the thin road on the other side of which was a wall of trees, beyond which was the river – or so I was to learn.

This knowledge was brought about by stirrings and lappings, and the nudge of hull against pontoon: you'll recognise the hollow clonk next time you witness such an event. Through the trunks of the narrow line of trees I could see the jigsaw shape of Quill lifting oars and coming about having made a mess of his first attempt.

Having finished my sartorial adjustments, I whispered down to Studely. "There's Quill."

"Sir?"

I dropped from the cart. "Quill is mooring." I nodded in the correct direction and collected my cane from atop a churn.

"I'll take Mrs. Glendower in and get the tickets," said Studely.

"First class, Studely." I smiled at my housekeeper. "I trust your socialist sentiments will not be wounded, Mrs. Glendower."

The stout woman shielded her breasts with her carpetbag. "Come the day when all comrades can travel first class, Pelham."

Satisfied she had said what she wanted to say she did a smart about turn and led Studely down the slope on which Larrison had parked his mares. They headed to the centre of the lengthy station, to safety.

I took another riffle through the straight limbs of the beech and birch trees to see how Quill was fairing. He was giving the old round turn and two half hitches of the lanyard to the post, bending low with feet wide apart and rear end greeting the morning sun just as Hammer came zooming in with the velocity of a shark homing in on its seal pup lunch.

Hammer's bow cut into Quill's hull, leapt up and whacked Quill amidships. Quill, lifted from his tying routine, did a double somersault not quite to Olympic standard but enough for an audience to give hearty applause for effort. Down he went, headfirst into Hammer's craft, sending all concerned tipping into the drink. Clencher hulls rolled, oars flipped and dropped, and waterfowl sped from the scene.

You may think, with Quill and Hammer up to their waists in Mead, I could take a breather. Not so. Having shifted my gaze from the riparian roustabout I caught sight of the two Americans scooting from the trees and out onto the lane at the far end of the station. They brandished machine guns. With their trench coats flapping, hats tipped, and teeth shining brilliant white, they snarled between thin lips. "Kill…goddam Limey."

I jumped from the tarmac of the slope and skidded down the grassy bank between summit and bricks of the station. I must have lost some sense of what I was doing – only for a fraction of a second, I assure you – but that fraction of a second had me squeezing a trigger of my cane.

What it was that made Larrison's two horses rear, I cannot be too sure. Was it the sound of the guns firing, or was it the bullets zinging and cracking into the churns? The giant beasts rose like tsunamis, bringing the front of the cart with them. It heaved and jolted, sending the churns down like struck ninepins. They thundered to the gritty tarmac and spewed warm creamy tidal waves down the slope. The clanging-bell tones rose as they emptied and jostled, rolling, rolling towards the gunmen.

The horses came down and tugged at the cart, flipping Larrison onto his back, feet in the air, whip swishing and cracking, spitting like lightning. The horses veered and dragged the cart around with them before they tore off, back down the slope, hooves splashing through milk and striking against the rolling churns as if calling for early matins.

Above the cacophony, I heard the whistle of a steam engine. I ran down the bank to the wall of the station then along to the door through which my housekeeper and Studely had squeezed only moments before.

I slammed the double doors behind me and brought down the crossbar to keep them secure.

CHAPTER 11
DOLLY ORBS

I stood in the olive green and cream gloss-walled cube of the station entrance; two paces to my right was the ticket office and facing me was the gaping doorway to the platform. I caught the high-pitched whistle of an over-stressed kettle and the post-climactic puffs of a steam engine rolling into the station. It slipped its way along the groove of the platform before coming to rest with an exhaustive belch of cloud and steamy wind.

I took a moment to brush myself down, straighten the line of my coat, adjust my cravat, and light up a well-deserved gasper.

A shutter shot up. A red face appeared at the ticket window. The face snarled. "You with the Glendower party?"

I shuffled to the window. "Yes, I am," I offered. "Good morning."

The man straightened his tie and pulled his cap down a fraction so the peak could shade his eyes. With both hands warming, he lifted a teapot and agitated it in smooth circular motions as if to create his own little whirlpool of tea. "Morning. You making that rumpus out there, was it?" He downed the teapot and jerked a thumb. "You what locked my doors?"

"I'm afraid so," I answered, unsure of his attitude. There was a gruffness to him that could have been that jovial country but solid working man thing or the sharpness of a man who had more important things to contend with than irritating people who clutter his station and injure his peaceful existence. "For safety's sake," I added. I eyed him, searching for some substance to his gaze. "We are being..."

"Pursued?"

"Yes."

"Foreign agents?"

"I suppose you could say..." I said, wondering what Mrs. Glendower might have told this man.

"Best be going then," he said. He leaned forward, palms flat on the surface of his counter and head at a jaunty angle. I turned to follow his line. I heard the clock clunk behind me. He pulled back from his brink. "You got only seconds."

I was about to offer thanks when the double doors rattled, and shots rang out. Holes exploded in the woodwork and splinters spat. One round zinged and ricocheted from a beam. I ducked, but still lost my hat owing to a passing bullet whizzing through it with the vengeance of an aggravated hornet.

A long whistle upped and downed and upped.

On my hands and knees, and scrabbling for my hat and cane, I saw the ticket office shutter being slammed down. I heard the hiss of steam and the squeak of steel against steel. I flipped to a seated position. My neck did the owl thing as I looked from the ticket office window to the shuddering doors to the olive green and yellow carriages of the train. The bally thing was moving. Slowly, but certainly moving. I whipped up my hat and cane and hoisted myself from the cold concrete. I made a dash for the carriages.

Now, here I beg you to understand my miscalculation. It's all to do with perception, you know. My previous actions of falling and rolling and sitting had led me to believe I was but a few hearty strides from the footplate of a carriage. The rub: I was on the wrong side of the station, on the wrong platform.

Did I mention earlier I was once something of an athlete? I stepped back and studied the drop then looked up to my right to judge the height and length of the footbridge. The footbridge, iron grey with the cruel embroidery of rust, was too much to combat and the last carriage was passing beneath it. I had only seconds.

I leapt and dropped onto the track. I hopped, skipped and jumped as I crossed the lines, almost touching the end of the carriage, almost…so back up I went, scrabbling onto the opposite platform. Then came the sprint before managing to slip a leather sole onto the footplate. I grabbed the handrail of the last compartment of the last carriage.

I flattened myself against the door and peered, with squashed nose, through the window, across the compartment through the facing door window and to the platform from which I'd just launched myself. There, with ungainly gait were our two Americans: one as rotund as a barrel, the other a lanky gangling stick-insect of a man. It struck me at that point – and we do think of the oddest things in the oddest of moments – that perhaps the great watchmaker had invested so much material in creating the first creature he was forced to skimp on the second. Bad planning, if you ask me.

There I was, doing the gecko thing against the door, as flat against the carriage as I could make myself, fearing the whipping from branches and railway paraphernalia such as tunnel walls and mailbag catchers.

Those readers among you with more than the average number of rings to count will understand my next problem. The carriage had no corridor; it was made up of separate compartments into which one could only enter or leave from a platform, by their respective doors.

I did not fancy travelling all the way down the outer edge of the carriages, eight in all I think, to find Mrs. Glendower and Studely. I recall prompting Studely to purchase first-class tickets and my bet with myself was that the said carriage would be right up there at the front hugging tightly to the tender.

Inching about, somewhat akin to an undecided Wall Street jumper, I reached up with my cane and hooked the handle onto the edge of the roof, judging it to give me more purchase. By squashing my head against the door, I managed to avoid the embarrassment and mild heartache of losing my wounded fedora.

It was at the point where my fingertips had whitened as if to never receive blood again, my knuckles locked fast to never open again, and my arms stretched beyond natural elasticity, when someone pulled the leather strap and the window slid down with a clatter.

Above the crescendo of the clickety-clack of straining fishplates came a satiny voice. "My dear boy, do come in. Park me your lills."

I sucked in the cold wind-rush of the speeding train and the mellowness of Sobranie Turkish. There, as if posing for a portrait within the window frame was a handsome face, with misty eyes, lightly oiled slick-back hair and a thin mouth squeezing an ivory cigarette holder.

I freed a hand and launched my cane into the compartment just as the kind fellow grabbed me by the lapels and pulled. His Sobranie Turkish missed my nose by an inch as he tugged and I ducked and wriggled, eventually making my way through the window and down onto the floor in an ungainly heap as my hat rolled to nestle against a pair of dainty ankles, opposite which, clamped together in virgin rigidity was a pair of stout and sturdy, sensible leather clumpers.

The soft-voiced gentleman with flat, clipped vowels helped me from disgrace and brushed me down with some velvet 'that's betters' and 'there theres.'

Still a little *kow-tow*, I saw my hat loom towards me. It was held by a small kid-gloved hand, a hand which I'm sure lingered in the air for a while after I took the fedora and used it to cool my face, which was most assuredly of the raspberry hue. The owner of the clumpy shoes passed me my cane and went back to clasping her shopping basket. Above the clatter of the train I heard her cluck of contempt.

The voice of my saviour came again. "Dear boy, you are in a muddle." He tweaked at the creases of his light woollen slacks, straightened his paisley cravat, enveloped himself in his camel coat and straightened the trajectory of his cigarette holder and its half-smoked stick of pungent tobacco. He sat down, crossed his legs, swiped a copy of *Variety* from the vacant seat at his side, opened it and hid his face.

"In a bit of a pickle, I'm afraid," I answered, watching a smoke-ring creep over the top of the weekly gazette before it stretched and swept away in the draught.

A new voice: "In not too much of a pickle for it to be an impediment to your closing the window, I hope."

I looked to my left and studied the owner of the voice. I went from toe to head. As for the heavy brown shoes, you know about them. Above them were thick gravy-brown socks failing to hide the bumps of varicose veins. Then came the starchy pleated brown skirt and the tightly buttoned herring-bone tunic. The ensemble was topped by a hat, a collection of twigs and flowers above the rim of what could have been a rusty dustbin lid; the thing had something of a moribund acanthus about it but it did not hide her scowl, the scowl of someone who had omitted to eat her prunes that morning. Her voice, the voice of this large overripe woman, put me in mind of someone trying to let the air out of a balloon as slowly and discreetly as possible – but failing miserably on the discretion aspect.

"I'm sorry," I said as I lifted myself from the floor and leaned to grab the leather strap. I pulled the window up to bring some semblance of calm to the compartment. "It slipped my mind."

"As no doubt…" the woman continued, "…the purchase of a ticket also slipped your mind." The handles of the basket creaked as she gripped and twisted. From opposite her came the lightest and sweetest of giggles. That dainty glove went up to hide the face. "Laura," the older woman complained. "It is no laughing matter." She added to it one of those '*I don't know what the world is coming to*' tones.

I saw the dainty gloved hand rest on a lap. "Well, what an adventurous day, Dolly" said the owner of that sweet hand and those dainty ankles. At this point I was in no position to look the owner in the face, but I'll come to that.

Dolly clucked again then picked up some earlier conversation with her travelling mate the way a woman of her sort can pick up a dropped stitch while doing that pearl one, knit one thing so beloved of her species. "Well, he certainly was very good looking."

"Who?" asked Laura.

"Well, your friend. Doctor whatever his name was."

"Yes, he's a nice creature."

"You've known him long?"

"No, not very long. I hardly know him at all really."

Dolly droned on. "Well my dear, I've always had a passion for doctors. I can well understand how it is."

She was answered with a sniff. A little sniff, the sniff that comes with tears nearing the lip of the well.

I must have groaned or squeaked…or something. The copy of *Variety* opposite was given a crisp rap. "More woes, dear boy?" asked my smooth-talking saviour.

I had been seated but bent almost double since closing the window, with my hands to my face, a heel of one kneading an eye socket. "Got something in my blasted eye," I said. I held back my head, blinking and squinting, just able to see the fellow rising from his seat.

Having dropped his newspaper, he removed a neatly folded handkerchief from his inside coat pocket. "Allow me." He loomed. "That's it, head back, let me varda your dolly orbs." With one hand on my shoulder, the fellow aimed the corner of the handkerchief at my face but was stopped by another hand: a gloved hand.

"May I?" Laura had homed in on the scene. The brim of her large black hat touched the brim of my fedora. She took the handkerchief from my rescuer, opened her sweet red lips and licked the aforementioned corner. We continued to rub brims.

I blinked hard, and fast, hoping for the mote to remove itself. I wanted a better view. "But he's a doctor, isn't he?" I enquired. "Surely…"

"He's no doctor. Besides, I have a much gentler touch," she said. "Now, don't move."

I surrendered. "Well, that's awfully kind of…"

She dabbed. "Just a piece of coal dust." She pulled the handkerchief away. "Have a good blink."

I did just that, and tried to focus; and there she was, radiant, beaming, like an angel – unless angels are chaps, I've never been too up on the cherubim, seraphim thing. Her hair was as raven black as her hat, her skin as smooth as porcelain and her eyes like glazed saucers. Although natural, her eyelashes were long enough to warrant a *punkah-wallah*. But, in the flickering sun-dappled light of the compartment I could see the smallest of tears, a tiny wash across those beautiful eyes.

As she handed the handkerchief back to the chap who had resumed reading his *Variety*, I checked the outline, the three-quarter length black coat, the slim waist belted in, and the padded shoulders. For a second, and only for a second, I wondered if I'd seen that figure before. In London, in my mews, in the rain, and perhaps before that.

Another thing was niggling me. I had been accused, most unfairly, of travelling upon Southern Railways *sans billet*. The matter needed to be addressed. I lit a gasper in an ostentatious way to advertise my nonchalance. I turned to Dolly the frump and puffed a cloud. "Madam, I can assure you that I am journeying quite legally. Owing to a fracas beyond the gates of the station I was unable to board the train before it was in motion, before the whistle was blown, so to speak."

Three pairs of eyes studied me. One pair, almost loving and tender, another pair still glazed with choked tears.

The third were slits of hate and bile. "Produce it, man."

I coughed. "Produce what?"

"Your ticket."

I glared. I am a good glarer when glaring is called upon. "Madam, the ticket is in the hands of another. A first-class ticket, I might add."

The kindly fellow threw me a straw. "I thought something was taking place at the station. There you were, leaping like a gazelle across the tracks, only to be hotly pursued by two no doubt roguish sorts." He smiled above his *Variety*. "I could not help but notice a billow of black smoke rising from the other side of the station." He tapped ash.

"So, who has your ticket?" the old woman demanded. "I shall make it known to the station master at the next stop. I know him and he knows me. I am the secretary of the WI, you know."

While making my riposte, I wondered how often she shaved that upper lip. There was more than five o'clock shadow about it. "My aged aunt has it nestled in her carpetbag amongst her wools and needles, dear lady."

Laura leaned forward and tapped the harridan on the knee. "Oh, Dolly, we saw her with that plump chap. You remember? You said she had fat ankles." Laura looked across to me. "She was marching along at quite a brisk pace. I'm sure you'll find her in the front carriage when we stop. But then again, I trust you. I see no reason for you to reclaim your ticket until we have reached our destination."

Let it never be said that my heart is apt to melt at the merest hint of warmth and compassion, but there was a softening behind my waistcoat and the faintest of hardening below. "Well, thank you. But I must hop off at the next stop and race to the front. My aunt may be in danger."

The WI secretary stabbed. "Well, just see that you do. Fancy leaving your aunt to fend for herself..."

"She is with a friend," I replied. I bit my lip. And she is quite capable of fending for herself, I thought.

The gentleman in front of me took his cue. "The two men following you, they headed for the front of the train. Lilly law?"

"Sorry?"

"Policeman, dear boy. I was enquiring as to whether they were policemen, or perchance they are hoodlums. There is the possibility they were driver and stoker."

"Hoodlums," I answered. "Pretty rough ones at that." I was nonplussed for a moment. "Driver and stoker?"

"Has it not occurred to any of you that we have just rushed through the next station?" He smiled across to the woman in brown. "My dear, Dolly, your friend the station master was nothing but a blur. It prompts me to assume that someone other than a Southern Railways employee is in control of the engine."

"Hell's teeth," I blurted. "We are undone."

"This is your doing," growled the old woman. "I shall be late for my coffee morning. I have never been late for a coffee morning."

"Oh, Dolly, you cannot blame this poor man for what has happened," pleaded Laura. I wanted to smile a thank you, but she avoided my gaze. "Besides," she continued, "you can always catch the train back from Southampton. I'm sure your members will understand."

Dolly clucked with contempt.

It was as I was trying but failing to avoid Laura's eyes that she caught my eye. "You know my name. Laura, Laura Jesson. May I…"

"Good to meet you, Laura." My mind raced, and my mouth blurted. "Alec. Alec Harvey."

Dolly spat disdain. "It's Miss Jesson to you…"

Grinning was a temptation unto which I had no choice but to give in. "Well, thank you, Dolly."

The dragon was inhaling extra gas for the next shot of flame and fury when Laura intervened. "Well, Mr. Harvey, what do you propose to do? Wait until Southampton? You must do something to help your aunt, and Mrs. Messiter will look upon you more favourably if you save her from tardiness."

That chap Eric Blair, an interesting fellow, could at times stick the knife in. What he said about heroes: *We sleep safely in our beds because rough men stand ready in the night to visit violence on those who would do us harm.'* That's all well and good, but I was no hero. Not for me seek out the dragon or poke the Cyclops with a burning stick. I would rather let the beasts lie. What is worse? The woman. How could I sit there in the snugness of the compartment knowing that Mrs. Glendower was protected only by Studely? To add to my predicament, I had Laura gazing at me with hope in her heart, hope that I would prove her companion wrong. The aged Dolly expected nothing from me except cowardice, sloth, and deception, but Laura was sitting there wishing for me to do good, wishing for me to be someone before whom she could swoon. You see, it's not the being in love that women go for; it's the very idea of falling in love: the novel within their breasts that demands so much of us poor chaps. It's the final chapter they love. They have no interest of beyond it; they have no care for what happens after he has sweeps her off her feet and carries her toward the rose-petal aisle.

I had to make a move, do something and do something good. Press-ganged by the fluttering eyelashes, dash it all. "You think they've taken over the train?" I enquired, trying to add some innocence to my tone. I didn't want her thinking I was an out-and-out scoundrel and common prowler of the mean streets. I was on my feet in a flash but spent the next moments dithering.

The gentleman, my rescuer, brought me back from my hum and haw. "Well, do make up your mind to do either something or nothing, dear fellow. Then do it. I am due to play some new songs on the white strillers, reserved for my good self, and the people will be gasping for me." He smiled up at me. I thought he was going to blow me a kiss. "As long as we stop at Southampton without careening into the Solent, you must do as you feel fit."

"White strillers?" I enquired.

"Verandah Grill. First-class, goes without saying. They have a delightful white grand." I must have been looking dopey. That 'goes without saying' thing has always puzzled me. If it goes without saying, why say it at all?" He had more information to dispense. "RMS Queen Mary, dear boy. Broadway calls. I do wish you could find your way to join me for a *soixante quinze*."

I clicked my fingers and warranted a tut and cluck from Dolly Messiter.

I clicked again. "Of course, The Queen Mary. I should have guessed. Hammer had everything planned down to a T. Oh, my giddy aunt!" I tugged at the leather strap and the door window dropped. I sucked in fresh air, flicked my cigarette out and watched it fly back in to nestle neatly in the nursery atop Dolly's head. Laura smiled as I put a finger to my lips, begging for her collaborative silence.

A chorus of three: "Hammer?"

"No matter," I said as I watched the smoke thicken from Dolly's hat. "I must get to the front of the train."

The pianist abandoned his *Variety* for good, having, I mused, found something much more captivating. He put a hand in his coat pocket and drew out a small, and dare I say it, rather feminine pearl-handled charm. "It's only a .22 Beretta, suitable for a lady's evening bag or a gentleman's jacket pocket. It doesn't ruin the line, you see?"

He tossed it across the two feet of space between us and I caught it rather deftly. "But…"

"You won't go far with that thing," he said, tapping my cane with a highly polished toe.

I flipped the Beretta in my hand the way one weighs and checks an apple for insect nibbles. "Well, if I can get onto the roof and make my way…there's no way I can go along the side…"

Laura was on her feet by this time and flapping around at Dolly's hat as she spoke. "Oh, Alec, it's too dangerous. You mustn't..."

You see? You see? One minute they are giving you the dead eye because you haven't the spunk to stick your head above the parapet and next thing, they are berating you for running toward the guns. I've often considered it a much better scenario when they simply ignore us. Perhaps we should just go our own way and ignore them.

It was one of those *'a man's gotta do as a man's gotta do'* moments and I told her so. She was quick to relent, the way a pretty filly is when assured of a queue of saps kneeling at her feet should you get one in the neck and fail to return. "Well, if you must," she said and addressed all her concentration to Dolly's apparel.

While Dolly flapped about, dividing her attention between the beating her head was taking and the assured toppling of her shopping basket, Laura whipped the hat from her head, tugged at the door window then tossed the flaming cornucopia into the overgrown embankment of the railway. It was at this point, the job having been done, when she noticed something and voiced her apprehension. "We are slowing down." She stuck her head out of her window, keeping a sweet gloved hand on her own headgear for decency's sake. I must say, she looked a marvel. Back in came her head. "We are between stations."

I eyed her, searching for advice, and perhaps a little more support, for her to tell me there was no need to put life and limb in danger. "But why would they slow down? Surely, speeding on would be the objective," I said.

The gentleman was fingering another Turkish or Moroccan, ready for insertion into his holder, when the words trickled from his mouth. "I imagine it is far easier to decouple carriages from one another when the engine is not pulling hard. Less tension, you know?"

"Decouple?" I quizzed.

He donated to me the smile those of an IQ nearing the two hundred score offer those struggling in the high seventies. "Most assuredly something to do with coupling, uncoupling, or decoupling."

"There are differences?"

He lit his stick and puffed mellow. "Am I to take it that your giddy aunt is in the process, or was in the process of being kidnapped by these rogues?"

"There is that possibility," I said. I looked to my three companions for support.

Support was voiced by all: "Get on with it, man."

Upon that order I slipped the Beretta into my coat pocket then stuck my head and an arm out of the window. I hooked my cane upwards for purchase.

Laura tossed me some final strings of encouragement before offering advice. "Best to take the roof. They'll see you making your way along the track."

CHAPTER 12
STRANGLERS ON A TRAIN

On hands and knees, I took a moment to congratulate myself as I enjoyed the fresh morning air and grabbed an eyeful of the south of England. It was young and green and fresh, as England should be, with a bright morning sun casting long hard-edged shadows. It was going to be one of Jan Struther's Wedgewood days and the air was already delicious: wonderful, despite the chilly, dewy tempest around my ankles. So, on with the mission.

My main area of concern was not so much falling off; these carriage roofs, though convex and rather slippery, were wide enough to give a chap a decent runway. That said, they left one the minimum amount of space between themselves and the jagged flint undersides of bridges and tunnels: I advise you to keep this in mind should you embark on such an endeavour.

I managed the full length of the carriage before having to throw myself face down with hands clasped over my hat. The roaring rush of sucked cold air played along my body for the moment of darkness. Back in the golden daylight, and straining to look up, I could see the length of carriages narrowing to a point, with no further bridges in sight. I was up and moving on.

Leaping from carriage to carriage was easy and I soon made my way along the second carriage where the smoke was denser, the chips of coal dust thicker, and the thunder of the engine louder: an angry and urgent metronome.

Flattened once more, I edged to the front of the carriage and was about to peer down between the second and first carriages when I heard an angry cry. It was not whence I'd expected.

"Why the hell ain't this rattler stopped yet?"

It was from ahead, down and to my right, from a carriage window or door. I wriggled around like a rattle snake, coat buttons catching and snatching as I did so, the bottom end of my cane in my right hand to hook it onto the guttering and give me extra leverage. A fat bald head was sticking out from a window, but not as far as the gun hand was. I think it was a snub-nosed revolver but didn't wish to enquire.

Another voice coughed a hoarse reply from where I'd so recently been perched. "Hold on, will ya? Don't blow your wig. These Limey couplings…"

I unhooked my cane and wriggled back to look down between the carriages to see a thin man crouched and balanced on a buffer. With one hand holding onto a handrail, he was leaning out to disengage the turnbuckle device: not a simple task when a train is moving, no matter what the speed. Below him, sleepers flicked and juddered like a motion picture reel jumping spools.

I called down. "Spot of bother?"

As he looked up, I had the smallest of interludes in which I could take in the surprise on his face; I even noticed the broken bridge of his nose. I swung with my cane, a sort of low one-handed teeing-off shot. I must confess, I shouted a spirited "Take that, you rotter!" The handle landed him a good one on an ear, but he was made of strong stuff and held on to the rail as he twisted and flattened against the end of the carriage with the free hand nursing the biffed lobe.

The gunman from inside the carriage – he of the fat, balding head – called out again. "Wilbur Hayes, pull your finger out and get us unhitched before I drill the broad."

"Got a goddamn cinder dick interfering," Hayes replied with a shrill but rather nasal shout once he'd got his breath back.

"Well, plug 'im! And I'll plug the broad."

As Hayes balanced on a buffer and hugged the end of the carriage a sickness crept into my stomach, not so much from the scene below – I've never had a problem with height or speed – but from the fact that our other friend, the fat gun wielder, had omitted a character in his impatience. Sure enough, the broad must be Mrs. Glendower, and she would certainly find that term unacceptable. Why no mention of Studely? Where the heck was Studely? Had I lost another ally? I was certainly leaving a wake of wakes behind me: Clackett; Sam the Spot, perhaps Hammer, and now Studely? I pulled back from the edge of the abyss to give my eyes a chance to recover.

I'm not sure if it could be put down to grief or anger, but a rage surged up inside me, and perhaps panic jabbed in some extra adrenalin. I cried out. "Studely!" Then, just in case Hayes had gained second wind and recovered from his earbashing, I edged to the end of the carriage roof once more and launched another swing with my cane. I copped the blighter a good sharp smack just as he was pulling a gun from his coat pocket. He didn't let go of the gun, but he howled with pain and cowered. I called out again. "Studely!"

I was answered with a shout from far behind. It wasn't Studely. "Stop swinging about and shoot him!"

86

I took a forward glance to check for bridges then squiggled around to peek behind. There, standing at the end of the carriages was Laura, with the low sun blanketing her silhouette as I'm sure that streetlamp had done when I'd spotted her only hours before. Yes, it was the same woman.

"Shoot him?" I called back with a croak, watching her stride toward me along the carriage roof.

Her long black coat was open and wafting in the stream of air like the wings of an angel who'd gone off the rails. She was swiftness and grace personified as she danced from carriage to carriage: the sexiest mountain goat I'd ever seen. "You have a pistol," she said softly – well, at least it came across as soft through the roar and racket of engine and rails – as she neared me. "We have provided you with one." The front of her hat flipped back and fluttered, and her black skirt wrapped around her pins.

I addressed both legs, up and down. "We?"

She dropped flat on her face seconds before the next dark whoosh of smoke and steam as we entered a tunnel. "Where's the old lady?" She shouted above the roar and hiss. "Concentrate on the job, Hardimann, not on me."

I buried my head in my hands and waited for daylight. "The job?" I screamed. We rushed into daylight and the flickering overhang of trees from the embankments. Her hair whipped my cheeks, her small gloved hands only inches from mine and gripping the edge of the roof. I did my best to look her full in the face. It was no easy; coal dust and smoke made squinting compulsory. "What do you know about the job, and come to think of it, how do you know my name?"

"You haven't got very far, have you?" She slithered on her front and peered over the edge.

I grabbed an arm and pulled her back. "He's got a gun."

"As have you." There was a touch of impatience in her tone. "Which one is it?"

"Excuse me," I said. Never let it be said I forget my manners. I leaned over into the deadly abyss once more to see the flickering sleepers. I checked my timing with the clickety-clack as a countdown and gave another savage swipe with my cane. I landed well and the thin man ducked, letting off a cry of pain that could have put the engine's whistle to shame. I pulled back from the edge and addressed my addresser, "Sorry, you were saying?"

"Fat or thin?"

"Thin," I said. "Chap going by the name of Hayes."

She rolled her eyes with that 'oh, him' look on her face? She rose like a goddess and leapt across to the first carriage before calling back. "Whack him again. I'm going to find the old lady. Abyssinia!" With a flirtatious wave, she was off toward the front end of the first carriage and the tender.

I watched her sashay away then drop down between front carriage and tender before I pulled myself to the edge again to have a chat with Hayes. He was almost ready with his pistol, but I got my stroke out first and knocked it from his hand, sending it rattling, clanging, and bouncing against a buffer before dropping to the sleepers, gone forever.

"Shoot!" Hayes shouted. "My hand, my gat, darn it." He waved a fist up at me before lowering it to caress it and blow upon it. "Shoot, shoot."

"I'd rather not, old chap. Wouldn't be fair," I called down through the few feet between us, and were I so inclined I could have reached out to assist the fellow up to discuss things. I thought better of it and decided on the offering of advice. "Why don't you just jump?"

"Whaddya mean, jump?"

I pulled the pearl handled Beretta from my coat pocket and aimed it down at the fellow. I must admit the weapon did look dainty and ineffective in my hand, but I assumed one shot would be enough if needed. "Jump. Come on, Hayes," I implored. "It's not as if we're travelling very fast now, is it? Hardly running speed. Don't forget, bend your knees and roll." One must never miss an opportunity to be helpful, no matter the situation.

He had both feet precariously balanced on a buffer and both hands gripped fast on the rail. He jiggled and wobbled, the motion adding a warble to his voice. "We need the suitcase, Limey. We'll get it one way or ..." And with a neat little twist and a tiny hop, he was gone.

I lowered myself to take the recently vacated space on the buffer. There was a shaky moment as I made it from one buffer to another, to the next carriage, the carriage containing the dear Mrs. Glendower, and hopefully, Studely. I was about to creep around to the outer side of the carriage when something crossed my mind. In a flash I was up onto the roof of the first carriage and heading for the tender. I dropped just as we passed beneath a bridge.

My basic knowledge of train engines – gained during my halcyon spotting days – reminded me there would be a narrow passageway along the side of the tender through which I could get to the engine. I opened the door and squeezed sideways along the thirty-inch corridor to open the next door.

I found Studely. He was aiming a pistol at the driver and stoker, both of whom were standing with flagging but raised arms. "Studely, what the heck are you doing, my good man?"

Studely, taken aback, had little room to move aback. "No choice," he said. His aim wavered as he shrugged. "Them Yanks...they told me to keep a gun on them to make sure they'd slow down without stopping."

"In order to unhitch the carriage, no doubt," I said. I nodded to stoker and driver. "Put down your hands, men. Get this machine moving as fast as you can."

Studely launched a complaint. "But, sir…my aunt…if we don't…"

"Your aunt?"

"No, no, I mean to say, my giddy aunt, lawks a mercy, sort of thing. Mrs. Glendower will be snuffed out."

I raised a grubby hand. "Not to worry, Studely. They will not shoot her. They need her. She may get slapped about a bit, but she's already had some fortifying practise in that quarter thanks to Hammer." I hopped out of the way as driver and stoker set to work. "To Southampton as quickly as you can possibly make it, gentlemen. Don't spare the…" I looked to Studely. "What is it they don't spare on locomotives?"

Studely just shrugged.

The driver busied himself with dials and levers and the stoker set to shovelling coal.

Studely rammed the service revolver into his trouser belt then offered me a neatly folded handkerchief. "Bit of soot on your face, if you don't mind my saying so. Actually, quite a lot of it."

"May as well use this, it's ruined anyway," I said, refusing the handkerchief, deciding to use my now grey lovely white silk dress scarf.

"Such a shame, sir," said Studely. "Were you to know the trammels to befall us I'm sure you would have dressed more appropriate."

"I would have worn my black scarf, Studely, but no matter. We have work to do." I knotted my scarf and tucked it in. "We now have two ladies to save."

"Two?"

"We must get into the carriage before Mrs. Glendower gives way."

Studely, portly as he was, found it rather a struggle to get through the skinny tender corridor, but he popped out eventually and followed me across the space to the first-class carriage.

Something crossed my mind as I balanced. "Studely, old chap, how did you get from carriage to tender?"

With his huge boots balanced on the ledge just a couple of feet above the sleepers, Studely leaned around a little before pulling back. He jerked his head to add a sense of ease to his answer. "Simple, sir. This first-class carriage has a corridor because of the buffet at the end. It's easy enough to get around the corner and in through the first door."

So that's how Laura got in, I thought. Well, if she can do it… "Well, we'd better get on with it."

Studely stuck his head around once more. "Just one more thing, sir. There's some bugger hanging onto the far end of the train."

I gave a cursive glance to his revolver. "You have bullets in that thing?"

He grinned. "I do, sir. No need to fret yourself."

"The bugger to whom you are referring is a blighter going by the name of Hayes and he has been kicked off the train once already. Let's hope he didn't find his firearm." It's not that I didn't trust Studely; never let that be said, but you know how it is when one cannot resist looking, the way one turns to peek when a fellow has just told you '*don't look now but…*' I stuck my head around the corner, caught the wind in the back of the neck and my fedora caught a bullet. I lie, it didn't exactly catch it in all true senses of the word; the bullet went straight through it. "Blast. That's the second shot it's taken," I said as I pulled back, forcing Studely to budge up a fraction. "Other side, Studely."

"You can get another titfer, sir, but you ain't gonna get another crust of bread. Worse still, you could be brown bread. Mind yerself."

Studely had his back to the end of the carriage and it took some careful shifting, slithering and balancing to get past his vast protrusion of a stomach. I peeked down the other side of the carriage. "Come on. All clear."

It was only a yard or so to the first door of the carriage, but it was a hairy yard. There could have been a tunnel or bridge at any time, and it is no simple matter travelling with one's body spread-eagled against a cliff of speeding steel. And it was filthy.

It crossed my mind that Studely's *natis* were as proud in proportions as his *stomachus*. I gave an order. "You wait there at the end, until I'm safe inside. Give me a chance to get a good look to see if all is clear."

He shouted above the whistle of the engine. "Very good, sir. That whistle, I think that means there's another…" His warning was lost in the smoky darkness of a tunnel, a long tunnel.

Once more I had my hat and head and face pressed like a shoulder of cold ham against a butcher's slicing machine, my knees shaking under the strain and my fingers slipping. Just in time, we were back into the clear morning and I was able to grab the door handle, slap the other hand on the window and pull it down with a smack.

After a quick look back – back really being forward to the front of the train – to check I had room for my legs, I stuck my head through the window then slid head-first into the first-class compartment to land ungainly on some polished brogues and the rubbery end of a walking stick and one hand grabbing for dear life on a knobbly knee.

Despite my exertions, I was up in a flash, adjusting the fedora, the cravat and the brush of my coat, and offering my sincerest apologies.

"Think nothing of it, dear fellow," said the man. He closed his good book and smiled up at me with one of those Wilfred Hyde White faces to match his languorous tone. The dim yellow of the glass lamp shade grazed across his forehead. He blinked and gave his pince-nez a prod. "Been in the wars, have we?"

"Not for some time, but the peace has been unsettled of recent," I answered before reaching back to the door to open it fully. I doubted Studely could have squeezed through the window and preparations had to be made. I gave one of my best grins. "Just need to allow my compatriot in and we can leave you to your reading, Vicar."

"Fine, fine, carry on." said the chap.

Decent sorts, these C. of E. bods, you know. Always there with the tea and cakes, and never a harsh word, never any wrath or thunder. Amazes me how they do it. Be that as it may, and I know the meek shall inherit the earth, but it did seem a little early to be resting in the heavenly luxury of first-class; I put it down to him having delighted in a weighty collection plate the previous Sunday.

I stuck finger and thumb into the mouth and let out a shrill one.

As soon as I'd removed thumb and finger, Studely was there at the doorway. "Morning, Vicar," he said, loosening a hand to doff his cap, forcing me to shoot out a hand of mine own to stop him from flopping backwards onto the tracks as we rattled over a set of points.

"Come on, Studely, in you come."

I was about to give an almighty tug to launch him into the compartment when he pushed me away. "Think I'll keep going, sir. Take 'em by surprise, if you get my meaning. Just make sure you get the window open for me." With that explanation, he doffed his cap once more and did the crab thing until he was out of sight, making his precarious way along the outside of the carriage.

Our man of the cloth, made a cross of smoke and offered a "Bless you, my son."

I closed the door and calmness filled the compartment. "Fine chap," I informed the reverend fellow. "One of the best."

I tapped a finger on my brim, slid open the compartment door, stepped into the side corridor and slid the door back to leave the man to his linen headrest cover, his comfortable dog-toothed seat, his very small cigar, and his *H&E* magazine.

I looked down the length of the corridor. All was clear. I made my way cautiously from compartment to compartment, my head forward enough to get just a decko into each one before bringing the whole body into play.

At the penultimate compartment, which contained a snoring pin-striped and bowlered businessman, I had my bearings, knew where my prey and his victims were enclosed. All there was beyond that was the small buffet area, a counter and a few chairs, and a steward whistling along to Carefree's *Change Partners* as he screwed a teacloth into a tumbler.

I was feeling quite bucked at this point, making progress, and the only negative was my thinking of poor Studely having to make the whole length of the outside of the carriage. There were surely more bridges and whatnots zooming towards us as the train picked up speed.

Quiet as a slippered mouse, I inched to the compartment window and peeked in. There was Mrs. Glendower sitting starch-backed, knees clasped together, her chin jutted in defiance. Standing over her was a huge bald man in a Macintosh. He was holding a pistol in one hand, his other hand pressed against a seat wing as he leaned in.

I cupped an ear, at the same time wondering what had happened to Laura. Had she done some fantastic disappearing trick? Had she lost her nerve? Perhaps she'd entered upon the scene all full of grit, bravado, and womanly gusto, before being over-powered, defeated and ...defenestrated. I'd heard no scream, but then again, she didn't come across to me as a screamer. Something for later; baldy was doing his routine.

"I'm gonna give ya another ten seconds, lady." He pulled back and seemed to jiggle himself to full height. "You like hoofing, do ya?"

"Hoofing?" Mrs. Glendower enquired.

"Yeah, hoofing, dancing."

"Not so much these days, young man...but in my time I was..." Her fingers danced in the air for a while.

The villain thumbed back on the revolver. "If you don't start playing canary, I'll whack some lead into a drumstick."

Mrs. Glendower dropped her hands onto her carpetbag, thumbs and fingers at the clasp. Her face flicked from dark to light as trees flashed by and the sun stabbed to light up the wisps of grey sticking from out of her tweed hat. "Drumstick?"

"Legs, lady, legs. One and then the other if I don't get no answers. Try doin' the two-step when..."

Old, watery eyes locked in a steely gaze. "You had best start shooting then, you capitalist hoodlum. If you think I am ready to hand over any weapon that could be used against world socialism, you are truly mistaken."

A question flashed through my brain. A weapon? There had been no mention of a weapon. Mr. Churchill said something about engineering but nothing about weapons.

Mrs. Glendower's hoodlum spoke again. "What are ya, some kind of hero for the workers? You think I'm gonna get all emotional over drilling a commie broad?"

I took my cue. I hooked the crook of my cane over the door handle. With the Beretta in my right hand I slid back the compartment door and stepped into the compartment with a heroic a stance. "Hold it there, mister," I demanded. "Get back and stick 'em up."

The square-jawed thug whipped around and shot me a fiery look. His face relaxed. "Stick 'em up?" he said with the widest of grins and the largest selection of teeth I'd ever seen in my life, behind which was a lump of gum rolling like tumbleweed. He took his hand from the seat and clasped Mrs. Glendower by the neck, forcing her to lift an inch or so, her chins folding over his ham-like fist. "What you gonna do with that peashooter? Ping me to death?"

"You'll get the same as Hayes," I said.

"Yeah? Well, Hayes is about as threatening as a glass of warm milk, so that don't get you no medal, buster. An' if you think I'm gonna start shaking in my boots at the sight of some pansy like you all togged up to the bricks you've got another think...Aah!"

The Aah! was accompanied by the crack of a pistol as the fat man fell back into a seat and loosed lead into the carriage ceiling. Stuck through his bloodied left hand was a knitting needle, a size nine as Mrs. Glendower later informed me. It's not easy to clasp a hand when the other is holding a pistol. Another shot went through the window before the weapon was dropped to the floor and kicked away by Mrs. Glendower, then picked up and pocketed.

I gave orders, and I must admit, I was impressed by my sudden forcefulness and fortitude. The hour and the man and all that rot that cometh, I suppose. "Mrs. Glendower, open the door."

She scowled. "What on earth for? We have to question this man," she said as she strained at the handle to let the door swing and crash open.

"Don't worry, he'll be giving answers." I stuck my Beretta into the man's chubby blubbering face and commanded him to kneel. He slid down, now whimpering like a child. "That's it, face the open door."

He knelt lower than I'd requested, rocking, and squeaking out his pain, the gust from the open door sucking away his words of spite and promises of retribution.

I was about to whack the first volley of my inquisition when Mrs. Glendower dipped forward in a flurry of tweed and whipped her knitting needle back with speed and malice. She wiped the blood from it, using a clean handkerchief in a perfunctory manner as though wiping a single tine of blemished dinner fork. It was put back into her bag where it belonged, and I must say, where I hoped it would remain.

She eyed me coldly. "Better start with names, Pelham. If he doesn't give up wait for an oncoming train and boot him out."

I cleared my throat, stuck the Beretta into the white band of the man's black wide-brimmed zoot suit hat and began. "Name?"

He must have rustled up some spunk from somewhere or another. "Take a hike, Limey."

Before I could ask again, hopefully with an added morsel of menace, Mrs. Glendower was up on her feet and raining down blows upon the man's skull with a vengeance, using the butt of the retrieved gun.

"Enough," I cried, having to move sharply to push the woman back into her seat, and she was no easy mass to move. "What on earth do you think you are doing? That's no way to behave."

She growled. "Pull his fingernails out. I can have another few goes with these," she spat, pulling a knitting needle from her bag. "That's the only way to treat these capitalist scum-sucking pigs."

I gave the kneeling fellow a gentle tap on the shoulder. "Excuse me one moment, please. Just stay there and enjoy the fresh air while I sort this out." I turned to Mrs. Glendower. "We do not cross these borders, Mrs. Glendower. I thought socialism was a creed of peace. Put the needle away."

She waved the weapon at me. "It's a war, Pelham, and you certainly don't have the guts for it."

I gasped. "Well, stone the flippin' crows."

She kicked out and landed the man one in the rump. "Who are you working for, you human leech, feeding off the poor and…who are you working for?"

"For whom."

She kicked again. "Why are you after the suitcase?"

"Mrs. Glendower, please leave this to me. This is my mission and I have no recollection of anyone asking for your involvement."

"You're a weakling, Pelham Hardimann, just like your father, no gumption, no balls…just another runt from the pestilential litter of the ruling classes…"

"Enough!"

A drawl came from the kneeling hoodlum. "You tell 'im, lady."

"And that's enough from you." With that, I gave the fellow a hefty boot to send him flying from the carriage. His flight was followed by a screeching whistle and a terrified voice calling out.

It wasn't him who called out, but Hayes. "Claude!"

I whipped around, but not with enough of a crack, to find a pair of arms telescoping from their sleeves and a pair of hands spreading toward my neck. The next thing I knew, I was on my back. From the shoulders upward I was sticking through the door with my head back, inches from a passing train.

The urgent rhythm of spinning steel thundered in my ears and my fedora was snatched from me in the storm of compressed air. As the hands tightened around my throat I stared into the wide mad eyes of

Hayes, who seemed unaffected by the beating on his back from Mrs. Glendower.

My Beretta was of no use to me; Hayes had landed a hard knee on my gun wrist and my other hand was clinging on for dear life to the frame of the seat. He spat venomous revenge. "I'm gonna scatter you down the line, you Limey fink. Where's the suitcase?"

It was in those moments, while trying to catch what little breath was allowed passage through my neck, that I pondered a few questions: one must go up to the pearly gates with a clean slate and all matters resolved. Why was Mrs. Glendower following the trail of the suitcase with such ardent enthusiasm and why was she so determined to keep her secret? It was none of her business, surely. And what did she know about my father? Were they just the anti-establishment ramblings of a fervent political activist?

The passing train has passed, and I was on my final philosophical cough when a vision appeared: an upside-down vision. With my head down, lolling, and the train having passed, I looked up the thick black trousers and up to the wide leather belt of Studely. I couldn't see his face clearly owing to the expanse of stomach, but I recognised his voice and it was as dulcet as a chorus of angels.

"Aunt Phyllis!"

"Eh?" was all I could say as Studely stood astride the open doorway, clinging to the frame of the train, his donkey jacket flapping and blocking out the light.

He reached across me and into the compartment, grabbed Hayes by the hair and yanked him out. He sidestepped and, hanging on with one hand and balancing on one boot, he gave space as the gangster somersaulted onto the track.

It was time to have my own sweet hands upon my own neck as I folded and rolled into the compartment, coughing and spluttering. Mrs. Glendower pulled Studely in and the saviour of the hour closed the door behind him. Peace, albeit an uneasy one, reigned.

I settled into a corner and strove for sartorial regrouping as Mrs. Glendower slumped back full of gasps of relief. Studely pulled at his belt and glowed in the aftermath of his heroism.

"Studely," I began, "whilst I must offer my sincerest thanks for your playing cavalry and all that, it does come as a bit of a surprise to hear you addressing our Mrs. Glendower as Aunt Phyllis."

Studely eyed me suspiciously the way one does when one is being eyed suspiciously.

Mrs. Glendower pulled a thin silver flask from her bag. "Here you are, boy, have a snifter. Clear your mind and straighten yourself out, you look an awful mess."

Studely accepted. "Slip of the tongue. Mrs. Glendower here does so remind me…"

I waved soot from my scarf and hid behind the cloud. "Enough, Studely. I understand. Wet your whistle. We are entering the New Forest and will soon be in Southampton."

I expected no reply and was offered none. I watched Mrs. Glendower play the proxy doting aunt and Studely playing the proxy dutiful nephew; both playing their roles well, as we all do sometimes, for how often are we merely just playing roles, never allowing our true selves out? We are nothing unless we have somebody or something to care for, and at times we pounce upon the opportunity to do so if our lives are empty or we have been cheated of those chances; it's old ladies with cats. Mrs. Glendower? Yes, she had been cheated; a man had cheated on her, had fallen head over heels in love with Queen and Country: the most pernicious and greedy mistress of them all, so she once informed me in those rare moments when a chap shows some interest in an employee's life.

I shall leave that question for another time. I had other things on which to ponder. Where was Laura, who was Laura? And how in the name of all that's holy do we board the Queen Mary without Hammer handing over a wad of boarding cards? What had become of Quill? Quill, a nasty sort, that goes without saying, but a lazy sort who is happy to cut corners, bend rules and pocket bribes, going to such lengths to collar me, me, an innocent man. Was he also after the wretched suitcase?

Deep in thought, I played twirling baton with my lethal walking cane. I tapped at the Beretta in my trouser pocket, unbeknown to me that the next time I used it in anger it would be pressed against a waistcoat button belonging to Hammer.

CHAPTER 13
A SUIT AND A SUITE

It was near eleven-thirty. My lips were calling for a stiff one and my stomach was wondering when the nosebag would swing into view. I had spent a good thirty minutes reclining in the sumptuous black leather back-hugging barber's chair a stone's throw from the Western Docks. A real barber's shop mind you: none of that styling and waving business where my Barnett is concerned. I like a proper haircut and a hot, close shave, some murmured social intercourse, a gander at the local rag, and questions concerning my need of something for the weekend.

I was given the final flick of horsehair around the neck, the mirrored rear view, and the apron was lifted and shaken. I stepped from the chair and dropped a florin into the man's palm. I'm a good tipper when a job has been done well.

"Know of a good tailor?" I enquired.

Like any good barber, the snipper was adorned with the thinnest of oiled combovers and that dour pasty look of a man who has spent his life in a cave. But his smile was gracious enough, and he made no more than half-a-dozen furtive looks up and down at my distressed apparel. "You are sailing this evening, sir?"

"If my wind is up and the tide is right," I answered cheerily. "Mislaid the togs on the way and need to re-stock."

"There is a Dunn and Co. gentlemen's outfitter on the high street, sir. As good as their Oxford Street store, I am reliably informed."

With that information planted in my brain and wondering if my Oxford Street account still stood wholesome and dependable, I unhooked my cane from the hat stand, rubbed shoes against calves in turn then hopped from the shop with the doorbell giving me the lightest of cheerios as I stepped into spring sunshine and thick, salty, Southampton air.

I used a few shop windows as ad hoc mirrors to gain a few squints at the new cut, walking tall and proud, though with that odd feeling in which one is always enveloped having just vacated a barber shop. I, as I'm sure you do, spend the next few minutes convinced I am being scrutinized, for we know that when we've had a trim all and sundry has heard about and is checking on our behalf. The passer-by says nothing, gives nothing away, but he or she is judging.

I was still in need of a whisky, a late breakfast or early lunch, but felt it would be better served to me if I were more suitably attired. The brisk walk, accompanied with some whistling – I am rarely a whistler – lasted ten minutes, added some glow to the cheeks and filled me with optimism.

It also gave me time to mull things over concerning Mrs. Glendower and Studely, both of whom had gone off in search of sustenance, a wash-and-brush-up, and I suspected, a bit of a *tête à tête*. It occurred to me during the last minutes of the train journey, once all the flap and flurry was over, that they had some history together. There had been an air of conspiracy in the compartment, but I'd left it well alone, having my own concerns on which to dwell. What had happened to Laura and why had the piano player handed me the Beretta? As for Mrs. Glendower and Studely, I had time on my side and we would soon be close-quartered once more, giving me the opportunity to delve.

That '*all is well with the world*' feeling I'd had darkened as I turned into the high street and headed for Dunn and Co. The brightness was dulled not by storm clouds or an easterly gale but by the creeping tingle up the spine, that tingle one gets when one feels one is being followed. Had I caught sight of a known reflection, a known hulk of a shape? Believing that turning around to check would only make the fear become solid reality, I skipped on to cross the street, dodged cars and carts, slipped between newspaper sellers and smoking chestnut stands, and bounded into the outfitters.

When comparing your barber and your tailor, beware. We are with a different kettle of kippers altogether. Time with your barber is short and he gets his slim, soft fingers around the half-crown as soon as he is done with the steaming towels, Yardley English Blazer and gentle cheek slaps. I'm an *eau de cologne* man, but that is of no import here.

Your tailor, on the other hand, is in for the long haul and he is sizing you up the moment you press a dab onto the brass handle of his emporium. Are you, he is cogitating, the snappy dresser, the up-with-the-fashions *nouveau riche* with hips bursting over with stacks of white fivers, or are you the staid and steady man of old money, slow to cough up, looking for that jacket to last a lifetime, perhaps viewing a purchase as something more akin to an heirloom to pass on rather than something to get him through the season?

With your barber there are few rules and even those few rules can be slightly bent. I have always been a little further to the left of your classic Ramon Novarro; I've always found him a little too near the centre. No matter, these things can be changed and passed off as lightly as a dance craze or food fad. Not so with your gentleman's outfitter. He is fixed in his opinions and his opinions are fortified by traditions of biblical magnitude.

The fellow eyed me as one would study a chap who'd just returned from a coast down the Amazon and forgotten to remove the leeches, non-categorized insects, bits of tangled undergrowth and spillings of native nosh from his vest.

"There is a seafarers' retreat on Victoria Dock Road, sir, if one is looking to redress the balance of one's vestments. They offer hot soup and bread, and they are blessed with an assortment of apparel suitable for a gentleman who has spent time in many ports. They will even supply you with headwear."

"Sorry?" was all I could splutter.

He hadn't finished, and I tended to lean towards the belief that this greeting was a well-rehearsed and well-used spiel. "I have heard of late that they have also acquired a clinic, sir, for those voyagers who have…"

"No, no, no," I hammered. "Don't let this fool you." I let my hands waft over my coat and even made a point of pointing to my ruined shoes. "I have been in some scrapes, upon these shores mark you. I am not from abroad."

Most decent fellows, those who acquiesce and fall into conversation, lend an ear to one's troubles and all that sort of thing. They move forward a step to draw you in, to offer support and encouragement in the sharing of your woes. Not this fellow. He was as inanimate as his mannequins. "Sir?" he said with the stiffness of a starched collar.

I made my case. "I have not fallen upon hard times, as may appear to you, but difficult times have recently come crashing down upon me."

He summoned up the strength to raise an eyebrow. "Sir?"

In the hope of drawing the merest of glints into his eyes I added "I have an account in Oxford Street."

There was no glint, but there was smarm. "I am sure you do, sir."

"The name is Hardimann, Pelham Hardimann. I suggest you get on the blower and make enquiries." I added mustard to the retort with a resounding "my good man."

With that he went hell for leather and lifted both brows before turning away. "One moment, sir."

As he did his stuff behind a curtain in his cramped telephone booth, I took a cruise around the stands, glancing over slacks and jackets, shirts and ties. "I'm in need of a total refit," I called out. I flapped along an array of Harris tweeds and then onto a rather crisply cut blazer. I moved on, keeping in mind the geography I was about to walk, drive or sail across. "This black cashmere topcoat, how much?"

The man slipped out of his booth. "Your account has been confirmed, sir. May I suggest we begin with the…" He put a hand to his mouth and let out a gentle cough.

"Smalls? I enquired.

"You will require something immediately."

"I will."

His face took on the expression one would have imagined on Noah, who having closed the bow doors and battened down the hatches with the sense of a job well done was informed that he had an odd number on board his vessel. "Something off the peg, sir? I was thinking perhaps we could begin with your trip before going onto the more modern and stylish habiliments suited to the Americas. They are not of my taste, of course…"

"Of course."

"But one does need to…"

"Blend in?" I unhooked a Kent suit jacket, scrabbled along the line for the matching trousers then helped myself to a sheaf of Shangtung shirts. I delved towards the fitting room to begin my metamorphosis. "Will only be a tick."

You may find all this very abrupt, too swift and lacking in care. I apologise. Though no great fan of 'off the peg', I was in dire need for a starter as far as this clothing meal was concerned. I have never been one for spending a whole morning trying on clothes and shoes; I leave that sort of thing to the fairer sex, which is more judgemental about these things.

I was given no answer to my ultimate remark; the man was slinking off with what I took to be almost Pavlovian reactions towards the opening door. He had another customer with which to deal.

I was out of the booth and striding about to test the cut and comfort fast enough to surprise the cardboard cut-out of an outfitter, but the surprise was all mine.

"I would suggest a black fedora and a grey scarf, sir."

Had his voice changed? No. It was Hammer. I would like to add, in all his glory, but glory would be the *mot* not *juste*. "Hell's teeth, Hammer," was all I uttered at first breath, but I was quick to collect my wits. "Good to see you. What happened to you?"

He was holding my cane, not so much in a threatening way, but in a way that said '*this could be a threat.*' "Happened to me, sir?" he said.

Certainly, I had taken into account some of what Mrs. Glendower had said about Hammer and his forceful questioning techniques and I had kept in mind Studely's discovery of the monocle, but let it never be said that I fall victim here, believing everything, creating my own little scenarios. I am ever prepared for Mr. Ponzi and his ilk. Standing before me was a Nazi. Really? Wasn't it just an old retainer, a man who buttles and buffs?

"You were off, Hammer. You left me in the clutches of Quill. And I'd like to know what the heck he's up to if truth be told, but we can leave that until you have accounted for your own actions."

Ever the Boy Scout, I had taken precautions, more out of fear of Kennedy's boys, but the result was the same. I had slipped the Beretta into the side pocket of my new Kent suit. I pulled it out quickly, kept it at waist height and gave Hammer time to take it in.

Hammer was shadowed by the shop assistant who hovered with his hands in the air as if trying to guess shoulder measurement, still living in hope that Hammer was a customer with the readies at the ready.

Hammer took a step towards me. "And what do you propose to do with that device, sir?" he asked a little too smoothly for a chap with a pistol aimed at his waistcoat buttons.

I jiggled the Beretta and caught the outfitter's nervous eyes. "I need a dozen shirts, two scarves, black tie and some socks with suspenders. I need some handkerchiefs as well." I jabbed the Beretta at the middle of Hammer's midriff. "Put the cane aside, Hammer, and stick your hands up." I gave the Beretta another menacing jiggle. "Cuff links, I'll let you choose, but nothing to garish. Sam Cooper Jockeys, some collars…" I tiptoed to catch a glimpse of the far corner of the shop, "…and a selection of cravats. Any Panamas?"

The outfitter minced an invisible circular chalk-mark. "A little too early, sir."

"Never mind."

"Anything else, sir?"

"Shoes. Three pairs. Deck shoes, a pair of grey brushed suede, and a pair of black Brogues."

"Very good, sir." The man hovered.

"Get on with it," I commanded, keeping a steely eye on Hammer who had his hands in the air, having hooked the handle of my cane over the arm of a mannequin. It suited it.

The outfitter was dancing a little by this time, knees knocking with the urgency of a child who'd put his hand up too late in class. "Measurements, sir." A measuring tape appeared. "I need to measure you."

I shrugged and slapped a free hand against a flank. "Same as these."

"But with different cuts…"

"Well, get measuring," I said. I was a keen watcher. Thinking I had been distracted, Hammer was slipping a hand into his coat. "Hold it, Hammer. Keep those hands up in the air."

"I was just…"

"Clam it," I snapped. I liked that. It had something of the Bronx about it and I considered a good way of warming up for when the old colony greeted me.

"Very good, sir."

I stood a little at ease to allow the outfitter room to manoeuvre and make the usual enquiries demanded of his profession. "Might I enquire as to which side...?"

This is, I must confess, a question that always grabs me by the gizzard. How much do they really want to know? Do I wiggle and wangle it out to the side for a sneaky peek, nip it over the top or just pop it through the Y? I settled with a hoarse: "The left."

"Very good, sir. Does one carry a holster?"

"I could acquire the habit," I answered. I was back to Hammer in an instant. "Okay, Hammer, why did you make a break for it? Trying to get to the suitcase before me eh?" He was slipping a hand to the inside of his coat once more. "Stop. Next time I see that hand move I'll put a hole in it."

"Very good, sir, it's just that..."

"That what?"

Hammer gave the faintest of smiles as he put the hand in and drew out a piece of paper. "I'm sure this would reduce the gentleman's tedium, and your discomfort." He waved and flicked the paper to open it and made to pass it. "While you are down there, my good man..."

The outfitter, crouching with thumb and forefinger nudging at my gentleman's vegetables to check I hadn't lied, peeked around the slim but sturdy trunks of my legs to grab a gander at the script coming towards him. "Sir?"

Hammer let go the paper. "These are the gentleman's measurements, and you'll find his shoe size; add an inch to the heel if you'll be so kind. I trust all the items will be delivered on board by early tomorrow afternoon."

"But..." began the outfitter, straightening and studying the paper.

"Before she weighs anchor. The suite is written at the top of the page."

The outfitter made the faux pas of squeezing between the muzzle of the Beretta and Hammer. "But what about a fitting...I usually give two and there'll be no time..."

I pushed the man aside. "Get it right first time," I said. I gave my hips a twirl just to loosen things up and rid myself of the memory of a chap handling the goods. I've never been comfortable with that sort of thing. At least the barber goes no lower than the neck. It's not that I am unsure of my sexuality, or that I feel threatened by another chap...you know...but one cannot but wonder if the old fellow has or hasn't responded in some way. It is such a sensitive arrangement and, unlike the brain or the eyes, cares little about the explorer. That said, I often wonder how any member of the species cannot gaze upon that young chap Cary Grant without enjoying some stirring in the loins.

The outfitter quickstepped to his shop door and turned the '*open*', '*closed*' sign to '*closed*'. "Very good, gentlemen. Should you wish to continue your discussion…"

I tried another bit of the Bronx, or was it Chicago? "Beat it."

The man wafted past us. "I'll be in the back room should you need…" and he was gone.

"Right, Hammer, let's get down to brass tacks," I said. "Hands down." It wasn't until this moment that I noticed the gloom of the place, the low lighting, and the dark woods with the mannequins adding to the eeriness. I dismissed the thought. "Hammer, I have a selection of questions and you have answers for all of them, I trust."

"I shall do my best, sir."

"No multiple choice. Straight answers. The truth."

"As I see it, sir."

"As you see it," I added in the hope of moving things along.

Hammer had more. "Have you partaken of luncheon, sir?"

"Not yet."

With his hands fully relaxed he stepped back and turned as if to leave. "Might I suggest we partake of luncheon and some light refreshment on board?"

I dropped the Beretta into my new side pocket and picked up my cane, feeling it would be enough should Hammer try any of his Nazi strong-arm shenanigans. "But we are not sailing until tomorrow. At least, I am not sailing until tomorrow afternoon. And you have not yet satisfied me of your allegiances. So, no funny business, Fritz."

"Fritz, sir?

"Well, there's some Bavarian blood in you somewhere, Hammer, there must be."

"There is none, sir, and might I say I find the inference offensive."

I pointed my cane towards him then looked along a row of shoes. "A jest, the merest jest. Lighten up. You see? German. No sense of humour."

"Be that as it may, sir, I am most assuredly of good English stock. The assumption that the members of the Third Reich have no sense of humour is one without foundation. For a nation to choose a supreme leader sporting a Charlie Chaplin moustache, there must be some ribs not averse to being tickled somewhere in the land. It is also somewhat ironic when studying the Englishman, would you not say, that a nation with such an abhorrence of all bodily functions can laugh most heartily, hold splitting sides and rock with mirth at the simplest peep of the passing of wind while feeling immense superiority over others who do not?"

"Yes, well, we'll see, Hammer. All in good time. Until I know what's going on, you and I are to be joined at the hip."

He hovered about half-way to the door. "I trust you will be fully satisfied once I have clarified certain aspects of the case, sir. As far as boarding is concerned, there is no need to worry on that account. Mr. Churchill can have words in the right ear, if you gather my meaning."

"I gather, I gather. And what of Studely and Mrs. Glendower, Hammer? And what of Quill? He's up to some rummy game, I can tell you, and I'd bet my bottom dollar you have some inklings."

"I have no inklings as far as Quill is concerned, sir. He is of no importance to me...of no interest whatsoever.'

That was interesting. Why so much stress of the negatives? Overegging the denials, wouldn't you say? All a bit *methinks the lady doth protest too much* or whatever Hamlet's mum accused Gonzago's missus of. I would get to the bottom of it, trust me, dear reader. You know me well by now. I am tenacious, a terrier with a tibia if nothing else.

'You claim to know nothing of Quill, Hammer, and I shall let that matter rest for the while, but what of Studely and Mrs. Glendower? Do not feign ignorance with me."

"I chanced to come across them earlier in a tearoom, sir, and advised them I would do what I can to find them accommodation aboard the vessel by tomorrow morning. I am led to believe they are happy with a bijou B&B for this night."

"And Mrs. Glendower was amenable?"

"As amenable as someone of her ilk can be, sir."

"But she classes you as the enemy, Hammer, and you most certainly do not view her as an ally."

He smiled, as far as he could smile. "As the Chinese militarist, Sun-Tsu once said, sir: *keep your friends close and your enemies closer*. Besides, it is she who knows the look and the whereabouts of the suitcase. The Queen Mary is a formidable vessel and we could find ourselves lost in a maze of corridors and chambers while searching for it. We must allow her to lead us to it, unintentionally, of course."

"And what did you make of Mrs. Glendower and Studely, Hammer? Their manner, I mean, together."

"Familial, sir, if that is what you mean."

"I see. It had crossed my mind. You think they are in cahoots?"

"Cahoots, sir? I could not say, but I doubt it. I am under the impression that Studely knows little of her leanings and is escorting her out of some sense of duty."

"My thoughts entirely, Hammer." I gave a shrug, believing things must be allowed to pan out; winging it seemed to be the option, the only option.

One thing I did deem worthy of keeping close to the chest, even from Hammer, was my brief meeting with Laura.

Do not misunderstand me here. It was not a matter of the heart. I just had the notion that perhaps too many bodies were cluttering a small library.

Hammer made it to the door, pulled down on the latch and opened it for me, adding a discreet ushering hand. "There will be a small party of us already aboard for this evening, sir. I hear Mr. Coward is to be giving us some renditions. I believe rendition is the word, one must be so careful about the misuse and bending of our lexicon. It can get us into such hot water."

"Up to our necks," I said with an extra spring in my step. Things were going in the right direction. "One moment, Hammer. Let me change my shoes."

"Very good, sir," he said, exiting the establishment.

I joined him in a trice, having wriggled into comfortable shoes. I sucked in late-morning salty air and stamped to loosen the leg of the trousers. I like the turn-up to rest with the crease directly above the knot of the laces.

As we walked, brisk of pace, with a sense of urgency and purpose, I turned things over in the head. I needed to make enquiries without giving too much away. That is not an easy task. "Hammer," I began. "This business of Quill?"

He played for time. "Quill, sir? As I have already stated..."

"Yes, Hammer. Quill. I saw his motor vehicle near Mrs. Glendower's abode and saw it fragment in a ball of fire. Remember, Hammer, the conflagration? Ring a bell?"

"It rings loud and clear, sir. I am suspect he was spying upon Mrs. Glendower, perhaps under the misapprehension that I was in the cottage."

"But you were, Hammer. You were in the cottage. You gave the poor lady the third degree, by all accounts."

He skipped down from the pavement then up again as we passed a nanny with perambulator. "All accounts or her account, sir?"

"I saw you, as clear as crystal, standing over the woman with a Luger." I gave him a gentle prod with my deadly cane. "A Luger, Hammer."

I have to say that Hammer could give the freshest of cucumbers a run for its money when it came to being cool. He continued his march, forcing me to break step with a hop, skip and a jump in order to catch up as we swerved around a corner and faced the sea.

"Has it not occurred to you, sir, that if Quill were to arrest Mrs. Glendower for the murder of your old and recently departed comrade Mr. Spot, she would be out of our reach. I had to improvise. It was necessary to frighten her, question her." He stopped. We collided. "I beg your pardon, sir."

"Continue, Hammer, continue." I was finding myself adept at this commanding business by this time. Practice was nudging me towards perfection. "Speak up, man. Explain yourself."

We parked ourselves near a greengrocer's store not many yards away from the entrance to the Western Docks. Hammer backed up to the brick wall, putting him in the shade of the striped canopy. "If I might say so, sir, you look upon Mrs. Glendower as a harmless old spinster with a craving for petty scandals and adventures, but you must remember that as one of Stalin's little foot soldiers she is as much a danger to the empire as any other foe."

"You are still convinced she is a murderer?"

"I have my suspicions, sir, and they have foundation."

I tucked my cane under an arm and searched for a smoke. "So, tell me, how come she assisted me in my journey, forwarded the suitcase to the destination prescribed by Sam the Spot, and defended me from two of America's finest thugs?"

"Hardly America's finest, sir."

"Good enough for me, Hammer."

The picture of Mrs. Glendower shoving the knitting needle through the man's hand sprung to my mind, an image followed swiftly by that of Sam the Spot lying on my Persian with his own selection of implements. I lit a gasper and gave a puff of smoke towards Hammer: something of a finale, a full stop, an '*answer that one if you can*'.

"I have to admit, sir, it puzzles me, but we cannot assume her innocence. I'm sure she has her reasons."

I took my cane in hand and made to move off. "Be that as it may, Hammer, I am still alive and she is still about, as is Studely, as you know." Another thought crossed my mind, but I left it unspoken: *And what reasons do you have, Hammer?*

After cadging some silver and copper from Hammer, I skipped across the road to Timothy Whites, popped in for a minute or so to gather up the sort of thing a gentleman needs in his bathroom while travelling, then was back out to buy a newspaper.

Hammer was talking, talking about something, but I must admit I was rather too engrossed with my '*catching up*' on world events, world events being something that had become of interest to me over the last couple of days.

There was a brief column about the failure of the January negotiations between Germany and Poland and the likelihood of a German invasion of Czechoslovakia within the next few weeks;

refugees fleeing to the rump of Czechoslovakia had already reached one hundred and fifty thousand.

Geronimo was on the warpath again but there was no cause for alarm and the world would soon return to peace and prosperity because John Wayne was sorting him out in *Stagecoach*.

There was a headline concerning the American Ambassador's declaration that the American people were opposed to minority status for Jews in the Holy Land.

And, by Jove, members of the glorious Third Reich could now purchase a VW Beetle on the never-never for five marks a month. It's strange, I mused, how civilization, technology and science, and all that can do well for the common man can at the same time sup with the devil.

Perhaps the most interesting article was a few lines concerning the escape from H.M.P of a certain Dangerous Dan Gully who had, after numerous attempts, managed to dynamite his way to freedom and was now on the run, supposedly to cross the pond and give his beloved Greta Garbo a cuddle. I could not help but wish the fellow luck as my eyes planted themselves on another story. I must have exclaimed '*I'll be jiggered*' or some such nonsense, forcing Hammer to come to an abrupt halt. We collided once more.

"There is an issue, sir?"

I flicked and stretched the broadsheet so he could see the photograph. "This chap, Hammer, I know him. He was on…"

"Mr. Coward, sir?"

"So, that's the blighter."

"Blighter, sir? I believe the BBC is planning a televisual broadcast of his stage play, *Hay Fever*, later this year."

"You're an aficionado of the television, Hammer?"

"I have viewed the expensive apparatus on occasions, sir, mainly for the news and programmes concerning the natural world and the sciences, something that should be offered to all at lesser expense, and soon will be, I hope. The masses, I am sure, thirst for education and will scoop it up with vigour once widely available. It may even keep them from the dross of the penny-dreadfuls and gossip columns."

I hissed. "Well, if you want to sit in a darkened room staring at a goldfish bowl, Hammer, there's nothing I can say. It won't catch on, you know."

He put his hand to his mouth and did one of those '*if I may interrupt*' or '*if I may get back to the matter in hand*' coughs. "I was wondering, sir, if you could enlighten me further about your brief encounter with Mr. Coward."

I pulled the Beretta from my side pocket. "He donated this quaint toy to the cause. Strange, don't you think?" I slipped the thing back home.

"His Majesty's Government does employ the oddest people at times, sir. They have, after all, employed you."

"Mr. Churchill is not a member of His Majesty's Cabinet, Hammer."

"As is regretted by so many, sir." He gestured for us to put best feet forward.

We found ourselves in a melée, a pell-mell mass where skeletons of cranes leaned and swung in a macabre ballet. Trams and trolleys trundled through and along, and stevedores diced with death beneath hoisted loads and between shunting trains. The sun was blotted out for a moment as a Rolls Royce was loaded. We stopped near a pile of sacks: coffee, tea, and sugar if I remember correctly. My eyes fixed upon one thing: a white grand piano lifting then gliding, its white sheen turning mother-of-pearl in the sunlight as it rose above the vast black walls – the hull of the Queen Mary. Her black and red funnels were already coughing black despite not having to sail until the next day.

"Boarding cards, Hammer?" I asked as we stepped away from the coffee, sugar, and tea against which we'd been catching breath.

"No need for concern, sir. Follow me."

I followed Mr. Churchill's henchman up the gangplank, finding us jammed between a convoy of loin-shouldering butchers. We were stopped by a fellow in a black frockcoat and blue cap; his sleeves sported gold rings.

"Mr. Hammer, sir, welcome aboard." Hands were shaken, or were they shook? "Mr. Hardimann's suite is ready."

I ducked and popped out from between the meat that carried on along the deck. "Good day," I chimed in a nonchalant manner. "And you are?"

The fellow spoke softly. "I am the second officer, sir." He had the goodness to shake my hand firmly once more then guided me further onto the ocean-going city.

"I need to make a call. You have a telephone on board?" I enquired.

I'm not sure if the expression was one of hurt, disgust or contempt; perhaps it was a cocktail of all three. "I'm confident you'll find the telephone in your suite as good as the other eight hundred and ninety-nine on board, sir." The man moved off and I shadowed him with a youthful and enthusiastic step.

As a threesome, we made our way along the side of the ship with me turning from time to time to find Hammer close behind and me managing to catch a glimpse of his face, with the feeling that here was a man who had just shared a joke with a fellow sufferer of fools. The bee was still buzzing in my bonnet concerning Hammer's inclusion of me in his collection of 'oddest people'. Does upstairs ever realize how much it is mocked by downstairs?

CHAPTER 14
THE SUIT IN THE SUITE

I could have donned the old nosebag in my fabulous suite, but I am never one to put the workers out, especially when taking into consideration that all systems are not yet up and running. Backstage chaps were still rushing around setting up stall for sailing the following day. Bunting was being looped up and through and all about, floors and banister rails were being polished, and the first-class shopping emporium was being stocked with an array of items that made one feel one was bowling along Burlington Arcade.

I was not armed with the collection of dining or cocktailing clothes suitable for mingling with the great and the good of first-class, so I felt it necessary to slum it for a day. I am adept, if nothing else, and can rub shoulders with all aromas and sounds of humanity.

Hammer and I settled at a table in the sparsely populated third-class Dining Lounge where we were offered a cold collation and average wines, but the company was quiet and civilized.

The lower classes, in their Sunday best, possessed an air of starchiness, sprig-of-holly backs, and hushed tones as they guardedly selected the correct scoffing implements and played hesitant chequers with the assortment of drinking vessels. It has always given me comfort to know that those with aspiration, the devout wish to enhance their station in life, take the niceties of polite behaviour more seriously than those of us who have landed at High Table without breaking into a sweat. After all, as a historian of these isles you'll be aware that the largest group to come to their demise once Titanic had hit her iceberg was the lower-middle class male; fellows armed with good manners and a sense of duty to their society, doing the *women and children first* routine. What does cause me disappointment and some degree of concern is that those for whom life has been nothing but a continuous flow of winning lottery tickets display little need to hold the standard, thus letting the side down and failing to shine as worthy examples. A keen and winning team is nothing without a first-class captain.

I sensed things were not wholly tickety-boo, tinkerty-tonk and '*all's quiet on the Western Docks*' between Hammer and myself. I put that down to the chagrin he must have felt concerning my previous accusations combined with finding himself sitting at table with me. Conversation was terse, not blunt or stinging, but uncomfortable and I was glad to retire to my suite for a well-deserved afternoon nap and he could busy himself with all the details necessary to be covered when arranging the comfort of one's master. Fine fellow that he was, even under such strained and strange surroundings, he softened my sleep with a warming mug of cocoa, pumped my pillows, closed the curtains to hold back invading light and harbour noise and left me to my slumber, a slumber untrammelled by dreams and hauntings despite what had occurred over the last hours.

I woke up the next day, midday. Hammer glided – I'm sure it should be glid – into my bedroom just as I was opening the peepers. He was armed with an overstretched smile and a tray containing Eggs Benedict, some freshly squeezed orange juice and a pot of black coffee.

"I could draw the curtains for you, sir," he said as he straightened from the tray delivery then made sure my smoking requisites were in easy reach on the bedside table. "It's a perfect day for sailing." He stood to attention at the end of my bed, giving cursory glances towards the window. I expect you want me to call it the porthole, but sorry, it was a huge square window, nothing as romantic as a porthole. I think third-class get those.

I stabbed an egg with a fork, picked up a Hollandaise-soaked muffin and rammed the clog of sleep from my tonsils. After half a cup of coffee the lungs were ready for a gasper. I lit up. "Sweep them aside, Hammer," I ordered. "Let the golden orb flings its rays in to chase away the gloom."

I blew a cloud to the ornate light fixture above my bed and took time to take in the room, as if seeing it for the first time, realising I'd previously entered it close onto exhaustion.

Hammer shimmied. "Very good, sir." He opened the curtains. "I have taken the liberty of running a bath. Your soap and brush are at the ready."

"Many thanks, Hammer," I answered. "Everything else running smoothly?"

He came back to the foot of the bed and clasped his hands, a little more at ease this time. "The tailor will be here in an hour, sir. I suggest you remain here in your robe, in your suite. I have some calls to make and trust you will be without need of me for an hour or so."

"Errands, Hammer?" I enquired. "Duties?"

He did that hand to the mouth and gentle cough thing. "I feel Mr. Churchill will appreciate some communication from me."

Realising he could have used the telephone in my suite, and with the jigsaw of a plan in my head, I gave him the nod. "Off you go, Hammer, and give my regards to the old man."

"Very good, sir." There was the hint of clicking heels before Hammer did a smart turn then marched from my room.

Now you may see sloth as my partner, my shadow, but do not be mistaken. When action is called for the springs uncoil with vigour, with snap. Some clandestine work was afoot. I pushed the breakfast tray to the end of the bed and swung my legs out to land my feet into the coddling wool of the bedside rug. Upright, I pushed myself into slippers and eased my arms and torso into the thick QM-logoed dressing gown. I took a gander in the *cheval* mirror, brushed my locks with fingers and palms then left the bedroom for the living room of the suite.

Hammer's room was through a small door to the right of the living room, and a boudoir much smaller than mine own but enough for a manservant to swing his own class of moggie. He was even blessed with a window, albeit a small one. On the single bed was a suitcase. I hadn't spotted it before and had failed to see him carrying it at any time, thus assuming he'd had it piped aboard while we were *in absentia*. Hammer was, after all, a man accustomed to planning.

I checked the clasps of the suitcase for signs of talcum powder. There were none. I flipped up the lid and did some gentle riffling. The usual things, socks, ties, handkerchiefs, collars and studs were there, along with a Luger. And burrowed deep beneath all this was a small box which on opening revealed a couple of monocles, a passport, and what I could only guess to be other forms of identification, in German.

I shuddered the shudder of a man who on seeing the blade rushing towards him is rendered immobile by the knowledge that he lacks the time to duck or step aside and must therefore accept his fate. I gathered my spirits and closed the box, taking care to tuck it back as deep down as I had found it. I headed for the wardrobe.

I pulled at a hanger, freeing a heavy covered and zipped-up garment from the thinly populated rack. Holding the hanger up high I used my free hand to unzip. Inside the black canvas cover was a neatly pressed grey uniform; the first insignia I noticed were the diamonds on the left sleeve, and I had seen enough. It was time to put the garments back next to the black leather coat. The zip was half-way up when I heard the click of a hammer being thumbed back on a pistol. My blood went to cold porridge.

"Put it back," said a familiar voice.

I turned. "Studely, what the blazes…you are pointing a pistol at me."

"I know, sir." He shook the damnable thing the way a polite gangster does when he wants his victim to march off and plant his feet in the prepared bucket of concrete. "You should have locked the door. Hammer could be back any minute."

I looked the service revolver in the muzzle then Studely in the eye. "He's off to the bridge to report in."

"Why doesn't he phone from here?"

I replaced the garment, closing the wardrobe doors firmly. "Security, perhaps," I offered. "Doesn't want me earwigging."

Studely tucked the revolver into his belt and backed out into the living room of my suite. Within moments his eyes were darting about, and I guessed them to be in search of a morning throat warmer. I am quick to notice a man's weaknesses and I am discreet enough to acknowledge them without being obvious.

"A snifter, Studely, before luncheon?"

"Don't mind if I do, sir."

"Help yourself old man, and please, Studely, I wonder if we could drop the *sir* business. I'm all for cordiality and chaps knowing their place but I feel we are now…"

"Partners, sir?"

"Comrades?"

He looked a little disappointed, forlorn, the way a chap does when he's standing alone and all the favourite players have been picked and the jerseys placed for goalposts, sure in the understanding he is sent to Coventry by way of being despatched to stand in goal, on a limb, far from the action. "Very good, Mr. Hardimann. Comrades."

"Hardimann will do," I said. "We public school chaps never go in for the first names or Mister malarkey, and nicknames may only blossom after the seasoning of friendship." I stepped into my temporary living room and closed the door of Hammer's room behind me. "Drinks are over there by the window."

"To who, Hardimann?" Studely asked as he wandered over to my drinks, giving his fingers that flexing and stretching exercise pianists do before attacking the keys. "To who is Hammer reporting?"

"Whom, Studely. To whom." He didn't thank me for the snippet of education, so I continued. "As I said, he said he was to report to Mr. Churchill."

Studely turned, having warmed a tumbler with scotch. "You believe him?"

I used the old secret agent trick, narrowing my eyes the way they do when they do their secret agent thing. "I trust no-one, Studely. After all, it is you, my comrade, who has just pointed a pistol at me."

He sniffed, smiled, and sank a gulp. "Just precautions, Hardimann. How am I to know you two are not in cahoots?"

Judging attack to be the best form of defence, I unsheathed the blade of interrogative riposte. "Tell me, Studely, apropos of cahoots, how are things between you and your aunt?"

It was not easy to notice the whitening of a face in the gloom of my Queen Mary first-class suite living room, even with the curtains pulled back and tied, but there was blanching. "Mrs. Glendower is not my aunt."

"So, what have you gleaned, Studely?" I signalled for him to replenish. "Has she given more details, taken you into her confidence?"

He gave a bit of a wobble, the wobble of a man wondering how to answer, how to get his story right when he is towering lie upon lie without the scaffolding of near truths or reliable evidence. "We didn't talk much."

I gave him one of my 'now, now' looks. "Come, Studely, the two of you were as thick as thieves on the train. I also have it on good authority that you luncheoned together yesterday before scouring the city for a B&B."

"It was a quick lunch, and then she was off on her errands, things to buy and tickets to collect."

"You did not accompany her, assist her with her bag?" I asked, remembering Mrs. Glendower's well-stocked carpetbag, the one loaded with knitting needles.

Studely helped himself to another whisky, which he took with less rush this time, savouring, giving himself time to enjoy and think. It was as though he'd crossed the Rubicon when he spoke again. "I followed her, Hardimann. Deliberately, I gave her space and time to be alone."

"You mean you gave her enough rope?"

"Something like that," he said. "There is more to Mrs. Glendower than the suitcase."

"There is?" I quizzed. "More than hits the eye?"

"She could be a murderer."

I guffawed. A small one, but it was a guffaw. "Oh, come now. Don't you start."

"Me, start?"

"It was bad enough having Hammer hammering on about her."

Studely borrowed one of my lines: "Be that as it may." He took his time to amble back to the drinks cabinet before skipping about and heading for the main door of my suite. He opened it a fraction, stuck his head out and looked up and down the corridor. Satisfied, I suppose, that we were not being spied on and there were no keyhole peepers and listeners about, he closed the door and locked it. "She ain't no innocent. I followed her to the ticket office where she was to collect our boarding cards and then around the corner to the left-luggage office."

I lifted an eyebrow as the intrigue wormed its way into my head. "Interesting stuff. Playing cloak and dagger, eh?"

"We planned to meet after a couple of hours at a B&B we'd seen earlier, one very near the station. I told her I wanted to explore, see the sights…"

"The sights? Of Southampton?"

"I wanted to report in at the local police station to see if there was news of Quill."

"Ah, Quill, master and nemesis in one," I jousted.

"Well, I had to report in, Hardimann," he said. "I am working for the force, you know?"

"But is the force with you, Studely?"

"Come again?"

Sensing he'd been making sense, and let it never be said I block the flow of a man who is making sense, I pulled him back to the track. "And what news of Quill?"

Studely stood in the centre of the living room, disconcerted, as if not all his plans were running like the proverbial Swiss watch. I had noticed before that when girding his loins and collecting his thoughts he was a thumbs-into-belt man. There he was, his thumbs jabbed and locked into his belt as he rocked gently in his boots. Eventually, he did the manly thing and looked me in the eye. "Nobody knows. He hasn't reported in since…"

"Since he set off for Hammer? Since he was caught with his snozzle pressed against Mrs. Glendower's window, since we saw him doing the Oxford, Cambridge thing on The Mead?"

"He hasn't reported in since knocking on your door."

I mulled then offered my thoughts, lighting a gasper as I did so. "But you'd lay odds on he's about somewhere, here in Southampton, or even ensconced within our dear queen here?" I gave the pile beneath my slippered feet a rhythmic but muffled tapping. "He's on the ship? Below decks, scouring the engine room and the third-class saloon bars?"

Studely shrugged. "Dunno, but wouldn't put it past him."

"We must be on our guard, Studely," I commanded, "or at least, I must be on my guard." I wagged my finger-squeezed smoking gun at him. "Back to Mrs. Glendower. You were shadowing. I think shadowing is the term." I sucked good clean smoke, sending a buzz to the grey matter then let out a cloud big enough to fill a sack. "You had your suspicions?"

"Still have. She collected a suitcase from the luggage office. I thought she'd keep it with her but she…"

"She didn't carry it to your B&B?"

He shook his head. "No. I mean, yes."

I took a stride or two and reached over to flick ash. Darn it, the window was secured tightly. I used a plant pot. "You mean yes or no, Studely? Has your brain already shrunk in the pond of my whisky?"

"She carried it to the B&B, but it only contained knitting patterns, some balls of wool and other, other…"

"Other what," I prompted. "Other what?"

"Womany bits, Hardimann. The sort of things a woman keeps, you know …accoutrements."

"Ah, yes, Studely. All the talcum powder, lavender bags, potpourri, pin cushions, spare spectacles and perhaps the odd sachet of tisane?"

Studely brightened for a moment as if finding himself locking arms with a man who understood, shared his fears and secrets: a man who had arrived so he should not face the world alone. "Exactly, and bathroom stuff. Nothing scientific or mechanical." He freed his thumbs from his belt and stuck his hands deep into his pockets. "I checked the suitcase while she was in the bathroom preparing for bed. But…I know the suitcase had contained something else, something heavy. I could tell by the way she staggered from the luggage office with it, all lopsided."

"Lopsided?"

"Yes, holding the handle with both hands like it was gonna topple her over. Heck of a struggle for her."

"And no porters to hand, no gentlemen diving into the breach?"

"Stubborn cow refused assistance."

"And she took it where?"

"Well," said Studely, scratching his head. "She went into one of them warehouses, them warehouses full of stuff to be loaded on the ship."

"You believe the contents of the suitcases are rehoused in another container?"

"Must be."

I went back to my pot plant to flick more ash. "And where is she now?"

He beamed the beam of the thick boy in the back row who on having been asked to offer up his declensions is pleased there is nothing more demanded of him than *amo* to *amant*. "She's got her feet up in our third-class compartment. She was a little tired this morning, put out, and needing a warm, dark place where she can avoid one of her migraines."

"Your third-class compartment is warm and dark?"

"Very much so, Hardimann," said Studely. I expected an edge to the answer, some bitterness or class envy, but bless the man, there was none. "Very cosy, and I like the vibrations."

"Vibrations?"

"From the engines."

"And Mrs. Glendower is happy with them?"

He smirked. "Says they remind her of her gallivanting days."

I killed my cigarette and apologised to the plant. I've never been one for stabbing dog-ends into nature and it is something that irritates me as much as a fellow – usually a woman – using an ashtray in which to deposit all other garbage not associated with tobacco: sweet wrappers, usually. I gave the clap of a man nearing the end of his cerebral crescendo, ready to dive into the climax of a plan. "Keep a beady one on her, Studely. Do not let her out of sight."

He grinned, patted the sides of his donkey jacket to remind himself of his notebook and pencil then dropped the hand to touch the butt of his revolver. "Always at the ready, Hardimann. You know me."

"Yes, Studely, I know you."

"I see you has a telephone in here," he chimed. "I can keep in touch with you that way."

"You have a telephone in your cabin?"

Studely was a man with few expressions. He beamed, he smiled, he did the odd scowl, and he was a common employer of forlorn. He tried forlorn this time. "No. There's one in the corridor near us."

"Well, use that one and keep your fingers crossed there's never a queue of émigrés suffering from homesickness before we hit international waters."

"Righto," he said. "So, what now?"

"I suggest you join Mrs. Glendower and put up your own feet. As I said, keep one eye open. My theory is she has an accomplice somewhere on board. Watch her at mealtimes, watch her closely this evening as we weigh anchor. Eye contact, Studely, it may only be eye contact but there'll be someone here to help her."

"And you?"

"I am waiting for one of Mr. Dunn and Co.'s brightest and best." I shot a glance to the carriage clock sitting on the fake mantelpiece above the fake hearth of my suite. "He'll be tapping a gentle tattoo on my door at any moment."

Studely made a couple of strides towards the aforementioned door. "There is one other thing, Hardimann," he said.

"Yes, Studely?"

"You know I was following Mrs. Glendower?"

"I'm taking your word for it, yes."

"I was not the only one."

"Don't tell me that little stick of a man Hayes and his rotund friend escaped from beneath the wheels of the steam engine and followed us here."

"Not them. It was Hammer."

The name hit home like a...well, dare I say it...a hammer blow. "Well, I'll be blowed!"

"That's what I said when I saw him peeking over a stack of condensed milk, watching her from a distance. Perhaps we'll bump into each other at the ball tonight, after we set sail. I'm told it's a fancy-dress thingummy."

"I doubt it, Studely."

"I'm sure it's fancy dress."

"No, Studely, I doubt we'll bump into each other. I'm not one for fancy dress balls or any other sort of ball. I will be in the cocktail lounge, listening to some melodies. No matter, just you keep your eyes on Madame Defarge."

"Very good, Hardimann." He chuckled. "I was thinking of dressing up as a police constable, or even a sergeant."

With that, he was gone. Moments later, the gentle rat-a-tat of the tailor's knuckles sounded on my door.

CHAPTER 15
AN INTERLUDE

I would have preferred a few leisurely hours with my friends Anderson and Sheppard, but I was in no position to choose. The fitting of my wardrobe was swift, whirlwind, leaving me a little out of puff and in need of a snifter to be followed by a gentle stroll.

By late afternoon, when party lights flashed their reds and yellows, I was sauntering along the pennant-decorated side and onto the forward deck where a brave couple played badminton. The gleeful couple smiled, retrieved their wayward missile, and continued in bad light, oblivious to the organized chaos down below on the dock as tugs whooped with gusto, ready for a tough job to be well done.

Stragglers were boarding, filing up the gangplank, already travel-weary and ill-tempered. Assuredly there were those full of hope and promise, seeking better lives in a new world; the noisy bustling ones, cheek by jowl, jostling for position in the fear there would be a shortage of bunks.

A crowd had gathered; flag-wavers and handkerchief-flickers jerked fingers to wipe away tears. A brass band marched up and down the Western Dock side, cutting a wake through the throng. Stevedores scurried and heaved at bundles and ropes. White-wall-tyre cars pulled up to spill out their rich and famous, those languorous journeyers convinced any form of transport can wait for them until they arrive.

I propped myself against a railing on the sun deck for a few moments to wave at the anonymous faces below. It is strange how landlubbers wave at seafarers and vice versa, perhaps with more pathos and heartfelt wishes than those who wave at trains slashing through farms and cuttings, don't you think?

A pair of gentlemen parked themselves near me, sharing their pipe smoke and banter. These two, not yet an arm's length from English soil had already started their patter. You know the sort of patter I mean. *'What about the cricket; the ashes, sunny afternoons on the village green, supping warm beer,'* and all that guff. I think guff is the word. These chaps have probably never walloped leather with a stick of willow in their lives, let alone worn whites on tonsured lawns. *'Will we be able to get the Thunderer?'*

is a common question cracking at the back of the throat. Then comes the talk of marmalade and HP sauce; Werther's Originals – unbeknown to them that they are moulded in a steam-powered factory in the Teutoburg Forest: the Englishman is masterful at making anything good his own. Then there is talk of afternoon tea, peasoupers, and mist-clothed water meadows. They drive me nuts, homesick before leaving home, glorifying in the unreal: the imagined Eden of their homeland. There is nothing more damnably irritating than the Englishman striving to be the Englishman when abroad.

I moved away and pondered events to come. I felt the rumble of turbines through my bones, and a sense of adventure and danger tingled up my spine. There was no call to calm myself, bring my fears and passions under control; there's never been any worry there. I am the most sangfroid of any English sangfroid. But, that said, I felt a docile evening in a bar was called for. There were still a few hours to kill before we broke free from the ropes and chains, with the hawsers unlooped.

I was in a clean-cut blazer and cream strides, with a yellow cravat and new dark blue sailor's cap. Overdressed, underdressed? It was difficult to tell. I was not as tightly wrapped as other seafarers, but I have always been a lover of the bracing salty breeze. I shivered and ducked through a door in search of a dram, one floor down on the promenade deck. I was getting my bearings by this time, at least on the upper decks, the three of them covering the main areas of importance: my first-class suite, the cocktail bars, and the better dining rooms.

"Dear boy," came a creamy voice I recognized but could not place as readily as I would have wished.

I halted, cane in hand, exuded nonchalance and waited for a face to appear. I gargled a spirited "what ho!".

"How are you, dear boy? Settled into your cabin, as snug as a bug in a rug?"

"I'm fine," I looked once more into that gentle face, those kind eyes, the hand drifting towards me. We shook. "Ready for the off."

"Good, good. Are you a sailor?"

"I've dabbled and paddled," I said, hoping it was something of a jest, but his mouth did not turn or crease. Well, I mused, we can't all be Ivor Novellos.

He squeezed harder. "And you did promise to join me for a cocktail. Remember?"

"How could I forget?" He let go my hand and we headed along a corridor, me glancing up from time to time at the wall maps, the deck plans. I've always had a good sense of direction but when it involves the vertical as well as the horizontal, I become somewhat muddled, bemused: lost, I suppose. "And you are off to…?

Mr. Coward ran a palm over his oiled scalp, twisted a cigarette into a holder just a fraction shorter than an extended telescope and lit up as we cruised parallel, like old conspirators who had misplaced the intrigue beneath their conspiracies. "Having taken some Hampshire air, I am ready to lie down in the comfort of my suite to write some ditties."

"New ditties?" I asked. A dumb question, I know, but how easy it is to mouth the sublime and the ridiculous when tongue-tied, when only shallow blubberings trip off the tongue, burble from the lips.

"People always want, and ceaselessly expect, dear boy," said Mr. Coward, gracious not to condemn my crassness.

"But what about joining in with all the fun?" I pushed.

"Work, dear boy," he said as he swept along, "is much more fun than fun."

We hit the apex of a corner, stepped aside with the niftiness of well-trooped dancers to avoid a luggage trolley and its white-washed porter, before coming to a halt.

"Mr. Coward...?"

"Dear boy?" He cocked his head and waited with the patience of a knowing saint.

"The Beretta you gave me, I was wondering if..."

He placed a hand on my shoulder, massaged and pressed. "Keep it. I have a feeling you may need it still." He slipped into his suite as though he'd hardly opened the door, with the softness and magic of a silk scarf slipping through a magician's ring.

I ankled, running ideas through my head, hoping to find a bar where I could plant the brain and warm the cooling cockles. It had occurred to me on my journey to the optics and decanters that poor Studely could be clanging the alarm bell at that very moment with me not in earshot. I put the worry aside, feeling no murderous mouse would stir until we were at sea. After all, if one is to throw a body overboard it is best to wait for the dimmest of dark skies and a decent depth of salty water.

I entered the Long Gallery: a gallery adorned with shades of greens and browns, with splashes of beige to add colour, or was it tone? I weaved through some sticking-out soles and knees before I slumped into a bucket chair and hoisted my feet onto a small table where they settled into a 'V' shape through which I could get sight and take aim at a waiter.

I'm not a finger-clicker so I waited to catch his eye and give a gentle call. "Waiter, if I may..."

"Steward, if you would prefer, sir," said the thin white pencil of a man as he glided – I'm still sure it should be glid – over to me and stooped to catch my order and show off his burgeoning bald patch.

"A large whisky in a moderate soda," I said as I dipped a shoulder and crooked an elbow, my fingers delving into my pockets searching for a smoke.

The decent fellow flashed a flame at me and waited for me to purse the lips. "Ice, sir?"

The cigarette wiggled as I ruminated. I was tempted to blurt a '*hell's teeth, man*' as is my wont when some straw of a man too accustomed to the other side of the Atlantic feels he must ruin everything with a Titanic-scraper. I let the twitching cigarette settle for him to light before I smiled and offered him my wisdom. "I prefer it unencumbered by a berg," I said, wishing Mr. Coward had been near enough to hear that one. I'm sure he would have enjoyed it and jotted it down for later use.

The flame died. "Very good, sir, shall I charge...?"

I gave him my suite number. He reversed his glide then pirouetted before wafting down the wide runway of the gallery.

I took the interlude between order and arrival of refreshment to get a gander at my fellow travellers. There were few of them, but I put that down to most passengers gathering at the rails to bid fond farewells to the dockside and England and to sing golly and gosh at the firework display that seems mandatory at these scenes.

I was using my cap and cane as plate and stick, doing that twirling thing enjoyed by conjurers and was getting the cap going at a jolly good rate when I was forced to cease.

There, not more than a half-dozen or so yards away from me was a huge black hat with a heliotrope band. It was tilting back with the grandeur of a rising west-end theatre curtain – before a proper play of course: something grave by that Norwegian fellow who slams doors.

Light from a low table lamp crept beneath the brim. At first, I found myself paddling to the waist then higher in the deep pools of Laura's eye. The truth dawned on me. It was Milly. Yes, Milly from the bathroom, Milly from beside the kitchen range at Chartwell. And...and bear with me here...it was Laura.

Your hero flipped his cap from his cane and laid it to rest on the arm of his bucket chair. He coughed a gentle greeting crackle to draw her attention, but her attention was already drawn.

She rose gracefully, swept fine hands down fine heliotrope silk then kicked an elegant spangled shoe out into the runway.

By the time she arrived afore me I was standing tall and strong, holding out a welcoming hand and flashing more gnashers than an American toothpaste advertisement. "Milly, I must say this is a surprise to beat all surprises and I have experienced more than a modicum of surprises in recent times."

"Mr. Hardimann," she said with a sweetness in her voice that I had not enjoyed when she bellowed up the stairs to inform Mr. Churchill of the whereabouts of his reading glasses. "I am so pleased to see you safe and sound."

"Not run aground, as yet." I released her warm fingers and poked at a chair. "Please join me. You'd like perhaps a…"

She tucked her hands behind her to flatten her dress and nested serenely into the bucket chair. "I have already ordered something," she said. "I know it is not the thing for a lady to order her own…but…"

I waved the concern away as I sat. "Think nothing of it," I commanded. "A lady alone needs sustenance and far be it from me to demand it is proffered solely by the male of the species. Those old ideas should go hang."

"Thank you, Mr. Hardimann," she said, tugging at her chair a little to get her knees closer to the table. I would like to think closer to me. But hold your guard; I was holding mine. I am ever the gentleman and ready to treat a young lady with civility and grace, but let it never be said that I let things go to my head. Many a man's downfall has been a pretty face and a shapely ankle: not mine. I had memories, certainly, but few scars. A man must go his own way, never to swerve from course in the vain attempt to please a woman.

"Tell me," I began with a smile. "Which of three are you really? The woman in black who roams my mews, the giggly and mischievous Laura, or Milly?"

She placed an evening bag on the table where my feet had moments before been resting. It was compact but I guessed it large enough to carry a pistol. I would have wagered my favourite niblick and jigger on it. We trod water in a hiatus as the drinks arrived and I was sure her sparkling eyes sparkled even more as she scrambled her brains for an answer.

She thanked the steward then sipped at something tall and green and laden with tropical fruits. "My name really is Milly, Mr. Hardimann. I really do work for Mr. Churchill and I really am here to assist you. I have been…"

I was willing to offer some assistance of mine own. "Seconded?"

"Yes, really." she said.

I warmed my teeth with whisky and soda. "And armed with an awful lot a reallys," I added for her.

She gave one of those charming twists of the head and dipping, coy smiles commonly used by her ilk. "You must think I am rotten to the core."

"To the core, no. And Mr. Churchill knows of this?"

She hid behind a wedge of pineapple. "I volunteered," she said. "I was concerned for your safety."

Down came the glass and into view came the smile. That did it. Blast. I would not let it win. "What were you doing at my mews?" I did not mention the gruesomely adorned Persian. I thought it better to confront her with the stiff at a later juncture; one must pace things.

"Looking for you," she said as she leant forward, extremely forward and devilishly low to place her upside-down Vesuvius of a drink on a coaster. "I was not sure if Mr. Hammer would stick by you."

My German accent was not of the level to get me a bit part in *All Quiet on the Western Front* but it was accurate enough. "You mean Field Marshall von Hammer...?"

Up went the hand. Her Laura giggle had been no affectation. "Von Hammer? Oh, come Mr. Hardimann, you mean to say..."

I was sharp. "I have seen the uniform."

She rapped out a fingernail tattoo on the small table before nestling back. "There is a fancy-dress ball this evening. As you know, we love to dress up as our enemies, especially those tyrants from history: Napoleon, Caligula, Genghis ...I've heard tell we even have a Joseph Stalin aboard ship."

Not historical enough, Joseph Stalin. The present can be a little too close for comfort when it comes to tyrants. I know the English love to prod and mock the bumptious, the over-inflated ego and the megalomaniac, but I was urgent. "There is more. Hammer is up to no good. And Quill, come to think of it."

"I can't answer for Quill, although he has been known to rub shoulders with Moseley and his mob, but Hammer, no, unlikely to say the least."

"Could be fifth column, a spy, the enemy deep inside..."

Milly blew upwards, jutting her bottom lip, giving her hat ribbon a playful waft and flap. "And dressing up in Nazi uniforms? Not exactly going deep undercover then, is he?"

She had a point, but having a point is not the same as being right. 'A bluff, a double bluff, a triple bluff, even."

"He gets a twitch when I mention my SS...my SS100. He knows I'm onto him...while he does that *I know that you know that I know that*...sort of thing. He's just playing me along to get his hands on...and I'm letting him think he's getting away with it. Doing my own bluff."

"No, no, Pelham, you are way off the mark." She scooped up her drink. "Apropos of his getting his hands on...did you get the dope on the suitcase from the old lady?"

That Raymond Chandler fellow has a lot to answer for. "The dope? No, well, she is securely guarded, have no fear there. My man is with her."

"Your man?" Her smile was a touch Mona Lisa, but I let it pass. I am used to being ribbed.

"My new man. Studely."

Milly gave her hat ribbon another puff of excitement. "Is he also a German spy?"

"No," I said, and I said it in all honesty and complete assuredness. "Studely is straight as a die, solid."

Her response was flat. "Very good." The glass went down again. "You think we'll get the suitcase from the Glendower woman before she hands it over to the Russians?"

I downed my whisky and soda, lifted the head to search for the steward, caught his eye and beckoned him over. I ordered another: a larger one. "Hand it over to the Russians? You don't imagine she'd do something like that, do you? She's just a mad old woman, a housekeeper with a tendency to filch trinkets and items of bone china. Batty is the word I feel most suitable."

"Let's hope so." Milly turned to look back through the various heads in the thickening crowd of the Long Gallery. Her turn back to me was sharp. "Don't look now, but down at the far door...I said don't look now."

I looked. "Well of all the...over there?"

"Over there."

"The Yanks are coming. Hayes and Clench." I lifted a hand to hide my face as the two men; let's call them our Ollie and Stanley, waddled and tripped their way down the centre of the Long Gallery. They sported thick pinstripe Zoot suits, spats, and white-banded fedoras. I mumbled through the corner of my mouth. "They're carrying violin cases."

The cornucopia of flora in Milly's drink was more than enough to hide her face. Me? I leaned back and slumped low, reached for my captain's cap and placed it across my face. I did the snooze thing.

"Where are they now?" she whispered before slurping in a rather unladylike fashion.

I prodded a finger at my peak and caught a wedge of the scene. I gave a shallow nod in the right direction. Hayes and Clench did the full length of the Long Gallery and parked, sitting their violin cases on the tables, in a corner shielded by a pillar. I pushed my way back up the back of my bucket seat. "I can't believe they are dressed as gangsters."

"They are gangsters."

"But..."

"All set for the fancy-dress ball. You know what they say, the best place to hide a tree is in a forest."

"What do we do?"

Milly's padded shoulders lifted and dropped. "KBO."

"Eh?"

"Keep buggering on."

I'm sure I blushed. "Who on earth taught you...?"

"My employer."

"Not Mr. Coward?"

She was not amused. "No."

My scotch and soda needed attention. My mind wandered for a while; I was peckish.

"Pelham?" Milly asked after some moments. "You are going, aren't you? I think you must attend this fancy-dress ball. Everyone who is anyone will be there."

I dwelt upon the question and suggestion. "I was thinking of going as an English gentleman."

She was still not amused. "I am going as Britannia," she said after a long spell of silence during which time I exercised my neck, ducking and craning to get a better view of Hayes and Clench who appeared to be locked in their own bout of quietude.

"Hmm?" I said coming back to our own little cameo. "I'll think of something, but I don't enjoy dressing up. Not comfortable amongst crowds."

"But you will be incognito."

"I wish not to be in anything." I turned my ankles to get blood to my feet, to relieve myself of the cramp about to set in. I am not a fervent sitter. "Well, if you'd like to meet up later, we can view the fireworks together. Then dinner, perhaps? It would be jolly and comforting, as we set sail, to have someone on my arm."

Milly was a master at flattening the mounds of hope, the mountains of optimism. "I'll have a shield on mine."

CHAPTER 16
MANIFESTATIONS

At least seventy feet above sea level, overlooking the stern upper deck and offering a view of the wake, the first-class Verandah Grill was an elegant semi-circular cave with the broad clean sweeps of art-deco, from the chairs to the ceiling. It was a theatre of silver and gold, and red velvet curtains. At the far end, over near the bay window was a white piano, the one I'd seen mid-air as it was hoisted aboard. Mr. Coward was not yet *in situ*, but I put that down to him still busily scribbling away on his new ditties.

By eight that evening the Queen had backed out of her dock, whistled and hooted goodbye to land and was creeping her way up the Solent to edge around the Isle of Wight. Tugs had tooted goodbye and were scurrying back home.

Dinner was a quiet affair. Milly, elegant and slim, picked at her food and, as any woman views it as her prerogative, sneaked a taste of mine from time to time as we did the small-talk thing. I lay off the wines and spirits, feeling I would need a clear head later. By eleven we were back in our separate cabins preparing for the ball; at least, I was.

Taking a long and convoluted detour back to mine own suite after dinner I called in on Studely and Mrs. Glendower.

My progress was speeded up by a helpful steward who accompanied me all the way, commenting at intervals as we dropped a flight or two that it was all akin to journeying to the centre of the earth. He was not far wrong; D Deck was close to scraping the bottom of this steel barrel. My lungs felt the air thickening with each step. That served me right, I suppose, for refusing to use the lifts, for professing my agility and addiction to exercise.

Despite my having taken the trouble on her behalf to obtain a pair of tickets to the ball, Mrs. Glendower was grumpy; she informed me that such events were a way for toffs to gorge themselves on the wealth stripped from the backs of the proletariat.

Studely kept his head down in his own little corner, putting the final additions to his uniform, making himself a member of the constabulary dressed as a civilian who had put it upon himself to dress up as a member of the constabulary. It suited him.

I left them and headed for my suite.

On entering my suite, I was greeted by Hammer who was brushing down his SS uniform with soft horsehair. The uniform fitted him well, worryingly so.

"You really need the holster, Hammer?" I enquired as I turned on the hub of the shin-tickling circular rug, giving him time to close the door behind me.

"It is commonly viewed as the most acceptable place in which to keep one's pistol, sir," he said with added edge to his consonants.

"I trust you are not going to spend the night speaking German, Hammer," I pressed. "I like my verbs early. And let's be frank, the accent doesn't really wash, does it?"

The disappointment on his face almost moved me. "I understand, sir, but I would be most gratified if you allowed me to retain some aspect of the language, the accent, for the ball, at least."

I smiled and gave a smack to my thighs. "If it thrills you, Hammer, if it thrills you."

"Thank you, sir." He crossed the room, pulled at the curtains and peered out into the darkness. "There is no longer land in sight, sir."

"We are all at sea?"

"I wouldn't put it quite like that, sir."

I slumped down in an armchair, crossed my legs, and let a loose foot jiggle, with my cane straddling across arms. "I fear we'll get nothing from Mrs. Glendower," I began. "She is intransigent. She will not give way. Studely has his eye on her."

"As do the Americans, sir," said Hammer.

"You've seen them?"

"They entered the Long Gallery as you were taking refreshment with Milly, sir. If I am not mistaken, the rotund person, Mr. Clench, is moulding himself along the lines of one of the Southside O'Donnell Brothers while Mr. Hayes displays a penchant for Mr. Capone, who, if I have studied with enough vigour is now residing at Alcatraz and dying of venereal disease."

"A high price for not paying one's taxes, Hammer," I quipped.

"An astute observation, if I may say so, sir. It is an affliction with which many people in power have suffered throughout history, an unforgiving affliction causing mental instability, thus exacerbating their monstrous desires and temptations towards the iron fist of totalitarianism."

"The disease or the tax issue, Hammer?"

"I feel the rule could apply to both, sir."

"Quite so, quite so," I remarked. I always feel one must give a fellow a spoonful of encouragement when he feels he is educating a friend or employer. "The Italians and the Irish eh? That Jo Kennedy fellow is pulling out all the stops."

"I take it, sir, that he works on the principle that if the United States is to dismantle the British Empire it is best to begin with Britain's foremost colony, Ireland, or at least its unification. Keeping the Italians happy will also give succour to Il Duce, thus warming him even more to Herr Hitler."

I gave a start and a phew, jerking a little and inwardly thanking Hammer for failing to provide me with a pre-ball scotch and soda, which would certainly have splashed all over my legs and chest. "Dismantle the British Empire?"

"Empires are always at the mercy of those trying to dismantle them, sir. Were it to be done by the United States it would be slow and anaesthetized, clouded in the ether of friendship. If done by Germany it would be short, bloody, and painful."

"With the old cold steel, eh?"

"Precisely, sir. There are, of course, those who would deem the fall of the British Empire as a moral necessity if the betterment of humanity is to be wished for."

"What rot," I coughed. "Mr. Churchill is aware of these concerns?"

"He recognizes the need for friendship, hands across the sea and all that goes with it, but I doubt he has yet felt the strangeness of the chloroform-soaked cotton beneath the nostrils. Great men are somewhat akin to great liners, sir. They have a course by which to steer and it takes a mighty wave to veer them."

I shivered and wondered if I should call for a drink. "Hammer, why did you not join us in the Long Gallery?"

"In polite society three is invariably regarded as a crowd, sir." He tugged at his lapels and ran a flat hand across his medals, giving extra attention to his Iron Cross.

"Mrs. Glendower, Hammer." I switched legs. "Any idea of her contacts?"

"I have taken such things into consideration, sir, and believe she will contact an agent once we have docked in Cherbourg. There is no reason for her to continue to New York. I sincerely doubt her finding any comrades in those quarters, whereas in France there is an abundance of both extremes."

"Well," I said with haughtiness brought about by knowledge born of recent investigations and received announcements, "she does not have the suitcase about her person and it is not wedged into her cabin locker or tucked beneath her bunk."

"I am aware of these facts, sir. I took the liberty of searching her cabin as she slept."

"You did, did you? Dangerous escapade?"

"Not entirely, sir. Mr. Studely was here and had failed to secure their cabin door by use of the lock. Also, I would remind you of what I relayed to you as we were introduced at Chartwell. I have been well trained."

"The British Secret Service?"

"Amongst others, sir."

"Nazis?"

"I feel it unwise to divulge, sir, if you'll allow me that indulgence."

Still seated and pleased to be so after such revelations, I picked up my stick and beat a rhythm on a palm. "The wheels need oiling, Hammer."

"Very good, sir. A glass of champagne?"

"Yes, Hammer, that'll do nicely, wet the whistle, so to speak."

He hoofed into the dinette or kitchenette area of the suite and raided the refrigerator. His voice took on a hollow tone as he called back from within the cold tomb. "We have a very pleasant special *cuvée*, sir, courtesy of Jacques Bollinger, from his most recently acquired Tauxieres vineyard."

I'm sure I raised my eyebrows. I must confess that these things are beyond me and connoisseurs would be shocked by my ignorance, but Hammer seemed happy in recognizing some educated prejudice on my part. "Just the ticket," I called to him. "Join me."

He returned and smiled as he 'popped'. "Very gracious of you, sir." Not a drop was spilled, a skill fortified by frugality. Hammer was no waster. "We do have some hope, sir," he continued.

"There is always hope," I said as I received replenishment for my confidence." I sipped and gave a hearty aah!

Hammer parked himself over near the door, one ear only inches from the wood of it as if expecting wiggers. "I spent time earlier this evening, after my telephone calls, talking with the captain, sir."

"A decent chap?" I enquired after a more sedate sip of the bubbly stuff.

"A fine gentleman, sir. Under the pretext, or should I say pretence of our need to locate an item of luggage that has gone astray or become intermingled with others on the way to Southampton, I questioned him about the chances of finding such an article."

"He was forthcoming?"

"Most certainly, sir. He allowed me a perusal of the ship's manifest."

"Manifest, Hammer?"

"Yes, sir. It is a list pertaining to those articles, large or small, brought aboard the vessel and placed in the cargo hold somewhere far below us, beneath the Plimsoll line, I would imagine."

"In the bowels of the queen?"

"I would say so, sir. The captain referred to the area as the deep-down cargo hold, invariably on decks G and H. It is an area where large items

129

and crates of smaller items can be loaded aboard ship without the need of a crane."

The man gave the impression he was ready to hold sway for a few moments. I put this down to my waving. Hammer, and yes, I must confess I did not know him well at that time, tended to prattle along all sorts of lines with constant irrelevant references to such minor parts of the issue instead of getting to the nub, the crux of the matter. There is nothing worse than a fellow rambling on when the tide is coming in, the light is fading, the matches damp, and the last swig has been sucked from one's flask. I was waving him to hurry along, but he had taken it as a signal for my need to pause. "Move along, Hammer," I jostled. "Did any manifestation spring forth from a glance of this manifest?"

Hammer continued with the ribs not tickled. "It did indeed, sir."

I wiped a cool hand across my forehead. "Speak up and speak speedily, Hammer. Time is thrashing on."

"Well, it comes down to this, sir. Mrs. Glendower was in possession of two trunks, purportedly loaded at the eleventh-hour, and these were loaded along with vehicles and a selection of farm machinery."

"We can reach the damn things, can get down there without causing any suspicious double-takes or awkward questions?"

"We have permission and are invited to do so, sir, if that is the basis of your enquiry. The captain did offer us a gentleman to guide us but I pressed him on his need for all hands on deck during the festivities, promising I would have no trouble in finding the items of which you are in urgent need."

I downed the remainder of my Bollinger and stuck the glass out to be recharged. "Of which I am in urgent need?"

"Precisely, sir."

"Well, let us finish the bottle and be on our way, Hammer. On with the hunt." He replenished my glass. I drank away, the veins cooling, the heart warming, the muscles flexing and willing to get on with the venture. "By the way, Hammer. Did you give the captain any idea of the ...?"

"I informed the captain that you were bent on wearing your favourite costume this evening, sir, and that you would not be happy unless you could enter the ball in splendour, donned and armed in the vestments of your favourite English hero."

I turned to slip the empty champagne glass on the small sideboard – at my side. "My favourite English hero, eh?" I ran through the gamut of Englishmen who could be blessed with such an honour, and as you are no doubt aware as a keen historian of these isles, there are many on which this honour could be bestowed. "Richard the Lion Heart?"

"No, sir, and I think you have let it slip from your memory that the gentleman was in fact a Frenchman. He may well have entered the world in Beaumont Palace, but we cannot overlook his forefathers or even his mother, Eleanor of Aquitaine. His soubriquet of *Couer de Lion*, his failure to speak English, preferring to speak and write in Limousin or French weakens the merit. It is generally understood that Henry V was the first English king to attempt the English Language since Harold, Earl of Wessex."

"Quite so, quite so, Hammer. Henry VIII?" I bowled. "I can see myself now, cloaked, caped and capped as the heroic wrestler or strapped in shining steel leaving my tent at the Field of the Cloth of Gold as the young king ready for a joust."

"With your stature, sir?"

"Stature, Hammer?"

He must have caught my wild eye. "I meant his figure. I was referring to his bulk."

"Of course. Good Queen Bess would be a better bet." I chuckled and gave my chin a rub before voicing inspiration. "Cromwell?"

"You are hardly the puritan, sir, if I may be so bold."

I clicked the fingers and gave a hurrah. "King Arthur."

"Ah yes, sir. A name derived from the Latin, *Artorus*, although some historians would go back even further to the Messapic or even Etruscan dialects. That is of no real consequence though, is it, sir, when one remembers he is generally considered to have been a Roman?"

I sighed a long one full of despair. "Is our England such a barren waste, forested only by stout and hearty men of misty myth, folklore and legend, with no truth in sight? Have we no decent, fit and worthy heroes of our own to pluck from the basket of history?" I asked, feeling the chest and throat stiffen. "Next thing you'll be telling me is that some of our greatest Anglo-Saxon brave-hearts came from German stock and that we have none at all of our own true English blood."

"Well, sir, talking of Anglo-Saxon...you do have..."

"You mean *we*, Hammer."

"*We*, sir?"

"Yes, Hammer. *We*. Were you to be an officer of the notorious SS, as your love of such a uniform seems to imply...your use of *you* leads me to infer..."

The Machiavellian stirrer of cocktails and presser of trousers smiled. It was not the sort of smile I warm to. "*We*, sir."

"Good, and it is pleasing to hear. Your interest in uniforms does not go unnoticed, mark you. I am always keen to give a fellow the benefit of the doubt, but I shall hold sway on believing your commitment to the English cause..."

"British, sir."

"We were considering *English* heroes, Hammer."

"And struggling, if I may be so bold, sir."

I let loose a sigh. "Yes, struggling. The way things are panning out, it seems my best bet would be to ankle into the fray as Ephraim Gadsby."

"A hero unknown to me, sir."

"Well, I am at a loss so throw the name at me. Then we can scuttle below decks and have a rummage."

"I'm not sure if scuttle is apropos in this situation, sir."

"True, Hammer. The name?"

Hammer gave one of his gentle coughs. "I took the liberty, sir, of placing in one of our other trunks a rather fetching combination that would suffice as a recognisable portrayal of that great legend Robin, Earl of Huntington. The manifest shows that the said trunk arrived and was put aboard. You can go as Robin Hood."

"Robin ruddy Hood! Hell's teeth!" I leapt up, stammered a while, clenched fists and shook one of them. I am rarely a shaker of the fist, but I'm sure you'll agree with me when I claim the moment warranted such an action. "I am no wearer of green stockings, Hammer." I flopped back down into my chair and held my head in my hands. After a couple of fortifying breaths, I looked back up to give him a volley. "And I'll be damned if I'll go prancing about like a popinjay in buckskin boots or attempt the Charleston and Breakaway or any of those newfangled Balbaos, Snakehips, Cakewalks and Jitterbugs with a feather jutting out of my pointy hat."

"You have a Terpsichorean bent, sir?"

"As a matter of fact, and for your information, Hammer, I do not," I steamed. "I am without any bent of any sort. I leave all that swivelling about for sleeker, more athletic and younger models of the species. The dance floor is not my arena. I prefer the sidelines, the bar, where I can look upon the goings on and offer up witticisms while serving and returning snappy banter."

I expected Hammer to cast a frown of disappointment or even sorrow and apology across his brow, but no; there was, if anything, a smirk. "I am sorry to hear that, sir, although I am sure that in your youth…"

I was ready for action. "Enough, Hammer. We must get below." I was up in a jiffy, the coiled spring, the eager beaver. "I think we should grab Studely by the collar and drag him along with us."

Hammer's face did not express complete confidence. "You think that it wise, sir?"

Now, you can imagine that Hammer was under the illusion that I was something of an idiot, and you may perhaps feel I should have disabused him of this belief. Let us step carefully here. It was far better to have Hammer regarding me as the fool, a man lacking his Machiavellian techniques. I was not for one moment going to allow Hammer to see me as no fool. I would let his weakness of observation be my strength, my power. I can play the fool. I'm sure you'll understand. The satirist often falls for the ruse of the stiff-upper-lipped fellow being a complete ass, but the stiff-upper-lipped ass has kept hold of power for centuries and is far from letting it go.

"I think, Hammer," I continued, feeling I should press home a point, "that we may need a bit of the old brawn as well as brain. Studely has a strong arm."

"But can we trust him, sir?"

Huh. Of all the…Hammer questioning the honesty and loyalty of my new friend. Talk about the pot calling the kettle…and taking the cake…and what have you.

I kept those thoughts to myself and played along. "I believe we can, Hammer. He has jerked me bodily from the jaws of death on a couple of occasions, and our acquaintance is surprisingly short for such a record."

Hammer shuffled and looked down to his highly buffed jackboots. "And what if he is siding with Mrs. Glendower, sir?"

Laying it on with a trowel now, accusing others…I kept my peace. "Mrs. Glendower will be left locked in her cabin. I am sure she is in the land of nod. These old women are early to bed and early to rise."

"Wise?"

"Perhaps, but not as wise as we, Hammer."

"Very good, sir. I feel we should take torches."

We took torches and headed along and down and along and back and down again towards Mrs. Glendower's cabin where we would find Studely standing stiff and loyal, on guard duty.

At first, we passed many revellers who were making their way toward the ballroom, dressed up in as many costumes as one could imagine of characters throughout history. Hammer earned a few strange glances, but he remained stiff-backed, monocled, and with his nose in the air: very haughty and Prussian. I just looked good and upright with my cane swinging gracefully.

The atmosphere, in all senses of the word, changed as we travelled downward; the thudding of the Queen's single reduction steam turbines strengthened, the reverberations twanged through my ears and the thinly-carpeted steel plates pounded through my feet and straight up my legs and vertebrae as though a doctor had fallen into a metronomic trance while checking for reflexes. I cannot ascertain as to whether or not the good lady was doing her expected 29 knots but judging by the noise and its tempo, she was making a good stab at it.

We arrived at the cabin of Mrs. Glendower and her companion Mr. Studely to find the door locked. I hammered and Hammer rat-tatted. No answer.

In the gloom of the narrow passageway, Hammer unbuttoned the flap of his holster and drew out a rather fetching firearm: his Luger. "Shall I?"

I was tempted give the fellow the back of my hand. "Hell's bells and heaven's bells combined, Hammer. You'll cause such a rumpus should you fire that thing. People are at their sleep, in the land of…and it seems many are partying, but you'll still cause uproar."

I was on my hands and knees and peeking when Hammer uttered next. "I've always suspected the lower classes to be accustomed to noise and violence, sir," he said with a strange tone, as if he really believed what he'd said.

I rose and squinted at him; the squint being what remained of my attempt to peek through the keyhole. "Not a man of the people, are you, Hammer?" I released the facial muscles.

"I have always endeavoured not to be so, sir." Hammer slid the pistol back into the holster and buttoned up with what seemed a rather petulant click. There stood a man who had been accused of putting the milk in first. "And up to this point I feel at liberty to congratulate myself on my success."

I knocked again. "Can we push and lever?" I asked.

"We could do the old trick of placing a sheet of newspaper beneath the door, turn the key a little, push it through so that it drops and then pull the newspaper back to our side, sir."

I leaned on my cane and cocked my head at a jaunty angle for comic effect. I can play the straight man when the moment calls for it. "We could," I said, "but the door is *sans* key."

The truth fluttered down to Hammer. "That signifies the likelihood of the door having been locked from this side, sir."

I lifted a gloved finger. "Exactly. Come, let's shove."

Hammer braced himself against the opposing wall of the corridor and pressed a foot against the paintwork, ready to shoot forward with the gusto of a man of high calibre being blasted from a circus cannon.

As one usually does when one is launching a shoulder at a door, I folded a hand around the handle and turned it. The door gave way and swung inwards, causing me to tilt before catching up with it, although I managed to reach up and flick the light switch while doing so. I had no time to announce my success to Hammer.

Once launched, he flashed across the corridor, flew through the open doorway, and covered the few yards of the cabin in a split second before careering into a bunk. Judging by the sound the bunk was wooden framed, and Hammer could count that as a blessing. I informed him of the pertinent fact as he picked up his cap, rose, brushed himself down, checked his forehead for a bump and patted at his cheeks with a handkerchief.

"The door was not locked, Hammer."

"I am now cognisant of that fact, sir."

"What the bleedin' hell!" cried Studely from the morass of bedclothes on the top bunk. His head appeared and his bleary, puffy eyes, strained to open. "Who the...? What the...?" He swung hefty boots about and dropped to the carpet just behind Hammer. "Where's Auntie...?" His question was almost drowned out by the crackling of a monocle being crushed under foot.

"Auntie, Studely?" I enquired.

Studely tried again. "Where's Mrs. Glendower?"

Hammer turned with the slow calm of evil mastered by Bela Lugosi. "A question we should be asking of you, Studely."

I could only see the back of the man's cap and head, but I'd lay a big white one that he was sneering. His head tilted forward, and I hazarded a guess he was surmising what had been defeated by Studely's great clodhopper.

Studely did his own about turn and rummaged in the bedclothes for his helmet, which he duly placed atop his head. I was expecting a salute, and one came. "I came over all seasick and needed a lie down. I read somewhere that lying down is good for seasickness."

"As is the wearing of silk underwear," said Hammer. "Perhaps..."

"Shut it," jabbed Studely as he shifted, causing more scraping sounds to call out in the overcrowded cabin.

"Perhaps your aunt has some..."

"Hammer, that's enough," I said, albeit rather too softly.

Hammer had not finished, and his sharp ears must have sent their message to his brain. "My monocle."

"Not to worry," Studely piped up with a grin. "You've got plenty more where that one came from."

The SS officer's voice boomed up from the depths of the deepest of tombs, challenging the thunderous rumbling of the engines yards beneath our feet. "And how would you know?"

"Oh, come off it, Hammer, we all knows what you're about, so don't give us any of that old macaroni," said Studely with a gust of confidence I had not before seen in him.

Hammer turned to me. "Macaroni?"

"I think he means baloney, old chap. Studely is getting his lingo lined up for the Bronx. Did you like my 'Clam it' yesterday?

"I could smell The Hudson, sir." Hammer turned back to face his impudent challenger. "However, that does not answer my question."

"Saw a load of them in the glove box of your Roller," said Studely. He added an extended 'old chap' for good effect. "You love dressing up as one of Hitler's finest. A strange hobby, but each to their own, as they say."

It may have just been an apparition brought about by the dimness of the yellow lamp above Hammer's capped head, but I had the strangest of feelings his hand was making a beeline for his Luger. It was clear to me, as an astute voyeur of *homo hominis* that Hammer and Studely were never going to regard each other as fellow brothers-in-arms. I was to take control before all fell apart. "Steady, Hammer," I called out. "Let's not fall out now. We have work to do and we are surrounded by enemies." The man's gun arm relaxed. I addressed Studely. "Get your torch at the ready, we are going below."

Studely was fine enough to salute me again and offer a fine 'righto' before he tugged a torch from deep down in one of those long pockets members of the constabulary enjoy. "Let's hope we don't go bumping into the sergeant-at-arms," he said as he stepped around Hammer and headed for the doorway.

Hammer was next to move past me. "He is patrolling the upper decks," he said, following Studely out into the corridor. "Perhaps he's looking for your lost aunt."

Studely lifted his weighty torch and waved it beneath Hammers long, sharp nose. "Any more of that and I'll bleedin'…"

I stepped into the corridor, dived between them and bellowed an intemperate "enough!" I am quick to come off the boil. "Now, let's just get along. Studely, you stop taunting Mr. Hammer here, and you, Hammer, please try to refrain from referring to Mrs. Glendower as some long-lost relative of Studely. Can we agree on that?"

I was offered the solemn nod you spot on the weakened head of a schoolboy commanded by his mother to hold her handbag for her while she dallies around the haberdashery, the poor youth knowing that such an enterprise will cover a good sixty minutes or so.

In the stained, or even strained silence, if one takes the persistent throbbing of the engines as the nearest to silence one could attain, a cabin door slammed shut nearby. I was aware of other voices, music and revelry, shouts of a card game, and the call of mothers to their wandering young. Doors were opened and closed as people passed each other in gangways, squeezed into each other's cabins, whooped, and howled as a hundred parties warmed up.

"It appears all the world is travelling to the earth's crust while we are heading for the core," I said, trying to bring a lightness of tone to the situation the way a leader needs to when the going gets tough and relations between the lower ranks are about to snap.

I assumed Studely was ready to spring another tease upon Hammer when his mouth opened, but it was not to close. He gaped and did what I think Messrs. Zanuck and co. would call a double take.

"Trouble, Studely, seen a ghost?" I enquired. "Spotted the tastiest of cheesecake?"

He pointed his unlit torch. "That was auntie's uncle."

"Uncle?" All I saw was the black hair and very wide-shouldered white-jacketed back of a man pinching his way between tarted-up young ladies sharing a bottle of London's finest gin.

"Uncle Joe," Studely said with a gasp. "I remember the photo of him in Mrs. Glendower's cottage." He prodded me with his torch. "At St Mary Mead, you know, Hardimann."

"Mind your manners, Studely," snapped Hammer. "Mr. Hardimann to you."

I held up a calming hand. "Not to worry, Hammer. We have covered that issue." I faced Studely and searched his clock for tell-tale signs of derangement. "Explain yourself."

"The photo. You told me it was of her Uncle Joe." He gave another point with the torch in the direction of where the wide figure had retreated having once passed the young ladies. "That was Uncle Joe. I'd recognise that moustache anywhere."

I backed away from Studely and Hammer to let a young couple squeeze by. "You mean Joe Stalin?"

"Yes," insisted Studely. "Uncle Joe."

I gave a nonchalant shrug. "Seems some chap has got it into his head to swan around the fancifully dressed masses in the garb of the Soviet leader," I said. "A strange choice, I must admit." It also occurred to me, not for the first time, that I must get to the core of this auntie and Mrs. Glendower business increasingly rattling around poor Studely's subconscious. Let it never be said that I fail in my duties of friendship when a fellow's mental health is at stake.

Hammer gave one of his coughs. "How ridiculous. Who in their right mind would go to a fancy-dress ball dressed as...?"

I looked Hammer in the eye then up and down. "And this remark is coming from a man in his sixties all togged up in the uniform of one of Corporal Schicklgruber's...?"

"*Schutzstaffel*, sir."

CHAPTER 17
CRISES AND TROUBLE DOWN BELOW

"We must go through the crew accommodation, but I imagine all hands are on deck," said Hammer as we turned a corner and headed for a door.

I took a moment to lean and take a breather. "Dashed hot in here," I said. I whipped out my top-pocket handkerchief, flicked it from its pyramid shape then wiped it across my brow.

"We are but a few feet above the number one boiler room and the water-softening plant, sir," said Hammer with that weary pedagogical tone that bears with it a touch of the '*as you would know if you'd bothered to study the plans*'.

Studely gave his head a rub by rocking his helmet to-and-fro, from time to time pressing it down and giving a tug at the strap. "Getting quieter, anyhow, apart from the bloody engines," he said once he'd ceased that exercise and started on meddling with his torch, bashing the end and giving a '*bloody batteries*' or two. "I suppose everyone's up on the top deck now, jigging about and filling their faces...well, all those who ain't kipping." Worry sped across his face. "What if we got top-heavy?"

Hammer rested a hand on the rail. "At a gross tonnage of nearly ninety-thousand tons, complete oil tanks, four steam turbines, twenty-four water tube boilers, thousands of tons of water plus cargo, four propellers weighing thirty-five tons each, along with motor vehicles and a wine cellar larger than that at Buckingham Palace, all below the Plimsoll line, I feel we shall be safe, Studely." He patted the man on the shoulder. I was convinced that had Studely not been adorned by his helmet the soothing hand would have been laid upon his head. "Does that put your mind at rest?"

Studely grunted, flinched, then tapped his torch against the door we were to enter. "Why are we going into the bogs?"

Hammer stiffened, missing Studely's smirk. "A miscalculation on my part owing to the delays and deviations brought about by your ill-timed slumbering, and Mrs. Glendower's absence."

Studely was not too unsporting with his tuts and groans, but he did lick a finger and chalk up an invisible score for himself. "Looks like we gotta go up a few decks, go towards the front..."

"The fore..."

"The front," continued Studely, "then work our way back down from there."

I was about to follow them as they started on their way, but I had matters to take care off. I was certainly in need of an angle at the Armitage, so much so that it put my teeth on edge. I made my excuses and disappeared. Having done what a chap has to do, ending with no more than the obligatory two shakes, I checked my armaments. I had only three rounds left in the handle of my cane. The Beretta had its six .22 rounds in the magazine. If push should come to shove, I had nine little friends with me, that's if I had the gumption to pull the trigger and not let the villains scarper as I had done with Hayes. Talking of Hayes, I wondered what he was up to. Was he on the same little trail? Had he found Mrs. Glendower scowling at the indulgent bejewelled toffs as she wandered about on the upper deck?

I pocketed the Beretta, tugged at the lavatory door and stepped out into the corridor with the stride and cane-swing of a man at ease, full of confidence and prepared for the worst. I gave Hammer the nod to proceed. "Lead on, MacDuff,"

Hammer paused before marching off. "I think perhaps you are referring to The Bard of Avon's Scottish play, *Macbeth*, sir, MacDuff being the usurper king's nemesis, a man untimely ripped from his mother's womb. And if you are, and should you take the trouble to study the text you will discover that it is in fact '*lay on*' that Macbeth cries out to MacDuff."

Studely turned to give me that Christian look of a man who recognises another's suffering.

"As you wish, Hammer," I said. I am not a violent or ill-tempered man despite my having experienced violent and ill-tempered times, and I have oft turned a blind eye when a fellow oversteps the mark, but that searing '*untimely ripped from his mother's womb*' cut deep. In a moment, I was back to the nursery floor, the lead soldiers, wooden trains, and nanny's fussing interrupted by the scolding bile of my drunken father and his hatred of me for the death of his beloved wife.

Hammer had not finished. "It is a common error, and therefore one to be expected but I feel…"

"Shift!" was all I had to say.

"Very good, sir."

With ice in my veins I gripped the handle of my cane and curled a finger around a trigger; either one would do, bullet or blade, I thought. It's no sin to shoot or even stab a Nazi in the back – just first check he or she is actually a Nazi.

As we made our way up the stairs and along gangways, I ran the plan through my head. "Hammer, through which cargo hold were the later motor cars boarded?"

Although ahead of me and refusing to twist his head about to face me, Hammer was clear. "Hold number two then through to the larger cargo hold, behind the anchor and just below the forward mast, sir. I believe we should veer to our right on entering F deck, otherwise we shall find ourselves within a maze of sacks and crates to no avail."

He checked his watch and it occurred to me that he had been doing so with some frequency of late. "A date, Hammer?"

"Not at all, sir. It is just that I have been on my feet for some time. I will be happy if we get this done, go up to the top deck and the ballroom, find Mrs. Glendower and contain her, thus giving me the chance to enjoy some respite."

"Jolly good," I answered with less coldness than I had administered beforehand, feeling it better to lighten up and choose my battles and times for my battles. I still needed Hammer as an ally, even a false one.

Having worked our way back up to B deck, passing a few other fellow travellers heading for the ballroom and bars, we slipped into the crews' rest rooms and kitchens just aft of the radio rooms. We were unchallenged as we continued, although Hammer did get the odd second glance. Studely, adept at improvisation, claimed once or perhaps twice that he had left something in his car.

The stairways and furnishings in the crews' quarters were cold and metallic, more utilitarian. Everywhere was whitewashed, or of shining steel, putting me in mind of what an old member of the senior service had once reported to me.

'*If it moves, shoot it; if it doesn't, paint it.*' A simple rule for your simple seaman, I supposed at the time.

We descended to the gloom of the second cargo hold. All I could hear was the rhythmic thunder of engines and what sounded like jets of steam whistling from holed pipes or open valves. The floor was oil-slick slippery, the walls and pillars glistered with condensation.

Studely gave a whistle, wolfish enough for me to suspect he'd spotted a tasty torso. "Stone me, look at the size of them girders."

"They are structural beams on which each deck is replaced once the cargo holds have been filled by derrick," said Hammer, a man whom I'm sure would not spot a tasty torso if it fell upon him on a buttercup-laden English meadow. "You had better switch on your torch, Studely. We have to make our way through the motor vehicles."

Studely, I am pleased to report, turned to me for the affirmative. It's good when a chap knows where the real authority lies. "Go ahead, Studely," I said. "Mind how you go."

I switched on my torch. Our beams flicked and fluttered through the gigantic cavern of a car park; the sparks from polished chrome winked back at us. There were scurrying rats by the dozen, but I suppose one cannot have them leave a sinking ship unless they are aboard in the first place.

Studely started his way down between a row of limousines and speedsters but stopped within seconds, frozen to the spot.

"Problem, Studely?"

As he does when armed with a torch, Studely splashed a golden one straight into my eyes. "Thought I heard voices."

Hammer gave a tut and I gave a wave. "Move on, you're imagining things."

I pushed past Hammer and side-shuffled between two Rolls Royce, one of them similar to the black and yellow model in which Hammer had driven me from outside the prison gates; you remember, the one Studely and I used to rush down to Saint Mary of the Mead. Then I heard the noise. I put a finger to my lips and turned back to Hammer, to flash him. "Hear that?"

"Yes, sir. I believe I did."

"Sounded like a scream, a faint scream, but a scream nonetheless."

"It did indeed, sir," said Hammer rather flatly, and I detected a smirk on his illuminated visage.

There was another scream, not piercing or guttural, but certainly a scream and what must surely have been sobbing. "We should help," I whispered.

Hammer parked up against me. "I feel that would be unwise, sir."

"Don't be so damn cowardly, Hammer. We are armed, and we cannot stand by while a young lady is being..."

"You misunderstand me, sir," said Hammer. "I believe the *'calling out'* you have heard, if I may describe it as such, is nothing but the calling out of a young lady experiencing a *'crisis'*."

"Then we must save her from it," I snapped. "We must unearth the blighter responsible, take him from behind and give him a jolly good seeing to."

"Hardly, sir."

Studely was back. "There's a Roller rocking about over there," he said, giving a flash of beam down the line of cars to land a circular spot on a rear bumper that rocked, rose and fell with increasing speed. "Looks like...and the window is all steamed up...so..."

I suspect Hammer interrupted for decency's sake. "I would imagine that a young couple have freed themselves from the bonds of their parents and made their way down here to enjoy some privacy, and what I believe our American cousins now describe as *'quality time'*, sir. I am sure they are not the first to take advantage of such a situation."

"Yeah," giggled Studely with relish and a bending of the elbow which sent his beam up into the dark, ribbed roof of the cavern, "a bit of 'ow's yer father."

"I wouldn't put it quite like that, Studely, but you have penetrated his meaning," said I. "Let us proceed with caution and discretion." I gave him a gentle shove. "Move on."

We crept along the line, keeping low as we passed the steamy, now furiously rocking, Rolls Royce. The need for absolute stealth need not have been considered a must; our quiet footfalls would not have been heard. "Them springs need oiling," said Studely.

"Keep going and shut up, you idiot," I prompted, fearing he would resume his giggling.

After passing another four or five vehicles we found ourselves against a wall of trunks and cases stacked as high as the temporary ceiling. "Hell's bells and by Timothy," I gasped. "Talk about needles and haystacks."

"Shine the torches, starting from left to right," said Hammer. "I have some clue as to where it is. Mrs. Glendower's case, along with yours, was loaded late in the day and should be near the front."

For a full minute at standstill we shone the torch lights against the wall of leather, canvas and wood, and studied, reading labels in the weird drub drubbing of engines and gurgling waterpipes in the belly of the vessel. I used my cane to count my way along the rows.

"Here's one with your name on it, Hardimann," piped Studely. "Want it?" He reached for it and tugged with all his might. It was as though he'd removed a keystone from a stone bridge or a hefty slab of concrete from low down Boulder Dam. Cases, boxes and trunks tumbled upon him and did not cease until he was buried, apart from one hand sticking out from the pile, and in that hand was the handle of my rather squashed suitcase.

I bent, urging him to loosen his grip. "Thank you, Studely."

The first spray of bullets zipped over my bowed head and splattered their way into what remained of the wall of luggage behind Studely's pile. The deafening cracks of echoing machine gun fire bounced around the steely cavern. On my back, with one hand still clutching my suitcase, I let go my torch. It rolled, rocking for a while before coming to rest, sending a beam down the length of an alley between the cars. The young girl's crisis reached a high C.

A savage voice called out. "Stick 'em up, Limey. And you, Adolf."

Never let it be said I lose my cool amidst my own crises. "Not too easy to stick them up when lying in this position," I called back.

Hayes stepped into the light. "Well, get up then stick 'em up." He jiggled the machine gun at Hammer. "Step over there and stand with your back against the trunks, Adolf."

I scrambled about, feeling for my cane, still holding on to my suitcase. I think I stepped on Studely's hand, quite by accident of course, and bless the man: he did not call out, in anger or in pain. As I came to full height, I levelled my cane and sent two shots between the cars, well, not quite between; I broke one windscreen and removed a headlamp from its bracket.

"Throw the peashooter down, Hardimann. You ain't got a cat in hell's." It was a second voice and it came from the front of another line of cars. The stout fellow was armed with his own machine gun; a machine gun almost hidden by the football-size mass of bandages wound around his injured hand, the hand so neatly needled by Mrs. Glendower.

"Good evening, Clench," clipped Hammer who was standing with his hands held high.

"Higher, Adolf," called Hayes. "That's snazzy, now keep still or you get drilled."

Clench must have been feeling left out. "And you, Hardimann, or this Chicago typewriter is gonna turn you into a pepper-pot lid. And don't go trying to work no angles."

Dropping my cane, I raised one arm but felt it unnecessary to raise the suitcase as well. I turned my head a little to find Hammer. "I didn't get..."

"I believe he is voicing his preference for you to remain still and silent, and not to attempt anything heroic, sir."

"That's right," said Clench as he took a few paces towards us. "Now, you, gunsel, shake a leg and toss the valise over here." He gave his own jiggle to his own machine gun. "Nothing fancy, Hayes's got you covered."

I tossed the suitcase into the gloom and watched it slide beneath a front bumper. It didn't glide far enough and Clench, although straining a little owing to his bulk, retrieved it. Hayes, some yards away, took advantage of the interlude to peek through the misted windows of the Rolls Royce to his right. Clench rose as another scream bounced against the metal walls. Juggling a little to hold machine gun and suitcase, he snapped an order. "Hayes, get that canary and slap her quiet, then wrap her up."

"There's no call for that sort of thing," I said.

"Button it, Limey."

A whistle came from Hayes as he opened the door to the Rolls Royce. "Hey, what a sweet patootie. Come on doll-face and bring Romeo out with ya." I blessed the gloom, for her sake, but the courtesy light came on as the girl stepped from the limousine dressed only in mother-of-pearl French silk, followed by her boy who it seemed had managed to grab enough time to pull up his trousers. Hayes pulled the lovers to face each other, handcuffed them together then gagged them with what looked like the girl's headscarf and the boy's cravat. He shoved them back onto the rear seats. He slammed the door shut. "Now, you two lovebirds keep nice and quiet until we gone or I give ya both lead poisoning." He chuckled as he ambled his way down toward me. "Clenchy, as for these two pills, tie 'em up. Find some rope. I've used up my cuffs on those two canoodlers back there."

"Why not drill 'em?" asked Clench with some sadness in his drawl.

Hayes clucked. "You can't go drillin' everyone you meet, Clenchy. You gotta have style, class and deportment, and manners. There's more to this malarkey than Zoot suits and spats. Besides, we ain't got no result yet. Open the case."

As Clench fumbled about, Hayes breathed Bourbon over me. "Kinda quaint of you not to plug me on the train, Hardimann. Bet you now wish you hadda done."

I said nothing as I watched my suitcase spill open. Out came clothes, nothing but clothes.

Clench, hunkered with the machine gun across his knees, dipped into the contents, flipping garments into the air like a magician struggling with his multi-coloured handkerchiefs. "What the hell is this? Where's the goddamn...who's garbage is all this...Peter Pan's, Errol Flynn's?" He rose in a rage. "Where's the real suitcase, you punk?"

I shrugged. "No idea, Clenchy."

"Mind your lip, Limey. Only my buddies call me Clenchy." He turned to Hammer with menace. "What about you, Adolf?"

"Only those of very close acquaintance call me Adolf," said Hammer. "I must say, I am with you on that matter."

"The suitcase," said Hayes, wishing to join the chat. He snarled, or grinned; it was difficult to tell. He threw one last garment. "Not to worry. We got time." He pointed his machine gun at the pile of fallen luggage and the remaining cases and trunks still stacked tightly against the walls. "You two can go through this lot."

145

"I would not be surprised if Mrs. Glendower already has the suitcase, gentlemen," said Hammer.

"Mrs...?"

"The old lady you molested on the train."

"Oh yeah?"

"She has given us the slip. We have searched all the cases and trunks. I feel we have been on a wild goose chase."

"Yeah, well yours is cooked," stabbed Hayes. "Clenchy, tie 'em up and tie 'em up good."

Hammer looked up and twisted a hand to check his watch. "Sorry we could not help you, gentlemen."

"Well ain't you cute?" said Clench as he gathered up some twine from a pile of ropes, string and straps at the foot of the luggage wall not far from the pile. "Looks like you gonna spend the rest of the trip keeping each other warm. It gets chilly in the Atlantic, and New York ain't so cosy this time of the year." He looped the machine gun strap over his shoulder and began binding Hammer and me together. Back to back, for which I nearly thanked him.

Hammer's leather coat squeaked as we were squeezed together. I did my best not to touch hands. No need for that sort of thing, no matter how desperate the situation, as I'm sure you'll agree.

Clench stepped back to admire his handiwork, and I was tempted to congratulate the man for his skill considering his bandaged hand. He had used his teeth. He brought the machine gun back around to waist height and gave me a prod. "An upper-class twit and a Nazi. Is there a difference?"

"Some, I'd imagine," I chirruped. "Although, and this is no disrespect to Hammer here, I would find Madeleine Carroll a lot more comfortable."

Hayes, taking advantage of my inability to duck or swerve landed his knuckles across my jaw, causing my teeth to rattle; another crack was added as Hammer and I knocked skulls. "So long, Hardimann. You should think yourself lucky we ain't up on deck or we'd be feedin' ya to the sharks…"

I was still giving my head and jaw – my whole head – a shake to remove the ache. "Hardly," I quipped. "Only basking sharks in these waters and they, I believe, feed only on plankton."

Hayes tried humour. "They'll love you then."

I had not until that time ever been gagged, even in the more exciting bouts of bedroom Olympics, so you will understand my concerns. It was a shock to have my new cravat strapped across my mouth then tied in a shoddy knot at the back of the neck. I mumbled something and was given a wagging finger by Hayes. He added a full stop to the wag with another sock to the jaw. All a bit much, I remember thinking at the time.

With that, both men slouched a slovenly turnaround and headed back toward the lines of cars. They knuckled the windows of the inhabited Rolls Royce and wished something vulgar.

The vaults and caverns of ocean liners bang and strain like steel drums, creak and groan like the sheets of a galleon, and I was able to hear every footstep and clang as Hayes and Clench made their way to the other end of the cargo hold.

Hammer and I spent a few moments struggling, wriggling our sweaty hands and chafing our wrists. I began to spit hopeful but muffled '*pssts*' that came out as monotone hums.

Hammer, not suffering the humiliation of being gagged, was more vocal. "Studely," he whispered at first then followed it with more, getting louder as he did so, pulling me round and round as he tried to hop. We tottered. I am glad to say that Hammer took the brunt of the fall, like a felled tree into a leather thicket.

Our collapse caused a groan or release of wind to come from deep down in the core of the baggage pile. I could not say if it was a '*bleedin' 'ell*' or a '*cor blimey*' but there was wind and there was rustling.

Hammer and I rolled as the leather and canvas mountain rose with the gentle heave and wriggle of a mole searching for the daylight-seeking worm.

"Can't bleedin' breathe in 'ere," gasped Studely as he popped into view, his helmet jammed down over his eyes.

Hammer urged again. "Come on, get yourself sorted out."

The rotund constable Studely, dressed-as-a-civilian-now-dressed-as-a-constable, staggered and wobbled, hands to helmet as if soothing a headache. It took a full minute of this waltz before the helmet came off with a slurp of released suction. "What 'appened to you two?" he enquired as he adjusted his attire. "Come to think of it, what 'appened to me?"

"Some would claim it to be fortuitous, Studely, but you were knocked out and hidden by the avalanche of baggage, thus leaving you free to untie us."

"Eh?"

Hammer spat the corner of a luggage label from his mouth. "Untie us, Studely."

With Studely heaving, Hammer and I managed to gain some dignity, and stand.

Hammer was still in urging mood. "Quickly, Studely, release us. We must get up to the ballroom to find Mrs. Glendower."

"All right, all right, keep your hair on," said Studely. I'm sure, although it wasn't easy to tell in the strange light, that he was smirking and taking great pleasure in the man's discomfort as he wedged the SS cap down onto Hammer's thin but wayward hair.

I dragged myself up and stretched limbs, untied my cravat and put it back into the position for which it was designed. "Good show, Studely. Now where is my cane?" I spotted it peeking from beneath my opened suitcase. "Here we are." I stooped to pick it up, taking a moment to sweep a couple of rounds from my trouser pocket to re-arm it. I waved it towards Hammer who was adjusting his cap and giving his lapels and cuffs a tug. "Works well, but I need some practice with the aim, don't you think?"

"Most certainly," said Hammer. "Now perhaps we can get on with things. I think you had best take this opportunity to change, sir."

I cocked an enquiring eyebrow. "Change, Hammer?"

He checked his watch. "We must get to the ball. It will be in…"

"Full swing?"

"Precisely, sir, and that is where Mrs. Glendower will make contact. I am sure of it."

Studely skipped a little. "Hope they serve beer."

"I'm sure they have taken it upon themselves to cater for the working man," said Hammer.

My shoulders sagged a little, not so much from weakness but from the very idea of having to dress up. Don't get me wrong here; I am not the jug of cold water that loves to splash across the happiness and mirth of human contact, but my heart sinks when the clarion call is made for us all to have a laugh for the sake of going out and having a laugh. It is mock happiness, as cold and mercenary as prostitution, force-fed and tasteless. I like humour to spring from the unknown, from the situation. After all, is not life already a big enough joke upon us all without us having to manufacturer it?

I dragged my feet with school-boyish sloth and went back to my suitcase. "I think you should nip over and unchain our two lovebirds in there, Studely," I suggested as I scooped up clothing.

"No keys," he said, patting at his tunic.

"I'm sure the young lady has misplaced the odd hatpin or hairpin. Do some jiggling."

Studely jumped to it.

I took a few minutes to change, finding odd places in my jerkin to house my pearl-handled Beretta, smokes and lighter, and the other odds and ends a gentleman needs to carry. I was pleased to make use of my cravat, leaving me with some sort of dignity. The green tights were a thick and woolly affair. "I'll come out in a rash, Hammer," I complained. "And, I shall need my cane, but I don't recall Robin Hood swishing one while robbing the sheriff of Nottingham."

"Quiver, sir."

I let the word rattle in my head before responding. "Quiver?"

"If you take a look in the closed and zipped portion of the suitcase lid you will find a bow, a quiver, and a half-dozen arrows, sir."

He strode with impatience, clutching his lapels like a headmaster considering the choice between a hundred lines or six of the best. I thought it best to allow him to get on with it. From the lid he took a dainty quiver with arrows no longer than two feet in length. Then he pulled out two lengths of wood bound together with a string.

"My bow?" I enquired.

He was upright and fiddling, unravelling. "Yes, sir."

"My *long*bow?"

"It will be, sir," said Hammer, searching for the threaded ends before screwing the two lengths of wood together. Once that was complete, he strained a little to bend the bow in order to loop one end of the string over a notch. "There we are, sir," he said with not a little triumph in his voice. "Ready for action." He had one other thing to offer. "Your hat, sir."

CHAPTER 18
DON'T SHOOT HIM; HE'S ONLY THE PIANO PLAYER

It seemed an age getting back up onto the sports deck. Then we made our way aft, virtually the full length of the ship. It was a bloody long ship.

"I promised to pop into the Verandah Grill and clink glasses with that Mr. Coward fellow," I said as we hastened, skipping past partygoers, many of whom had already downed more than a good dozen tilts at the yardarm.

"Very well, sir," said Hammer rather frostily. "As long as we keep an eagle eye out for Mrs. Glendower."

"Checking your watch again, Hammer?"

"Force of habit." He put out a hand to check the lift doors as I stepped out to get the fresh air in my lungs, giving the bellboy a thank-you nod. "To your right, sir."

"I am aware, Hammer. I have been here before."

From the open deck, I could see distant lights. Strange dots of light, not the strings of pearls one sees running along a cliff-top or skirting the horseshoe of a small quay or harbour, just odd single pricks of different colour. Were they moving? It is difficult to tell when one is moving oneself; it is the effect one gets as a train alongside starts making off when one is in the railway station.

"France, Hammer?" I asked as we jostled along with Studely who was behind us, wheezing, and calling out for his well-earned pint. Above the chatter and squeals of fun I could hear *Has Anyone Seen Our Ship?* from the Red Peppers if I recall correctly: not a current number but a fun-filled favourite. An odd number to be playing unless there was some irony somewhere or other; I have never been good with irony. Why would we be looking for our ship if we were sailing upon it, upon her, if you catch my drift.

As for my enquiry concerning the French coast, Hammer had nothing to say. "The Verandah Grill, sir," he said as we stepped into the warmth of the throng. "Mrs. Glendower."

"Any sign of her?" I asked, tiptoeing and rocking from side to side to get a decent view through the boas and boaters.

"No, sir, but I have just espied our ersatz Mr. Stalin sitting over there near the piano, to the right of the dance floor at the far end…"

"Well, that's our man, surely," I said.

"Her man, you mean, I think, sir."

"He's alone? I can't see too well from here. Get pushing, Hammer, work your way through."

Hammer began gliding and weaving his way through the crowd, and he did it with panache. Was it the leather coat and the cap? Drinkers and scoffers backed away, turning as he passed, to get a better gander at the Nazi in their midst. There were comments varying from '*look at that Nazi*', '*strange fellow*' and '*he does look dashing*'. One filly even admitted to adoring a man in uniform and declared that none can wear them with such style as the Germans. As for my costume, nothing was said.

Following in Hammer's wake, I took in the faces and costumes. There was a Napoleon, a little too tall, but the cuffs and collars matched. A few Henry VIIIs jigged about, showing off their muscular calves and great girths. There were pirates galore as one would imagine on a sea voyage and I supposed that many had plumped for the easy option of a thick leather belt, an eye-patch, and a stuffed parrot.

One fellow did catch my eye and I felt compelled to scuttle through a space to prod him in the stomach before congratulating him on his choice and accuracy. I gave him a good poke with the end of my cane before flipping the hat from Marie Antoinette's head as I swung it over my shoulder and stabbed it back into my quiver. "Excellent," I called out above the hubbub and plonking piano keys. "Almost perfect, the baby face, the heavy jowls, the cigar, the hunched shoulders." Feeling my cane had done enough work I gave the fellow a hearty pat on the back then swung down to dig a few fingers into the padded stomach. "Could have made that bigger. You'd be better off with a large brandy balloon as well. That little schooner of sherry is far off the mark."

The gruffness was there and down to a T. "I beg your pardon?"

"The belly, old chap. I should know. I broke bread with the man only a day or so ago."

Piggy eyes glinted specks from the glitter ball. "Is that so?"

"Absolutely, old chap." I tried to pull the fellow away from a huddle to continue the chat, to give him some more pointers. "Bluster, my man, you need more bluster. More wind, even. Wind-son Churchill." I laughed and expected an echo from him, but the poor chap appeared disappointed, at a loss. He had done his best and I had wandered in only to pour scorn upon his efforts. That said, he was a willing student as many are when I offer tutelage.

"Anything else?" he asked. He turned a dining chair, plonked down, pushed his schooner away across the table in disgust and spent a moment to re-ignite his cigar. He unhooked his stick from his elbow and leaned forward with the stiffness of a man whose back is telling him to slow down.

I gave him time to settle before giving him more. "His best friend is a pig, which is fitting. He told me…the real Mr. Churchill, that is…he told me that pigs treat us as equals. That's unless I misheard, and he considers himself equal to pigs. Damnably insulting to the poor sow if you ask me. Come to think of it though, he does lean into the trough with the enthusiasm of a Gloucester Old Spot. Cigar and spoon in one hand and a bucket full of claret in the other."

He looked up with furrowed brow. "Would you be considered as an equal?"

"Good question, old man." I leaned against a pillar and kept one eye on the pianist who was enjoying a flourishing finale, leaning this way and that with his elongated cigarette holder sweeping smoky half-moons. "Perhaps an equal. An advisor, most certainly."

"I was enquiring on behalf of the pig." With that, the fellow followed the words of Mr. Benjamin Hapgood Burt: *The pig got up and slowly walked away*. A *'much obliged to you'* was not offered.

I gave a half-hearted goodbye wave and took another glance across the sea of bobbing hats. Coming towards me, clasping trident and shield and armed with a growling scowl, was Milly. I executed a deft gentlemanly *'hero of the forest'* bow and was about to come over all medieval and romantic with a touch of the Blondel – the French *trouvère*, not the Miss Pinkerton one – when she launched her tirade.

She puffed and wheezed rage then pronged me. "Do you realise what you have…have you any idea? You utter fool. You idiot. He's a foul tempered monster at the best of times."

To say I was taken aback would do my surprise no justice. "You are blithering, woman. What on earth are you talking about?" I brushed her tines aside and stepped away to save my tights from unwanted ladders. "We're searching for Mrs. Glendower. Have you…?"

I had never been hit, swiped or even nudged with a shield before, and a hefty swipe it was. Milly, still raw with rage, kept it at full whistle. "He has a meeting with some French officials when we arrive in Cherbourg and I am expected to spend from dawn onwards taking notes, so do not involve me in the search. We're on a bloody boat…"

"Ship, I think you'll find."

"I don't care if we're spinning round in a bloody bathtub. You lost…"

"Misplaced," I interjected, watching her bosom heave for an intake of anger-fuelling oxygen.

"Lost," she stamped. "Find that suitcase before we arrive in Cherbourg. As for Mrs. Glendower, I don't care if she's swimming the channel lengthways. And if I can't report to Mr. Churchill within the next ten minutes that you've recovered the equipment you will find yourself doing the crawl alongside her."

"And what is he doing visiting French ministers of state?" I enquired. "He is not in the Cabinet, despite the wishes of many."

"He will be," said Milly. "The only reason he doesn't hold an official post is because Mr. Baldwin did not wish to make Mr. Hitler cross. Chamberlain, the same."

Despite my apparel, I felt this was not the time to slap oneself on the thigh, stick fists to hips and lean back with a forest-piercing laugh. The mollification of Milly was called for as a prelude to some sucking up to Mr. Churchill. "I shall apologise and dissolve his dudgeon, if that's what one does with dudgeon. It sounds as though it should be. Worry not," I said. "It was an easy mistake to make. It is, after all, a fancy-dress party."

The shield was pressed against me once more. "I wouldn't if I were you, Pelham. He is off to the bathroom."

"Just go and tell him," I said, giving her a gentle prod. "Please. I must make amends."

After letting an *'all right then'* sigh, Milly left me standing with her trident and shield as she swept off to catch up with the grumpy bear that was staggering through the crowd. I watched as she caught up with him to stop him for a moment and plead on my behalf, stroking her long black hair and sending me furtive glances. She was back in a thrice.

The look on her beautiful face did not inspire optimism on my part. "And what did he say?" I enquired as I watched Hammer's SS cap floating towards the dance floor. Following in his wake was another, albeit shorter, figure: that of, I am sure, Mrs. Glendower. I looked back to Milly for her explanation and was greeted with one of those *'butter wouldn't melt in her mouth'* or is it one of those *'from the mouths of babes'* moments?

"Mr. Churchill," said Milly, "had the pleasure of telling me that he would be busy on the lavatory for some time and wished me to inform you that he is capable of taking only one shit at a time."

I didn't spend too many seconds with the mouth open. I rested the weighty shield on the warmed but now vacant chair, handed back her trident, grabbed her by the arm and dragged her from the throng and out into the darkness of the deck. Well, when I say darkness, there was darkness on the other side of the rail.

As she leaned against the rail and stared up at the stars, I took the opportunity to fumble around in my leather jerkin for my smokes. "Made a hash of things, haven't I?"

"You are a bit of a baboon at times, Pelham," she said.

"A baboon?"

She did some finger-pointing stuff involving the top of her head and her mouth. "Good idea to get this in gear before using this, don't you think?"

"I'm a buffoon, all right. Fancy doing such a stupid…" I didn't get the chance to finish my self-admonition. Her lips were suddenly on mine, albeit for a moment: less than seconds, in fact.

"Mr. Coward's playing my song," she said wistfully after releasing me from her grasp.

I am good with shock once the spluttering and gasping is done. I bent an ear. *Stardust.* I must say I prefer the original with Hoagy, Mr. Siedel, and the Dorsey brothers. Theirs is a little more up-tempo."

"I asked for the Isham Jones," she said.

"Really? I don't have you down as the romantic sort. I have you down as more of the knife-in-the-back sort."

Now, I wouldn't say she relented or softened, but she did pass a hand over mine. "I thought you would like it," she said. "That's why I requested it. Mind you, I asked before you decided to insult my employer."

They never let it lie, do they? I was not going to be tricked. A Hardimann, especially this one, is always on his guard. It takes more than a kiss and a swift grapple. "I think you should fill me in a little more, old dear," I said after a couple of good drags of my smoke, feeling my manliness coursing through my veins once more. "I don't mind signing some official secret code of silence note or whatever is deemed necessary when employing a fellow in the art of hiding beneath the cloak and swashing about with the dagger. I am, after all, attired to swash and buckle."

She withdrew the gentle and loving hand. "The Official Secrets Act, 1889," she said with a generous dash of venom.

"That's the fellow," I said. "I sign, you speak." I looked up to search for the plough or that Orion chap, the one with the big belt and sword.

She pointed her trident towards me, one eye closed and the other wide to make sure of her aim. "No need for that, Pelham," she offered. "The merest hint of you opening your plummy pie-hole and I'll shoot you through the head myself." She added an extra '*have you got that*' jab with the trident.

Losing the pleasure in the taste of my smoke – such indulgences should be enjoyed in quiet and temperate company – I flicked my dog-end into the thickening darkness and watched it drift away. As I lifted my head from the study of the dog-end's descent I caught a glimpse of lights about us. Small lights, perhaps of the net-wielding sardine man chasing the silvery shoal. I looked back to Milly. "So, speak up."

She softened with as much speed as she had previously hardened, took me by an arm and led me on a perambulation which I felt would go from stern to…the front bit.

155

"You've heard of the Air Ministry RDF development centre at Bawdsley?" she asked. My silence informed her of my ignorance and prompted her to continue. "Range and direction finding. We are preparing ourselves for the Luftwaffe with a link of stations known as Chain Home, or CH. This chain will give us warning and advantage as German bombers and fighters head for our coast. A major improvement on the old acoustic mirrors, I can tell you."

I was pleased she could at least tell me something, but I wanted more. I gave a polite nod and gentle 'hello' to a languorous and amorous couple as they passed us. One of them was wearing a rather fetching Nelson patch and missing arm, the other more than amply filling her Lady Hamilton costume.

My tones were hushed. "Sounds like a sound idea to me," I said. "Somewhat akin to the beacons sending old Drake off to fight the Spanish Armada," I added to egg her on, to show her I was lending a keen ear.

"Effingham," she clipped.

I had only moments before been introduced to her darker side, that side of her accustomed to the language of the saloon bar, and I may have misheard owing to a sudden gust of channel breeze or slap of an over-enthusiastic wave against the hull way down below. I felt compelled to ask. "Effing whom?"

"Effingham. Lord Howard of Effingham commanded the English fleet. He sailed on the Ark Royal from which he defended Plymouth, allowing Drake, Frobisher, and Hawkins to give chase and set the Spanish fleet alight."

"I see, offence and home defence," I said. "So, this chain...?"

"The system is effective, but we are hampered by size. There is a broadcast aspect and a reception aspect, both of which require towers exceeding two-hundred feet or more."

"Easy targets," I said.

"Certainly. But we have other concerns."

We swapped arms as were turned to head back whence we'd come. I assumed she didn't want to go all the way. I took the brunt of a wind that seemed to be sizing up for a gale, taking pleasure in swirling around my green hosiery. "Other concerns?" I urged.

"Submarines, Pelham. Germany's *Unterseeboot*. What Mr. Churchill calls Hitler's Grey Wolves could starve us into submission should a war last for more than twelve months, which it most likely will. We need a hunting and detection system for our fleet."

"Without the need of those great big towers."

"Precisely. We have tested Rawlinson's Surface Warning System and we have a range of nearly fifty miles. We are developing something better, stronger, something smaller that can be housed in all our aircraft and ships. If we can develop a system capable of picking up a U-boat periscope at least a mile or so away we will be able to protect our shipping: the convoys we will rely on for everything from oil to tea."

I forced us to stop as the picture entered my head. I drew her closer to me, taking care not to get a tine in the eye or scrape my forehead with the edge of her helmet. I turned to look out to the greyness of the sea and sky. It was now grey with brushstrokes of pink, no longer the inky blackness of night, as though a curtain had been partially lifted. The truth dawned on me as gently as the dawn lifted from the horizon. "Something small enough to fit into a suitcase?"

Milly adjusted her Britannic helmet, brushed loosed hair from her eyes and joined me in my perusal of what could have been distant cloud or the French version of our own white cliffs of Dover. "The cavity magnetron is our greatest secret and we have to hand it over, along with Mr Whittle's jet engine."

I recalled something Mr. Churchill had said that day in Chartwell about paying a heavy price. The matter deserved some pressing. "I'm to hand it over."

This woman could change tack quicker than a dinghy in a maelstrom. "If you ever get your hands on it," she replied sharply. "Our prototype version of the cavity magnetron is more advanced and more powerful than the American one, thanks to Messrs Randall and Boot: much smaller, generating microwaves much more efficiently, operating in frequencies between three and thirty GHZ. This centimetric system, should it work, will allow us to detect smaller objects from a much greater distance."

I didn't want to get too technical because technicalities were the swamps into which I easily find myself being sucked and entombed like those fellows who occasionally get themselves dug up by archaeology students on field trips in the flatlands of eastern England. I gave some thoughtful hums, the way a good student should when relying on the fact he could perhaps swot up later, after class and in the privacy of the library. I was tempted to add an '*I see*', but I saw something to kick a kink into my train of thought. "That's Quill," I snapped. "Quill doing Quasimodo."

Milly did a slow head-turn and looked down the length of my straightened arm and past the pointing finger to where a once tall but now buckled and hunch-backed hobbling man was nosing his way through a doorway and into the Verandah Grill.

"Richard III," said Milly. "It appears you are not the only one who enjoys wearing tights."

"Be that is it may," I jabbed back at her, "that is Quill, demon detective of The Yard." I pulled her away from the rail and levered her in the right direction. I reached back and whipped my cane from its quiver. "What the heck is he doing here? I knew it. He wouldn't go to all this trouble just to collar me. He's after that damned suitcase as well, ready to auction it off to the highest bidder. Damnable traitors. We're surrounded by them."

"Really, Pelham?"

"You think I'm paranoid…"

The question wasn't wholly rhetorical, but Milly took it as such. I was about to offer some hypothesis, without mentioning the stiff on my Persian, when screams rang out from the Verandah Grill. They were not screams of merriment, mirth, or even crises. They were screams of fear accompanied by rapid gunfire.

Stock still in the doorway, we did some surveying, and what a scene it was to survey. The music tinkled away into nothingness as a macabre silence fell upon the scene. Bits of plaster fluttered from the ceiling. Partygoers played statues, some caught in the strangest and raciest of poses.

A weighty and rotund Hollywood mogul wheezed with his crossed eyes set firmly upon the teetering ashy end of his cigar. A slim girl, left buttock in mid-squeeze, looked up into the handsome face of her squeezer and beamed contentment, and I guessed, despite her embarrassment, wished the fellow had the prowess to remain gripping for the allotted time – however long that was to be.

A handful of people were still standing straight, the most noticeable being Messrs Hayes and Clench with smoke drifting from the muzzles of their machine guns. They had their backs to the velvet curtains as if posing for a passport photograph or a second bow after a heady opening night.

Opposite our two hoodlums stood Quill and Hammer. Hammer was stiff and proud apart from the right arm bent and the hand inches away from his holster. Quill must have experienced some miracle of modern medicine and was just as straight and tall, making the hump a little more humped though dislodged and more crudely apparent. These two men may have been quartered side by side in a dilemma, facing death and all the eternal darkness that goes with it, but that did not hinder them from scowling at each other, somewhat akin to Joe Louis and Nathan Mann during the weigh-in and pre-match square-up.

In the centre of the scene, sitting neatly around a small table was Mrs. Glendower, and Studely who was trying to lean as far away as possible from Stalin without tumbling from his chair.

Mr. Coward was the first to speak. "I am accustomed to the occasional critique, gentlemen," he began, "and while I rarely find need to take notice of it, I feel it is always better received when in writing as opposed to being in the form of a mural daubed with lead."

Clench stepped forward and shook his machine gun. "Shut it, you Limey pansy." He sprayed a couple of rounds into the piano stool to make his point. "We do the gabbing and you keep your lugs pinned back until someone gives us an answer." He lowered the muzzle. "Hey, Marie Antoinette, quit the snivelling."

"I am Queen Elizabeth," came the petulant reply. A tiara dropped from a beehive of red hair to the polished boards with an expensive clatter. The snivelling and whimpering stopped. Tears were dabbed and a nose wiped amidst a huddle a few paces in front of the doorway where Milly and I were waiting.

I was tempted to take a step back, put a guiding hand around Milly's slim waist and draw her with me to safety, and in a tactical retreat hunker down to scrub the old grey matter for a solution to the stand-off. Too late.

Clench gave voice once more. "Hey, Errol, come and join the party. Bring Maid Marion with ya." He gave a sneer and turned to receive some applause from his partner. None came.

Now mark me well here. I have never been one to enjoy bathing in the limelight so you will understand the reddening around the gills as everyone in the room turned to me. I had been called upon and sensed a *'cometh the hour cometh the man'* moment, so into the room I stepped.

"Don't be shy. Join the merry throng, Mr. Hardimann," called out Clench. He beckoned with his weapon. "Shake a leg, go stand over next to the old bim and drag the chippy with you. That's it, that's it. Good boy."

I hovered a moment, the brain fuzzy as it searched for meaning.

Clench let loose a bullet; it smacked into a seascape. "Come on, ya Lincoln Green Limey,"

Into the hush came the dulcet tones of Hammer. "The gentleman requires you to stand next to Mrs. Glendower, sir, and advises you to bring the young lady with you."

"Yeah," sniggered Hayes. "For a group shot."

"A shot?" I enquired.

Hayes was swift. "Yeah, like for a holiday snap, and do it quiet or you'll be collecting shells. And they won't be off Jones Beach."

Milly and I followed orders and parked – still standing – behind the seated triune of Mrs. Glendower, Studely, and the Stalin fellow to whom I had not yet been introduced.

Studely twisted a little to look up. "All right, Hardimann, not to worry, we'll be okay," he said. "She's hidden it well."

Clench snapped: "Clam it, copper."

Studely clammed it. Quill gave a deep growl of nervous and wintry discontent. Hammer checked his watch.

In the eerie silence, something dawned on me. There was a quietude not expected when travelling aboard an ocean liner. Obviously, owing to the violent interruption of the proceedings by Messrs Hayes and Clench, feet had stopped tapping and fingers had ceased snapping; paper kazoos lay limp and unblown, hats and costumes no longer rustled, and the piano was silent. But that was not all. I wondered if anyone else had noticed. They had other things on their minds: the two hoodlums and their respective machine guns. Hammer checked his watch again. Yes, dash it all, he had cottoned on.

I chanced a swift message to Milly on my right. "The engines have slowed."

"They've what?"

"Slowed. We can't be far from Cherbourg."

A mass gasp of fear followed some plinks and plonks – I can't recall the notes – as Mr. Coward adjusted the lie of his cream smoking jacket, accidentally knuckling a key or three.

Following the gasp was the crashing rat-a-tat-tat as Clench spun like a top and fired a dotted line down the flanks of the piano. "Another note out of you and you'll be wearing a wooden kimono. Got that, tootsie?" He rat-tatted another row of dots into the stage floor.

Good Queen Bess, *sans* tiara, still recovering from her blubbering, was the first to beginning screaming. A sharper scribbler would have said that all hell broke loose, but it was mainly noise. Milly and I took advantage of the commotion to slither between legs and under bending bodies towards the doorway through which we'd recently entered. Hayes and Clench were wheeling and jigging, spouting bullets in great leaping arches, mostly at the piano and enough to let decent draughts through the velvet curtains. Windows cracked and tinkled, and two ornate chandeliers plummeted to the floorboards.

I pulled myself up from the floor at the doorway, gave some assistance to Milly then dragged her behind me to safety where we could watch things take their course.

The noise died away, except for the irritable clicking of triggers as the two hoodlums became conscious that they had discharged all their ammunition. They looked up, bemused and befuddled, searching each other's face for some solution: a plan B, I suppose. They had none. Their gaze shifted in unison and I followed the route: to Hammer who was standing stock still and tall with his trusty Luger pointing its ugly black snout towards them.

"I think that is sufficient for this evening, gentlemen, don't you?" he said with excellent polish and the sort of demeanour I could never muster in such circumstances. "Now, I suggest you follow my wishes." He checked his watch and continued to hold court. "I would ask everyone to remain exactly where they are for the time being. This will only take a moment."

Hayes and Clench dropped their impotent weapons to the pitted floor and growled. "What'ya gonna do, Adolf?" asked one of them; I can't recall which.

"I intend to finish what I am here to do, gentlemen," said Hammer.

Hayes wanted more. "And what you gonna do with us?"

"Nothing, gentlemen. Do you have gum with you?"

Clench curled a lip and spat. "What if we do?"

"Well," said Hammer, "I suggest you unsheathe a stick of it each and spend the next ten minutes or so masticating. That should keep your tiny brains safely occupied if you don't attempt anything hazardous."

"Hazardous?" drawled Clench.

"Such as trying to walk at the same time." Hammer gave the Luger a wiggle. "I think the accepted mannerism in this situation, gentlemen, is to lift one's hands and place them gently atop your heads."

Hayes snapped, "Ah, shove it, Adolf."

A bullet cracked and zinged its speedy way across the dance floor, perhaps an inch or so above Mrs. Glendower. It whipped the white-banded hat from Hayes's head. He squealed, and Mrs. Glendower shrieked. I gather by this time Good Queen Bess had run out of puff and had nothing else to offer.

Peace reigned and we all looked to Hammer for our cues. He did not keep us waiting in the wings for long. "Studely, Mrs. Glendower," he began, "and you two" he added, giving a nod to our hoodlums, "outside, now." He looked a little nonplussed for a moment, and I remember at the time thinking that being nonplussed was certainly not like him at all. "You," he said, "Mr. Stalin or whoever you really are, go with them." He turned a little to watch Mr. Coward who was clearing daggers of broken wood and shards of chandelier crystal from his piano. "Mr. Coward, please open the lid of the piano stool."

I heard Mrs. Glendower gasp. Stalin growled. Gasp over, Mrs. Glendower spoke out. "How the hell...?

"Now, now, old woman," said Hammer. "You and your moustachioed friend have been all hugger-mugger and eyeing that piano stool for the last ten minutes."

"You sneaky underhanded..."

"Enough." Hammer fired another shot and Clench, who fortuitously for him had let his hands down by his sides, lost his hat. "There are many ways of finding answers to questions, Mrs. Glendower."

Mrs. Glendower shot up from her chair and shook a fist. "I'll get you for this, you bleedin' Nazi."

"Tut tut, Mrs. Glendower," said Hammer. "Your accent is slipping."

"Why, you good for nuffin'..."

Studely tugged at the babushka's sleeve. "Settle down now, Auntie, we'll sort it out."

She ripped her sleeve from Studely's grip. "And you can shut up an' all, you big fat lummox. I don't know why I ever bothered with the likes of you."

Suddenly, and I must say that I rarely use suddenly but feel it most apt at this juncture; suddenly she was staring across the Verandah Grill from Hammer to Quill in turn. "Or you two. Typical bleedin' Hardimanns you are. Not much blood but plenty of stain."

I'm well enough used to the old *'filius est pars patris'* and had spent many years deeming it as a compulsory remark offered by distant relatives, but, "*What the...?*" was all I could say in hushed tones. There was no need to knock me down with a feather; my body could have happily keeled over of its own free will. Hammer and Quill, brothers?

Hammer was calm, frighteningly calm. "The three of you, go and stand over by Mr. Hardimann."

Mrs. Glendower was already standing. Studely and Stalin rose from their seats. The threesome shuffled, cut a diagonal across the room, and stepped over cowering party goers towards me. Hayes and Clench followed with as much swagger as their embarrassment would allow.

By the time the ensemble arrived at me, Mr. Coward had lifted the lid of the piano stool and taken out a small suitcase from within. When I say small, it was small: perhaps the size of case one would use for carrying items of correspondence while travelling during the summer season. It was of red leather, with brass corners.

I felt a gentle nudge from Milly, and the gentle breeze of her whisper in my ear. "I told you it was small."

I had nothing to say, so I said nothing and concentrated on the unfolding scene.

"Over here with it, Mr. Coward, if you would be so kind," said Hammer.

Judging by Mr. Coward's lean I guessed it to be weighty despite its diminutive dimensions. He plonked it down at Hammer's feet and it gave a thud.

Hammer smiled. "Thank you, Mr. Coward. Now perhaps you can go back to entertaining your followers. Bring them back to their light-heartedness. You were playing something light and romantic."

Mr. Coward straightened from his toil. "I've heard tell that your Mr. Hitler detests jazz and all forms of music that reflect so-called inferior races and persuasions, Mr. Hammer. I may call you Mr. Hammer?"

Hammer gave a little bow. "Mr. Coward, Herr Hitler detests jazz and is infuriated by the sound of whistling." With that said he dipped fingers into his pocket and pulled out a monocle, which he lodged into his right eye socket. "As for me, I love to whistle along to jazz. Back to your piano, Mr. Coward. You were giving a rendition of *Stardust*."

Mr. Coward headed back to his piano.

Hammer did a half-turn. "Mr. Quill, you have an explosive device to deal with, am I correct?"

The crowd drew breath as Quill nodded. "You've got another thirty minutes," he said with his pencil moustache rippling beneath the false hook nose.

Hammer faced his audience to give some explanation. "Ladies and Gentlemen, you are alarmed. I can assure you there is no need. Do not fret. The captain and much of the crew is secured on the bridge, expertly bound and gagged by Mr. Quill here…"

"Detective Chief Inspector," grumbled Quill.

Hammer gave the Luger a wave just in case a handful or so of the now motionless dancers were unaware that Richard III was Detective Inspector Quill of The Yard. "As I was saying, when I have completed my small task Detective Chief Inspector Quill here will disarm the explosive device and allow you all to continue on your merry way. Have I made myself perfectly clear?"

I am sure the chorus of yes was not as effusive as he would have wished for. It was given, nonetheless.

Hammer faced Quill once more. "I shall leave you to get on with it once you have helped me transfer this to our waiting vessel, and I'm sure you have your other explosive device well in hand," he said with a dark and brooding politeness that sent a shiver down my spine. He bent to pick up the suitcase, spent some seconds as if weighing it to check its contents before straightening then backed away from Quill. Everyone watched Hammer in silence, some eyes following the line of his Luger which was now pointing towards Mr. Coward. "Come on, Mr. Coward. *Stardust*."

Mr. Coward settled down onto his piano stool after giving his smoking jacket a flip-up at the back. "I'm not sure if a second time would be…"

"You played it for her, you can play it for me. Now play it."

With that, Mr. Coward flopped his fingers down onto the keys and let them prance about as he whistled, much, from what I could see on his face, to the delight of Hammer.

The partygoers who had not been in much of a party mood for some time began to straighten up, come out from corners, from behind bullet-holed velvet curtains, and from beneath toppled tables, with an air of business as usual.

I turned to Milly to rattle off a list of my accumulated astonishments when a large figure loomed between us, and a deep, gravelly voice boomed.

"Who the hell is that whistling? Bloody din! Bad enough having to put up with that honky-tonk racket. Milly, come on, we've got that blasted frog to see in a couple of hours."

My head span for some time but eventually came to rest. I could see Hammer standing but a yard away from our little gathering with his Luger pointing directly at us. We all backed out onto the open deck and into the brightening dawn. Hammer followed. He aimed at Mr. Churchill. "There will be no Frenchman." He addressed the huddle. "If you follow my orders, no one will be harmed." He was preoccupied with Mr. Churchill once more. "Do not point your walking stick at me, old man. It is most aggravating."

CHAPTER 19
ON CONSIDERING THE THREE

"Hell's teeth, this wind." I backed away from the huddle on the deck, trying to batten down the flapping tail of my jerkin over my green tights and exposed rear end.

"Shut up and stop complaining, Hardimann," snapped the jackbooted butler.

"It's all fine for you with your leather coat on, Hammer…"

"Herr Hammer to you. Another word and I shall shoot you dead where you stand."

I refrained from voicing the opinion but viewed Hammer's remark as something of a turn up for the books. He had gone from latent to blatant, had nailed his colours to the mast at a stroke.

I managed to wriggle my way through the pack – the pack being Mr. Churchill, Milly, Studely, Mrs Glendower with her new Stalinesque friend, and our hoodlums, Hayes and Clench – until my back was jammed against something solid: the ship's rail. Quill, he was next to Hammer and enjoying a medley of smirks.

We were grouped in an open-air alcove beneath the ends of curved white roofs, the underside of lifeboat hulls hanging from davits from the deck above. These shapely hulls blocked out most of my seaward view, hid the horizon, and gave only a strip of grey sea to survey. The near silence of dawn was spoiled only by the rhythmic shush of Queen Mary cutting through waves at what must have been her minimum speed.

I turned back to peer over heads and shoulders, and in sight was still that tall leather-coated figure of Hammer with Luger in one hand and small suitcase in the other. Against the rail, behind the group, I felt, to some extent, safely hidden from his glare.

On feeling a sharp jab in the kidneys, I turned to see the top of Milly's head bobbing at an angle with which a young lady of good upbringing and education such as hers should not have her head bobbing about in public. She wasn't kneeling, but she was nearly there. I guarded my honour as she pulled once more, this time at the front of my jerkin. I gave a "*sshh*" and then a "*what do you want, what are you doing?*"

She rose to whisper in my ear, her trident an inch from my eyes. "I've got to get him away from here, Pelham."

"Who?"

"Him." She gave a thumb over her shoulder to where Mr. Churchill was waddling away from the small throng, jabbing his walking stick down onto the iron of Queen Mary then wandering back as though having forgotten why he'd left in the first place, only to repeat the shuttling promenade. "I'll get him to port," she said.

"To port?" I enquired. "He'll never make it." I'm not one to question the abilities and stamina of the older generation but a furtive glance as we left the Verandah Grill told me we were still a few miles from the French coast. The deep, dark, waters were most surely not conducive to an early morning dip, let alone a lengthy Canadian crawl to shore.

"The port side," she hissed. I enjoyed the warmth of her breath in my ear as she added, "You keep Hammer busy."

"Isn't it he who is keeping us busy? I still had my cane with its few rounds and was wondering when I should use it. Maybe I could get a decent shooting line through the huddle before me. Carving a few nicks and grooves into the hoodlums would cause no consternation. The Beretta was rubbing where I do not care to be rubbed in such a manner: well, not so sharply, anyway.

Milly hissed again. "Mr. Churchill is more important than the case. Remember that. There's an accident boat up at the front, near the wireless room…"

"The bridge," I said. "He shouldn't be here in the first place."

Too late. She was gone.

Hammer, having spotted Mr. Churchills meanderings, dispensed clipped orders. "You, you there, the fat imitation of a warmongering aristocrat. Stand still."

I had to pipe up. "I say, Hammer, old chap, steady on. Do you have any idea whom you are addressing?"

Hammer's next address was to his brother, his new right-hand man. "Lower a lifeboat, Quill."

Quill could not resist a petulant "Detective Chief Inspector." That said, with the speed of a man used to taking orders, he made his way along the deck and up a flight of stairs to the topmost deck from where he would be able to operate the lowering of a lifeboat.

Hammer raised a hand to adjust his monocle. "And by the by, if any of you are contemplating jumping overboard, I urge you to consider the drop of eighty feet and the likelihood of your landing on the steel deck of a U-boat. The water is also very cold, and this part of the channel is most hazardous. None of you are fit enough to endure such

166

trials." Dissatisfied with the state of his monocle he withdrew it from his eye only to realize that to give it a swipe with a handkerchief he would have to holster the Luger and put down the case. He pocketed the monocle.

As this little scenario played out, I chanced a lean over the rail and there, down below, was a U-boat. It looked nothing more than a small pencil nestling against its pencil box: the great black cliff of Queen Mary's hull.

I pulled back from the edge and stared a good long one at Hammer. "You're a traitor, Hammer. A damnable Nazi and a traitor."

"Yeh," called Hayes. "You're a stinking traitor. At least we do it for the dough."

Hammer took a step forward with his arm out straight and pressed the muzzle of the Luger against Hayes's forehead. "Another word from your foul mouth, Hayes and I'll throw you over the side."

Hayes held his hands up to surrender. "Okay, okay, you Limey nut, I got the lay, the racket ain't flopped yet. We can deal."

"No deals. Right, now, all of you, into the boat."

Hayes had not finished. "Aw, come on, Hammer, old bean, we all want the same thing."

"The same thing?" asked Hammer. "Explain yourself. Be brief."

Hayes gave a shrug. "We both want the downfall of the British Empire."

"We do?"

"Sure. We're gonna do it with God-fearing Christian capitalism while you guys can do the guns and bombs thing. Me and Clenchy here can throw some greenbacks your way."

"Be that as it may, Hayes," said Hammer before Hayes could continue on his theory, "get into the boat."

You may wonder what your hero was doing all this time, watching these two aggressive powers squabbling over the precarious future of our great peace-loving nation. Let it never be said I remain cowering in the darkness of my foxhole with enemies all around; I am ever at the ready to swell the pages of England's history.

Hammer had forgotten about me. There I was, tucked in behind the heavy shoulders of Clench and Studely, and even the pointy shoulders of Hayes gave me cover. Mrs. Glendower and her new moustachioed friend were grumbling hatred against all around them, although the grumbles did not seem to reach Hammer.

Just as the gloss-white clencher side of the lowering lifeboat clonked against the rail a few inches from my elbow I took the opportunity to raise my cane. Up it came, straight and true between the legs of Hayes and Clench. I fired one shot and the round struck Hammer in the chest, forcing him to take a step back. He did not fly, he did not fall. He flinched, raised an eyebrow, and fired a shot from his Luger. The bullet whizzed through my green hat and trimmed a feather.

"Back, back," Hammer shouted, signalling with the Luger. He fired a warning shot into the air. The bullet zinged against a davit, causing Quill to skip back and holler profanities.

I leaned back and toppled into the lifeboat, striking my head against the engine cover before falling between seat planking. I was up in a flash and staggering about. I peered from the other side of the lifeboat to the cold waters of the channel below and the glinting steel deck and conning tower of the U-Boat. I managed a glance forward to where Milly had gone some moments earlier, and there she was with Mr. Churchill, sitting in the emergency boat as it dropped slowly to the sea. Milly gave a wave; it had more of the '*adieu*' than the '*au revoir*' about it. As for Mr. Churchill, all I could see of him was the Astrakhan, a black hat and the billowing fumes of a cigar. I could be safe in the knowledge that the escapees were out of Hammer's eye line, but should the fellow who had just popped out from the hatch of the submarine conning tower have spotted them, I could not vouch for their safety.

Hammer was still letting off warning shots and firing off orders with as much spit and venom as the lead hitting the steel girders and overhangs of the ship. Keeping my head down was the sensible option and this keeping-the-head-down was given some assistance as a weight fell upon it. I was in sudden and uncomfortable darkness as Studely came sprawling over me, forcing me to lift my cane and fire an aimless shot. I missed Mrs. Glendower by an inch or so. Mrs. Glendower's arrival set the lifeboat swinging to-and-fro, banging against the Queen's hull, and I was still far from gaining any form of balance.

What I did ascertain was the rough trajectory of the next round I fired from my cane; it was in the direction of Quill some twenty or so feet above us and his call from behind the davit gave me reason to believe he had judged the missile as meant solely for him.

He was beginning to take things very personally. "Hardimann, you..." The remainder of his sentence – some question of my parentage and its legitimacy – was muffled beneath the crack of the service revolver he poked between the girders of the davit. One round dug a bright groove out of the polished handrail of The Queen before it skipped over my head.

"Hell's teeth, Quill," I exclaimed. I tottered. "Is that a way for an officer of the law to behave?"

Hammer answered on Quill's behalf. "Sit down, Hardimann, you're rocking the boat."

Rocking was the right word. There was plenty of banging and clonking as the lifeboat swung out from the hull of The Queen only to charge back against it with gusto. It was a very large lifeboat, large enough to accommodate a hundred or more souls should the need arise.

I was almost the stick rattling around in the empty barrel, from time to time careening into other members of the newly appointed seafarers, namely Studely and Mrs. Glendower.

It was during one of these collisions that Mrs. Glendower's friend and comrade, the strange fellow masquerading as Mr. Stalin, surrendered to Hammer's wishes and made his crapulous exchange from larger vessel to smaller. I did my best to play the goodly host but was still dodging the venomous lead of Detective Chief Inspector Quill of the Yard who had taken it upon himself to be judge, jury, and hangman in the pursuance of justice concerning your hero, Pelham Hardimann.

I am all for a man striving for a job well done and would support pedantry and perfection, but I was beginning to see this onslaught as nearing the frozen limit. I called out once more. "Enough, Quill, we are following orders." I shook a fist then pointed upwards and to the right to all I could see of Hammer: his SS cap. "Hammer's orders."

I was about to add fervent elucidation to my well-founded ministrations when the lifeboat surged in a lusty swing back to the hull of The Queen. Wood and steel met with a bang and a jolt, sending me backwards and toppling, the violent action given more venom as my cane flipped between my legs. In the thinnest split of a second, I was somersaulting, dropping to the icy grey of the English Channel.

It was one of those slow-motion moments – the descent that is – and myriad thoughts streamed through my brain. There was no life flashing before me. I did not waste travelling time. I considered my portions and proportions of the three and their existence. You know the three?

It has always been my belief that a man needs three staples with which to lead a life of contentment. I think contentment is the *mot juste*; happiness is such a far-off star.

The three. A chap needs gainful and enjoyable employment. Gainful in that it pays for more than bed, board, and clothing. One needs little treats in life, such as an SS100, a decent tailor and a well-stocked wine cellar.

An abode where one is happy to dwell alone, or to invite guests without them dropping the jaw. Have them uplifted by your taste in furnishings and works of art, learning as they revel in your hosting.

The most difficult one: the better half, the companion, the good woman, the good man –companionship to your tastes. Someone with whom you could spend a wet Wednesday afternoon in Rhyl when it is coming down in stair rods, the public houses are closed, and the cat's whisker has snapped on your wireless.

Of these three, a minimum of two makes life bearable. With only one of these one must surely be emboldened by hope and the promise of a better future. Without even one of them, I can understand a man doing the

Beachy Head thing in the certainty he is going to a better and less stressful place.

And with how many of these three had I been blessed? I considered employment. It had been gainful and enjoyable until halted by the arrival of a local flatfoot leading to my incarceration. Employment since my release can only be computed as hazardous, painful, and confusing. Plots were thickening at an alarming rate. Gainful as in useful? Who is to know until the final scores are released? I was not gushing with optimism. The employment matter can be left open for the time being.

A decent abode. I had only viewed it momentarily since my release and it had been damaged, desecrated by the uninvited living and the uninvited dead.

As for the companion? Now it may be some time since my emotional wave has crashed upon an embracing beach, but never let it be said that I am frosty and mean of spirit. But I have never come across – in all senses of the word – a woman with whom I can suffer the breakfast repartee. The questions asked the night before by most young ladies are explorative and trifling in their probing, blessed with the lightness of flirtation and expectation. Over breakfast the questions become needling in their search for deeper truths. The night before, she is gasping open mouthed and bubbling with admiration as her eye lands upon your Picasso, Royal Doulton, and the way you pluck a bottle of champagne from the refrigerator. Come the morning, she is calculating with the speed and accuracy of that Mr. Babbage fellow and his wonderful machine. Are you or are you not a safe bet, her haven for life, her meal ticket? Is there a future or just a short spell of happiness before she robs you of your investment, your past, your future and half of all you possess? Call me cynical if you wish, but I had of recent felt it best for a man to go his own way.

With all that said, someone may have punctured my balloon of self-preservation. And just when I find someone I want, see happiness in all its long-legged and pouting beauty, it sails away from me. Not so much sailing but motoring. With Mr. Churchill hidden below canvas in a motorboat, Milly was speeding toward England.

I hit the water.

CHAPTER 20
YOU CAN SWIM BUT YOU CAN'T HIDE

As I surfaced, the time was not wasted. I used it to go over some moot points. Bear with me a while.

I'm not sure if you are familiar with terminal velocity and I must admit these things are a little over my head. Let us consider for a moment that the human body – any form of body – will double its speed per second per second every thirty-two feet or so. That initial thirty-two feet could have you dropping at around forty-five miles per hour. Take this into consideration and you will see that I must have been travelling at least two-and-a-half times my initial launch speed when I hit the water: from nought, plus a bit, to over ninety in seconds. This may seem trivial to you, but I feel it deserves some consideration.

The other factor is the water. Jump into your bath; bounce from the springboard and perform a supreme swallow dive into your municipal pool, slip from your punt into the Cam, and you will find the old H2O embracing, even comforting, certainly not a threat. How hard is water? I am not talking about the dissolved bits of calcium or magnesium sloshing around in it. A descent of over one hundred feet or so and water starts to harden; it fails to move out of your way fast enough for it to cease being a solid mass. It's at about fifty feet when it starts to smart, somewhat akin to hitting the pavement. Three feet if you are an ass and do a belly flop. Some choppiness in the water can help; it's the break-up of surface tension. Falling from a great height into a mill pond is not as serene an action as it may sound.

One more quick calculation. Tumble at thirty-two feet per second and you will plunge below the surface – should you be going like an arrow as opposed to a hippo – to a depth of ten feet or so. If you double the entry speed you do not necessarily double the depths before coming to a full stop and the beginning of your ascent. The water compresses beneath you and closes in all around you.

I guess I went to a depth of fifteen feet before using the tangled and flailing ascent to get my brain in gear and congratulate myself on having taken precautions: the arms close into the sides of the torso, the head up so as not to get a hefty smack in the face, and the hands cupped firmly around the gentleman's vegetables to avoid severe bruising and a day of doubling up in agony.

I hit the water well with feet pointed but my jerkin shot up with the woollen tights and jumper fluming up as if to squeeze me out like icing from a cake maker's funnel. I struggled for a while to clear my face of the wool that had taken on the weight of chainmail. And above all else, despite my perfect drop the *'landing'* stung like hell; my rear end re-living my Eton days.

Through the murky depths I saw bubbles rising and expanding. The thrum-thrum and swish-swish of great steam engines and turning screws clanged around me but seemed to be heading away.

As I popped up into the wavy surface I caught glimpses of Queen Mary's towering stern, the white foam of her wake, even shorter glimpses of far-off land and for a moment what looked like a slab of straight and shiny steel skimming like a slide-rule across a ruffled page. Jutting from atop the straight metal was a conning tower. A larger swell blocked my view as soon as I espied it.

I coughed salt, wiped the eyes, and removed my jerkin and woollen top. Removing the tights was a flurry of acrobatics, water-swallowing, and more dipping and rising.

I'm sure the older reader – and welcome to you – will remember the days of woollen bathing trunks and how one had to roll them down the legs before tugging them off in preparation to squeeze the gallon of sea from them. A swift pull was never enough, even with mother's help – if you had a mother, that is.

So, there I was, developing goose-pimples and treading water in a cold swell in nothing but Sam Cooper Jockeys as civilization steamed into the distance.

A swell lifted me, giving me another view across the water, allowing me to spot something most bizarre. At the stern rail of Queen Mary was a figure firing potshots. My bobbing up and down made Quill's aim wayward, but his voice carried across the ever-stretching stretch of channel between us. "You can swim, Hardimann, but you can't hide!"

Working on the principal that there are no echoes at sea I can only surmise that Quill must have repeated this threat at least half-a-dozen times. No matter.

Quill's other utterances were more disturbing. "He's there, in front of you!" he shouted. Another shot rang out and zipped into a wave some yards from me, but that gave no worry.

As for the *'he's there, in front of you'*, some kind fellow should have called out to Quill *'he's there, behind you.'* A figure loomed upon the policeman, lifted him bodily, and launched him like a rag doll from the stern of Queen Mary to be churned up in the huge blades of her screws.

Quill's call, before his own demise, made it clear I had a pursuer. Hammer must be on his way. I would have to spend much of the time below the surface. I understood my position in the hunt, for hunt it most surely was.

I am quick to adjust to my surroundings. Drop Pelham Hardimann anywhere you wish upon the earth and he will find his bearings, orientate, acclimatize, and assimilate.

I turned slowly in full circles as I grew accustomed to the swell, catching more glimpses of far-off land, a small white hull coming towards me, and a hundred yards or so away the steel slab of the U-boat that had some minutes before been nuzzling up against the sheer black hull of my recent accommodation, the now distant RMS Queen Mary.

I went under until the call for air was too strong. Kicking away to keep head above water, I was half-way through my circle of reconnaissance when I received a clonk on the mazzard from a loose fender. Down I went, as far as I could, doing the old discretion is the better part of valour routine as the lengthy lifeboat chugged above me toward the U-boat. I came back up to see the huge rudder cutting a watery furrow. Studely was at the tiller.

Hammer was giving orders as the lifeboat neared the U-boat. "*Matrose, wirf uns ein Seil rüber, damit wir neben Euch festmachen können.*"

A call came from the conning tower. "*Natürlich, Kommandant.*"

My rusty German told me that Hammer had this fellow Nazi ready and waiting for him on the conning tower of the U-boat. All he had to do was pull alongside, jump aboard with case in hand and batten down the hatches or whatever they do on such vessels. Then he would make his leisurely way to shake hands with the nasty corporal back home in Berlin. Such planning. Such forward thinking. But what would Hammer do with his hostages? Why did he need hostages? Could I leave Mrs. Glendower and Studely to their fate? No, I could not. There were questions to be asked and I was damned if I would go to a watery grave with them unanswered. And if truth be told I was still full of fervour to give Hammer a good smack in the daylights.

I ducked down and breast-stroked my way towards the U-boat, coming up at intervals for air, until I found myself on the other side of the vessel. With any luck, I could clamber up and get a decent perch from where I could view all actions.

"*Sie haben eine Menge Menschen an Bord, Herr Kommandant.*" I heard the sailor comment as I heaved myself up the rounded fat belly of the U-boat.

It was a bit of a struggle, but the gentle swell helped me gain purchase on the skinny ladder of the vessel, and I was hidden by the conning tower.

I listened for Hammer's reply. "*Es war nötig Geiseln zu nehmen . Wir können sie ziehen lassen, sobald das Gerät sicher an Bord ist. Aber pass' auf Matrose, halt' die Augen offen. Da ist ein Mann irgenwo im Wasser, der nicht weit weg sein kann."*

It occurred to me that Hammer was cock-a-hoop to be gabbling away in his own tongue after such a long time, although the thought crossed my mind that he must have spent some time doing so in the radio room of Queen Mary while getting his German ducks in a row for this eventuality: his escape with the suitcase.

I smiled as I shivered. From what I could hear, something had gone adrift in his plans. That's always a good sign. These fellows are all at sixes and sevens when plans go awry. Your Englishman is always armed with plan B or perhaps C in the knowledge that plan A is certain to come a cropper.

Hammer was laden with hostages, an awkward thing on the high seas no matter how near foreign shores. Although my veins needed no ice, some other part of his speech cooled them further. I was the man who was missing but no doubt close at hand.

Still clinging, lying flat against the freezing steel like a starfish with an absent limb, I looked about. Small fishing boats bobbed cheerily – at least small enough to look dainty and cheery – in the low early morning sun about halfway between the U-boat and the shore. We were not far from Cherbourg, almost in daylight. Surely, Hammer would not add murder to his piracy so near to a foreign port where eyes must be upon him. U-boats popping up for a gander at the cliffs cannot be a common occurrence in these parts, so likely to attract an audience from either tiny boat or craggy cliff.

My heart sank. He had most certainly murdered Sam the Spot, and by this juncture, after his most recent display of thuggery, I wouldn't put it past him to have murdered poor one-armed Clackett. Was he about to dispatch his next brace?

I managed a peek. Hammer was watching his passengers scramble from one craft to another. He was no gentleman, allowing the two American hoodlums to be first from wood to steel. A better man would have given Mrs. Glendower right of way. But there you are, where is the difference in spirit between nation and its citizen? The latter is but a microcosm of the former.

Two things spurred me on. *"Was soll ich tun, wenn ich ihn sehe?"* the sailor had asked.

Hammer's reply was blunt and to the point. *"Erschieß" ihn!"*

That order to shoot me on sight combined with the bodily need for movement; I had to move. I was welded to the steel by the cold and my limbs were flagging. As any springtime or autumn swimmer will tell you, one may soon get used to the frost of the briny sea but the pain doubles once one is back in open air and skin-grating breezes. I was in danger of losing extremities: my favourite ones.

Still out of sight from Hammer and his crowd, and his sailor friend, I reached up to grip the bottom of the conning tower ladder. The thin rungs dug into my palms and soles and the chance of slipping was never far from my mind. I was atop the tower and but an arm's length from the armed sailor within seconds. It had been somewhat akin to climbing up the outside of a giant galvanized bucket. All I had to do was vault over the lip of the conning tower and take the man by surprise as I dropped down into it.

As I balanced atop the lip, I chanced a cheeky hello. The sailor spun around and I used the split-second to peruse the shock that swept across his hard-jawed fizzog. I whacked him a good one, a right-hander to the eye as hard as I had wished to offer Hammer. He shrieked. He dropped his weapon and I grabbed it with the adeptness of silly point catching that just-nicked half-hearted defensive stroke. Before he had chance to recover, I walloped him again with my free right hand: a hand closed tight and on the end of a good upward swing. The poor man toppled over the lip of the conning tower and headed for the channel, suffering a bounce off the bulbous hull of the vessel before reaching water.

I stood, shivering to out-quiver an aspen, looking down from the conning tower, watching Hammer help his last passenger, Mrs. Glendower, onto the deck of the U-boat.

I filled my lungs and readied myself to give the command any true-born Englishman worth his salt dreams of hollering. "*Schnell, schnell. Hände in der Luft, Fritz!*"

With shocking grace and the demeanour of a chap wondering if he'd just heard the May cuckoo, Hammer turned and looked up. "I beg your pardon, sir?"

It was good to be referred to as '*sir*' again; I suppose respect comes through the barrel of a gun. I jiggled the machine gun and pointed it towards the tall leather-clad figure that did look – dare I say it – resplendent on the deck of the U-boat. "*Hände hoch! Der Krieg ist für Sie vorbei, Fritz.*"

"At the risk of contradicting you, sir," replied Hammer, "I feel you are under some misapprehension. The war cannot be over for me owing to the fact it has not yet begun."

"Be that as it may," I professed, "stick your bally hands up." I felt some verbal vim was called for. "You damn traitor." I chanced a look over the side to see Hammer's compatriot flailing about in the swell of the channel. I called down. "You'd better help him out, someone."

There were no volunteers.

"Why the hell should we fish him out?" piped up Clench, waving that now familiar bandaged hand. "You're the guy who tipped the kraut into the drink. You get him out."

"Come, come, Clenchy. Where is your Christian spirit?" I pulled back the bolt on the machine gun. "Get him out. Help him, Hayes."

Clench had not finished with his complaints. "But my hand," he whimpered.

"The saltwater will do it good."

I looked back to Hammer to receive a confusing expression, perhaps a mixture of agreement and thanks. Was he surprised? Can we not always be gentlemen, even in times of conflict, large or small?

Ordering the two hoodlums to drag the poor young sailor from the sea was not an act of altruism on my part. I am swift when it comes to forming the ad hoc plan. With the two hoodlums busying themselves I had only Hammer, Mrs. Glendower, and her new Stalinist friend with whom to contend. I had one man down there on my side: Studely.

I was about to nip over the lip and clamber down the side of the conning tower when the earth moved beneath my feet; metal moved beneath my feet. The conning tower hatch opened, tipping me forward a little but I regained balance with astonishing speed.

"*Was geschieht?*" came the call as an oil-smudged face appeared down in the tubular hole. "*Wer sind Sie?*"

"I am Pelham Hardimann," I responded, sticking the muzzle of the machine gun down into the hatchway. "I need a chat with your boss."

"*Was sagten Sie?*"

"I said I need a chat with your leader."

"*Mein Führer?*"

"No, not that lunatic. Another lunatic, and a traitor." I jabbed the machine gun at him as he stepped up a rung on his ladder and lifted a hand to pull himself from the hatchway. "Now, if you don't mind…" I prodded at him with the muzzle. "No, back down you go, and mind your fingers. Down you go." I reached over to give a pull at the hatch. I kicked at his fingers and brought the hatch down with a hefty slam. I turned the wheel to lock it tight.

I had killed time when it was not mine to kill. I called down to Hammer who was overseeing the rescue of his comrade. "I wish your people would learn to speak English, Hammer. How the hell can chaps fight a war when they don't understand each other?"

Having helped Hayes and Clench pull his man from the sea and onto the deck of the U-boat, Hammer took time to turn and address me. "You are correct, sir. It is an aspect of human conflict our leaders should consider before embarking on any form of hostility in the future."

"I'm coming down."

"Very good, sir."

I wriggled my way down, lacking decorum as my Y fronts snagged against a bulky bolt on the side of the conning tower. Sensitive skin burned with cold against the steel and the self-inflicted wedgie tortured me with the acutest of chafing as the cotton tugged and strained. It took a moment for me to gather and readjust, not easy when armed with a weighty machine gun.

A call of shock rang out. "Pelham Hardimann."

I dropped to the icy deck of the U-boat and the metal slapped through my feet and pounded up my shins before I fell backwards, almost launching the machine gun into the sea.

"Pelham Hardimann," called Mrs. Glendower once more as she pulled at her black headscarf. "Such behaviour is not called for. Cover yourself."

"With what?" I asked a little drunkenly as I scrambled to my feet. "Have you arrived with my laundry?"

Clench drawled. "Ah, he ain't got nuttin' to show."

I turned to the man who was supporting his bandaged hand and wincing in pain as the saltwater bit into his wound. A sudden shiver trembled from my toes to my head and I launched into a hopping routine to keep my whitened soles from the icy deck. "It's cold. The water is freezing and the wind-chill cuts to the bone," I said. "It's all right for you wrapped up in your Zoot suit. I don't even have a hat."

"That's no excuse to be vulgar," said Mrs. Glendower. "Cover yourself." She turned to drag poor Studely into the domestic struggle. "Go and get a blanket from the lifeboat."

"But, Auntie..." began Studely.

"And you can stop this auntie business, you oaf. You are as useless as him, as all Hardimanns. I'll be happy if I never hear the name again until the day I die."

Hammer offered me a smile then a whisper. "One wonders, sir, if that day could ever arrive prematurely."

"Quite so, Hammer," I replied. "But while we are all here...most of us are here, I would like to get one or two things straightened out."

Hammer plonked the small suitcase onto the deck before holding out a hand to plead. "If we could just get this man aboard," he said, adding a jerking thumb towards the dripping sailor.

"But what of me, Hammer? The bones are splitting with cold."

"With all undue respect, sir, that is of no concern to me," said Hammer. "You are nothing but a nuisance to me, an irritation soon to be scratched away. You are, after all, standing on a German submarine, a submarine full of German sailors. Your only ally on board is Studely, and he now seems to be adrift."

It took me a second or so to cotton on, but cotton on I did. The sight of Studely drifting away in the lifeboat, waving a blanket with a sense of a job well done before looking down to see the widening gap of icy water between his vessel and the U-boat was not the only thing to jar. Above the lapping of waves, I heard the hatch of the conning tower clang back, a noise followed by the clonking of heavy boots, the clicking of machine gun bolts and the call of a German captain through a loudhailer. The main thrust of his argument was that I should down my weapon and point to the sky.

All I could hear from Studely's direction was the intransigent whirring of a diesel engine refusing to start. I was undone. I tossed the machine gun into the sea as ordered. "It seems you have won, Hammer," I said, peering down towards the suitcase. "You have me between…"

"…the devil and the deep blue sea, Hardimann? Not too deep and hardly blue." He added insult to injury with one of those grins so beloved of villains. "You put up a valiant fight. Mr. Churchill will be proud of you should he ever receive news of your heroism."

CHAPTER 21
HOME TRUTHS

"I am disappointed in you, Hammer, taking the side of these goose-stepping gangsters. Democracy will win in the end, you know?"

Hammer harrumphed. "Voting just allows you to choose the imprint of the boot under which your head is crushed, and it is usually a boot chosen by the false wisdom of the masses. And by the way, Hardimann, we no longer goosestep. We leave that to Mrs. Glendower and her ilk."

I was going to question Hammer of his swift change from '*sir*' to '*Hardimann*', but these things are self-explanatory. I was without weapons and allies. Studely was drifting further away into the channel. Something wormed into my mind, something Hammer had mentioned only moments earlier about Mr. Churchill. "What do you mean by *if he ever...?*"

"If he lives, Hardimann. If he lives."

I would have snapped fingers had they not been so spongy and wrinkly with that spongy and wrinkly business one suffers after a long, deep sleep in a cooling bath. "Quill."

"Precisely. Your nemesis, your staunch and stuffy Quill of The Yard."

"And your brother-in-arms."

"Not just in arms. He was my brother indeed."

"The bomb, the other bomb, that's what he was going to do. He was going to blow up Winston Churchill. Too late now, he's fish food."

"That's as may be, Hardimann, but we plan. Wheels are in motion."

My mind raced. I did thumb to chin and studied the suitcase before looking up to see Hammer lodging his monocle into an eye. "But why? He's not in the government. Why not Chamberlain or Halifax?" My question was ignored. I clicked back a few sprockets. "Your brother, Quill really was your brother?"

Mrs. Glendower sidled up and chipped in with nastiness. "Yes, his brother, another blot of scum popping up from the bed of an incestuous pond."

Hammer ignored her. "Because," he carried on as he pulled his Luger from inside his leather coat, "Winston Churchill is the only Englishman Herr Hitler fears."

"Give me the suitcase, Hammer." I chanced. "We can put all this behind us. I'll put in a good word on your behalf."

"It has gone too far for that, Hardimann." His concentration fluttered for a second.

Coming towards us was a small fishing boat, a sardine boat, or smack; I'm not too up on these vessels. "More of your friends, Hammer?"

"We have friends everywhere. You'd be surprised how many we have in England and France, some of them in very high places." He was about to continue but needed to wait for the fishing boat to give its '*whoop whoop*'. It drew up against the hull of the submarine.

"What you doing now, Hammer?" Hayes took a couple of paces towards the small throng. "Me and Clenchy here are still up for a deal. We can bring down the British Empire once and for all. The world will be ours to share."

"No deals," said Hammer. He addressed Mrs. Glendower. "This is your lift to France."

"France?" Mrs. Glendower exclaimed. "You should be taking us to English shores, you scoundrel."

"Hardly, madam," quipped Hammer with what a man of his type would call *schadenfreude*. "You will not be welcome on English soil after all you have done to steal this suitcase on behalf of Russia. You can go and live in the political Eden you have desired for so long. You and your new friend will fit in well."

Our friend Stalin, the chap to whom I had not yet been introduced, flinched a little unless the movement was solely to give his moustache a tweak.

Hammer had more for Mrs. Glendower. "Your communist friends in Cherbourg will escort you to Paris and then on to Moscow. They have been contacted."

"You contacted them?"

"Yes," said Hammer. "No need for thanks."

Mrs. Glendower, for the second time in my knowing her, let loose with a volley in an accent not suited to my common view of her. It was guttural and hard, from the streets, of the smoke and docks of London. "You are the bleedin' spawn of Satan."

Hammer removed his monocle and breathed upon it, taking time to compose his answer. "No, mother, I am the spawn of you and the man you hated from the day I was born. The man you murdered."

My knees knocked with shock, amazement, and anger. Confusion rattled around in the old onion. "You're his mother?" I swapped addressees. "You're her son?"

"That is correct, Hardimann."

"I rue the day," snapped Mrs. Glendower with a scowl to sour milk. "I rue the day when Hardimanns forced their way into my life, my family's life, my mother's life."

I punctuated my speech with hops, clasping both hands around the gentleman's area. "Your mother's life? You have lost me. I am all at sea."

Hammer pulled back the hammer on his Luger. "You have one minute should you wish to have your thoughts disentangled, Hardimann. The Royal Navy is on its way and this vessel must make haste, must dive."

Mrs. Glendower crossed her arms, squeezed her bosom in defiance, and marched past Hammer straight for me. "My mother, your father's cook. Remember her, do you?"

I sucked then gasped. "Mrs. Allingham. But...she was...well, she never..."

"Yes, she did, Pelham Hardimann. Out of wedlock. Sent into confinement she was, before I...less than a day old...was ripped from her arms and imprisoned in the cold and flinty walls of our ever so loving church. Born of sin, we become sin, remain sin, and are abused as sin, to be forever punished."

"But my father never..."

"Not your father. Your uncle. Good old Uncle Mortimer Hardimann, the hero of the family. Your Uncle Mortimer, Pelham, the scourge of all maids in the Hardimann household, and a little threatening to the stable boys if the truth be known."

There was silence, apart from the drumming of the fishing vessel, until Hayes stabbed a whistle into it. "You Limey toffs sure love to sow your wild oats."

"Yeah, in fields a little too close to the homestead," added Clench. "And there's no way you'll get me on a French beach."

Hammer shot him and sent another bullet over Hayes's head before the skinny hoodlum's open mouth let out its shriek of shock.

"Hell's teeth, Hammer!" I cried. "You can't just...you shot him dead... in cold blood."

"Should I have asked some questions beforehand?"

"He's a Hardimann," said Mrs. Glendower with the dullness born of unwanted knowledge. As for her glance towards the dead man, no eyelid was batted.

Hayes was glum, gazing down at his stricken compatriot, but seemed to charge his courage like a gambler with that one card up his sleeve. "Okay, Hammer, spill, I'm all ears. What's all this about?"

"Aboard the Queen Mary, in her cargo holds, are hundreds of cases of Gordon's Gin and Dewar's Scotch Whisky."

Hayes spat into the wind then wiped an eye. "So," he began with a shrug. "Business."

"The importer is a company going by the name of Somerset."

"Straight business, Hammer. Nothing sour, cleaner than the bathtub gin we used to sell, and high-class boozers pay up fast. No complaints. End of prohibition, in '33, we just carried on."

"An import company owned by a Mr. Joseph Kennedy, the same Mr. Kennedy who had dealings with Chicago gangsters Sam Giancana and Frank Costello. Am I correct?"

Hayes scowled. "Ain't you the swot?"

"I do my homework, Hayes. You worked for Giancana and Costello, didn't you?"

There was another shrug from the hatless gangster. "So, now I'm legit. Big deal. Whooppee doo!"

"Not quite, Mr. Hayes. It appears that you and your friend Mr. Kennedy, along with a few others including Mr. Jean Paul Getty, have overlooked one vital law."

Hayes sniggered. "We don't break laws, Hammer. We just knock a kink into 'em now and then."

"And who is defying the 1799 Logan Act? Mr. Kennedy or Mr. Getty?"

"The Logan Act? Where's that, Vaudeville?" Hayes laughed but stopped as he caught sight of his dead partner's body.

"It is an act forbidding any United States citizen to do business with a foreign power unless authorized by the state."

"Shipping booze don't break no rules, Hammer."

"But dealing with The Third Reich does, does it not? Especially when shipping oil, purchasing art confiscated from the Jews, and the buying and selling of arms."

"What's it to you?" demanded Hayes. "You ain't no friend of the Brits, and we Americans can help you, at a price."

"So, tell me, Hayes. Kennedy or Getty?"

"Aaw, come on Hammer. Take a long walk off your own submarine. I ain't squealing."

Hammer raised the Luger and fired off another round. Hayes stood stock still as if resigned to his fate. Hammer shuffled a little, stuck a hand into his leather coat and pulled out an envelope. He passed it to me. "Open it, Hardimann. Show the photograph to our hoodlum friend here."

I took the envelope and pulled out the photograph. It took only a couple of paces on the cold steel to reach Hayes who snatched it from me and glared as if willing his eyes to burn it."

"The photograph is of an official party held by the Third Reich, November last. Am I correct?" asked Hammer.

"Could be," sulked Hayes.

"In the foreground of that photograph you can see quite clearly Mr. Getty, and Hilde Kruge, a close companion of the Fuhrer."

Hayes flicked a back of a hand against the photographs. "What's that to me? Your Royal Eddie has shooken hands with him enough times."

"If you study with more care, Mr. Hayes, you will no doubt recognize someone in the background."

"Nope."

"It is you, isn't it, Hayes?"

"Could be."

"Take your time to study the second picture, Mr. Hayes. While you do that, I shall bring us back to what Mr. Hardimann here calls *the nub*."

"The nub?" I enquired.

Hammer ignored me. "There was one case missing from the shipment, wasn't there? Think back, Mr. Hayes, of the shipment that is now on The Queen Mary."

"What of it, Hammer? Get on with it, speak up, shut up, or shoot. I'm getting chilled to the bone here."

I had to interject. "You're getting chilled to the bone? Look at me."

Hammer tapped a boot against the suitcase between his legs. "One crate went missing from that shipment, didn't it? Inside that crate was this very suitcase."

Hayes snarled but it didn't work well owing to his chattering teeth. He tossed the photograph and watched it glide and swerve to the choppy channel. "So?"

"You eventually found the crate and the person who had removed it from the lorry transporting the load."

"He shouldn't have took it in the first place. Stealing, that is."

I had to make enquiries, but I must admit a truth was dawning on me. "Who had the crate?"

Again, Hammer ignored me, keeping his beady eyes on Hayes. "A man called Clackett."

Hayes was good with hatred and spite. "Had a name, did he?"

"Yes, he did," said Hammer. "You murdered him to get information. You beat and tortured a one-armed…"

"Clackett would have given nothing away," I snapped in. "Fine fellow. And being one-eared, he most probably didn't catch all the questions."

Hammer addressed me. "He certainly was a good and loyal man." He was back to Hayes. "All you got from him was Sam the Spot."

"Never got to no Spot," said Hayes. "Well, we did, but we didn't kill him."

"No, you didn't. But you murdered Clackett."

"Aaw…" began Hayes. He did not finish his sentence. The signals zooming from his brain to his mouth were cut short by a 9mm bullet spat from Hammer's Luger.

Hammer turned to me and spoke before Hayes's head hit the deck of the submarine. "Your American cousins are more poisonous than your Saxon brothers, Hardimann. You just haven't noticed yet." He signalled with the Luger, which I'm sure was still smoking. He barked an order to the young sailor who was suffering from chattering teeth.

The young sailor saluted and sprang into action, up the conning tower like a chimpanzee up a rope, his final exertion given some assistance by the handful of machine gun-wielding sailors watching over the drama.

"A man cannot have two masters, Hardimann. Clench and Hayes had many. We'll be on our way in a minute or so once we have dispatched these two corpses," said Hammer. "Perhaps your housekeeper would like to finish her own torrid little tale. I see no reason for you to die in ignorance."

Mrs. Glendower stood an inch or so from me and launched into her story with the gusto of a professor telling his favourite Greek tale. "In 1863, Mortimer Hardimann, stuffed to the gunwales with diamonds, sailed back from Africa. A hero of the empire. My mother had just turned seventeen and was happy in her work as cook's help at Hardimann Hall. She had not yet suffered the wandering hands and intrusive loins of your uncle. The gallant and valiant Mortimer was only back home for a week, brimming over with brave tales and drunken glory…before…"

"Before he pressed his manly needs upon…had his wicked way?" I proposed.

The slap of a wet hand on a cold wet face in a snappy breeze aboard the deck of a submarine carries a hearty sting.

"Let me finish, you buffoon. If you interrupt again, I'll shove a knitting needle through your head."

I nursed the cheek with one hand, the other left cupped over what was left of my iced manhood. "You are armed? But you have no bag with you."

Mrs. Glendower stuck a hand into her clothing and whipped out a knitting needle. "I am always armed, Pelham Hardimann."

The ghastly vision of Sam the Spot supine on my Persian inked into my brain. "Pray continue," I stuttered in the hope she would deem the impediment as result of lengthy exposure to the elements and not one born of sheer panic.

Continue, she did. "Had his wicked way? Oh, yes, he certainly did. After some months of confinement my mother was back working at

184

the house, with me shipped off to London to be nursed at Uncle Mortimer's expense. When I say expense, let's just say he managed to toss the odd penny or two onto the shiny, silver collection plate... "

"He did the decent thing..."

The fist-clenched needle rocketed to my neck. Another sixteenth of an inch and it would have punctured skin. "Let me finish!" she demanded. "What do you know of the decent thing, Pelham Hardimann? He paid enough for me to be sparsely clothed and lightly fed until I was at an age to take up my position. Have you ever suffered the hardship of a workhouse?"

"I have not. Your position?" I could see the next paragraph written out and ready to be voiced, but I felt the need to show a keenness of spirit, the urge to hear the tale of woe. She was giving old Dickens a run for his money.

"Yes, Pelham, old enough to reach the sink and the washing-line with the help of a library stool. Like them young, you Hardimanns, don't you? As long as their feet touch the floor while they're sitting on the bed – another pre-requisite."

"Well, I have managed to steer clear of ..."

"Your father couldn't steer clear, could he? Before he was out of short trousers he was snapping at the heels of the maids like a sheepdog on a Welsh mountainside. Just like his uncle."

Still guarding cheek and privates, I lifted a shoulder to add some sorrow and depth of concern to my question. "You mean...?"

She hissed. "Like Uncle, like nephew, and I was next."

I shot a glance to Hammer's stern face then back to Mrs. Glendower's quivering wattle. I could not summon the nerve to eye the needle. "You mean...?"

"Twins, Pelham. Twins, and both rotten to the core. I was shipped out with the promise of a monthly stipend and a sweet little story of a loving husband dying in the Sudan. People saw me as so brave, so stoic and heroic, bringing up the sons of a hero, a dishevelled Victoria, but still the sober hand of her crapulous family."

"You mean Albert...?"

"No, Pelham, your uncle Mortimer and my mother, the abandoned once more to be abandoned, all the way down the chain, link by link."

"So Mrs. Allingham – your mother – shot my father?"

She sneered this time but gave me some hope as she pulled the needle away from my neck. "No. She shot Uncle Mortimer."

"But...?"

"She shot the portrait, you dunderhead!"

"So, my father did shoot himself. Guilt, I suppose. He must have relieved poor Mrs. Allingham – your mother – of the shotgun..."

"No, I shot him. She didn't have the courage. She was too forgiving. All the money had gone, your uncle's money that had been put in trust, your father's money, and we were about to be left penniless with my poor aged mother thrown into the street. Mother fired at the portrait. I was outside, watching through the window. She didn't notice your father. She just left the library. Oh, the look of horror on your father's face. There he was in his chair with hands gripped, mouth wide open, shaking with fear. He knew his time was up."

"So, you...but he said something about the Purdeys when getting up from the breakfast table?"

"Not the balls to top himself, no. I charged in through the kitchen door and snatched the shotgun from Mother's hands. I finished the job, finished it properly."

Searching for some decency in such dire and sombre conversation, I hitched at my Y fronts, feeling them dry with that scraping saltiness sure to start a rash. Hands stayed in their protective position. The call of nature sprang upon me. I should have relieved myself earlier, when swimming. There's something sweet and warming about a pee in the sea, is there not? This is the why most seaside-holidaymakers go beyond paddling. Rarely do they swim. If your paddler goes beyond ankle depth it is solely to wade up to the waist with arms out like wings, and pee.

I pressed on with my interrogation. "But your mother was not in the library when I discovered the...the...the murder scene."

Mrs. Glendower jabbed again with the knitting needle, adding more pressure. "Mother came back in to see what I had done, that is all. I stopped her just as you entered the library. And what did you do? You went back to your breakfast."

"Nothing worse than cold eggs and bacon. Cumberland sausage with an extra splodge of mustard, you might get away with but..."

I anticipated a '*pop*' of skin and the squirting of Hardimann blood as another ounce of muscle was added to the needle. "You callous, heartless bastard, Pelham Hardimann."

"I say, steady on."

"Did you go and find her, comfort her, or even break the news to her? No, you knew damn well she would enter the library to see what all the noise had been about. Two shots, Pelham. Her shot was vandalism. My shot was murder."

"But she died, she fainted and died."

"What did she have to live for? Her story was over."

I shifted a little. I swapped hands. This action did not relieve the pressure upon the bladder. "Why did you not come to me?"

"What? You are joking, of course. I had a plan, Pelham, a plan. Your family had sown, and I was about to reap."

"I had never set eyes on you before you came to work for me."

"My wretched sons had grown up, and being typical Hardimanns, I couldn't turn to them for comfort."

"But how did you know...you just appeared on my doorstep the day after I had posted my card to the agency requesting a housekeeper."

"Exactly," said Mrs. Glendower. "Just as I happened to turn up at the Hardimann estate one day to find my poor exasperated mother standing in the library delivering the shotgun to your father."

"And Sam the Spot? What harm had he done you?"

She sniffed the brisk salty air and shot a look towards Hammer. "Ask him."

Hammer cut in. "That's enough."

An almighty crash of metal on metal broke through the chilly air.

"But I..." I started as I turned to see the young sailor coming down the conning tower. Once landed, he dragged the small piles of chains – the chains he'd tossed from the conning tower – across to the dead hoodlums.

"Enough, step away from each other," said Hammer.

Mrs. Glendower removed the knitting needle from my skin, giving me the opportunity to squeeze the knees together, hop, and wriggle a little more. She bared teeth with a hurtful grin. "Need the lavatory, Pelham?"

"Don't worry," said Hammer. "Relief is on the way. Mother, take your friend and get aboard the fishing boat. You will be met in Cherbourg. Think yourself lucky you are not to be shot for treason."

"Or murder," I chipped in. I received another slap, fortunately with the hand free of needle.

Hammer called to the conning tower as behind me the sailor wound the chains around four legs. There was a splosh and the corpses were gone. The sailor turned to Hammer for orders, orders that Hammer gave with the confidence of a man who'd given so many before.

"You're about to dive?" I asked.

"I am about to dive. You are about to die." He pointed the Luger at Mrs. Glendower then at her friend, fake Stalin. "Go, get on the boat."

Mrs. Glendower and her friend marched across the deck of the U-boat and reached up to the outstretched hands ready to haul them up and away, to France.

Hammer bent and picked up the suitcase. "Are you ready, sir?" he asked with gentlemanliness in his tone.

I watched the sailor scramble back up the conning tower. The other sailors had gone. The fishing boat belched diesel smoke and growled away. I stuck my hands in the air.

"Stand nearer the edge, if you would be so kind, sir."

I shuffled to the edge of the U-boat. "You realize Britain will fight to the last man, Hammer. I suggest you keep that in mind."

"Her mistake, whether against the Fatherland or the United States, will be to fight for her empire."

"The sun will never set..."

"Twilight already, I'm afraid. That greed for power and influence, that self-indulgence will be her undoing. Turn around, sir. Look out to sea."

I turned and heard the click of the Luger's hammer.

Out at sea, perhaps four or five hundred yards away, was Studely. He was running up and down the length of the drifting lifeboat. Halfway on each run he stopped and threw up his arms. Waving in despair, or just responding to my lifted arms, I had no idea.

"Look at that fool," said Hammer acidly. "Your Sancho Panza. I closed the fuel line as soon as we pulled alongside this vessel, just in case anyone tried to escape. He hasn't the wit to work that out. Planning, sir. It's all about planning."

"Fool, he may be, Hammer, but he is loyal."

He could not, and did not, deny that truth. "Any last requests, sir?" he asked. "I feel I owe you that much. You were, after all, somewhat press-ganged into...this affair."

I closed my eyes and waited. "Nothing, Hammer. Though perhaps if I could for once have the last word..."

Two shots rang out.

CHAPTER 22
THAT SINKING FEELING AND THE NORMANDY LANDINGS

I beg you to extend some forgiveness here if I am a little vague as to what happened next. You understand the pressures under which I had been subjected.

With my eyes clam-like, I felt low rumblings beneath my feet as the cold air whipped around my body. I welcomed the tickling at my toes, ankles, shins, thighs and upwards until blessed relief.

When I opened my peepers the flat steel deck of the submarine had disappeared and the conning tower was dipping beneath the surface, missing me by only a few feet. It was fortunate that I did not catch the now warmed and wetted Y fronts on the periscope.

Hammer and his chums were heading for the depths where they deserved to lie in perpetuate, as I'm sure you'll agree. That Cavity Maggie thing and the plans of Mr. Whittle within that little red suitcase would rot with them, but if truth be told it was clear I had failed. Hammer was taking the strangely scenic route to Berlin.

As for your hero, he would not be able to return to England's shores with head held high; his one-way ticket to Coventry was purchased and officially stamped.

After succumbing to the sinking feeling I recognized the need to get the old arms and legs swishing about.

I heard Studely's call before I caught flashes of the lengthy lifeboat, but I did not have wind to call out in reply. I had to swim, and swim as I had never swum before, in the hope he would not lose me in the channel. I could have taken a shorter route and headed for France, but I wished for English sand, soil, and grass, her meadows.

I was flagging within minutes. I passed out. There was no great white light, just a mental toss up as to my destination, heaven or hell, and perhaps worst of all, nothingness.

I came to with a throbbing head, my arms flapping about, a hefty weight on my torso, and the lunar-like face of Studely zooming towards me. The puckered lips nudged me away from the heaven route and prodded me toward hell.

I spluttered salty channel. "Stone the flippin' crows, Studely. What in the name of all that's holy are you...?"

He let go my arms and rolled away. "Sorry, Hardimann, I thought you was a goner."

I hitched myself up onto my elbows to get my head from the bottom of the boat. "A handshake or, should you feel the tide of your emotions swelling above the coastal defences, a hearty slap on the back would have sufficed."

Studely sat back, his frame slumped against the hull of the lifeboat. "I thought you was drowned. I was trying that..."

"I know what you were trying, Studely. Such things should not be ventured. It is best to leave well alone with your manliness, and mine, intact. Stick with the windmilling arms and the pressing, by all means, but..."

He sulked. "Don't know why I bothered."

His sullen face did not exactly warm the cockles or melt the heart, but I felt I had been remiss. I dragged myself up a little more and gave him a couple of pats on the nearest knee. "You bothered because you are a fine fellow. We have spent a few moons surrounded by villainy, inhumanity, greed, and the coarse dehumanization of social engineering. It has darkened my soul and blurred my vision. You have remained straight as a die."

"You what?" he enquired as he rolled forward to lay his hands upon the hull opposite him. He stuck a finger into a hole and opened a cupboard beneath the bench seat, from which he pulled out a couple of thick, rough blankets. "Here, you better get yourself warmed up."

I took the blankets. They itched like hell, but my shivering slowed. "A warm coffee would not be refused, Studely," I offered. "I'm even tempted to cup my hands around a steaming mug of Ovaltine."

"Nothing doing. I've had a rummage around already."

"Shame," I said. "You'd expect a slab of Kendal Mint Cake to keep up the energy levels, wouldn't you?"

"That's for mountains."

"Correct, again you are correct." I gave my thighs a slap as I stood up to get a panoramic view of the sea. "A day or so to England?" I asked as I tugged at my Y fronts. The drying salt was starting to do its nasty work. "Need a bath and some soft clothing."

"You ain't the only one who's wet. I fell in and all. Managed to get back into the boat though."

"Yes, Studely, it would appear so."

"The thing is, Hardimann," Studely began with a low and heavy voice of seriousness and deepest thought. "The thing is, do we have enough fuel to get to England and do we know which way to go?"

"As for fuel, I have no idea, but surely, north is the only thing we need to know. You have a compass?"

Studely surrendered a glum "nope." He folded his arms and kicked at the hull. "Dover to Calais is easy because you can see each coast, but we could end up missing England altogether if we veer off course. It's the tides. And," he added with some vigour and a flick of a finger, "if the weather cuts up rough, we could be dashed against the rocks."

"I suggest we go full steam ahead and charge upon a French beach, Studely. Tell me, as a member of His Majesty's Constabulary, do you have any judicial powers in Normandy?"

He shook his head again and rewarded me with another "*nope*." With that said he stepped to the stern and revved up the engine.

Upon regaining my balance, I shouted a question. "So, you managed to get her going, Studely?"

"Get her going?" he called back with one hand on the tiller and another cupped around an ear.

"Hammer closed the fuel line."

"I know. I saw him do it. Took a while to get her going again though, air in the pipes or something."

"Strange, don't you think?" I quizzed him as I made my unsteady way to the stern. I plonked onto a seat, wrapped the blankets tighter and kept my head down. "It's strange he didn't just shoot us dead, the way he shot poor Clenchy and Hayes."

"They deserved it."

I was a little shocked by such concrete conviction. "But playing judge, jury, and hangman is a little extreme and requires a certain propensity to cold-blooded murder, don't you think?"

"Extreme situation. Besides, if they ever find the bodies, you know who they'll blame?"

"Who?"

"You."

I am not a gulper, but I gulped like a booby with eyes too big for its beak. "I suppose you are right."

"I would say…" Studely began as he pressed an elbow hard on the tiller and creased up in such a way as to make it possible to undo his boots.

"What would you say?"

"He wanted you, us, to live. You, certainly."

"He didn't even shout '*dive!*' Why me?"

"Relationships, relations I suppose." Studely unbuttoned his braces. With some niftiness he removed his trousers then his tunic before shoving a hand back on the tiller. "He is your brother, or cousin, or something." He nestled down next to me where we could, stretching from time to time, get a view over the prow and watch the enlarging coast of France.

"Not what I'd class as a special relationship. And you knew about…"

"Mrs. Glendower gave me some story on the train, when you was asleep, after you dozed off…you know…some of it. I worked out the rest."

"The blood not thicker, just leaving a more stubborn stain, wouldn't you say?" I said.

"Could be. Must mean something. You shot him."

"Yes, I did," I said, recalling the moment I'd stuck my cane through the knitted throng on Queen Mary and let off a round. "Didn't leave much of a mark though, did it?"

"Not enough powder in the rounds, but it left a bit of a dent in his flask."

"His flask?"

"Yes," said Studely, craning his neck. "Hold the tiller so I can get me boots back on. Running up a beach in long-johns is one thing but I hate sand between me toes."

I took hold of the tiller. "He was saved by his hip flask. Well, well," I muttered. "You'd have thought he'd pop some lead into me just for that. Another shot of lead for the death of his twin would also have been forthcoming…"

"No love lost there. What I think is strange," said Studely pulling at his laces, "is how he got everyone, all the crew, back into the submarine before firing those two shots. It's like he wanted them to think he shot you dead. It's like he didn't want them to see what he didn't do but should have done."

"Perhaps he just changed his mind and considered drowning a more sadistic revenge."

"Might be that." Studely stood up and took back control of the tiller. "Better brace yourself. I'm gonna run her up onto the beach. With any luck we can keep dry. We're not far off now."

Studely, no great whistler, hummed a tune then whistled, soon to wander into the words. "*And a hay harvest breeze, blade on the feather, shade off the trees…and we all swing together, with our bollocks between our knees…*"

"I'd rather you didn't, Studely."

"Sorry, Hardimann," he said. "Missing a few notes, am I?"

"Not at all, old chap," I told him. "It's just that…"

"Memories, eh? Mind how you go."

We hit the beach. The jolt sent us careening almost the full length of the lifeboat. We managed to hop, skip, and jump along the seating planks to gain some control before flying onto the soft dry sand.

"Lucky the tide's up," I said as I lifted my face from the sand and blew grains from my nose. "Lucky we are on a French beach as well."

Studely rolled onto his back and studied the grey sky. "Lucky?"

"Of course." I heaved over onto my side and rested my head on a tucked-in arm. "Consider how it would be were we to arrive almost naked on an English beach at this time of the morning."

"Get arrested, I suppose."

"Not that," I advised. "The beach is empty. Not a soul in sight and no sign of human life at all, apart from that set of footprints over there on the harder sand."

"Too cold for bathing."

"Absolutely, but you can bet your bottom dollar that on an English beach there would be some masochistic maniac taking a bracing dip. There would also be a parade of stick-chucking dog-walkers leaning against an oncoming gale."

Studely let out a sigh and patted his stomach. "I'm starving. I could eat a horse."

"And there is another plus," I added as I gazed about. "We must scramble up that cliff and see what's the other side. There may be a smallholding." I watched him fidget for a while. "Having trouble?"

"My revolver, Hardimann. It's creeping down me leg, and it's bleedin' cold."

I looked away to allow the man some privacy as he fumbled in his nether regions to retrieve the weapon. "Well, once you've sorted yourself out we'd better get moving. We can't remain here for eternity." I was about to slap flat palms down onto the sand to push myself up and onto my feet when a wave rushed up and swamped us. We wriggled and jiggled, Studely fell onto me and jabbed a knee into my groin. We disentangled then crawled like crabs farther up the beach and onto dry sand just yards from the foot of the cliff. "That's just dandy," I exclaimed, trying to rub the beach from my body. "Just when I thought I was safely dry." The shaking commenced. "Why the hell people come here for their holidays is beyond me. We are in a blizzard of cutting wind and flailing sand."

Studely rose like a monster from the deep, wet sand covering him from head to toe. "Have to go back into the water to get clean," he grumbled as he studied the short gush then the droplets falling from his revolver. "This is buggered."

The cliff was a gentle, muddy slope and we conquered it within a matter of minutes, despite the occasional slide and wayward drift. The summit gave us a reasonable vista, out to sea where the fishing smacks did their stuff, then back round across a thin road on the other side of which were small fields dotted by the odd farmhouse.

I could also make out the shape of a small beached motor launch some hundred yards or so away. "Didn't see that from the beach."

"Other side of those rocks," said Studely. "So they couldn't have seen us, which is good."

"Correct again. Your old lemon is working well this morning despite the trials we have undergone. We can rap upon a door and beg for victuals. We deserve wholesome sustenance," I said as I skipped down the grassy bank onto the sharp stones of the lane. "Ouch! Some shoes would brighten the morning."

"And clothes," moaned my right-hand man as he braked beside me.

"While I can understand your consternation, Studely, you seem to forget that you are wearing more than me." It occurred to me at that moment that I had left many a rough but warming blanket down in the lifeboat. I was about to mention the fact when Studely cut in.

"Something coming."

He was not mistaken. Skimming across the top of a hedge was the black shiny roof of a vehicle, the 'phut-phut' of it getting louder. Eventually, for it was not going at record-breaking speed, around a tight bend came the gleaming radiator then the fire-engine red coachwork of a sit-up-and-beg Rosengart LR4.

I stepped into the middle of the lane with arms waving. Studely, no doubt feeling the barrier needed some fortification, joined me.

The brakes let out a gritty squeal as the vehicle swerved, leaving only inches of air between the hedgerows before it came to a skidding halt with the bumper but a finger-nail's width from my shins.

The driver, judging by the nearness of his nose to the steering wheel, was a short fellow. His face was round with that redness we associate with jolly farmers, country yokels, and the tellers of long fishermen's yarns. He was making strange noises. His shoulders jiggled up and down, the mouth opened and closed at great speed, and flecks of spittle splashed upon the windscreen. Fist shaking began.

"He's not happy, Studely," I said across the bonnet as I edged my way around a front wing to see if the driver was willing to drag down his window and converse.

"Got my revolver on me," Studely said. "I can stick it in his face, pull back the hammer and…"

"…drip seawater down his shirt? Just stand in front of the car."

The driver's window came down with a clunk. "*Sortez de la route, vous l'homme fou. Que voulez-vous?*" the driver ordered then asked with added animation. A stubby half-inch of Gitanes or Gauloise wobbled on his bottom lip and fumes drifted up into a watery eye.

"Awfully sorry," I began, knowing a bit of the old plum-in-the-mouth at full volume puts a foreign Johnny at ease when confronted by an Englishman. They expect it of us. We must play the stereotype.

"*Sortez de ma voie!*"

194

"Relax, old boy," I continued. "We are only seeking help, some clothing and a modest nosebag. We have suffered trials and would view aid with tribulation."

"*Ainsi vous êtes l'anglais. Pervers anglais!*"

I saw a chink of light. "Yes, English, *nous sommes* a pair of English."

"*Une paire de pervers anglais jouant sur la plage. Le sport anglais de flagellation, je suppose.*" He flicked fingers from Adam"s apple to chin. "*Pervers! Mon Dieu! Pervers!*"

"Ah, Father Green," I said, giving that inane grin one has to offer to those lacking in the English tongue; it is amazing how near our own shores the white man's burden has to be carried. I called across the bonnet to Studely. "Father Green, a man of God taking the morning air in mufti. Lady Luck has smiled on us. The charity of the all-embracing church has come to the rescue."

"Institutionalised bible-bashing and buggery, if you ask me," retorted Studely, rather uncharitably, I thought. "Get 'im out the car."

This was a side of Studely that had not so far come to light and I promised myself that I would, when the dust had settled, take it upon myself to dig into this gloomy chasm of his character. Putting away childish things does not only refer to the toys and games of callow times when we lower the voice and grow the stubble; we must also discard the horrors.

I chanced another stab at the driver. "*Bonjour,* and a fine morning to you." I leaned into the window and shoved godliness into my tone. "I feel we must fall upon your charity, your mercy."

"*Que? Que fait-il avec ce fusil? Sont vous les voleurs?*"

"Just some old clothes and a pair of sturdy walking shoes will suffice, dear fellow," I answered. "Naturally, should your housekeeper push a bowl of steaming onion soup across the rough-hewn vicarage table...a stick of bread and a wedge of Camembert..."

He seemed to be getting the gist. "*Vous me montrez un fusil pour voler le camembert? Ce n'est pas étonnant vous avez eu besoin des allemands pour vous aider à Waterloo. Vous êtes insensés.*"

"Eat, in a sense. A baguette, a wedge of Camembert, some onion soup. Waterloo?" I pulled back and looked across the roof of the Rosengart to give Studely, who had made his way to the passenger door, the good news. "Clothing and wholesome food is nearing us, Studely, and perchance, should I know the French, a decent table wine, the sort they don't export because they like to keep it for themselves." I dropped down a little to thank the driver for his promised donations. "Very decent of you, old chap, though I feel you should lay off the Waterloo thing. A long time ago, you know. Let bygones be bygones and all that. A country that wallows in the muddy nostalgia of lost empires soon finds itself wearing heavy boots."

He wasn't looking at me. He wasn't being rude – none of that Parisian stuff. Never regard a Parisian as a Frenchman: a different brush with different tar altogether. He wasn't ignoring me. Judging by the view I had of the back of his head I immediately ascertained he had his eyes fixed on Studely. Let us be accurate here. He had his eyes fixed on the spout of Studely's service revolver. His dog-end shot from his bottom lip and smacked the windscreen as his fingers stabbed the roof. *"Je capitule!"*

"Studely," I sighed through the window. "There's no need for that. I was pulling the man our way. He was relenting, offering. He was in the palm of my hand."

Studely lowered a little for us to face each other as we conversed. "How can we trust him?"

The driver had the decency to lean back a little with his head doing that left and right thing your tennis fan does – even when there is a fault one end and no chance of the ball shooting back over the net.

"Why shouldn't we trust him, Studely?"

"He's a frog. Bit of a coincidence him driving along here when we arrived on the beach, don't you think?"

"I'm sure he comes this way every day. Matins and all that."

The driver smiled and nodded. *"Oui, matines."*

Studely pressed. "What if Hammer signalled to him?"

"And why should he?" I asked.

"In case we made it to the beach."

"Enough, Studely. Get in the car. The fellow can drive us to the church. There are sure to be some clothes there. It's still early in the morning and we may travel unseen. Only farmers around here, and they'll be in their fields."

The driver smiled and I wondered if he was keeping score. His smile shifted to shock as Studely squeezed behind the tilted front passenger seat and into the back seats. Studely kept the pressure up by tapping the muzzle of the revolver against the driver's temple. "Won't keep you long, mate."

"Que faites-vous? Sortez de ma voiture. Je ne vous prends pas n'importe où."

"To the church," I called out as I skirted round the front of the car and to the passenger door. I hopped in and slammed the door, causing the window to drop with a clatter. "Sorry."

The driver did that French thing with his mouth; it's difficult to explain. I think it can be best described as that lippy thing a horse does while demonstrating the shot from a bottle of Sarson's.

I struggled to pinch the top of the window between my fingertips and pull it up but it wasn't giving way. As I busied myself this way the driver flung open his door and rolled out onto the road, ending up jammed into the hedge.

"What on earth...?" I looked back to Studely. "What did you do?"

"I just stuck my revolver in his ear. I was trying to get him going. I'm freezing here and..."

I was out of the car in a flash to run around and help the man from the hedge. "You frightened the life out of him, Studely. He near jumped out of his skin." I grabbed the driver by the elbow and began tugging.

"Jumping out of his togs as well," said Studely.

Perhaps tugging was not a good idea. As I straightened, I found I had removed his jacket, or at least assisted him in the removal of it. There was no complaint. Sitting, with his back in the hedge, the fellow unlaced his boots then wriggled to remove his trousers.

"*Voila! Prenez-les et laissez-moi la paix,*" he shouted as he launched a boot at Studely who by this time had popped out of the jalopy, still brandishing the revolver. "*Allez, allez, vous les bâtards anglais, vous corrompez, vous les voleur.*" Off came the heavy woollen scarf, followed by a collarless cotton shirt.

"Ha ha, clothes," said Studely triumphantly. "They'll fit me."

"You can't purloin the man's clothes, Studely."

My plump companion – clothed only in his cotton long-johns, vest, and boots – waved the revolver at the strewn garments. "It ain't stealing, he's offering them to me."

"To us," I corrected.

"They're not gonna fit you, are they? He's just my size, and you...a bean pole. You can have the scarf."

I shivered in my jockeys, cupping a little against the brisk breeze nipping down the lane. I eyed the boots. Disappointment did not take long to quash burgeoning hope. I could see they were far too small. "We have nothing to offer him in return," I piped up. "We have to do the decent thing."

Studely filled a trouser leg. "These is desperate times, Hardimann. Besides, he's not far from home. I expect he'll be back on the farm in the wink of an eye." He hopped and filled the other trouser leg.

"And alert the gendarmerie. They are armed, you know? The farm?"

"We'll be far away by then." Studely swept up the shirt and donned it with the ease of a man slipping into something comfortable after relaxing in a hot tub. "He ain't no priest. He's a farmer. Look at them boots...look at them hands."

"Well, that makes it all the more..."

"No such thing as a poor farmer." To add an exclamation mark to the remark, Studely pulled at his new braces and let them thwack against his ample torso.

As he swapped revolver from hand to hand, put on the jacket and pulled here and there to check the fit – with some pleasure – I looked down at the farmer crouching in his hedge and considered my own actions. Here, I had been the thieving partner arguing over the spoils when the spoils would be of no use to me. Had they been of use to me, would I have been so adamant in my condemnation of Studely's ill-gotten gains? Who is to know?

I was offering some gesture, an apology I suppose, to the stricken farmer – although I was still the least dressed – with shrugs and open hands when something caught my eye.

My first thought was...it's a crow, a rook, one of those big black birds...

Perhaps it was the noise that made me turn my head.

CHAPTER 23
FRENCH LEAVE

"And you can drive one?" asked Studely as he bounced, his head knocking out a wobbly rhythm on the canvas roof of the Rosengart, the squeal of squashed springs adding melody.

"The word is pilot, Studely. Pilot."

He chanced a speedy turn of the head to grin at me. "And you're sure it was an aeroplane, not a lolling crow looking for morning snails?"

"Morning snails on thorns?" I tapped an impatient hand on the fascia just as Studely jerked the wheel to get the thin tyres out of a rut. "It was an aeroplane, Studely. There's an airfield nearby. Judging by the speed and angle of the crate, there must be."

Studely crashed gears as we hit the top of a hill. He aimed for the apex of the bend and stamped a boot down on the accelerator.

I let out a gentle, but staccato murmur of hope and satisfaction. "I'll soon have you back on England's green and pleasant…"

Studely screamed.

I shouted. "Stop!"

Studely hit the brakes, we skidded for twenty yards and spun to a grinding halt across a gateway. After falling back from the windscreen and slapping back into his seat, Studely spent a few seconds stroking his forehead.

"Injuries?"

"Just another bump. That's a lot of bulls."

"They are cows, Studely, cows," I informed the man as the herd closed in around us like a low rain-stuffed cloud bullying a mountain top.

"They got ruddy horns."

"*Froment du Léon*, Studely," I advised as bovine steam misted my window. "Pretty little things, aren't they? Look at those lovely white rings around the eyes, and the lashes…remind me of… Many a farmer will keep two or three of them in a herd to boost the fat content of the milk. Good meat as well."

Studely fiddled with his revolver. "I'm starving. We won't get around them."

199

I shouldered my door to find it barred by tan flanks. "No need to. We can ankle our way across this field. There's a windsock in the next one. Shift over."

"Can't budge. We're jammed in." Studely flinched as a horn prodded into the vehicle. "Buggerin'..."

"Toot."

"Toot?"

"Yes. Toot." I leaned over and jabbed at the klaxon. There was no withering blast: just a useless parp.

Studely growled. "Now what?"

"Sunroof."

He looked up and smiled. "Posh motor for a farmer."

"Praise be, they are rich," I added to his observation as I grabbed the roof handle and twisted.

After a scramble through the roof we used the backs of the odd cow or three as shifting stepping-stones before launching ourselves over the five-bar gate into the field. Studely landed well and advertised the fact with pumping arms and volleys of *'yes', 'yes.'* I made a mental note that in a quieter moment I should address the issue of magnanimity with the fellow.

I let off a variety of sucking noises as I unfolded from the emulsion of Normandy earth and fluid *Froment du Léon* dung.

"The mud is always worse by the gate," said Studely with the air of authority one gets from an idiot who's just finished reading his first book and delights in the fresh knowledge he now has to bestow on lesser men. "At least your underpants don't show up so much."

"Thank you for that, Studely," I said as I scissored and slid, stiff-legged with arms outstretched like Dr. Frankenstein's homemade chum, to firmer and less muddied grass.

The sky was clear now apart from some wisps of high, scudding clouds, and the air was warm enough to brush away the sharp chill I'd suffered on the lifeboat and beach. The dewy moss played soft on my tender plates – much of a relief after the grit of the road – but the silver lining had a cloud – thistles and nettles. I looked across the field and judged a diagonal march would bring us to the edge of the airfield within five minutes. In the distance, some way past the windsock, was the roof of what must be the shack of an office and the longer roofs of small hangars. I pulled back the shoulders, drew the stomach in – it doesn't have far to go – filled the lungs and thrust a spurring-on arm to show Studely our goal. "Come, Studely. Let's get on with it."

I marched, the gazelle barely bending blade or stalk.

Studely was heavy of foot. "I'm ruddy famished," he whined at the back of my head. "That man could of fed us."

I didn't turn. I have a clear voice and can project like a Shakespearean warming to the riotous stinkards. "Could *have* fed us, Studely, could *have*."

"Exactly."

"You were in your undergarments as you shoved a pistol in his face, Studely, and the man was to infer only one thing from such an action. Plus," I reinforced with a finger like a sea-dog checking the wind before tipping the swill bucket overboard, "owing to the lack of support offered by your discarded constable's tunic, the rotundity of your belly would signal to all onlookers that you are a well-nourished man. One cannot blame him for believing that all you required from him was his rustic apparel. He was not to know you wished to be fed."

"Well I'm bloody fed up now."

I halted between two pats, did a skittish about-turn with fists firm on the hips, and confronted my subordinate. "Is this the Studely, man of the hour who exchanged blows with hoodlums, pulled me from the tracks and dragged me from the clutches of Davy Jones' Locker?"

Studely kicked at some dandelions. "I'm cold and hungry."

"You are warmly clothed and overweight. A brisk march on minimum rations will do you good."

"No rations. I haven't eaten since..." He did that twirling around the finger thing with his revolver as he did his calculations. "Since..."

"Since dining on Queen Mary with Mrs. Glendower," I prompted. He was still twirling so I held out a hand and patted him on the shoulder. "Come on, Hoot Gibson, we'll soon be back in Blighty, eyeing the waitresses and hollering for more chop sauce."

He looked up. "Hoot Gibson?"

The pat I gave him was followed by a friendly punch. "Yes, surely you remember, *Pride of the Range, His Only Son...*"

"He crashed his plane in a race."

A truth dawned upon me. Never let it be said that I cannot root out a man's fears and phobias; it is a skill to arm the ally and disarm the foe. "We won't be racing as he was, Studely. It'll be a jaunt, a hop over the channel in bright blue skies with the sun behind us as it dapples gold on grey waves."

Had I won him over? He lay off the dandelions and took a kick at an innocent looking *Dactylorhiza maculata*. "And you can drive...fly?"

"I did some hours in my younger days, Studely. Sop Pups, Sop Camels..."

He stilled but would not look me in the eye. "On the western front? More people died learning to fly them than got shot down..."

"Absolutely. Seat of the pants stuff, I can tell you."

He made to move away. "Well, seat of your pants is all you got now, innit?"

"Very droll, Studely," I said as I quickened the pace. "Let's see if there's an old crate we can use, something I can fly. It's a bit like riding a horse, you know?"

He stopped. "You know the penalty for rustling?"

"Be that as it may, we can't stay standing in the middle of this meadow no matter how glorious it looks. We must make haste. Lives are at stake."

"Lives?"

"Important lives, Studely." I flicked and scraped at the dried mud of my underpants. "Hammer implied there is a plot afoot to assassinate the one man in England feared by Hitler."

"The plotter?"

"Quill, it had to be Quill, who else but Quill?" I said with certainty. "Remember Hammer's comment about the other bomb? It can't be Hammer. He is playing Captain Nemo. My guess is Quill has already planted the explosives. We must get back to find them."

"I know Hayes and Clench murdered your old friend Clackett, Hardimann, but what about Sam the Spot?" asked Studely with a squint of surliness. "Those knitting needles."

The second dawning of the day came to rest upon me. "So that is what all this foot-dragging is about, is it? Mrs. Glendower."

"I don't know what you mean."

"I think you do, Studely, and now is the time to get down to brass tacks. Mrs. Glendower, your aunt?"

I must admit there was some foreboding in my question. I had recently acquired – or found – two long lost relatives, both of whom I could eye with nothing but contempt, and I was in no mood to learn of another no matter how worthy a man Studely may be.

His confession needed walking pace, which I counted as a bonus. We were moving, but most importantly, I didn't have to look the man in the eye. There's nothing worse than looking a fellow in the eye when he's spilling his all, opening his heart and all that malarkey. I dread the day when the Englishman feels the need to weep and wallow in the sickly fragrance oozing from the heaped bouquets of grief. That E. M. Forster chap got it all wrong, you know: all that guff about the English having untrained hearts. The Englishman has a trained heart and a trained heart keeps the lachrymose at bay. Be that as it may, never let it be said I am not ready to listen when a fellow human being has things to remove from his stricken chest and the need to shove the heart upon a sleeve like a scouting badge.

"So, explain all, Studely. Keep it trim. I am all ears."

"Wait."

I stopped and displayed some leaking of temper with some chivvying.

Studely fussed with jacket pockets. "That farmer bloke was smoking, wasn't he?"

"His vehicle was pungent, I'll admit that."

With the grin of a young magician who'd perfected his first act after months of rigorous training, Studely pulled a packet of smokes and a box of matches from the pockets.

"Good man, Studely. You see, the gods are looking upon us." I took one from the packet and we shared a match. "A smoke each will feed us well until we get beyond the windsock."

We moved on and Studely opened the pages of his history with Mrs. Glendower. "She's not really an aunt. She was a sort of aunt. I hadn't seen her for about ten years."

"You knew Hammer and Quill?"

"You gonna let me tell the story or what?"

"Tell, Studely, I shall keep mum."

"She was a sort of aunt who looked after me when I was a kid, when my mother was working at the kilns. She was a filleter and barrel packer, because my father – her husband – left us and never came back."

"A smoker, Studely," I mumbled. I'm not sure if he heard me. I called back a little louder to lift his spirits. "What I'd do for a plate of fine oaky kippers. Even a bloater or buckling would not be pushed aside."

"They was salmon," he snapped before suffering a coughing fit. He stamped and jumped the pollution from his lungs before retrieving his stride. "Days and nights, she used to work. Mrs. Glendower…"

"Aunt Phyllis…"

"Aunt Phyllis would do me breakfast and tea. When I asked about her husband…when I asked about her husband, she told me he got struck down with the cholera in India."

"Happened to many, Studely."

"She had enough money to get by, a pension and that, but she always needed a few extra coppers so as to get her twins educated."

I spat loose tobacco from my bottom lip and swerved to miss a bushy thistle. "The twins being Hammer and Quill?"

"They was twenty years older than me at that time…"

"Perhaps still twenty years older…"

"I didn't see them much. Hammer…"

"His real name, Studely?

"Quentin."

I didn't smirk. Well, if I did, Studely did not see it because I was making good speed some yards ahead, making a beeline for the corner of the field.

"He changed his surname name to Hammer because…when he joined the expeditionary forces."

"And Quill?" I called out, letting the question float behind me on the gentle breeze flowing from distant hills.

"Nasty piece of work. A bully. Used to pull me ears."

I couldn't say for sure but there was the distinct thwacking sound of Studely's boot taking it out on impudent flora that had the audacity to smile at him.

"Good copper material, would you say, Studely? The sort of chap who loves to meet and beat?"

"He signed up as soon as he could and passed all sorts of exams. One thing about Aunt Phyllis, she was one for educating her sprogs."

"But not you. You, the son of a..."

"My mother was a kindly soul, Hardimann. A kindly soul, as was Aunt Phyllis really. She was nice to me."

"But Quill was..."

"Called me a runt."

"Ah," I said as I corrected my bearings. "We bind the adult with the words we use to clothe the child."

"I joined the force as soon as I could, but I couldn't pass no exams."

"Any, Studely, couldn't pass any."

"Right, none."

We stopped in the corner of the field and leaned against posts as we finished our gaspers. Studely continued with his tale as I studied the scene in the next field.

There was not a soul to be seen, which was surprising for what was promising to be a good flying day, but there were some crates sitting about. I noticed a couple of Gloster Gauntlets over in a corner tucked in-between a bevy of Amiot 143s. "Well, there are some craft there, Studely. We have wings at our disposal."

We stamped our dog-ends into the sod. Well, Studely did the stamping, I just flicked.

"Quentin went into service after the war. I think he liked all that dressing up smart, wearing black clothes and bow ties...knowing all them posh wines and stuff."

"Let us hope they are sufficiently fuelled," I said as I began a wobbly attempt to get into the next field.

"Quill went up through the ranks very quick. He got promotion quicker than I got socks."

I pressed down on the barbed wire and lifted a leg over before staggering and hopping until the other leg was free from peril. "We will have to use the private planes, Studely. Can't chance flying across the South Downs waving French colours."

"He was on the fiddle, always getting bungs from the pubs and gambling dens."

I looked across the hundred yards or so to the first building. "Let's have a butcher's in the hut first. There's bound to be something useful to us, me especially, such as a flying suit and a pair of boots and gloves."

"He stitched up a few an" all. Surprised he didn't get your friend Sam slammed up. But then again..." Studely continued as he climbed over the barbed wire. "...I know Sam used to bung him fivers to keep him sweet."

"Come on, we are but yards from home now."

"Quentin sent Aunt Phyllis money from time to time, but Quill... he never sent nothing, the skinflint."

The wooden hut was small and square, like something a weekender would hire on a Hampshire beach in order to poison himself with a leaky primus stove while waiting for some flatfish to come fluttering by. I peered through the square four-paned window at the side to see a small desk with lamp and charts. Hanging from nails were jackets and flying suits. Beneath these garments was a selection of boots. I sank back from my peeking stance and smiled with satisfaction. "We are in luck."

"Oh," said Studely. "So, we really are gonna fly."

"You will be home before lunch. All we need to do is get in."

"You go in. I'm staying out here," he said. "I'll have me last smoke, if you don't mind."

With 'oh ye of little faith' almost spilling from my pursed lips I made my way around to the hut door and shouldered it. I was swift to regain an upright position and ran an eye along the selection of flying suits. I picked a blue one and it fitted me well. I was heaving on the second boot with my back pressed against a wall when there came a tap at the window.

Studely's nose was squashed against the said window. "See if they've got some of them life saver things, you know, the ones you blow up. And parachutes."

I banged the wooden wall with the back of my head, gave another heave to become fully shod, and stuck my face to the window. "Studely, we shall not crash into the sea." Chance of crashing into a white cliff, I thought. I chose a fleece-lined flying jacket and it fitted me well. I exited the little hut and made my way around to the back to find Studely sucking hard on his condemned-man's Gauloise. I pulled on the pair of gauntlets I'd swiped from the ops. desk. "Ready for the off?"

"Suppose so. You think Aunt Phyllis murdered Sam the Spot, don't you?"

My shoulders dropped. "Studely, I have no idea. For all I know it could have been Quill...could have been Hammer."

"Quentin."

"I refuse to call him Quentin, Studely. We met as his being a Hammer and we parted company as his being a Hammer. Hammer he shall remain.

Anyway, for all I know, Hayes or Clenchy could have done the needle trick on Sam."

"They said they didn't."

"And you believe every word they said?"

We made our way across the field and past the small hangars to the array of aircraft. I did my *'eeny, meeny, miny, moe, please sit down it's time to go'* until my eyes fell upon an old favourite with spats. "A Westland Lysander," I said, adding a leathery gauntlet clap. "Just the ticket. Short take off, short landing, and can be piloted by an idiot."

"Things are lookin' up."

"Sorry, Studely?"

"When will we get up?"

"Soon. A piece of cake. All we have to do is…"

My explanations were cut short by the thunder of an 890hp Bristol Mercury XII radial engine, the swish of a spinning propeller, and the bronchial spluttering of exhausts.

"Buggerin' 'ell," exclaimed Studely. "Someone's in it."

"Your revolver," I snapped. I whipped off my right gauntlet. "Hand me your revolver."

"But it's going, it's moving,"

"He's just taxiing his way through the other crates to get to the end of the field. Give me…" The revolver was slapped into my ready palm. "Keep up, Studely, you'll have to get in first while I negotiate. Get your headset on as soon as you can."

"Negotiate? Headset?"

"Yes," I said, sprinting. "There's a fuel tank between pilot and navigator. We'll have to communicate…looks like she's got two twenty-pound bombs under her."

We reached the taxiing Lysander within ten seconds and I soon had a hand on a wing strut and a boot on a spat. I shoved back the rear cockpit canopy just before Studely leapt up and gripped the fuselage, just behind the wing.

Balancing precariously, I pushed the revolver into the open front cockpit. "A lovely morning," I declared to a fresh face with rosy cheeks.

The middle-aged pilot went into a bit of a grounded spin. I held well with my boots jammed tightly between the wing struts and my gunless arm wedged through the ladder-like sidebars of the cockpit.

"*Oh, mon Dieu, pas un autre,*" shouted the pilot as he eyed me then owled his neck to see who owned the fingers behind him.

I poked at him with the revolver. "Come on, out you get. Defenestrate!" I liked that and had to smile although the wind from the propeller made it something on the macabre side, or so I would imagine.

"*Qu'est-ce qu'arrive ce matin? Se trouve présent une guerre?*"

I shouted above the roar of the engine. "You'll get it back. I'll deliver it, air mail. Out you get."

"*D'abord, un officier allemand fou et maintenant un Anglais fol avec un fermier gros.*"

"Out! *Allez!*" I yelled. "Come on, Studely. Pull."

Using the grips of the rear guns, Studely yanked himself up and dived into the rear cockpit. Through the corner of my busy eye I saw him stand to turn and face the tail-end, drop down into the seat, ram the headset on then give me a hearty thumbs-up.

The pilot threw his hands in the air, slapped them down, removed his headset then strained to lever himself up from his seat. "*Mon Dieu, le monde a fait des folies encore une fois.*"

Within seconds I was seated in the cockpit and had full control of the Lysander. After sorting out my headset I donned my right gauntlet, gave a selection of finger-taps to various dials then waved to the extracted pilot who was lying face down and pounding upon the sod of his homeland.

I heard and felt the jolt of Studely's canopy closing. I pulled the top over on mine and corrected the spin of the plane. We bounced and trundled on the rough field, with a lovely stretch of green before us. The blades of grass swept past into a blur as we picked up speed and were soon airborne.

Studely did not take long to settle down, to quiet down, to finish vomiting, or so I imagined from the noises coming through the communications.

Take off was sharp and at a fast and acute angle for which the Lysander is so famed. I soon saw the sea to my left, the town of Cherbourg sprawling before us, and sitting large as life in its harbour was Queen Mary.

"This thing's good for two-hundred miles per hour, Studely. Sit back and enjoy the flight."

Some crackled grunts from Studely informed me he had heard, if not understood.

I had another good look about; the Lysander gives such clear views of the land below, the air above, and all around. I must admit a sense of glee washed over me. "We are blessed with guns and bombs, Studely. We may have to fight our way through."

There was no answer. I guessed he was busy, familiarizing himself with his surroundings and the toys at hand.

"I would ascertain, Studely," I continued, "if we head north east until we sight land again then run east along the coast until we see the white cliffs we can follow the roads through England's garden."

Studely's reply was muffled but I assured myself it had something to do with his empty stomach.

It also dawned on me – a third dawning of the morning, you could say – that the aircraft in which Studely and I were flying was adorned with French Military insignia. The British wouldn't shoot down a low-flying French aircraft if it crossed the line, would they? The problem is, I supposed, is that one can never really be sure of the identity of one's enemy.

CHAPTER 24
THE HAMMER BLOW

There is nothing worse for the reader when glued to the plot and thundering through the pages, the heart pounding with excitement as we run in our hero's shoes, to find it has all been but a dream.

Many times, I have given a typhoon sigh and lobbed the book through the bedroom window when the author springs it upon me that none of the above has happened. He, or she gives us the routine: the waking in a cold sweat, the realization it was only the door banging in the wind, the cat purring at the end of the bed, all because of a late-evening Stilton and water biscuit washed down with a heavy claret. I shall not do that to you. That said: I did emerge from a reverie.

I had been assisting Rudy Vallee with his *Vieni, vieni* as we sped above the waves, wing-tipping from time to time as we rushed over sauntering fishing boats and lumbering freighters. I'd also done a couple of rounds with Art Gillham – the Whispering Pianist – and *I'm Sitting on Top of the World*. My compass and horizon line had stayed firm and steady for a good half-hour or so.

My reverie was broken by the hard line of land growing thicker, and more colourful, until the white sides of the Isle of Wight were clearly apparent. One could be forgiven for thinking the Isle of Wight is so called because the chalk cliffs are white, but wouldn't that point the finger at the locals and accuse them of illiteracy? The Wight part is some Olde English, something to do with creatures. The Isle of Creatures – perhaps even more insulting to the locals, don't you agree? These Jutish fellows, once pagans, turned to the goodly path of Christianity at the point of a sword, only to revert to their old ways as soon as the Mercians departed. How foolish and vain it is to force a greater culture upon a smaller.

Then the Needles: time to turn to starboard and follow the coast for ten minutes or so, leaving Hampshire, before tipping a port wing over Brighton and following the winding high-hedged road through the patchwork, multi-coloured counterpane of Sussex, over Burgess Hill, East Grinstead and Godstone, before tipping starboard and taking the straight for Westerham in that quaint and scented rind of north west Kent.

"There she is, Studely," I piped up. "There is Chartwell."

209

I did not hear Studely but above the throbbing of the Bristol engine I could feel the man rousing. Eventually there was a shout in my ear. "We made it. We went over a couple of airfields, you know?"

"I am aware of that, Studely, but I wish to land on the doorstep, an arm's reach of the brass knocker. I can run along the tree line and use the lower fields," I called out, almost breathless, reducing my revs and taking advantage of the remarkable slat-and-flap system which allows such slow airspeeds without stalling.

I hedge-hopped at fifty miles per hour, keeping a lookout for a reliable stretch of unploughed field. I may have failed in my mission, but a tidy and professional arrival could do me no harm.

I was marvelling at my skills and having one of those *'it's just like riding a bicycle'* moments as we skimmed along at thirty feet or thereabouts when something caught my eye. "Hell's bells" I shrieked.

Studely's bellow of "what!" slapped me in the ears.

"Through the trees, look. In the car. Can you see?"

"Bugger me."

You may well say *'bugger me'*, I thought. We were only seconds from a failure greater than that of losing the suitcase. "Take another gander, Studely, a good one in case my eyes deceive me."

"They don't deceive you," shouted Studely. "That's Quentin, all right."

"Hammer, Studely. Hammer."

The flickering of sunlight between the tree trunks and budding branches would have been romantic, perhaps idyllic had it not been for the hard-edge figure of Hammer speeding along in a roadster up the two-mile long straight, heading for Chartwell.

"Strafe the bugger," demanded Studely. "You said we got guns. I got some here."

"Strafe? But we're past him now. Use yours."

"Go around again, loop the bleedin' loop or something," called my co-pilot and rear-gunner. "Bomb him."

I was ready and willing to educate the fellow in rudimentary physics, the stresses and G-forces of aerobatics, but Studely's enthusiasm pressed me into action verging on the daredevil. I revved the engine and veered hard to the right and up at such a rate as to send my blood to my feet. It had not crossed my mind that although the fuel tank balances the Lysander perfectly, the added weight of Studely behind me made the crate a little tail-heavy. I corrected my error but found myself at two-thousand feet before I felt safe. In less than thirty seconds we were half-a-mile back down the tree line and steering a perfect course along the road with wing tips snapping high twigs and knocking crows' nests like coconuts at a shy.

Hammer's roadster grew, but there was the risk of getting too close and over-shooting. I was too low and without room to dive. I slowed as much as I dared then let rip with the two 7.7mm machine guns mounted in the wheel fairings. I blazed a trail, a railway track of shattered tarmac and grit. Too low and too fast. The lines zipped either side of the roadster.

My only hope was that Hammer would swerve from left to right; if he were to do so he would hit a tree and end it all in a mass of crumpled steel and gushing, oily steam. I knew he was too cool to commit that error. I released a twenty-pound bomb and it thumped a crater into the road just yards in front of the roadster.

"Missed," called Studely. "He's shot between the trees. He's swerving all over the place."

"Use the rear guns."

I heard the fluttering rat-tat-tat of the rear guns spitting as I pulled the Lysander up and to the right once more, filling the swirling air with smoke and the sweet stench of hot oil.

"I can't shoot low enough."

"Just don't hit the tail, Studely." I pulled harder, bringing the Lysander into a sharper angle. Another fly-past was called for, and a damned quick one if we were to get Hammer before he reached Chartwell. "We've got one bomb left."

For a few seconds, I had a good view of Hammer's speedster digging ruts into the field as it slewed and swerved, sending Fresians in all directions. I could even see his gloved hands fighting for control of the wheel. "We've got him now, Studely. A sitting duck on an iced pond."

I let rip with the machine guns, but too late. Hammer fought hard and got the roadster back on the road. If I could calculate in yards it would have been only the low hundreds, two or three; Hammer was not far from the gates.

One more burst of machine gun fire ripped another tramway up to the gates as Hammer was about to squeeze through. I pulled at the second bomb release just as I realized my speed and height. Had the release jammed? I wasn't sure, but all too apparent were the red-bricks and tall chimneys of the house zooming towards me. I pulled back and pictured the spats of the Lysander streaking either side of the tallest chimney.

We cleared the architecture, just, and I heard the explosion, felt the shockwaves judder through the undercarriage of the aeroplane. As I turned again to find a place to land, I could see smoke rising in a flume above a cloud of dust and falling brickwork. "We got him?"

"Can't see, there's too much smoke and dust," Studely bellowed. "Maybe Hammer's in the middle of it."

"In fragments if there's any justice in the world." I pulled round once more to bring the Lysander down along the tree line, hoping to come to a standstill near the wall of the estate.

We bounced and trundled, and before the crate came to a stop Studely and I were discarding our headsets and fighting to get out of our seats. I landed reasonably well and rolled as the rear wheel brushed past me. Studely followed suit. As we stood, we saw the circling Lysander correct its line and start going straight for the last tree before the gates as it coughed and spluttered its final drop of hot fuel. It came to a thumping halt, and startled rooks – or crows – fanned out from the branches.

"She'll blow up?" panted Studely as he leaned with hands on hips to get his vertebrae back into line.

"No, she's okay. Fuel line is off," I said. "Quickly, let's get in and see what's happened to Hammer." The Lysander blew up in a ball of orange flame and inky black smoke.

I pulled the revolver from my flying suit and raced off through the gates, up the gravel drive and past the front door. The sight was something to behold as the smoke and dust cleared.

In a huge crater, the hissing roadster let off steam, nose down and tail up like a spoon in a soup bowl. I stepped and kicked through the strewn bricks and plants with the revolver at the ready just in case the driver was still breathing. If I had learned one thing about Hammer over the few days I'd known him, it was that he would fight to the last, get the job done at any cost.

I stopped at the lip of the crater. Hammer was sprawled over the broken windscreen and across the bonnet of the roadster. The force of the explosion and crash had sucked him from his boots, and there before me was one sockless foot with a missing toe. The feet wriggled, hands moved. Up came the head, followed by the strange backward motion of a cat waking from a nap. He rolled over to face me and slowly rose from the carnage.

"Stick 'em up, Hammer. It's the end of the line for you. And don't go doing any of that German accent business on me."

With the sombre gait of a man who'd strained every muscle and cracked every bone, Hammer made his tentative way from the front seat, over the back of it and onto the boot lid of the roadster where he remained with his hands in the air. Bits of red brick dropped from his leather coat as he peered up past the lip of the crater to the man he could not defeat: your hero, Pelham Hardimann.

His peering did not last for long. It occurred to me as I stood there with the revolver pointed at him that he had changed his gaze and was looking beyond me.

I recognized the sound of the Riley Big Four with its 2.44 litres drumming as tyres crunched gravel and split half-bricks: I have always been good with engine sounds.

I didn't look round. Perhaps I knew what was about to happen. Out would come Hammer's friends, his semi-aristocratic chums, House of Lord's buddies and Moseley mates, ready to whisk me off to some nowhere land where ditches are dug and filled, never to be ploughed.

For the first time since standing at the mouth of the crater I noticed Studely at my side. "Sorry to put you in this bind, old chap," I said without the courage to look him in the face.

"Not to worry, Hardimann. Besides, you can still shoot the bastard where he stands."

I gave my head a solemn shake as I glowered down at Hammer. "Not the right thing, execution, Studely. He is not armed. His friends however..."

A car door slammed.

"Pelham, oh Pelham," came a cry, a voice I knew, a voice that sent shivers up and down my spine.

Studely was the first to turn around and dish out "Gordon Bennett and Cor Blimey, would you credit it?"

I had hardly done my own one-hundred-and-eighty degrees when arms were flung about my neck and the soft silk of Britannia's flowing robes pressed against me.

"Milly," I gasped as she squeezed. "How the..."

Another door slammed.

Milly kissed before she spoke, all in one rushed breath. I suspect, though I cannot be too sure, there was a lifted leg. "A Sunderland picked us up and dropped us off at Dover, from where we were flown to Biggin Hill. We've only just..."

"We?" I could have passed an age swimming in the deep pools of her eyes – apologies for the cliché, you'll have noticed I use them rarely – but more vital things were taking place. I pushed her away and looked over her shoulder.

My heart sank as the voice growled and the Astrakhan-wrapped bear rumbled into the scenario. "You're alive, damn it all, Hardimann. You're meant to be dead."

"Dead?"

"Of course, dead. If you are not dead, it signifies they did not buy it."

It's difficult to invoke the interrogative when the jaw has dropped but I did my utmost. "Buy it?"

Mr. Churchill rolled past me like a slowing boulder on the lower slopes of an avalanche. He stopped at the crater to wave his stick at something. "My wall, my brick wall." He hissed rage. "What in hell's name have you done to my wall, Hammer?"

Hammer lowered his arms. "I was... it was bombed, sir."

"Do you know how much time and effort I put into building that wall during my Black Dog days?" He stabbed his stick at Hammer who I felt was starting to lose his footing on the boot of the roadster. "Get out of there, man. Why in God's name are you still wearing that ridiculous uniform? Just can't get enough of it, can you? Do you intend for all the staff to be versed in your foibles?"

It had not until this time crossed my mind to take a gander at the porch of the building. On doing so, as prompted by Mr. Churchill's remark, my eyes fell upon members of the Chartwell household staff. kitchen, laundry, garden and otherwise. They were in a line, purveying the goings on as a crowd would do when a monkey does more than the organ grinder usually requires outside a Lyon's Corner House. One would have expected cheers or at least some stifled gasps, but there was silence: I assumed that was because the master had spoken and had more to say.

"Get out of there, Hammer. Explain yourself, if you can," commanded Mr. Churchill. "Who scooped this hole in my drive, smashed my wall, and rammed an aircraft into one of my copper beeches, burning it to a frazzle?"

Hammer, unassisted and with arms waving for balance, climbed from the crater, and brushed himself down a little more. I could almost feel his pain as he spoke, studying his one remaining redbrick-dusted boot. "I am afraid, sir, that Mr. Hardimann was under the misapprehension that I was...a traitor...a German..."

"As he should have been, Hammer, which is the main cause and reason for his need to be absent, absent from here, and if possible, absent from the face of the earth."

I'm sure you can understand my confusion and I must admit that my brain was getting a little fuzzy. I had not eaten for some time and the limbs were feeling a little stretched from their joints. Mr. Churchill's insistence that I should have been dispatched to the spirit world at some time or other during the last couple of days was also weighing heavy on the mind. I was in need of gentleness and soothing words.

"I do feel his demise is something possible to avoid, sir," said Hammer. "All that passed on Queen Mary and the deck of the U-boat was quite convincing."

Milly had taken hold of a hand and it was warm. "So, you really think he's one of them?" she asked in a conspiratorial whisper.

"Damn right he is," I said. "Tried to drown me before making off with the suitcase."

"Oh, come along, Pelham. You were meant to be confused." She had the audacity to giggle and at any other instance it would have riled me, but...

"Now what?" Studely hovered, revelling in Hammer's discomfort.

His question was answered by Mr. Churchill. "We shall all go into the house, make use of baths then meet on the lower lawn to untangle this web. I fancy some Darjeeling and a large Scotch with my good news." With furrowed brow, he thrust another remark for Hammer to parry. "If there is any good news."

"We are blessed with some good and there is some shadow of bad, sir," said Hammer.

"I could do with some suitable clothes," I chimed. "Perhaps a light brown tweed and a pair of brogues...?"

"That has all been arranged, sir," said Hammer. "Your wardrobe, the selection in your Queen Mary suite, should be arriving within the half-hour."

Mr. Churchill left Hammer, Studely, and I still perusing the destroyed brick wall, the crater and the smashed MG. He shooed his staff into the house then bellowed for Milly.

My Britannia swept away only to turn as she hit the shade of the doorway to send me the sweetest of smiles. For the first time in my life I blew a kiss.

"Stroll on," said Studely with folded arms and a rolling-eyes look to the sky.

"Studely," I said, "you have no heart, no soul." I was about to educate him about gentlemanly ways and the way a chap must go along with these womanly wiles when I heard a familiar cough; remember that cough that coves use when they want to interrupt and offer their three-pennyworth? "Yes, Hammer."

"You no doubt feel I have a great deal of explaining to do, sir."

"We could spend some time crossing a few Ts and dotting a few Is, Hammer," I said "But, have you failed to keep in mind that we have something much more urgent with which to contend, something far more important than family squabbles?"

"Sir?" Hammer asked, brushing dust from his SS uniform.

"We are expecting an assassin at any moment."

"Lawks a mercy," cried Studely. "Bloody Quill."

"Bloody indeed, Studely..." I eyed Hammer in the hope he had some solution up his dusty sleeve. "Quill had a plan, you said. Any idea as to...?"

"I'm afraid not, sir." He reddened at the gills. "I would be grateful, sir, if we could keep this from Mr. Churchill for the time being. I shall inform him in good time. He does not know of Quill's former allegiances and remaining allies."

"Maybe not," snapped Studely, "but I've had a sneaking suspicion for some time."

To say I was taken aback does not do service to the expression '*I was taken aback*'. "You have, Studely?"

He shrugged with insolence. "Why do you think I tagged along on this caper?"

"Really? You must advise me later, Studely. First we must deal with his plot."

"We do have some time to prepare," said Hammer. "We have connections, other agents. I received a message over the radio as I was flying back from…"

I quizzed him. "Where we flew from?"

"Yes," said Studely with some gusto. "The beached motor launch and the footprints; you made it to the airfield only moments before us."

I gave a finger snap. "And, Hammer, it was your plane I saw taking off."

"Yes, sir. I was fortunate enough to be using a Hurricane, one ready and waiting for me. Owing to the superior power of the Hurricane I was at Biggin Hill before you were halfway across the channel."

"But, the U-boat, Hammer. You were in the U-boat."

"For a while, sir. The captain took me as far to shore as he could possibly go. A German agent came out in a small boat to fetch me. I was at the airfield before you were ashore." Hammer did something rare. He smiled.

"Tickled, Hammer?"

"Sorry, sir. I was just remembering the face of the French pilot carrying out pre-flight checks on his Lysander. He was not amused to see an SS Officer marching across his airfield."

"And what was the message concerning the imminent arrival of a deadly assassin's bomb? Please pass it on, Hammer. It would help."

Hammer checked his watch and seemed pleased it had not suffered in the crash. "By my reckoning, sir, Quill will have arranged something monumental. It'll be in the next few days or so. A car bomb, perhaps. Maybe something in the post."

"Well, you'd better get on with it before we have to batten down the hatches, pull down the shutters, and up-end the tables."

"I can assure you, sir, the wagons are already in a circle." Hammer took long strides towards the front door. Gravel crunched as he stopped and turned. "Would you like further details of this escapade before, during, or after your bath, sir?"

"Um, well, I suppose we could kill two birds…"

"Very good, sir. I shall make haste and run your bath immediately."

"Just one other thing, Hammer," I said. "Someone tipped Quill into the briny. Any news on that?"

"I have been informed, sir, that Chief Inspector Quill of The Yard was launched into the channel by a certain Mr. Gully. A convict, referred to by the tabloid press as Desperate Dan."

"So, it was him I saw..."

"Most likely, sir. It seems Mr. Gully was desperate to make his way to the Americas in the hope of meeting his only love..."

"Greta Garbo."

"Precisely, sir. Having made his explosive escape, after many attempts, from His Majesty's Prison, he crossed country by bicycle before making use of a Cadillac parked at Saint Mary Mead. The conflagration you witnessed was caused by him in a dramatic attempt to remove all possibilities of a chase."

"The blighter blew up my SS100."

"He did, sir."

"And where is he now?"

"It is assumed he is still on his travels, sir."

"But why ditch Quill?" I quizzed.

"Well, sir, Mr. Gully, so I have been told, had always pleaded his innocence, and it was Quill who..."

"Got him banged up," said Studely.

Hammer nodded. "Precisely. Mr. Gully wasted no time and took the opportunity to meet out summary justice in his own inimitable style, and in doing so assisted you to some extent."

"Well, I never," I exclaimed. "And he's heading for the good old USA. What the heck will he get up to there?"

Hammer smiled. "With his penchant for explosions and destruction, sir, I am sure our American cousins will find some use for him." With that he entered the house.

I thought Studely was about to give me one of his '*lord luvva duck*' exclamations as he faced me, having watched Hammer disappear into the gloom of the house, but all he had to offer was a shrug and a "beats me."

CHAPTER 25
EQUALS

Hammer turned off the wireless as requested, and I sank deeper in my tub to give the face and hair a good swilling. He leaned across my bath and carefully placed a half-tumbler of whisky on the small table a few inches from my elbow.

"Well, well," I said, "that's a turn up for the books, the young Pelham Hardimann being found washed up on a Normandy beach, drowned, having fallen off Queen Mary in a drunken stupor. Very rummy, but all part of the charade eh?"

"We thought it best to broadcast the news of your demise as soon as possible, sir. It lends credence to my position while lessening dangers to your person."

"Was the drunkenness really necessary, Hammer?" I asked. "I'm all up for some cloak and dagger and matters concerning my safety but, while not wishing to appear peevish, I do feel the Hardimann character somewhat blemished by the scenario."

"We had two choices, sir," said Hammer. "Drunkenness or suicide."

"And the other choice?" I enquired.

"I beg your pardon," sir."

"You said two choices, Hammer."

"Indeed, I did, sir. Drunkenness or suicide."

"Not two choices then, Hammer." I wormed a little finger into an ear and gave it a hearty shake. "A choice has a minimum of two options, and you offered me only two, you offered me a choice. Two choices would surely involve more than two options."

I think he sighed as he lifted his shoulders and walked to the doorway of the suite for a rummage in the airing cupboard. "Very good, sir. Shall we say we had a choice, of two?"

"And you needed credence to be lent?"

"The Third Reich is under the misapprehension that I am working for Germany, sir, while being warmly ensconced within the Churchill household."

"At the heart of the matter," I prompted.

"Precisely, sir. My involvement with the suitcase was simply to bolster, reinforce, and add weight to the subterfuge. It took some months of planning, I can tell you."

"Certainly you can tell me, Hammer." I swapped fingers and ears. "Am I to assume the suitcase contained nothing but a couple of radio valves, a rainbow of wires, an assortment of gold and blue tinplate strips, and plates of Meccano?"

"Something a little more complicated than that, sir. We had two choi…a choice. We could lead the enemy to believe we are way ahead, more scientifically advanced in military matters or convince them we are trailing far behind the level at which they presently believe us to be."

"And we plumped for…?"

"Owing to the failure to invest in military matters over the last decade or so, sir, we felt the latter to be more realistic. It works on the principle that if someone is looking for something, they do not yet have it. It also gives us some clue as to what technical and scientific resources our competitors have, and how advanced they are in some areas."

"Pity the poor blighters on Queen Mary, Hammer, and you certainly led Hayes and Clenchy on a wild goose chase."

"There was a handful of people on Queen Mary who were aware of the plan and willing to take part."

"And did we succeed, Hammer?"

"I believe we did, sir. One must realize that Britain has three clear enemies, three threats to her safety. Nazi Germany, Communist Russia, and of course, The United States of America. It is good to know how they all stand and which way they will jump. It is also vital to have some knowledge of who pulls strings and who has influence in their midst."

"Clasping both friends and enemies very close and keeping an eye on the serpents within their bosoms?"

"Absolutely, sir. I trust your bath is comfortable."

"Warm as toast, Hammer." I did a bit of face-washing to convince him of my pleasure. "Your suspicion of our American cousins surprises me."

"If you think back, perhaps you will recall, sir that in 1916 the United States was but a whisker from fighting alongside Germany and the Austro-Hungarian Empire, though preferring isolationism. It was not until a plot by the Kaiser to support a Mexican attack on the United States that the Americans chose sides. Can we be sure of them when Europe erupts once more?" He stroked a folded towel before coming back to my bathtub and placing it next to my whisky. "She does, for the moment, seem inclined to cover her eyes and ears. Her present creed is isolationism."

"Isolationism?"

"Not getting involved in the affairs of other nations, sir."

"Can you blame them, Hammer?"

"Certainly not, sir. We believe they have but four divisions at their disposal while the Third Reich has a minimum of a hundred-and-fifty to hand for instant use. What she does have, however, is a vast industrial base and Mr. Roosevelt has the urge to put it to good use."

"Well, we must pull them to our side, Hammer."

"Absolutely, sir, which is why the real articles are on their way, to be placed in the correct hands."

"The real suitcase." I downed what remained of my whisky. "I was…"

"A decoy, sir."

"Well," I said, feeling a little sore in the head as the ideas rumbled about, "I've never known the decoy mallard to be shot at so often. The poor goat tied to the tree, on the other hand…"

Hammer gave one of his gentle coughs. "Talking of mallards, sir, you will be taking tea down at the pond. Mr. Churchill likes to sit and admire his handiwork, his new duck house. He has also been doing much of his painting from there recently. I will join you later when I have finished my own *toilette*."

"Very good, Hammer," I replied.

I could tell Hammer was itching to move on, to leave my presence and get on with his own bath so I gave him a gentle wave then a halting hand as one more question sprung to mind. "Tell me, Hammer," I commanded as I fished about for the soap. "What will become of your mother?"

He filled the doorway. "Mrs. Glendower, sir," he replied then paused for a moment or so with a finger to his chin. "Well, sir, while she may be viewed by some as a traitor, one can understand her leanings."

"Leanings?"

"Leanings, sir. After all, life has not treated her well and her belief in the noble cause gave her strength. Were she to remain in England, she would be…"

"Hanged, I suppose."

"Yes, sir, hanged for the murder of your father and Sam the Spot, although mitigating circumstances could be taken into consideration. But, for treason there is no excuse."

I squeezed the sponge and enjoyed the soft water trickling down my chest before I stuck out an arm to grab the towel. "A shame, Hammer, a shame," I said. "Life does more than deal some of us bad cards. It plays the very game for us and decides on the stakes, knowing we will lose our very all."

Was he getting into this new habit of smiling? "On the other hand, sir, we do now have our own serpent in the bosom of the Soviet Union."

"Young Studely described you as Machiavellian, Hammer. He is not far off the mark, is he?"

"One could say that, sir. By the way, sir, if you don't mind my saying so, I feel I ought to come clean."

"Well a wash and brush up is most certainly called for, Hammer. Look at the state of you."

"Quite so, sir. As I mentioned earlier, I have a bath run in the other suite. I was referring to another matter."

"Pipe up, Hammer," I said as I lifted the Hardimann torso from the bath and started patting it with the towel. "Good to get the stubble removed, I can tell you. You can't beat the soap and badger and a good bubbly soak to set things right."

I waited for him to speak up and he appeared to need a few seconds or so to collect his thoughts. By the time he was ready I had dried the body and was giving the hair a good rubbing.

"It concerns our relationship, sir."

I paused my rubbing and looked him in the eye. "An interesting but rocky one considering its duration, wouldn't you say?"

"Indeed, sir, but one has to keep in mind that my acting as your manservant…"

"My man's man," I interjected in the hope of putting him at his ease and budging him along.

"…was only acting."

"You are not a man's man?"

"I am not a servant, sir."

I wrapped the towel and knotted it around my waist. "So, to whom do I turn for the timely breakfast, the perfectly run bath, and the neatly pressed flannels?"

"There are agencies, sir."

"But not your agency?"

"Precisely, sir. During your stay here you can rely on the services of Lucy, one of the maids."

"Not Milly?" I enquired with disappointment tugging at the heart.

"Hardly, sir."

I slapped some cologne on the chin and cheeks. "From this time on, Hammer, I'm expected to refer to you as…Quentin?"

"I am happy with Hammer, sir."

"Very good, Hammer. In the future we shall face each other as equals."

He turned to exit the bathroom and I bid him farewell with a nifty "So long, Hammer."

"Catch you later, Hardimann," he replied, and I knew that had he been facing me I would have spotted an upward tilting eyebrow and a self-congratulatory smile.

CHAPTER 26
DUNDEE CAKE

From the top of the bank, with the stately home behind me, I looked across the lawns towards the table and chairs placed neatly a few yards from the pond, a pond the size of a small lake.

A couple of strides or so from the table and chairs was the hunched-over figure of Mr. Churchill in a boiler suit and straw hat. He may well have been an artist and a fan of the landscape, but he was no wearer of hooped jerseys, knotted necktie, and beret. He was stabbing a brush at an easel, stopping now and then to do that thumb against brush thing the well-trained artist does to size things up. I'm no critic but I was wondering if he could see anything through the cigar smoke chugging into billows as he gave breath.

As for the subject matter, it is all well and good painting trees and a lake, I thought, but how one can get an accurate portrayal of a duck is beyond me. There were dozens of them swimming about, bobbing and tipping, wagging tails, and snapping beaks.

"Ready? You scrub up well."

I turned to my left to see Milly standing by my side. "Milly," I said with joy sinking before the mouth had finished her name. "What has happened to my Britannia?"

She prodded at her horn-rimmed spectacles and folded her beige cardigan-clad arms. "Back to the usual graft and dress for me, I'm afraid, Mr. Hardimann," she said.

"I prefer…"

"Yes, you do." She looped an arm through mine. "Keep your fingers crossed. There may be a next time."

We walked down the bank and across the lawn toward the pond in a stately manner – I was wearing a light brown wool suit – and I was about to have another shot with the famous Pelham wooing routine when Studely made his presence known.

"All right, Hardimann," he called from a yard behind. He pulled up alongside.

"Studely," I chimed. "Good to see you spruced up. Ready for the Earl Grey and Battenberg?"

He gave a "ha ha" then licked thumb and fingers. "Too dainty for me, Hardimann. I just spent the last ten minutes digging into last night's steak and kidney pudding. I love leftovers. You should see the size of that larder." He bumped against me as he turned to look around. "Where's Hammer?" he asked, walking backwards for a couple of yards before turning to the front.

"Hammer is coming clean after having come clean," I informed him. "He is also, one hopes, on the trail of some dastardly plot hatched by the now deceased twin. It seems he has everything organized. A network of spies and a ring around the premises with armed guards behind every bush."

We arrived at the table and chose our seats. I did not show my disappointment when Milly picked one to place Studely between us.

Mr. Churchill levered himself up from his wicker chair and dumped his brush in a jar. "Ready to report, Milly? he asked before letting out a rumbling cough. He dragged his wicker chair to the table and placed himself where he could maintain a good view of his lake and none of Pelham Hardimann. "A bloody shambles if you ask me, but Hammer promises me it will turn out well in the end." He took great pains to lean his walking stick against his chair, ready for use.

"All set, sir," said Milly, prim and proper and straight. I wondered where she'd hidden her notebook and pencils.

Another rumble. "Studely, you play mother."

It was not that I was feeling left out of things, left on the sidelines so to speak – remember my Coventry remarks earlier on – but I felt I should make my presence known. "Keep an eye out for one of Quill's cronies lobbing grenades, or scrabbling beneath the hedgerows to take pot shots…"

Mr. Churchill addressed Studely. "There'll be no taking pot shots at people in Chartwell. This is my haven and I will not have it shattered." He acknowledged my presence with a glint of malice in his eyes. "It has been scarred enough."

Milly cut in to veer her master from the topic. "Tea is on the way."

Mr. Churchill had not finished. "I built this with my own hands, Hardimann. Sodding great digger, we had. A measly pond the size of a piss puddle to a tree-lined lake with ducks and swans…plenty of fish."

"Very impressive."

"Does a man good to work with his hands, get his back into things. This country was built by the gnarled hands of the working man, and don't you forget it."

I waited until he turned his back to me once more, to gaze at his masterpiece, before I rolled my eyes to the thin clouds and blue sky. "Yes. I'm sure you are correct."

"Bloody right I'm correct."

"Tea on the way," said Milly again. I half-expected her to comment on the weather. "And cake."

A look over my shoulder gave me a view of young Lucy, in her black and white uniform, pushing a top-heavy trolley across the lawn. Studely, fine fellow, was up in a flash to assist her.

Lucy performed a small curtsy before laying out the Spode cups and saucers, teapot, strainer and all the bits needed for afternoon tea on the lawn while Studely placed the marvellous centrepiece: a cake.

"Dundee cake, Lucy?"

"Yes, sir."

Mr. Churchill fiddled with his bow tie. "We are blessed indeed. Clemmie…your mistress has banned Dundee cake from the premises of late." He whipped up a napkin the size of a picnic blanket and shoved it down into the top of his boiler suit. "She has relented, realized all this belt-tightening is unnecessary?"

"I don't really know, sir," said Lucy, adding another curtsy. "I don't remember her ordering it. It got delivered fifteen minutes ago." With that she adjusted her starched headgear and the line of her blouse. She soon had sensible shoes making whispering noises on the lawn as she headed back towards the house, swerving a little like a moth having lost sight of the moon as she passed Hammer who was marching towards us in a dark suit and conservative tie.

"News, Hammer?" Mr. Churchill called out. "Shot your assassin? Far away from Chartwell, I trust."

"Nothing sighted yet, sir," said Hammer. "But not to worry, we have the grounds well covered."

"Good, good," grunted Mr. Churchill. He gestured for Hammer to sit. "Join us, we have Dundee cake today."

Hammer did not use the pause to answer and Mr. Churchill's smile was cut short as I leapt up, whipped the yellow scarf from around my neck, leaned across the table then ambushed the cake. I placed flat palms on its sides, lifting it as though lifting a crown from a royal head. I wrapped my scarf around it. I kicked back my chair and skirted around the table to the lake, with the cake hanging in my yellow sling. I whirled and whirled like a dervish until releasing it. I'm sure I put a decent spin on it.

The cake flew in a beautiful arc, with yellow tail flapping, to the centre of the lake where it crashed onto the roof of the duck house. There was a call of infuriated fowl as the cake rolled for a moment until steady as if to chance a leap over the top edge of the roof before it started its slow roll back and sad drop – with a plop – into the water. It didn't float.

"My bloody Dundee cake," stormed Mr. Churchill. "Do you have any idea...?"

I ducked to avoid the swooping swish of his walking stick but as I rose was caught full in the face by the whipping napkin. I caressed my cheeks as I stated my case. "But the cake could have been a bomb. Quill could have..."

Mr. Churchill heaved to draw air into his lungs and turned to Hammer who was studying the ripples fanning out across the lake.

"Shoot him, Hammer. Shoot him dead, now!"

Hammer was as steady as a Cornish lighthouse. "But, sir, Quill is dead, drowned at sea."

"Not Quill, Hammer. Him. Bloody Pelham Hardimann." I stepped back a pace as Mr. Churchill flicked once more with the napkin, "He has ruined my Dundee cake."

"But, sir..." began Hammer.

A brilliant flash cut into the calm light of the spring afternoon as lengths of timber rushed like Agincourt arrows to the low-scudding clouds. The easel closed its three legs and tipped over, and the tablecloth cracked like a whip in the gale. A shower of planking and roof tiles followed.

Mr. Churchill flicked even more with his napkin and slapped the wrecked tea-party, the leaking teapot, the spinning cups, the unaligned teaspoons and the stricken vase that had shot its contents over the legs of his boiler suit. "Shoot him, now!"

"But, sir," said Hammer as daggers of wood stuck into the lawn and dived into the pond, some still cutting through the snowstorm of white, green and brown feathers. A mushroom of cloud billowed above the lake and drifted. "Him?"

I've never really understood or been able to recognize the colour puce, although I have oft heard it mentioned when a storyteller tells of his or another's wrath. The violent rush of lake water did nothing to cool him. Mr. Churchill pointed, and I was his bullseye. "Yes, him. Pelham Bloody Hardimann."

I turned to Milly and shrugged, hoping for a smile. "Oh well," I said. "Keep buggering on."

THE END

Pelham Hardimann returns in
The Plan on the Clapham Omnibus